YMIR LEGACY

THE SACRIFICE

ZOEY ALESTER

Buzzard Roost Ranch Books · Oklahoma

© 2015 Buzzard Roost Ranch Books

9119 E 12675 Rd

Dustin, OK 74839

Written by: Zoey Alester

Ymir Legacy - The Sacrifice

Cover Design & Layout: Nathan Jeffords

A CIP record for this book is available from the Library of Congress Cataloging-
in-Publication Data

ISBN: 978-0-9916126-2-8

First Edition December 2018

Printed in the United States of America

THE SACRIFICE

Prologue

The ForEverNever
The Land Beyond the Mist and Fog
Many years ago

Feing Digon…Feing Digon, the ancient battle cry of the Faeries was heard all throughout the ForEverNever, the Land Beyond the Mist and Fog, the home of the Faeries. The Faeries had been fighting each other for so long, none of them could remember a time when there was peace in their world.

The Faeries were created from elements of the Earth, shortly after the Earth came into being. Each Faerie was gifted with its own unique powers and distinct abilities. Along with the Faerie's powers and abilities came the responsibility of serving as guardians of the Earth.

Although the ForEverNever, the Land Beyond the Mist and Fog, or the ForEverNever for short, was physically separated from Earth, it was still connected to Earth. Many of the Faeries often traveled between the ForEverNever and Earth. Other Faeries' powers and abilities were so strong that they did not have to leave the ForEverNever to effect change on Earth, the human world.

The Faerie World was divided into seven Faerie Houses. Each Faerie House had its own ruler and no one Faerie House was created more powerful than another. As some of the Faeries began to forget about their responsibilities to Earth, they chose to succumb to the influence of their powers and abilities and became greedy and self-centered. Several of the rulers of the Faerie Houses were constantly fighting to increase their wealth and lands in the ForEverNever. These rulers thought it their right to rule the whole Faerie World. The other rulers fought to preserve their homes and protect their families. Since there was constant conflict in the Faerie World, there seemed to be little hope for the Faeries of the ForEverNever.

The "Power of All," who created the Faeries and their world in a time long forgotten, was tired of the fighting and called the rulers of each of the seven Faerie Houses to a gathering at the Cliffs of Moher. The rulers of the seven houses were told to bring every member of their family to the gathering.

The Cliffs of Moher, a sacred location, was chosen because it was a neutral location and one of the few places—along with the Isle of Iona off the West coast of Scotland, Anglesey off the coast of Wales, the town of Hafnarfjördur in Iceland, Granada in Spain, New Orleans in the United States, the Urubamba Sacred Valley in the Andes of Peru, Mount Kailash in Tibet, the Giza Plateau in Egypt, Axum in Ethiopia, Uluru in Australia, and an unknown place in Antarctica—that was shared by both humans and Faeries. But the Cliffs of Moher was the only location that was open to all Faeries. The "Power of All" decreed centuries before that any one Faerie House couldn't rule the Cliffs of Moher.

The rulers of the seven houses, along with their families, agreed to attend the gathering. The houses of Zephyrine, Azar, Ymir, Attewater, Ashbel, Pelagia, and Erion all met at the Cliffs of Moher on a sunny, yet rainy day.

As rays of light made their way through the drops of rain, the "Power of All" carefully watched the Faeries. The "Power of All" knew the Faeries were allowing themselves to be corrupted by their powers and abilities, and the choices they made. The "Power of All" could see there was very little goodness left in the Faerie World and expressed displeasure to all the Faeries concerning the way they were living their lives. The Faeries had completely neglected their responsibilities to the Earth and were becoming more self-serving with each passing year. Their actions made them and their world vulnerable to a great darkness and evil. The "Power of All" communicated to the Faeries, in no uncertain terms, things needed to change. If the Faeries agreed to the "Power of All's" plan they would not be harmed; but if they refused to agree to the terms presented to them, they would all be destroyed.

The "Power of All" required one Faerie at the gathering to relinquish his or her innate powers and accept a new power the "Power of All" would grant the Faerie. The courageous Faerie would know nothing about the new power, until after it gave up its innate powers. The Faeries were warned that the power would not grant them influence over others and it could not be used to their advantage in any way. In fact, the Faerie would not remember it had this power or any power.

All of the Faeries gasped at this request. Give up their powers... impossible; to the Faeries their powers were their identity and sense of purpose. A Faerie was nothing without its powers and to not even know it had a power was unthinkable to all the Faeries at the gathering.

No Faerie would step forward, each Faerie waiting for another to make the sacrifice. The "Power of All" wondered if it had waited too long to summon the rulers of the seven Faerie Houses to make its demands known. Was there no good left in the Faerie World?

Then all of a sudden, from the back of the crowd, a young female Faerie, the smallest and youngest Faerie of the group stepped forward. A young male Faerie standing beside her, grabbed at her clothing trying to pull her back. It appeared he wanted to volunteer so the young female Faerie would not. But before either of the young Faeries could speak, there was a roar of displeasure from the most gifted Faerie at the gathering.

The young female Faerie was the only daughter of the King of the Faerie House of Ymir. She had brought great joy to the Royal House of Ymir since her arrival.

"No," the King of Ymir yelled, "I will not let you make this sacrifice. I will give up my powers."

The "Power of All" smiled at the King's remark...it was not too late. There were still a few Faeries capable of good...and it seemed they were all from the House of Ymir. The "Power of All" wondered what made the House of Ymir different than the rest of the Faerie Houses—but did not ponder on the question. For the moment, the "Power of All" was simply very glad for the difference.

"No father, you can't give up your powers. You are King and must be able to protect all the Faeries under your rule. If you don't have your powers, how will you protect us?" the daughter asked not expecting an answer.

The young female Faerie looked directly at her father and gently smiled. "I am not afraid. I will give up my powers."

The young female Faerie then turned to the "Power of All." "I am tired of all the fighting and seeing Faeries that I care about vanish forever. What do you need me to do?" the young Faerie asked in a quiet, but confident voice.

The 'Power of All" gently gazed at the young female Faerie, "You don't look like much now, little one. However, I sense in time your powers would have been great, but lucky for all the Faeries, your sense of compassion and what is justice is even greater."

The "Power of All" then expressed in a loud clear voice for all those present to hear, "I will accept your sacrifice and I commend your bravery. State aloud you freely and willingly choose to give up your powers and I will do the rest."

In a loud, clear voice, the young female Faerie repeated what the "Power of All" said. Her father looked on anxiously. He appeared ready to interrupt his daughter's words at any moment. There was a bright flash of light and a booming noise that sounded similar to thunder. The young female Faerie's body started to shake and her legs gave way beneath her. She fell to the ground. Her father and the young male Faerie rushed to her side.

"How do you feel?" both asked her at the same time.

"I feel fine, just a little dizzy," the young female Faerie said as she rubbed her head and tried to stand. "Can you tell me how I ended up on the ground?"

The young male Faerie and the young female Faerie's father just looked at her with concern in their eyes. All the other Faeries looked on, not really concerned about the young female Faerie's wellbeing. They were just glad the crisis was averted and they did not have to give up anything.

"Why did you do it?" the young male Faerie asked in a questioning, almost hesitant voice full of concern. "I would have given up my powers… if only everything had not happened so quickly, I would have had time to stop you and volunteer instead."

"Time waits for no one," the young female Faerie said as she winked at her friend, trying to make him laugh.

"Now that you have taken her powers," the King of Ymir said to the "Power of All," "What is this new power you are giving her, and what are the rest of the terms of your plan for us? Is there anything else we must do to avoid destruction?"

"This courageous young Faerie has done what none of you would," the "Power of All" looked at all the other Faeries still standing crowded together behind the young female Faerie. As a result of her brave and compassionate nature, she willingly sacrificed herself for every one of you. She has done all that needs to be done, for your world to avoid destruction."

The "Power of All" looked at the young female Faerie with soft eyes and gently smiled. "As for her new power, it is the power of pure love and absolute goodness. From this moment on, she will not be able to think an unkind thought, say an unkind word, or do an unkind deed."

The King of Ymir confused, then angered by the "Power of All's" statement glared at the "Power of All". "How does that help anyone?" The King gruffed.

"Because of your daughter there is love in the ForEverNever. The goodness in the ForEverNever is now strong enough to balance or even stop all the corruption and greed. You Faeries will still have a tendency to be selfish, but now you will feel more compelled to choose good over doing things that are self-serving and hurt others. And hopefully you will all return to fulfilling your responsibilities to Earth," the "Power of All" authoritatively stated.

Before disappearing the "Power of All" told the King of Ymir, "Your daughter is a precious gift, protect her above all else. There will always be those who want to hurt her. If she should be lost, hurt or killed, the whole Faerie World could be in jeopardy."

The King of Ymir nodded in response to the "Power of All's" warning.

The young male Faerie stepped forward, and puffed out his chest to appear brave and more grown up than he was. "I will protect her with my life," he stated as he looked directly at the "Power of All".

Although the "Power of All" could no longer be seen, its laugh could be heard by the Faeries at the gathering and all the Faeries in the ForEverNever.

The "Power of All" refused to do anything else. It was now up to the Faeries to decide their own fate.

As soon as the "Power of All" disappeared a Dark Shadow emerged from its hiding place behind a tiny rock. The Dark Shadow wanted to get a good look at the young Faerie who had sacrificed all so her fellow Faeries, both friends and foes, could survive. She had ruined the Dark Shadow's plans. The Dark Shadow swore that someday it would make the young female Faerie pay. She would never be safe. The Dark Shadow would not rest until it had destroyed her and all her love and goodness.

However, the "Power of All" was not oblivious to the Dark Shadow's presence at the gathering. So the "Power of All" directed one of its most faithful and loyal servants to watch over the young Faerie for all her days and nights. The faithful and loyal servant was told not to make its presence known to anyone, especially to the young female Faerie. The faithful and loyal servant was supposed to remain close, but always out of sight.

Initially the "Power of All's" plan was successful. The day of the gathering of the seven Faerie Houses the Faerie rulers signed a treaty declaring peace in their world. The Faeries fairly divided the land in the Faerie World into Seven Realms governed by the rulers of the seven Faerie Houses. To make things simple, the lines in the Faerie World were drawn to parallel the seven continents on Earth, the human world. Each Faerie House was granted guardianship over one continent. For their sacrifice, the green-eyed Faeries of the House of Ymir were given first choice over the realm they wished to rule. They chose the realm that ran parallel to the human territory that included the Cliffs of Moher and the rest of Europe.

From the remaining Royal Houses, one member from each house participated in a tournament. The winner of the tournament was given the next selection of which realm it chose to rule. The remaining Royal Houses were able to choose which realm they wished to rule, based upon the place they finished in the tournament. The blue eyed Attewater's chose the land in the Faerie World connected to North America, the purple eyed Faeries of the House of Zephyrine chose the land connected to Asia and the gold eyed Faeries of the House of Azar chose the land connected to Africa. The Faeries whose eyes were multi-colored from the House of Erion chose Antarctica, the red-eyed Faeries of the House of Ashbel chose Australia, and the orange eyed faeries of the House of Pelagia were given South America.

After the gathering at the Cliffs of Moher, there was peace in the Faerie World for thousands of years; however, over time the Dark Shadow's influence began to permeate the Faerie World. Some Faeries from each of the seven Faerie Houses began to lose their will to follow the goodness the young female Faerie represented. These Faeries became very selfish and decided to unite to take the land from the Faeries that continued to choose goodness. Since the Faerie House of Erion was the smallest, the followers of the Dark Shadow decided to attack there first. Most of the Faeries of the House of Erion were killed during the battle; however, a few were able to escape and bring word of the attack to the other Faerie Houses.

The remaining Faeries of the House of Erion decided to make their new home in the lands of the Faerie House of Ymir, where they were welcomed with open arms. They joined the remaining Faeries in the other Faerie Houses in a coalition to defend their Houses against attacks from the followers of the Dark Shadow. They selected the King of the House of Ymir as the High King.

The Faeries who were still influenced by the goodness of the young female Faerie hoped their show of unity would deter the Faeries who had turned their backs on goodness from trying to take their lands. These Faeries also knew that if they maintained a coalition, they could call on each other if or when their realms were in danger. The Faeries of the Houses of Ymir, Attewater, Zephyrine, Azar, Erion, Ashbel and Pelagia, who continued to recognize the importance of the young female Faerie of the House of Ymir, made a pact to do everything in their power to keep her safe. If anything were to happen to the young female Faerie, they knew all love and goodness would vanish from their world and their ability to choose good and kindness over greed and self-centeredness could disappear.

The Faeries who continued to choose to be influenced by the goodness of the young female Faerie reaffirmed their pledge to their responsibilities to Earth. Some of these Faeries had the power to frequently travel between the Earth and the ForEverNever. Some made the choice to permanently leave the ForEverNever and made their home on Earth. These faeries maintained no connections with ForEverNever. Some of these faeries avoided humans and made their homes underground, in the forests or in the waters of Earth. They continued to use their powers to benefit the health of the Earth and humans. Others did everything they could to fit into the human world. These Faeries rarely used their powers. Since these Faeries maintained no connection to the ForEverNever and they didn't use their powers, they lost their ability to use their powers. Overtime, these Faeries began to believe they were humans and became vulnerable to the same afflictions as humans, such as aging, illness and death.

YMIR LEGACY

Why do things have to change? Why do those you love have to die? And why do I have to leave the only home I have ever known? I have never felt so scared and alone. Since my grandmother's death, there has been no one for me to talk to…no one for me to turn to. If only my father was here and I wasn't being forced to move to a completely different country, then maybe I wouldn't feel like everything was spinning out of control or like I was losing myself—not sure which direction to turn. I miss my mother so much…every day. Those who say time heals all wounds most not have lost a mother. And my father's actions have greatly hurt me. When am I going to feel like pieces of me aren't missing; when am I going to stop hurting?

- Sophie St. Clair

i : Saying goodbye

Dublin, Ireland 1958

"Had it only been a year," Sophie sighed as she watched the flames in the fireplace burn down to embers. She was not sure how much time had passed when a gentle breeze, caused by one of the servants opening the library door, brought the fire back to life. Although Sophie felt no warmth from the flames, the fire's brighter flames intensified, crackling gently, nudging her out of her mindless state and drew her attention to the photograph of her and her parents on the mantle above the fireplace. It was taken a little over a year ago—on her eleventh birthday—at her family's beach house on Long Island Sound in New York.

Sophie remembered it was a cold January day. Although they knew it was too cold to go in the water, her parents had brought her to the beach house because it was her favorite place. Her parents knew she enjoyed being around the water, and that singing with them as they walked down the beach was one of the things she most loved to do.

Sophie loved listening to her mother sing. Her mother had a clear, pure voice that could fill you with joy and move you to tears. She would sing what she called "Irish ditties," which were always fun to sing. She would also sing songs with words Sophie had never heard. When Sophie asked about the songs, her mother would say with a far way look on her face, "I learned them a long time ago when I was young." Then she would smile at Sophie and start singing another Irish ditty.

"The people in the photograph look relaxed and happy," Sophie thought as she continued to stare at the photograph on the mantle.

The individuals in the photograph wore enormous grins, as if they didn't have a care in the world. Her father, dressed in his favorite sweater, was very handsome with a big smile on his face. The sweater was one she and her mother picked out for him together. Her mother let Sophie choose the color. She chose green, her favorite color. She and her mother gave the sweater to her father for Christmas, when Sophie was ten.

A singular tear rolled down Sophie's face as her gaze focused on her mother. Her mother looked beautiful—just as Sophie remembered her. And although her mother always looked beautiful, she looked especially glamorous and alive in the photograph. Sophie's father's arms were around her mother and she had her arms around Sophie, their precious daughter. She was wearing the green dress Sophie loved. The dress matched her husband's sweater and complimented her green eyes, making them sparkle. Her eyes magnificently and almost magically, expressed her love for life and for her family.

Sophie paused, in sudden shock, as her eyes were drawn to the image of herself in the photograph. She was looking adoringly up at her mother and was actually smiling. She looked happy. Sophie couldn't remember the last time she was truly happy. In fact, it may have been that perfect day, when the photograph was taken. That day, a few weeks before her whole life drastically changed forever.

Staring at the photograph Sophie could not believe it was only a year ago that her mother was taken from her in a horrific car accident. Shortly after her mother's accident, Sophie's father, who worked for the United States Department of State, was transferred to Ireland. Her father left Sophie with her Grandmother St. Clair and headed off to Dublin, Ireland. He wanted her to stay in New York so she could finish the school year with her friends, but Sophie could not help but think her father may be trying to get rid of her. What she did not understand was why her father wanted to leave her.

Sophie's father only sent for her because her grandmother had suddenly passed away and there was no one else in New York to take care of her. She missed her grandmother very much and was sad that she was gone, but Sophie was glad she was going to get to live with her father again.

"If only he was moving back to New York, maybe things would start to feel normal again," Sophie thought. However, she knew her father had made his choice and she would be stuck in Ireland.

Sophie's father had been stationed at the American Embassy in Dublin during World War II. He never spoke about his life in Ireland, but that is where he met her mother. Before he left New York to return to Ireland, he told Sophie he would send for her when the time was right. He knew his job would be demanding and he would not have a lot of time to spend with her.

"I don't want to leave you, but my country needs me. Besides, I am no good for you right now." Her father looked at her sadly before he left.

"What does that mean?"

With a somewhat distant look in his eyes, Sophie's father replied, "I wish I could tell you more, but I cannot. I will send for you when I can. I promise." He pinched her nose.

Sophie stopped asking questions. "What was the point?" She knew she was not going to get any answers—especially not the answers to the questions she really needed answered. Besides, she did not want to take the chance of irritating her father with all her questions. "Then he really may never send for me," Sophie thought sadly. She felt she not only lost her mother, but was losing her father as well. She rarely saw him and now he was leaving the country.

Right before he walked out of his mother's house in New York, Sophie's father turned and looked at her. He smiled, "Sophie, I love you very much and will send for you soon. I suspect living in Ireland could be good for you; it will give you the opportunity to experience the rich culture of your mother's homeland and may make you feel closer to her."

Now that Sophie was being forced to move to Dublin, she doubted her father's words and whether moving would make anything better. To her, the move and all the changes were not a big adventure or a new beginning; they reminded her of all she had lost and completely closed the door on her life in New York with her parents, grandparents and friends. Just thinking about it made her feel sadder and more alone in the world. The changes couldn't bring back her mother. And New York was the only home she had ever known—the home that held all her memories of her mother and grandmother.

Seeing the smiling faces in the photograph made Sophie long for her mother, her father and their life in New York. She could no longer hold back her tears.

YMIR LEGACY

Life has become so complicated since my wife died. When I was given the opportunity to get out of New York and start again, I had to take it—especially when I heard what they wanted me to do. My country needs me and doing something important may help fill the giant void left from the death of my wife. However, I feel like I have let my daughter down. I know she needs me and I am trying my best, but how can I be there for her when I'm not truly whole myself? Does it ever get any easier?

- William St. Clair

ij : a new Beginning

Dublin, Ireland 1958
Hours Earlier

Sophie was so excited when she first landed in Dublin. She had flown by herself and could not wait to tell her father all about the trip. She was the only passenger on the private jet. And although, she had her own seat in the cabin, the pilot let her sit next to him in the cockpit. He even told her about some of the instruments in the cockpit and what they were used for.

But, Sophie's father did not meet her at the airport. In fact, she would not be able to see him for almost a week. He had to go out of town for work and sent one of his drivers to pick her up at the airport. The driver was a very stern, bulky looking man, who appeared to not know how to smile. Sophie was somewhat afraid to go with him—but he knew the code word, the word she and her father had invented, the word they were to use in emergency situations.

Sophie reluctantly left the airport with the man. The man was not friendly—to say the least. He didn't say a word to Sophie on the way to the car or after he started driving. Sophie was glad for the silence and half heartily looked out the window as they passed by the daily happenings of Dublin.

After what seemed like a considerable amount of time had passed, the driver dropped Sophie off at the curb in front of a large house. He emptied her two bags out of the trunk and looked at the door. "If you don't want to stay out here all night, you better knock on the door. It's my night off. I'm leaving."

"He can't even walk me to the door. Where was he raised—a barn?" Sophie thought as she looked back at the driver and then down at her bags.

"And how am I supposed to get these bags up the stairs?" she asked hesitantly.

"Not my problem," the driver shrugged.

"I really only get paid to drive and I've got plans tonight," he yelled as he got in the car and drove away.

Sophie tentatively walked up the steps to knock on the front door. Before she had a chance to knock, a very kind looking woman with sparkling green eyes and a big smile opened the door.

The woman looked to be a little older than Sophie's mother, before she died, but something about the woman made her seem much older, and almost "other" worldly. Maybe it was the way she wore her hair all tied back with a black ribbon, away from her face, or the black dress with puffed sleeves she wore. Or maybe it was the dim lines at the corners of her eyes, or something in her eyes themselves. Although her eyes were green, like Sophie's and her mother's, the woman's eyes were the deepest shade of green Sophie had ever seen. They had a strange sparkle.

"You must be Sophie," the woman said with a smile. "I would know you anywhere, child. You have the look of your mother about you, with your curly reddish blonde hair, green eyes and button nose. But I think you have your father's chin."

Sophie rubbed her chin as the woman continued to speak. "I used to know your mother when she was younger."

Sophie looked up at the woman and smiled. The woman smiled back and opened her arms to give Sophie a big hug. Grateful for the woman's kindness, Sophie eagerly stepped into the woman's welcoming embrace.

"Glad to meet you Sophie. I am Helen, the head housekeeper. We have been eagerly waiting for you all day. Welcome to your new home. Welcome to Evanswood. It may seem a little overwhelming and odd to you now, but I am sure the house will grow on you. It's a very special place."

Helen winked at Sophie, "I know you will fit in right away."

"What about my bags?" Sophie hesitantly looked over her shoulder.

"No need to worry about those," Helen responded. "I will have someone take them up to your bedroom."

Helen smiled and put her arm around Sophie. She then noticed Sophie's bracelet. It was a gold band with a unique removable medallion mounted in the center of the band.

"Where did you get that bracelet?" Helen stared at the medallion, which looked very familiar.

"My mother had it made for me for my tenth birthday. She said the medallion was very special and I should keep it with me always."

Helen gave Sophie an even bigger grin. "I have one too. Only my medallion has a slightly different design." Helen dangled her medallion before Sophie's eyes.

Helen showed Sophie into the library, located off the main hall and across from the staircase leading upstairs. As Sophie walked into the room, she noticed the enormously high ceiling and several large windows covering the wall to her left. She looked at Helen, who was behind her, and saw there was a set of stairs on both sides of the entrance to the library curving up to a landing above. Sophie turned back around noting that the landing wrapped around the room covering all the walls of the library except the wall with the large windows. There were several shelves of books on the landing.

Sophie continued to look around the room and saw a large, brightly colored tapestry under the landing on the wall to her right. On the far wall, in the center of the room, was an enormous fireplace with a marble mantle. There was a larger than average size odd looking egg shaped clock on the mantle.

Sophie thought it a little strange that the fireplace was not lit, but the room felt warm. There was also some light in the room, although no lights were turned on, and Sophie smelt something burning. She turned around again and saw two additional fireplaces on opposite sides of the large door she used to enter the library. The were on the other side of the sets of stairs curving up to the landing. A fire burned in both of the smaller fireplaces.

"This is the largest library I've ever seen. But, who needs three fireplaces?" Sophie thought.

Helen walked over to the desk in the corner of the room closest to the brightly colored tapestry. The desk had a lamp and a few items on it, and was in front of the same wall as the enormous fireplace in the center of the room. Helen pushed a button on a strange little black box on the desk. She then leaned over the box and asked for Sophie's dinner to be brought to the library.

Sophie gave Helen a strange look.

"It's an intercom," Helen said as she pushed the button again for emphasis. Sophie just continued to stare at her.

"You speak into it and the person on the other end can hear you," Helen responded to Sophie's quizzical look.

Helen then motioned for Sophie to sit on the couch in front of the desk. The couch was facing a roaring fire in one of the small fireplaces and there was a tray of snacks on a table between the couch and the small fireplace.

After making sure Sophie had eaten a few bites and was comfortable, Helen apologized for not being able to show her around the house. There was an emergency in the kitchen and she had to help. Helen turned and walked out of the library.

The house staff was preparing for a large party that Sophie's father had only informed them about that morning. The party was going to take place in the house the day her father returned to Evanswood. It was to be a big affair. Many had already labeled it, "the party of the year." Dignitaries and representatives from all over the world planned to attend the party. There would be music, dancing, and a formal dinner. There was still much work to be done. Everything had to be prefect—and they had less than a week to prepare.

Walking out of the library Helen yelled over her shoulder, "Sophie, your room is on the second floor, third door on the right. You can't miss it. The door frame is the only one upstairs painted green with gold designs."

As Helen reached the library door, she turned and looked at Sophie with kind eyes. "The room belonged to your mother, but it was re-decorated after she and your father left for the United States, shortly after their wedding."

Helen smiled at Sophie. "I hope you like it. We made a few improvements in anticipation of your arrival."

Sophie stared after Helen and thought to herself, "What am I supposed to do now? I am all alone and stuck in this big, ancient, drafty house." Looking around the room she added, "that's dimly lit with strange artwork on the walls."

Sophie knew her mother once lived in the house, but that did not make it feel any less strange or any more like home. From the little she had seen of the house, nothing reminded Sophie of her mother's warm and open spirit.

Based on a conversation with her father, Sophie knew her mother owned the house until her death and allowed her former guardian Mrs. MacTavish to live in the house with her grandson, Sean Ferguson. Maybe Mrs. MacTavish re-decorated more than just her mother's old bedroom.

"If she had decorated the house, Mrs. MacTavish needed to take a few classes in interior design," Sophie said to herself as she continued to look around the dimly lit library.

Sophie found it a little unusual that Mrs. MacTavish and Sean still lived at Evanswood. She didn't know them and she had never heard her mother speak of them. She didn't even think her father knew them. However, when she first learned she was moving to her mother's former home in Dublin, her father told her, "Your mother would have wanted Mrs. MacTavish and Sean to remain at Evanswood, their home, so I will let them know they are welcome to stay as long as they want."

Sophie's father stressed that her mother would have wanted Sophie to get to know Mrs. MacTavish, someone who was very important to her. Sophie learned her mother had kept in almost daily contact with Mrs. MacTavish when she lived in New York.

Sophie was a little surprised neither Sean nor Mrs. MacTavish was there to meet her. She thought begrudgingly, "They are probably busy preparing for the party. It seems THE PARTY is the only thing people care about in this house."

Sophie had to admit, part of her was glad Mrs. MacTavish and Sean were not there to greet her. She was not sure how she felt about sharing her home with strangers, even if one of them had known her mother. She needed time to sort through her thoughts. And she was too tired for a "surface conversation" concerning how she was doing and what she was feeling. Sophie didn't even know these people or anything about them—and she certainly didn't want to answer any questions about her mother.

Sophie also knew that whether she wanted to or not, she was going to meet Sean in the morning. The last time Sophie spoke to her father on the telephone, before she left for Ireland, he told her she wouldn't be leaving the house for school. Her father had spoken to Mrs. MacTavish and decided Sophie should be schooled at home in Evanswood. With his job and the recent changes in Sophie's life, her father thought the safest, most practical option was for Sophie to be tutored at the house with Sean. If she remembered correctly, Mr. Fitzpatrice, the tutor, would be at the house early the next morning to begin her first lesson.

As Sophie sat on the couch finishing her dinner, her eyes were drawn to an object on the mantle above the small fireplace. She stood up and walked over to the lit fireplace to get a better look. It was her father's favorite photograph of his family.

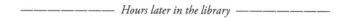

———————— *Hours later in the library* ————————

Collecting her composure, after staring at the photograph of herself and her parents on the mantle for what seemed like hours, Sophie left the library in search of her new bedroom. She thought about looking around the house, but she was exhausted. All she wanted to do was go to bed. And there was also a chance Sean would show her around Evanswood… or if she was lucky, her father would give her a tour of the house when he returned.

Right now all she wanted to find was the door on the second floor, with the green door frame and gold designs, her bedroom. Sophie moved her hands to her mouth to hide a yawn.

Thankfully, Sophie found her room with little effort. She stepped inside and could not believe what she saw. Her room was extremely large, and much bigger than her room in New York. The room was bright, unlike the rest of the house. It looked like it was recently painted. The walls were a light green—her favorite color—and matched the door frame. In the corner there was a portrait of her mother. Sophie had not seen this image of her mother before. Her mother appeared younger than Sophie ever remembered. She was wearing a dress and necklace Sophie had never seen. On her feet were an odd, but beautiful looking pair of blue slippers with strange swirly designs etched in silver.

Sophie told herself, "I'm not going to cry." However, seeing the portrait made her miss her mother dreadfully. And her exhaustion from the trip made it more difficult to hold back the tears.

If Sophie was truly honest with herself, she felt alone and a little afraid to be in this new house, in this new land. As she continued to think about her mother, Sophie could not stop the tears from falling.

Sophie wiped the tears from her eyes and reminded herself to be strong. "I'm glad Helen is here she seems very kind," she sniffled.

A subtle movement pulled Sophie from her current thoughts and brought her attention to the center of her bed. Sitting there on top of what appeared to be a new flower comforter was a small, white, fluffy dog asleep in a brown wicker basket. Sophie could not believe her eyes as she took a few steps towards the bed to get a closer look.

"How did you get here?" Sophie had never asked for a dog. She was not even sure she liked dogs. Maybe the dog was Sean's or Mrs. MacTavish's and somehow it had made its way into her room. But, if that was the case, why was it in a basket and why did it have a bow around its neck?

Sophie tried to gently and quietly sit on the bed without making a sound, so not to wake the dog. But just as she sat on the bed the dog raised its head and barked at her. Well it was not exactly a bark. It was more like a whimper. She could have sworn it was saying hello.

"But, how could a dog say hello? And the last time I checked, I do not speak dog," Sophie thought.

Attached to the basket was a pretty pink card. Sophie picked up the card and read:

> *My dearest daughter,*
> *Sorry, I was not able to meet you at the airport. I had planned to be there, but I was called away at the last minute on important work. I will be home in about a week and plan to take a few days off work to show you around Dublin. It is a great city with wonderful people.*
> *I know leaving our home in New York and saying good-bye to your friends has been tough on you. I am truly sorry for the added pain this has caused you, but I thought change would be good for us and new experiences may help us remember how to be happy.*
> *I also thought you may like a new friend to keep you company while I am away. Her name is Zoey and she is about five years old. She belonged to a friend of Mrs. MacTavish. She needed a new home when her owners moved to a new apartment. I hear she likes popcorn.*
> *See you soon.*
> *Your Loving Father*

Sophie crumbled the card in her hand as the tears fell freely from her eyes. As hard as she tried to stay brave, she could not keep from crying. She looked at the dog that continued to gently bark at her, a little louder this time. Sophie distinctly heard, "Please don't cry." Sophie supposed she was more exhausted and upset than she realized…or was she losing a grip on reality and hearing voices in her head. She reminded herself, "Dogs don't talk."

As she stared at the little dog with a red bow and the name tag Zoey, around her neck, Sophie started to cry even harder. All she could think about was what she had lost over the last year and the fact that her father was not here to tell her everything was going to be okay. Then Sophie began to get angry.

"What was my father thinking? I don't know how to take care of a dog. In fact, I don't even want a dog," Sophie thought as she hit the bed with her hand.

All Sophie wanted was her father to be there. She didn't want Zoey, "his guilt gift," no matter how cute she was.

"And what dog really liked popcorn?" she thought as she looked down at Zoey's cute little nose, white fluffy head and soft brown eyes.

Zoey was just small enough for Sophie to pick up and carry around. Before Sophie realized what she was doing, she reached into the basket to pick up Zoey. Sophie cradled Zoey in her arms and gently placed her next to her on the bed. She took off the bow and name tag from around Zoey's neck, removed the basket from her bed and then laid her head down on her pillow. Within minutes she fell into a deep sleep.

––––––––––––––––––––––––––––––––––––––

"Wake up, wake up, it's time to wake up!"

Sophie heard the words before she opened her eyes. Sophie rubbed her eyes and felt a little disoriented. For a few moments Sophie did not recognize where she was. She felt something cold against her nose and something fluffy against her face.

"Alright, I am getting up," Sophie said as she continued to rub her eyes. She thought, "If I could only remember where I am and why I need to get up."

Light was shining in the windows. As Sophie looked around her eyes focused on the portrait of her mother. She remembered she was in her new home in Ireland. She heard the voice again.

"You need to get up for your first lesson with the tutor. You have about an hour to get ready, and you better not be late."

Sophie was confused. She looked around, but did not see anyone else in the room. In a hesitant voice she said, "Who's here?" She did not really expect a reply, since no one appeared to be in the room.

Sophie looked at Zoey. "I really must be going crazy because the only other living creature in this room is you and dogs do not talk."

Zoey looked up at Sophie. "What makes you think dogs don't talk? I just woke you up didn't I? And who do you think was speaking to you last night?"

Zoey shook her head, slightly irritated by Sophie's disbelief and continued, "I would have said more last night, but you woke me from a wonderful dream and I really wanted to get back to it. However, it was kind of difficult for me to get back to sleep when you grabbed me during the night. You were holding me so tightly I had trouble breathing.

Sophie continued to stare at Zoey in disbelief. A dog was really speaking to her. And she could understand every word the dog was saying. "This cannot be happening," Sophie mumbled.

The next thing she heard was Zoey responding. "This is real 'little one' and I am here to stay. Plus, I think you need a friend." Sophie could not help but laugh at Zoey's comment, and the way she scrunched up her nose when she said it. And who was Zoey calling little? Sophie was much bigger than she was and older than her, not counting in dog years.

Sophie wanted to speak to Zoey longer, but what kind of things did you talk about with a dog? And she really did have to get ready, if she wanted to have any breakfast before her first lesson. Zoey warned her that she could not get through Mr. Fitzpatrice's morning lessons on an empty stomach. And with as little sleep as she had the night before, she knew she needed some breakfast for the extra energy, especially if she was going to meet anyone new and explore her new surroundings.

"Sorry if I picked you up in my sleep and held you too tight. I didn't mean to hurt you," Sophie told Zoey as she patted her head.

"I was a little winded when I woke up, but you didn't hurt me." Zoey wagged her tail.

"Mr. Fitzpatrice's lessons can be long and redundant."

Zoey stressed she heard a few of the lessons and they put her to sleep. Zoey advised Sophie that if the Greek Gods were on the agenda for the day, she should bring a book. She had heard Mr. Fitzpatrice practicing for that lesson and found it very boring.

"How could anyone make the Greek Gods boring?" Sophie thought.

Sophie did have one problem—other than a talking dog—she did not know where to go to get breakfast. At home in New York, she always ate in the kitchen. Except when she was at her grandmother St. Clair's. There she was required to eat in the dining room. However, she did not know where either the kitchen or the dining room was, in her new home. Sophie sighed; she still had trouble believing she was no longer in New York.

As Sophie was deciding whether to look for the kitchen or the dining room, there was a knock on the door. It was Helen with her breakfast. There was French toast and hot chocolate.

Sophie smiled: "Thank the almighty for Helen and her trays of food. But, how does she know my favorite breakfast?

After all my years of studies, this is the only job I could find—tutoring some well off children who cannot even make it to my lesson on time. I should have been a professor at a university or at least an elite private school. Well, it's possible these children will be good students and will be interested in learning. They always say you shouldn't judge a book by its cover. Maybe I am judging these children too harshly. And after the three years I took off to help my mother, I am really looking forward to teaching again. I need to just breathe and not get annoyed. She should arrive very soon. Then I will let her know that being late to my lessons is not acceptable behavior.

-Professor Fitzpatrice

iii : the first Day of School

"Whew, just in time," Sophie wiped her head. She opened the library door as the clock located on the mantle of the fireplace in the center of the room finished striking seven.

"What an interesting clock," Sophie thought. She had seen it the night before, but really did not take a good look at. Pausing after entering the library and focusing on the clock she was able to admire its uniqueness. The clock was shaped like an egg in an egg server, was made of wood painted black and divided into three parts. The top part of the clock was egg shaped and contained the face of the clock. The face had a gold background with a moon in the top right and bottom left corners, and a sun in the top left and bottom right corners. The roman numeral numbers on the clock were painted black. The hands on the clock were also black with fine pieces of gold and silver metal wrapped around them. The middle part of the clock was plain with two door handles carved into the wood. The bottom part of the clock looked like the base of an egg server. There was an image of a sun and a rooster on the bottom part of the clock, but it did not appear to be carved into the wood.

Looking at the clock got Sophie to think about how early in the morning it was. She stewed. "Seven AM; what a horrible hour to start a lesson. Why does Mr. Fitzpatrice have to start lessons so early? It's not like he has anything else to do during the day. And the lessons are in the house, we don't have to go anywhere to get to the classroom. Why can't he start later?"

When Sophie switched her focus from the clock on the mantle and walked further into the library, she saw a small table sitting in front of a blackboard on the far side of the room. The table was in front of the small fireplace closest to the windows. There was a man standing near the window in front of the blackboard. The man had to be the tutor, Mr. Fitzpatrice. He was not as intimidating as Sophie expected.

"Well, I am not sure what I was expected," she thought, "but I know it was not this man standing before me." The man was not short, but he was not as tall as her father. He was not over weight, but was a little round in the middle. He had brown beady eyes that reminded Sophie of a squirrel. His hair was thinning and she could see the sun reflecting off the top of his head. All in all, he was not bad looking.

"You are late," the man said in a nasal voice. Sophie couldn't help but cringe a little when the man spoke. She never heard a voice like that before. The sound of it actually hurt her ears.

"I am Mr. Fitzpatrice. Please take your seat, so we can begin."

Sophie opened her mouth to say the clock had just struck Seven, and she was not late, but decided against it. She wanted to get through the day with Mr. Fitzpatrice speaking as little as possible. Zoey was right; Mr. Fitzpatrice was a stickler for his schedule and punctuality. Sophie did not want to throw him off schedule more than she already had, from being late, which was another reason she decided not to speak up about her really not being late.

Sophie sat down across the table from a lanky boy. In his brown pants and jacket, both of which, looked too big for him, the boy blended into the brown chair. Sophie looked closer at him. She realized he was much taller than she originally suspected. He was just very thin. He wore a brown tie that fit tight around his neck. She thought, "the tie couldn't be comfortable."

Sophie could hardly see the boy's blue eyes hidden behind big black glasses. The frames took up so much space she could barely see the lenses. She wondered how he could see through them.

The boy did not look up when Sophie pulled out her chair to sit across from him. Even after Sophie's examination of him, he continued to avoid looking at her and didn't say a word. Sophie almost wanted to stick her tongue out at him to see what he would do, but she knew that was not very nice. However, the thought crossed her mind more than once.

The boy's dark blonde hair was slicked back, but the cowlick on the front of his head kept falling in his face. In the short period of time she had been siting at the table, Sophie saw him push his hair out of his eyes several times. It seemed he was used to this challenge and didn't appear annoyed by it. He also had a cowlick in the back of his head that kept trying to stand up straight. "He must have put a lot of water on that one this morning," Sophie laughed to herself.

As Sophie looked at the boy, the boy did not even look up to smile once. She couldn't tell if the boy was glad or irritated he had to share his morning lessons with her.

Mr. Fitzpatrice began his lessons with math, Sophie's least favorite subject. She moved her hands over her mouth to cover a yawn. Mr. Fitzpatrice looked at her with displeasure.

"What does he expect? I only slept a few hours the night before. I'm only human!" Sophie thought.

"What is one fourth of a hundred?" Mr. Fitzpatrice asked in his nasally voice. The boy seemed to really like math.

He sat up straighter in his chair, looked directly at Mr. Fitzpatrice and answered in a clear voice, "twenty-five."

"Correct." Mr. Fitzpatrice smiled at him.

Thankfully, Mr. Fitzpatrice didn't ask any more questions. Instead, he wrote twenty problems on the blackboard. He told Sophie and the boy they had thirty minutes to copy and answer the problems.

Sophie breathed a sigh of relief. "I'm going to have at least a thirty-minute reprieve from Mr. Fitzpatrice and his awful nasal voice," she thought, and then began to copy and answer the math problems.

"Time is up," Mr. Fitzpatrice announced.

Sophie cringed. She always tried to find the good in people and did not like to think anything bad about anyone, but Mr. Fitzpatrice's voice was really getting to her. It sounded worse than nails scratching across a chalkboard. Sophie wanted to cover her ears every time he spoke.

"I'm really going to have to work hard to get used to listening to that voice. But how do I go about getting used to that voice, when all I want is to avoid it?" Sophie asked herself.

The boy did not seem to mind Mr. Fitzpatrice's voice. He focused intently as Mr. Fitzpatrice wrote the answers on the blackboard. Sophie could not help but cover her ears when Mr. Fitzpatrice asked her and the boy to switch papers, so they could correct each other's work. Sophie thought that was the teacher's job, but she did not vocalize her opinion on the matter.

"Hi, I'm Sophie," she said as she pushed her paper towards the boy. "What's your name?"

Sophie knew the boy had to be Sean, but she wanted to get him to talk. She thought an introduction was the best place to start. Then she could stop thinking of him as the boy.

The boy tentatively looked up. "I am Sean. Nice to meet you," he said quietly as he handed Sophie his paper.

"At least he is polite and he seems kind, but he also seems very shy and a little uptight," Sophie thought.

Sophie began to correct Sean's paper. Of course, Sean answered all the problems correctly. She felt a little embarrassed because she missed ten out of twenty.

"Don't worry," Sean smiled. "His voice grows on you... and some of those questions were a little difficult. I can work with you and help you figure out the answers, so you get them all right the next time, if you would like?"

Sophie smiled back at Sean, "I may have judged him unfairly. Maybe he is not as stuffy as he looks."

"What's happening to me?" Sophie wondered. "I'm normally much kinder to people."

For some reason, at that moment, Sophie's mind wondered to Zoey. "And I have never heard a dog speak before. What's going on inside my head?"

"Losing my mother and moving to a new home must be making me a little less friendly," Sophia said aloud, as she threw her hands in the air perplexed. Sophie did not realize she had spoken aloud until both Sean and Mr. Fitzpatrice looked at her strangely. Thankfully, they were both distracted by Helen opening the library door with snacks.

"Praise Helen and her trays of food," Sophie thought. "She is always coming to my rescue. Food is a great distraction. Mr. Fitzpatrice and Sean completely forgot about my comment."

Helen put the food down on the table.

"I told you he was boring. And that voice, I am not sure how Sean sits through his lessons." Sophie looked over and saw Zoey had entered the room. Zoey jumped up on the couch, as Helen left the room.

"I just wanted to check and see how you were doing," Zoey said right before she lay down on the couch to take a nap.

Sophie looked at both Sean and Mr. Fitzpatrice. Sean was busy eating a chocolate chip cookie and getting milk on his upper lip. Sophie wanted to tease him about his milk mustache, but she was not sure how he would respond to her joking. Even eating a cookie, he looked so serious. And Mr. Fitzpatrice had flipped the blackboard. He was ready to begin his next lesson.

"How strange," Sophie thought as she scratched her head. "Neither Sean nor Mr. Fitzpatrice seemed to notice the talking dog lying on the couch."

Zoey shook her head and wagged her tail at Sophie. It almost seemed liked Zoey was laughing at the confused look on Sophie's face. When she got no reaction from Sophie, Zoey laid her head back down on her front paws to return to her peaceful slumber.

Sophie turned her attention back to the blackboard which read: Bram Stoker, James Joyce, Oscar Wilde, Jonathan Swift and W.B. Yeats.

"Can you tell me who these persons are and for what they are known?" Mr. Fitzpatrice asked.

Sean was still eating his cookie and could not answer. Sophie had no idea who the people were and yelled out, "They are Greek to me!"

Sophie was not exactly sure the meaning of what she said. She just remembered her father saying "it's Greek to me" a few times when he did not know the answer to a question her mother had asked. Her mother always laughed in response. Sophie liked the expression, but had never used it before. In her mind, she could almost hear her mother laughing.

Sophie's joyful thought was interrupted by Mr. Fitzpatrice clearing his throat very loudly. Sophie focused her attention on him and thought, "maybe it was not the right time to have tried out that expression."

Mr. Fitzpatrice looked startled and somewhat offended by her statement. "No young lady, they are not Greek," he said. "They are Irish and some of the best writers the world has ever produced."

Mr. Fitzpatrice then began what he called "reading time" and started to read aloud from one of the books by W.B. Yeats. Sophie felt like she was being tortured. She really enjoyed learning and the story was not bad at all, but Mr. Fitzpatrice's voice was just too much for her. After Mr. Fitzpatrice had not looked up from his book for ten minutes—Sophie was sure it had been ten minutes because she had been watching the clock—she looked at Sean and motioned to the library door with her head.

Sean shook his head, "No!" Sophie smiled at him and motioned to the door again. This time, he shook his head "Yes," and smiled back. Both Sophie and Sean quietly moved their chairs from the table and tip toed to the library door. By the time they reached the door, Zoey had jumped off the couch and was standing next to them.

"It may seem Mr. Fitzpatrice is deeply absorbed in the book he is reading, but there is no way you can open that door without making noise; you will get caught, if you try," Zoey said.

"There is another way out of this room. I can show you." Zoey continued in a clear voice.

As Sean reached up to open the door, Sophie shook her head, "no" and began to follow Zoey. Although, he was not sure what was going on, Sean followed. Zoey led them both to the wall on the far side of the room that was covered with a large tapestry.

Zoey tried to fit her nose between the tapestry and the wall. "Pull here."

Sophie put her hand on the edge of the tapestry and gently pulled it back a few inches, trying not to make any noise. She realized that there was not a wall behind the tapestry. It was an open space that appeared to be another room, with a door at the end. Sophie pulled the tapestry back farther. She let Sean and Zoey go first. Then still holding back the tapestry, Sophie squeezed behind the tapestry into the room on the other side.

Once they were all in the room, Sophie carefully and quietly let the tapestry fall back into place. The room went completely dark. Sean let out a slight gasp and Sophie grabbed his hand.

"It is okay," she whispered, "I remember seeing a door at the back of the room before I let go of the tapestry and the room went dark. Just follow me. We can crawl on the floor, running our hand along the wall until we reach the back wall. Then I can just feel for the door handle. And open it."

"Why do we have to crawl? Can't we run our hands along the wall while we are standing?" Sean asked.

"I'll get my pants dirty if we crawl."

"Because Mr. Smarty-Pants, if we run into anything in front of us, I would rather already be on the ground, instead of falling to the ground. And, it is more fun this way," Sophie replied.

"The dirt will brush off your pants."

Sean just shook his head and smiled. "Boy, this girl really makes me smile a lot. I can't remember the last time I smiled this much. This girl could be trouble, but I think we are going to have loads of fun together." He had already forgot about his pants getting dirty.

Before Sophie reached the back wall her hand hit something. "Smash in Squash! That hurt a little," Sophie whispered to herself. She moved her hands out in front of her and touched the obstacle with both of her hands. The obstacle felt hard, with sharp edges, and not very large. After a quick examination, she determined the obstacle was likely a box.

"I will explore you later, but right now all I want to do is get out of this dark room," Sophie thought as she pushed the box aside and continued to feel for the back wall.

"I think something just ran across my legs," Sean yelled.

"Shh...shh, we are trying to be quiet here. Do you want to get caught after all of this?" Sophie asked.

"But, it could have been a rat." Sean replied in his quietest voice.

"Don't be a baby. There are no rats in this house," Sophie stated.

"No, I think it was a rat," Sophie heard Zoey say from the back of the room.

"I don't want to hear anything from you either," Sophie said in a less confident voice, looking for Zoey in the darkness.

"What did you say?" Sean asked.

"Never mind," Sophie replied. "Let's just get out of here."

Sophie continued reaching for the back wall. This time, she was a little more cautious where she put her hands. Once she felt the back wall she moved her hand back and forth across the wall searching for the door handle. She remembered seeing the door handle in the middle of the back wall, so she concentrated her hand movements in that direction, praying she did not come across any cobwebs or spiders.

"Got it," she yelled as her hand turned the knob and opened the door.

Sean wanted to say something to Sophie about being quiet, but he was just happy he was getting out of the dark room...and away from the rats and whatever other dangerous things were in the room. He really disliked being unable to see.

A bright light streamed through the doorway. Sophie and Sean crawled out the doorway into a beautiful garden. The garden was double the size of the library. It was filled with bright flowers, and trees with multi-colored leaves. There was an elaborately decorated bench next to a pond. Strange statues that resembled some of the creatures from the books Sophie's mother read her when she was young decorated the garden.

One of the statues appeared to be a woman with a very long neck, and full, elaborate wings. Another statue looked like a man with webbed feet and a curly tail. He was sticking out a long oddly shaped tongue.

After Sophie and Sean entered the garden, Zoey came running through the door. "I thought I would let you figure out how to get out of there, before I moved away from the tapestry. I wanted to save some of the work for you. And why chance wandering around in a dark room when I know in minutes there will be light."

Sophie pondered Zoey's words and thought, "Yes, who would choose to wander in the dark, knowing the light is coming." Then she remembered Zoey's earlier words. It was true someone had to do the work. Sophie laughed at Zoey's spunk.

"Why are you laughing?" Sean curiously asked.

"Could he not hear Zoey?" Sophie wondered.

"That was amazing," Sean said. "How did you know how to get out of the library?"

"I guess that answers my question," Sophie thought. "Sean does not hear Zoey."

Sophie really wanted to tell Sean about Zoey, but decided against telling him. She did not want him to think she was crazy. And who would believe a dog could talk, especially if they couldn't hear it. This was one secret she was going to keep to herself; at least for a while, so she decided to lie. She hated deception of any kind. It went against her nature, but this time it was necessary. She did not want to end up in the loony bin, if they had them in Ireland.

"I found the hidden room when I was in the library last night." The tapestry looked a little odd, but very soft. I wanted to see if it was as soft as it looks. When I touched the tapestry it didn't feel like there was a wall behind it. I thought it strange, so I pulled it back a little and realized there was a large open space behind it. I did not check out the room. I had no idea there was a box inside it or this lovely garden."

At Sophie's mention of the lovely garden, Zoey looked around. She was in awe. "I saw Helen pull back the tapestry once or twice, so I knew about the hidden room. However, I had no idea this garden was here. What a wonder!"

"What box?" Sean gently shook Sophie's arm. It was the second time he asked about the box. He could not figure out why she was not answering. She seemed to be in some kind of trance just staring at the dog.

Shaking her arm got Sophie's attention. She responded, "that box," pointing at the box sitting on the floor in the middle of the now somewhat lit room. Sitting close to the box on the floor was a small green lizard with a long tail.

"Rats," Sophie shook her head. "I do not see any rats in there."

The door leading to the garden remained open allowing light to fill the room. With the light shining on the box, it sparkled. They could all see it was covered in ornate designs. It looked beautiful. Sophie went back in the hidden room. Since the room was better lit with the garden door open, she decided there was no need to crawl. She walked passed the lizard, bent down, picked up the box and returned to the garden.

Once she had the box outside in the light, she began to examine it. The box was a lovely blue and the designs covering it were etched in gold.

"How could anyone leave such a beautiful box in that tiny, dimly lit room, hidden from view?" Sophie asked not expecting an answer.

"The designs on the box appear to match the designs on the walls in my bedroom. It must have belonged to my mother," Sophie said as she looked at Sean.

Sophie shook the box. "I wonder what's inside." She pulled on the lid of the box, but it wouldn't open. She shook the box harder this time, but it still wouldn't open. There was no latch on the box holding it shut, so she could not understand why it did not open.

"May I see the box?" Sean asked as he reached out his hands.

Sophie tentatively handed it to him. She was hesitant to let go of something that may have belonged to her mother. Sean looked closely at the box.

"I have seen a box like this before," Sean smiled. "My grandmother has one like it, but her box is more of a pinkish red." He pushed on the back corner of the box.

"There you go," Sean said, as the panel at the bottom of the box moved aside revealing a keyhole.

Sophie grabbed the box from him in awe. She held the box close to her eye to get a better look at the keyhole. "It looks like a heart-shaped key will fit," Sophie said as she moved her finger over the keyhole.

"I may have seen a key similar to that before," Sean said. "Once when I was much younger, I was playing in my grandmother's room when I was not supposed to be there. I heard my grandmother coming, so I quickly hid under the bed. That's when I saw my grandmother open her pinkish red box."

"Did she use a heart-shaped key?" Sophie asked.

"I am not sure. I could not see the shape of the key," Sean replied. "But, I remember there were several other keys on the keychain, maybe one of the keys was heart-shaped."

"I know where she keeps her keys," Sean smiled.

"Where?" Sophie asked with her eyes shining brightly. "I really want to get this box opened." She pulled the box close to her chest.

"In her room," Sean replied. "I've not been in there in ages, but I don't think she moved anything. My grandmother is a stickler for consistency and tradition."

With a serious face, Sean said, "I bet the keys are still in a brown box on top of her dresser."

"Let's go get it!" Sophie declared.

Sean thought as he smiled, "This girl really is going to get me into trouble, but I'm having a lot of fun."

"If you want to check out Mrs. MacTavish's room," Zoey exclaimed, "The best time is at dinner. She is always away from her room for a few hours."

"Oh" Sophie uttered. She had almost forgotten about Zoey, she was so distracted by the box. Although, it was hard to forget about a talking dog…especially, when that dog kept talking to you.

At the same time, both Sean and Zoey offered to take Sophie to Mrs. MacTavish's room.

"I would love to look for the key as soon as possible. However, I think we should return to the library now." Sophie smiled and walked towards the door leading back into the hidden room as Sean and Zoey followed.

Sophie, Sean and Zoey all made their way back to the tapestry. Sophie slowly pulled back the tapestry to see if anyone was in the library. Thankfully, Mr. Fitzpatrice had left. She pulled back the tapestry so Sean and Zoey could follow her into the library. Sophie, Sean and Zoey then quickly and quietly left the library making their way upstairs without being seen.

Sophie, Sean and Zoey all missed dinner that evening to search for the box in Mrs. MacTavish's room. Sophie and Sean just found the brown box on Mrs. MacTavish dresser when the knob on her bedroom door began to turn.

"That was a short few hours," Sophie thought as she regarded Zoey with a look that said you could not have been more wrong. Sophie held tight to the brown box and grabbed Sean's hand. They both dashed towards the bed.

When Mrs. MacTavish entered the room she was greeted by a barking dog. Zoey jumped up on her leg and then proceeded to run three circles around her.

"Sophie better appreciate this! I am making a fool of myself. Hopefully, I have distracted Mrs. MacTavish long enough for Sophie and Sean to hide."

Mrs. MacTavish rubbed her forehead slightly confused. She bent down, picked up Zoey, held her close to her chest and scratched her head. "How did you get into my room? I do not recall leaving the door open when I went downstairs for dinner."

Zoey gave Mrs. MacTavish a friendly bark.

Mrs. MacTavish continued to scratch Zoey's head as she carried her to the door, to put her outside the room.

"Try not to get into any more trouble," Mrs. MacTavish told Zoey as she slowly closed the door.

Sean and Sophie had just enough time to hide under the bed, before Mrs. MacTavish walked back into the room and sat at her desk. Sophie breathed an inward sigh of relief. They had not gotten caught, but Sophie did not know how long they were going to be stuck under the bed. Luckily, Mrs. MacTavish had a king size bed, so both of them had space to stretch out a little under the bed.

Sean guessed his grandmother was looking at her mail. They could be stuck under the bed for a while. He started to say something. Sophie put her index finger over her mouth urging him not to speak. He motioned for Sophie to open the box that she still held tightly in her hands.

Sophie carefully placed the box on the floor between them and slowly opened the lid. Inside the box were the keys Sean remembered.

"We got it! Thank you," Sophie mouthed as she held up a small heart-shaped key.

Sean gave her a big grin and a thumbs-up.

Mrs. MacTavish sat at her desk rubbing her head. She only had soup for dinner, hoping it would help her feel better, but her head still hurt horribly. She wanted to lie down, but she could not go to sleep, yet. She needed to write a letter that had to go out in the morning mail. There was an old friend who needed to know Sophie was in Ireland. She wanted to invite him to the upcoming party at Evanswood.

He would blend in with all the people attending the party. No one would guess the true reason he was there and they would be able to speak in person. The party would also give him the opportunity to meet Sophie.

Mrs. MacTavish was anxious to see her friend. Although she heard from him regularly, she had not seen him in years. They had a lot to talk about.

Mrs. MacTavish quickly wrote, "Sophie arrived in Ireland a few days ago. I am not sure I can protect her on my own. I may need help. There will be a party at Evanswood in four days. This will be the perfect time for us to speak. Please come."

Mrs. MacTavish reread her words. "That should do it," she thought. She silently prayed that he would come. She then left her room to bring the letter downstairs, so it could go out with the morning mail.

"Is she gone?" Sean asked.

Sophie slowly poked her head out from under the bed and looked around. "It looks that way," she replied. Thankful, she and Sean were not stuck under the bed all night; she crawled out from under the bed. Sean followed.

Sophie removed the heart-shaped key from the key chain. She put the key chain back in the brown box and the heart-shaped key in her dress pocket. Next, she placed the brown box back on Mrs. MacTavish's dresser. Then she and Sean hurried out the door and ran to Sophie's bedroom, where she had left the blue box.

"Open it," Sean said as Sophie took the blue box out of her closet. She removed the key from her pocket, pushed the button on the corner of the box to reveal the keyhole and placed the heart-shaped key in the keyhole at the bottom of the box. The box popped open…like magic. Inside the box was a beautiful mirror and blue shoes with silver etching. There seemed to be a place for a ring, a small circular object and a long thin object, but Sophie did not see anything else in the box. Sophie took out the shoes and mirror and placed them on her bed. She shook the box, just in case the ring or circular object had fallen out of its slot and was hiding somewhere else in the box. She heard nothing rattling.

Sophie laid the box on her bed next to the shoes and picked up the mirror.

"What do you see?" Sean asked.

"How strange. All I see when I look into the mirror is a haze of black nothingness. I can't even see my own reflection," Sophie told Sean.

Sean opened his mouth to speak, but was interrupted by a knock on Sophie's door. Sophie quickly placed the mirror on her bed and threw a blanket over the objects on her bed.

"Come in," she yelled.

The door opened and Helen walked in smiling, with a tray full of food. "You missed dinner, so I thought you might be hungry."

At that moment, Sophie's stomach began to growl. She realized she was famished. "Thank you Helen. I really am very hungry."

"My Pleasure, young Miss," Helen replied. "I brought enough for two." She winked at Sean and turned to walk out of the room.

Before she reached the door she turned and looked at Sean, "you better hurry to your room soon. Your grandmother was looking for you. She seemed a little upset when she could not find you."

"Thank you Helen," Sean replied with a worried look on his face. "I will go find her right now."

"Do you think my grandmother knows we were in her room?" he asked Sophie after Helen had left.

"No, there is no way she could know. I am sure she did not see us. Plus, we put everything back the way we found it, and we did not leave anything behind."

Hoping Sophie was right, Sean took a few bites of food from the tray before he headed off in search of his grandmother.

I can't believe I finally met someone who can understand what I'm saying. I remember when my father told me about a young man he met many years ago—the young man who spoke to my grandfather and became his friend—but I didn't believe him. My father said the young man wasn't exactly human; but, Sophie seems to be human and I can have a conversation with her. I don't think she is the same type of being as the young man. She doesn't smell sweet, the same way my father described the young man smelling. Since Sophie appears to be human, I don't understand how she can hear me, but I'm very glad that she can. She seems sad, lonely, and maybe a little angry. However, I can tell she has a kind, loving heart and a strong spirit. And if things keep going the way they have been going since she arrived at Evanswood, we are going to have a lot of fun over the next few years. I think we will become great friends. I'm going to try to do all I can do to make her happy. Even if that means I have to be more sarcastic than normal.

-Zoey

iv : the Shoes

Sophie finished the dinner Helen left for her then moved the box and the mirror off the bed, so she could crawl into it with her Jane Austin novel *Pride and Prejudice*. Sophie planned to read a little before it was time to go to bed or she fell asleep…or whichever came first. She was very tired from her trip and yawned as she turned the page; however, she was still enjoying the book, regardless of her exhaustion.

"Wouldn't Mr. Fitzpatrice be surprised if he knew how much I enjoy reading, especially Jane Austin's novels. He would probably say something along the lines, 'You should not waste your time reading the writings of an English author,' which Jane Austin certainly was. 'You need to focus your time and energy on reading the masterpieces of the great Irish authors'."

As her mind drifted towards thoughts of Mr. Fitzpatrice, Sophie dreaded getting up early the next morning for lessons. Sophie decided she probably should give into sleep.

Sophie had just nodded off when from out of nowhere she heard "are you going to try on the shoes?" She opened her eyes and saw Zoey had hopped up on the bed and was now looking at her.

"Ah, the shoes," Sophie yawned as she rubbed Zoey on the head. "How could I forget about them?" She reached down to pick up the shoes.

"They really are a lovely shade of blue. These designs seem to resemble something, but I have never seen these shapes or patterns before," Sophie exclaimed as she picked up the shoes and examined them closer. In the light they sparkled. Sophie was now wide-awake, eager to try on the lovely blue shoes.

Sophie dangled her legs over the side of the bed so she could easily put on the shoes. "They look a little big. I wonder if they truly belonged to my mother?"

She leaned over to put the first shoe on her right foot. She reached for the left shoe and the shoe on her right foot fell off hitting the floor with a plop. She reached down and picked up the shoe, to try it on for a second time. This time she was able to keep the right shoe from slipping off her foot by focusing and curling up her toes in the front of the shoe.

After Sophie put on her left shoe, curling her toes to keep both shoes on her feet, she started to spin. The room around her began to disappear than reappear. Where her dresser once was, she saw a tree. Her carpet began to shimmer and turned into green grass then back into a tan carpet. The ceiling faded away into open sky then closed back up again. There were spots of bright light and vivid color shooting through the air. Then the colors settled and specs of red, yellow, blue, orange, green and purple drifted through her room, like bubbles floating in the air. An enormous amount of energy vibrated through the room and there was a buzzing sound. Sophie felt like she was in her room and outside all at the same time. She felt weightless and electrically charged.

"What's happening," Sophie heard Zoey say over and over again. But Zoey's words were breaking up and became faint and distant. Sophie tried to respond, but it was like she was talking into a big void of nothingness, no sound escaped from her mouth. As Zoey looked at Sophie, she saw a bright light. Sophie faded in and out, and almost appeared translucent, like particles of matter that were visible to the eye, but were floating on air, not connected to each other, leaving empty spaces where light passed through. Sophie was vanishing right before Zoey's eyes, but Zoey could still see the shoes sparkling on Sophie's feet.

Zoey jumped off the bed and began frantically pulling at Sophie's shoes with her teeth. The first shoe came off relatively easily and Sophie began to come back into focus. Zoey pulled at the second shoe, but had trouble getting the shoe off Sophie's foot. Zoey grabbed the shoe with her teeth again, pulling harder, but the shoe would not come off. She started to shake her head back and forth with a large amount of force. Finally, Zoey fell backwards on the carpet with the shoe in her mouth. Sophie sat on the bed scratching her head speechless, wondering what just happened to her. She was in awe of some of the things she had just seen.

"What a RUSH!" Sophie said when she finally found her voice. "How did that happen? Where did I go?"

"I haven't a clue," Zoey responded, "But you disappeared from this room for a while. I thought I was going to lose you for good. That's why I risked my life to pull off your shoes."

"Thanks for your help Zoey," Sophie said as she slightly rolled her eyes at Zoey's over dramatization of the risk she took. As far as Sophie could tell, at no point was Zoey's life in any danger. It was Sophie who had just encountered the most bizarre experience of her life. She had not been terrified though. A sense of peace had settled over her as she shifted from her room to that other place.

"It was so beautiful and enchanting... wherever I went. I have to go back. For the few seconds I was there, I almost felt at home," Sophie said.

"Are you crazy?" Zoey asked with widened eyes. "Maybe you should try to stay out of trouble and go to bed. I do not want to have to save you again—at least not tonight."

"Maybe you are right Zoey," Sophie exclaimed, as she made plans in her mind to try and get back to the magical place. Tomorrow couldn't come soon enough. For the time being, however, Sophie decided to take Zoey's advice and go to bed. Her head hurt. She still felt a little sick to her stomach and she was completely exhausted.

Sophie put her head on her pillow. Within a few minutes her stomach settled and she fell into a deep sleep.

———————————————————————————————

The next morning Sophie entered the library at 6:55 a.m., early for her lesson.

Mr. Fitzpatice looked directly at Sophie, "That was some stunt you and Sean pulled yesterday. I still cannot figure out how you got out of the library."

Sophie just smiled at Mr. Fitzpatrice and looked around the room.

"If you are looking for your partner in crime, you should know he will not join us until after lunch today. He has visual training this morning," Mr. Fitzpatrice informed her.

Sophie was afraid to ask. She knew if she did, she would have to hear Mr. Fitzpatrice speak longer, but curiosity got the best of her – it always did. "What is visual training?"

Mr. Fitzpatrice replied, "It is exercises for your eyes and brain to make them work better together – kind of like physical therapy for your eyes."

Sophie was confused by Mr. Fitzpatrice's answer, "physical therapy for the eyes… what did that mean?" She decided to ask Sean about this visual training the next time she saw him.

"Thank you for the explanation Mr. Fitzpatrice. It was very helpful and informative."

Sophie took her seat at the table and looked directly at Mr. Fitzpatrice, appearing as if she was ready to learn. All of a sudden, she let out a loud gasp.

"Sorry, I just remembered I forgot to take my medicine this morning. I was so concerned about being on time."

Sophie smiled charmingly at Mr. Fitzpatrice. "Would you mind if I went upstairs to take my medicine?"

"If you need your medicine, you may return upstairs. But hurry back downstairs so we can start your lessons. After your disappearing act yesterday, we are a little behind schedule for the week."

"Behind schedule are we, Mr. Fitzpatrice?" Sophie shook her head as she left the library. "We are going to remain that way for the rest of the week. There is no way I am going to return downstairs for lessons with just you and me – not a chance."

Before Sophie returned to her room she wanted to stop by Sean's room. She needed supplies for her journey. Sophie planned to travel to that other world and suspected this was the perfect opportunity for her to try on the shoes again. Sean was busy with some training she had never heard of before. And Zoey was nowhere to be found. She had probably headed downstairs for breakfast or went on another exploration of the house, looking for other hidden rooms.

If Sophie were honest with herself she would admit that the house was oddly unique with strange statues, paintings, doorways, windows, furniture and hidden hallways and rooms. She was really looking forward to exploring the house herself one day, but first things first…put on the magic shoes and get back to the other world.

Sophie was in luck. She found Sean's room easily, only two doors down from hers. She found a bag hanging behind Sean's door. She looked in the bag, but it was so dark inside she could not tell what it contained.

She sat on the floor and dumped out the contents of the bag where there was more light. A sealed container fell on the floor.

"This will be prefect for water," she thought.

A small knife, some matches and a lightweight jacket fell on the floor. "All set, the only other thing I may need is some food. Thankfully I have a few rolls left over from breakfast. I can pack those and I may have an apple on my dresser."

Sophie stuffed all the items on the floor back into the bag. She picked up the bag and returned to her room. Once she reached her room, Sophie went in her top drawer and pulled out a pair of tights and three pairs of socks. She changed into her nicest, casual dress. She wanted to look good and be comfortable wherever she was going.

Sophie grabbed the apple off her dresser and the rolls off her breakfast tray. She stuffed them into the bag. She then went into the bathroom and filled the container with water. She was not sure exactly where she was going, but she was going to be prepared.

Once Sophie had all the items in the bag, she put her tights on over the three pair of socks. She did not want her shoes falling off this time. She draped the bag over her shoulders and began to put on the lovely blue shoes.

Just like the first time Sophie put on the shoes, the room began to spin around her. There were vivid colors and bright lights. There was also a loud buzzing noise and different colored bubbles floated in her room. The walls and roof surrounding her disappeared. Sophie felt a jolt of electricity and her body shook. Before Sophie knew it, her bedroom transformed into an open meadow with the greenest grass she had ever seen. She felt a little disoriented at first and had trouble standing up.

Sophie knew she had to move around if she wanted to regain her footing and stop the spinning in her head. Currently, she was not sure where her arms were. She knew her legs were still connected to her body, but she could not feel them. Sophie stumbled around in circles. After a few minutes, she was able to walk normal and started to feel better.

When she finally looked up, Sophie realized she was right in front of the most beautiful and majestic horse she had ever seen. The horse had a long slender neck and muscular lean legs. It was about two times her size in height and was pure white. The horse also had a long flowing white mane and tail. It moved with a gentle grace. Sophie never had the desire to ride a horse, but looking at the horse in front of her she wished she knew how.

Holding her hand out in front of her, Sophie moved forward to touch the horse. When it did not back away or make any sudden movements, Sophie slowly moved her hand to pet the horse on the neck.

"How does that feel?" she asked the horse, not expecting a reply.

"That feels wonderful! Thank you! Can you scratch behind my ears as well?"

As Sophie looked at the horse surprised, it continued speaking, "Young lady, you have a face I have not seen before, but it looks a little familiar. Who are you and where are you from?"

Sophie decided that since she had been talking to a dog the last few days, talking to a horse was not overly strange. She laughed to herself.

"You know my parents told me not to talk to strangers. However, since you are a horse, I think it may be okay. I am Sophie St. Clair and I am from New York City, in the United States of America."

"Sophie St. Clair from New York City, in the United States of America, I am Polleux. Welcome to the ForEverNever, the Land Beyond the Mist and Fog." The horse bowed.

"The ForEverNever, the Land Beyond the Mist and Fog, I have never heard of this place," Sophie said. "Where is it located?"

"The ForEverNever, the Land Beyond the Mist and Fog, or just the ForEverNever as it is often called by those who live here, is the home of the Faeries," Polleux replied.

"The ForEverNever exists parallel to the human world, but it is invisible to the human eye. However, it is closely connected to Earth."

"Cool," Sophie exclaimed. "I am in a world no other humans can see, the home of the Faeries."

"What are Faeries?" Sophie asked.

"They are beings, similar to humans, but instead of souls, they have special powers and abilities…But, enough with the questions," Polleux expressed. "You know you really do not belong here child. There are no humans in the ForEverNever."

"I will take you to my friend Simeon," Polleux declared. "He may be able to show you around, and help you find a way to get home. There are many from this world who would be very irritated to know that a human had found her way to our land. They may wish to harm you."

"I may already know how to get home. Probably, all I have to do is take off these shoes and I bet I will be back home in my bedroom," Sophie thought. But she didn't want to go home yet, so didn't volunteer the information.

Polleux lowered his head and bent his front legs. Bowing again, "Care for a ride my lady?"

Sophie did not want to admit she didn't know how to ride a horse. She told Polleux she was not feeling well and thought it best to walk along side of him, which was partially true.

Sophie walked with Polleux on a windy dirt road. The dirt road felt a little odd to her. It was not exactly hard, more like a squishy sponge. It was also a strange grey color. When Sophie dragged her foot across the road, she did not kick up any dust. Sophie and Polleux passed several small, quaint, brightly colored cottages, the kind of cottages you would see in a storybook or in a painting. All the cottages looked similar, except they were different colors. They were one story with thatched roofs, a large front door and several windows. They had flower boxes in the windows and neatly painted fences.

Sophie was feeling a little thirsty from walking. She patted her back and said a silent thank you because Sean's bag was still there. She reached into the bag and took out the water container. She pressed the container to her lips to take a quick sip. Water spilled and trickled down her chin, cooling her face. Laughing she asked Polleux if he wanted any water. He was laughing too and shook his head back and forth indicating he did not want any water at that time.

Polleux and Sophie continued walking. Sophie saw oddly shaped trees and strangely colored plants. She heard birds making weird high-pitched sounds that were almost painful to her ears. She saw several strange looking, but beautiful animals. The flowers were bright and vibrant. The light surrounding her and Polleux seemed brighter to Sophie than the light from the sun in the human world. The wind also felt different in the ForEverNever. It seemed a little lighter, cooler and moved faster than the wind Sophie was used to on Earth. There was a sweet scent of lavender in the air.

After walking a short distance, Sophie and Polleux reached a cottage that looked identical to all the other cottages they passed. Polleux motioned for Sophie to open the gate and told her to go knock on the door.

I can't believe I finally got to meet her. I never thought I would have the chance, with her living in the human world. She is so young, but she seems so grown-up. She has lost so much at an early age. Looking at her is like looking at a miniature version of her mother. I know she is going to be a beauty when she's older. Simeon is going to be ecstatic when he sees her. But, I can't figure out how she got here. Being here she could be in serious danger and probably doesn't even know it. She is very lucky she ran into me instead of someone else. I wonder how much she knows about our world and her mother's past.

- Polleux

v : the golden Egg of Triumph

"Who is it?" A cranky voice asked from inside the house. Polleux nudged Sophie forward and told her to speak up. "Tell her you are a friend of Simeon's and you're wondering if he is home." Sophie followed Polleux's directions.

She heard the voice inside the house yell, "Simeon, you better answer the door, it's for you. Lord, knows how I can get through the day with this racket."

Within moments the door swung open revealing a grinning young man. He was several inches taller than Sophie and appeared to be a few years older. He had lovely green eyes with blue specs and wavy black hair that curled around his ears. He was muscular, appeared athletic, and had a casual but confident walk.

"Oh, it is you Polleux. Good to see you. It's been a while old friend... and who do you have with you?" Simeon asked.

"Simeon, meet Sophie St. Clair from New York City in the United States of America."

"New York City," Simeon let the name roll of his tongue. "I have never heard of it," he winked at Polleux.

Simeon looked at Sophie and smiled, "Hi, nice to meet you Sophie. He placed his hand over his heart.

Simeon then turned his focus on Polleux. "I am glad you are here Polleux. I was just heading out. Shortly before you arrived I got word from the King's royal messenger, the Crow. Someone has stolen the King's golden Egg of Triumph. According to the Crow, the rumor is the thief headed towards the Sunken Hollows. When I focus on the egg, I can feel the rumors are correct and the egg is at the Sunken Hollows. But, my senses are also telling me that if we don't get to the hollows quickly, the egg could be gone. I may not be able to track the egg if it is taken much farther past the hollows.

Simeon jumped on Polleux's back and reached down to help Sophie up. He stressed, "We must leave now."

Sophie hesitated and did not reach out her hand.

"Come on," Simeon stated impatiently. "We have to leave now if we want a chance at retrieving the egg."

Sophie made sure her bag was secure on her back and moved closer to Simeon, but would not give him her hand.

Simeon shook his head and hastily jumped off Polleux. In one swift motion he lifted Sophie onto Polleux's back then jumped onto Polleux in front of Sophie. "Hold on tight," he chuckled.

"Polleux can fly like the wind. And he is going to have to show off his speed, if we are going to make it to the hollows in time to catch the thief." Simeon patted Polleux on the neck.

"But, don't go too fast. I think Sophie might be a little afraid she will fall off," he whispered in Polleux's ear.

Once Simeon and Sophie were settled on his back, Polleux called out "ready". He then took off with haste towards the hollows.

"Hold on tight! I am told I must hurry," Polleux said in a playful voice.

"When have you known me to do anything less? I have never fallen off your back."

Sophie could not see Simeon's face, but it sounded like he was trying not to laugh.

"You can hear him?" Sophie asked surprised.

"Of course I can hear him. He is one of my oldest and best friends. I have been listening to him for years."

"How strange," Sophie mumbled as she scrunched her face.

Simeon replied, "It is not strange at all. Talking to animals is one of my abilities. What is strange to me is that you, a human, are able to hear him."

"Yes, I am a human," Sophie expressed slightly confused. "Aren't you?"

"Me, a human?" Simeon laughed. "Sophie you are in the ForEverNever. The only human here is you. And you really shouldn't be here."

Sophie was not sure what to say. Simeon looked like a young man to her. "If he looked like a young man, but was not human, than what was he?"

"Polleux did tell me there were no humans in the ForEverNever. Maybe he is a Faerie," Sophie thought.

Sophie was trying to take in all she had seen since she arrived in the ForEverNever. She tried to look around to clear her head, but Polleux was going too fast. She was frightened and had to close her eyes. She began to relax her muscles when her head suddenly jerked forward. Startled, she rested her head on Simeon's back keeping her eyes firmly shut. She held on to Simeon tighter, as Polleux raced down the windy path.

"Smash in Squash! Aren't there any straight roads in the ForEverNever?" Sophie groaned as she struggled to maintain her balance.

"No," Simeon replied with a big grin.

"He sure seems to be enjoying himself," Sophie thought.

"All the roads in the ForEverNever are windy or curved," Simeon explained, "that's one of the reasons riding here is so much fun."

"Just a little faster Polleux, we are almost there. I can feel the egg is close," Simeon whispered in Polleux's ear.

Before Sophie knew it, they had reached a large flat open area surrounded by hills on three sides and a stream and woods on the fourth. The air felt moist and smelled of a crisp autumn morning after it rained all evening.

"Welcome to the Sunken Hollows Sophie," Simeon announced raising his hands in the air. "You can't see them now, but in the evening this whole area is covered with tiny creatures that glow in the dark and light up the night with different colors."

Sophie looked around, trying not to move too much. She did not want to fall off Polleux. As she looked around, she did not see anyone. "It looks like we arrived too late. The thief must have gotten away with the Egg of Triumph," she said to herself.

"This is going to be much easier than I expected," Simeon chuckled.

"What do you mean? There is no one here," Sophie exclaimed.

"Not exactly," Simeon replied. "Do you see that bright light coming from the tree at the far side of the hollow, just on the other side of the stream?" Simeon pointed his finger towards the light.

"Well, I bet the thief left the egg there to be retrieved by the person who wanted it stolen.

"How do you know the egg is there?" Sophie asked. "If you can see it from here, you have super human vision."

Sophie paused and rubbed her head. "What am I saying? You aren't even human."

"No, I can't see it," Simeon replied. "But another one of my gifts, other than talking to animals, is finding lost items. If I focus my thoughts on the lost item, I am able to form a connection with the item and can feel where it is located."

"I can also see a light coming from the tree," Simeon said with a wink.

Simeon jumped off Polleux and firmly landed on the ground. He headed towards the stream that looked like it was glowing. Simeon crossed the shallow stream within minutes. Once on the other side, he could easily see the egg left in a hole in the old tree. He reached inside the tree and retrieved the egg. Holding the egg securely in both hands he headed back across the stream to Sophie and Polleux.

"Something is wrong," Simeon thought as he walked towards Sophie and Polleux. He could feel danger approaching as the hairs stood up on the back of his neck. As soon as he reached Sophie and Polleux, he heard yelling coming from the trees. An individual on horseback was riding towards him at full gallop.

"I guess this is not going to be as easy as I thought. He must be here to collect the egg." Simeon pointed at the individual riding towards them. "Too bad for him, or anyone else who comes, we got here first!" Simeon laughed.

Simeon stuffed the egg inside his coat pocket to free both hands. As the rider reached Simeon he quickly pulled the rider off his horse. The rider fell hard on the ground. Angry, he slowly stood pulling a large knife out of his left boot. He charged Simeon at full speed. Simeon was very agile on his feet and easily dodged the knife. Even though the rider was much larger than Simeon, he soon found his size a disadvantage when fighting a more agile opponent. The rider's size made him clumsy and slow on his feet. Simeon quickly jumped out of the way of the rider's second attack throwing the rider off balance. Simeon used the opening and easily knocked the rider out with a sudden jab to the head.

Simeon yelled to Polleux, "Leave now and take Sophie to the hidden cave. I will meet you once I have taken care of the other riders."

"Other riders?" Sophie asked.

"Yes, I can feel them approaching. I think three additional riders are close and there could be others behind them. I am normally much better at sensing danger, but I was so focused on retrieving the egg that I missed the warning signs. I was also busy answering someone's questions," he said to Sophie with another wink.

More yelling from the woods interrupted Sophie and Simeon's exchange of words. "You need to leave NOW!" He pointed to the approaching riders. He handed Sophie the egg and asked her to put it in her bag. Once the egg was secure in her bag, Polleux took off. He quickly reached a fast speed. Sophie held on for dear life and prayed Simeon would be alright… and that she wouldn't fall off Polleux.

"It is okay young lady," Polleux said. "All will be well and I have never lost a rider."

Sophie briefly looked over her shoulder and saw Simeon leap in the air and take another rider off his horse.

"If the individuals who approached them were Faeries, their powers must not be strong. Simeon was making easy work of them," Sophie thought. She saw another one of the riders was already on the ground not moving. With lightning speed, Simeon knocked out another rider who joined his friend on the ground.

As Polleux raced towards the cave Sophie looked back, barely able to see Simeon knock the final rider off his horse. They were getting ready to fight.

"Don't worry about Simeon! He is the best fighter I know," Polleux exclaimed. "I once saw him defeat 40-armed Faeries all on his own, without a weapon. It is because of his lightning speed, incredible strength, and skill on the battlefield, the King chose Simeon to guard his most precious treasures."

"We are almost at the secret cave. Simeon will meet us there. It may take him some time though. He will not kill any of the riders, but he will make sure they are all taken to the King to be questioned. It is important to know why the egg was taken. The King will want to know how anyone was able to successfully get the Egg of Triumph out of his castle. There may be Faeries close to him that are plotting against him," Polleux explained.

Fortunately, Sophie and Polleux were at the secret cave for only a short while when they saw Simeon riding up on a black horse.

"This is Thunder, and he belongs to one of the King's royal guardsmen. I was in luck. It was only the four riders who came to retrieve the egg. As soon as I had the four riders all tied up, the second group of riders, who I sensed earlier, approached. The second group of riders happened to be the King's royal guard. They are taking the four riders back to the King to be questioned."

"May I have the egg?" Simeon held out his hands to Sophie. She reached into her bag and carefully handed the egg to Simeon. Simeon held up the egg for Sophie to get a better look.

"It is very beautiful. I see it is made of gold, but why is it so important?" Sophie asked.

"The egg belongs to the King of the Faerie House of Ymir, who is the High King of the Enlightened Faerie. I am in his service and have been appointed the royal finder. The title is not very impressive I know, but I cannot complain about the benefits." Simeon laughed.

"Enlightened Faeries?" Sophie asked.

"In the Faerie World there are Enlightened Faeries, and then there are those who follow the Dark Shadow; the Shadow Faeries. Although both the Enlightened Faeries and the Shadow Faeries are capable of kind gestures, the Shadow Faeries have allowed themselves to be corrupted by their power and greed and rarely choose to help others. The Enlightened Faeries, on the other hand, generally choose to be less self-serving and rarely use their powers to hurt others."

"Many years ago the Faeries were assigned the responsibility of protecting Earth. In general, Shadow Faeries have turned their back on helping the Earth and the humans who live on it. Some Shadow Faeries even harm humans for their own amusement.

"There are seven Faerie Houses. Each Faerie House has its own ruler and royal court. Shadow Faeries existed in each Faerie House. Over time the Shadow Faeries from the various Faerie Houses united, chose a leader and started to attack the Enlightened Faeries. The Enlightened Faeries selected the King of Ymir as the High King of the seven Faerie Houses. They believed having a High King would make it easier for them to unite their armies to defend against the Shadow Faeries, and still have enough resources to maintain their responsibility to Earth."

"The Enlightened and Shadow Faeries are now often at war with each other. The Shadow Faeries are always trying to find ways to gain more power and territory in the Faerie World. The Enlightened Faeries do not want to fight, but they fight to defend their world and the Earth from the influences of the Shadow Faeries. Some of the past battles were very bloody and resulted in many Faerie deaths."

"If the Enlightened Faeries were to lose the war, love and goodness would disappear from the Faerie World and the Shadow Faeries would have free reign over the Earth."

Simeon pushed a button on the side of the egg and it opened. There was nothing inside, but bright flickering lights of varying beautiful colors.

"I know it appears empty now, but this egg can be full of spectacular images. It sits on a pedestal in the King's war room. Whenever there is battle the King can open the egg and watch the battle. It gives him the advantage of knowing where everyone is on the battlefield, so he can better direct his troops and anticipate the moves of his opponents. This egg has turned the tide of many battles. The King of Ymir is the only Faerie King with an Egg of Triumph. Although, there is peace in the land and power is now balanced, there is no telling how long it will be before the Shadow Faeries stir up trouble, again. We need to get this egg back to the King," Simeon declared.

"But, the King can wait a while longer. Now that the egg is safe, we need to find a way to get you home. And since finding things is my specialty, I don't think getting you home will be too difficult. How did you get here, anyway?"

Sophie started to speak than stopped. She did not want to go home. She was having too much fun!

"Do you know how you got here?" Simeon asked Sophie a little louder.

Sophie unenthusiastically replied, "It's the shoes. I think once I take them off I will return home. But do I really have to go home now?"

Both Simeon and Polleux looked down at Sophie's shoes. Then they looked at each other and exchanged a strange look. They both looked like they wanted to say something, but neither said a word.

Finally, Polleux asked, "Where did you get those shoes young lady?"

"I found them in my new home," Sophie replied. "I think they may have belonged to my mother."

"Who was your mother, child?" Polleux asked. However, he already knew the answer. He knew who Sophie was the moment he saw her.

"Emma St. Clair," Sophie replied. Simeon and Polleux looked at each other again.

Simeon wondered, "Could this child really be their Emma's daughter?" But, all he had to do was really look at Sophie to know the truth. She looked so much like her mother.

"Since Sophie was their Emma's daughter, they had to get her out of the ForEverNever immediately. She could be in serious danger," Simeon thought.

"We need to get her home immediately," Simeon mouthed to Polleux.

"The sooner the better," Polleux mouthed back.

Polleux turned to Sophie with a concerned expression on his face. "You need to be heading home. Let's get those shoes off your feet and see what happens."

"I really don't want to go home," Sophie said. "If I leave, I am not sure I will ever get back here. I have enjoyed meeting you and Simeon, so much. And the time we have spent together today was wonderful. I saw so many new things and it is so exciting here. I am sure there are many, more new things for me to see here in the ForEverNever, the Land Beyond the Mist and Fog."

"We enjoyed getting to know you too, Sophie. But, every good thing must come to an end. You really need to be heading home. Time passes much slower here in the ForEverNever. To you it seems like you have only been gone a few hours, but in your world, most of the day has probably already passed. There are sure to be people at Evanswood worried about you." Simeon's voice was firm, but kind.

Simeon could see Sophie's hesitation in wanting to return home, but he knew she could already be in danger. He could feel some powerful force moving closer, but friend or foe he could not tell. He didn't want to chance it.

"Can you please take off your shoes now?" Simeon asked in a gentle voice. "The willow trees have started to talk. Can you hear that sound in the air?"

Sophie shook her head as she thought, "Who knew? He speaks 'tree' too!"

Simeon interrupted her thought. "And once the willow trees have spread the word amongst themselves, all of the Faerie World will know you are here. Then no where in the ForEverNever will be safe for you."

"Well, how do we keep the willow trees from talking?"

"That, young lady, is an adventure for another day. It is quite tricky to get the willows to stop talking about something, once the wind of it has blown through their branches. Also, to get them to stop talking takes a lot of practice and a quick mind. The willow trees have to be tricked into not speaking about a subject. Some Faeries work at it for years and still can't master the challenge. The willows just laugh at their efforts. I don't think even Simeon can get them to stop talking," Polleux responded.

"Now, do you need my help taking off those shoes or can you do it yourself?" Polleux sounded serious. It seemed he would likely rip the shoes off her feet in any minute, if she did not take them off soon. However, since he lacked hands, Sophie was tempted to see how Polleux would get the shoes off her feet. She suspected he would have to use his teeth.

After thinking a few moments on it, Sophie thought better of tempting Polleux to remove her shoes. "No, I can do it," Sophie shrugged.

Sophie ensured Sean's bag was held tightly over her shoulder, she hugged Polleux and said goodbye to Simeon. Sophie then took a few steps away for Simeon and Polleux. Leaning down she removed the shoe from her right foot. She said one last goodbye. Careful not to drop the shoe she was holding in her hand, Sophie removed her other shoe.

The world around her began to spin. The bright light and colored bubbles appeared. She felt the electricity. Her surroundings disappeared. Sophie was not sure she would ever be able to return to the ForEverNever; but she hoped she would be able to return and that it would be soon. She also wondered if she would ever get use to the queasy sensations she experienced when shifting worlds.

I can't remember a time when I've laughed so hard. Why am I always so serious? I need to figure out how to lighten up and have more fun. Maybe I am so serious because I'm afraid that if I'm not well behaved my grandmother and those at Evanswood will try to get rid of me. If my parents did not care enough for me to keep me and just left me at Evanswood, then what's to stop my grandmother from wanting to get rid of me? I know she loves me, but I'm not always sure she likes me.

-Sean MacTavish

vi : the Grained Eye

The next thing Sophie knew, she was standing in the middle of Sean's bedroom. She was feeling a little sick and disoriented, and wondered how she ended up in his room. Sean was leaning over his desk writing something. He wasn't aware she was in the room. As Sophie looked at Sean, she could see out the window above his desk.

"Simeon was right," Sophie thought. "Time does pass slower in the ForEverNever. It's almost dark out. I was gone the whole day. I wonder if anyone missed me or tried to find me."

Sophie looked over at Sean again. "I must not have made any noise when I returned or else Sean would have heard me. But, how could he have not seen all the bright and colored lights that appear when I travel between the ForEverNever and Earth?" Sophie shook her head in amazement.

Trying not to make any noise, Sophie carefully moved the bag off her shoulders and placed it on the floor next to her. The floor squeaked, as Sophie took a step to get closer to the door. At that moment Sean looked up, surprised to see Sophie in his room.

"Oh, sorry Sophie, I did not hear you come in." Sean took off his glasses and laid them on the desk. Then he stood up to greet Sophie.

"Where have you been all afternoon?" Sean smiled at Sophie.

"Mr. Fitzpatrice was so irritated when you did not return for your lesson this morning. He was in a bad mood all day. I think I heard him muttering something about falling further behind schedule, but he was a little difficult to understand," Sean laughed.

Sophie said the first thing that came to mind, "I was in the hidden garden. Sorry, I fell asleep and lost track of time."

"Did you make the lessons this afternoon? Was Mr. Fitzpatrice irritated with you because of me? Maybe he gave you some extra hard math problems or he read to you from one of his books." Sophie looked at Sean with a mischievous grin.

"Yes, I made it to the afternoon lessons. And no, Mr. Fitzpatrice did not treat me unfairly. He barely even talked to me and gave me free time to read what I wanted," Sean replied in a playful voice.

"You know, I don't think Mr. Fitzpatrice is going to be so quick to trust you the next time you ask to leave his lesson."

"Do you really take medicine?" Sean asked Sophie in a concerned voice.

"No health issues here," Sophie joyfully replied. "I just had to come up with an excuse so I could get out of the library.

"Oh," Sean scratched his head. "So, why are you in my room?"

Sophie had to come up with something fast. "I...I," she said looking around the room trying to avoid eye contact. Her eyes caught the reflection off Sean's glasses sitting on the desk and remembered she wanted to ask him about his visual training.

"I was concerned and a little confused when Mr. Fitzpatrice told me you would not be at the lessons this morning. He said you were at visual training. I wanted to ask you about it. So I'm here."

"What is visual training?" Sophie asked raising her up-turned palms in the air.

"What is visual training?" Sean repeated. "It is hard to explain. I do exercises for my eyes a few times a week. When I look at written text on a page, my eyes want to jump around and sometimes the words fade in and out, which makes it hard for me to read. The exercises help my eyes and brain work together. They also help both my eyes work better together, so when my eyes focus on a point in space, I can see it more clearly. Before I did the exercises, my eyes had difficulty seeing things close to my face. I sometimes had blurred vision, got tired easily and got headaches. That is why I wear these glasses. The glasses help with my eyestrain. I can see the page in front of me without the glasses, but they help my eyes focus on the page or whatever I am reading."

"Are the exercises difficult?" Sophie asked.

"Not really, but sometimes they make me tired," Sean replied.

"What are the exercises like?" Sophie was now really curious.

"For one of the exercises, I just follow a pen. The eye doctor holds the pen out in front of me and I have to follow the pen as he moves it back and forth, up and down, in circles and in squiggly lines. I know it sounds simple, but I have a hard time seeing only one pen when he gets really close to my face. The pen often appears doubled, which I think is called, doubling. Sometimes I feel very uncomfortable and anxious when the pen gets close to my eyes.

Another one of the exercises is done with a string and three beads. You can do the exercise anywhere you can tie the string at eye level. You push one bead to the end of the string and the other two beads to different points on the string. You then hold the string firmly in your hand and back up about seven to ten feet holding the string tight to your nose. Next, you stare down at the bead on the end of the string.

Looking at the end of the string, you should see two strings all the way to the end of the string. The other two beads should also appear to have doubled.

For the exercise you choose one of the beads to focus on. The bead you are looking at should then appear as a single bead, while the string and other two beads appear double. You alternate which bead to focus on."

Sophie thought about it for awhile. "That sounds odd! You really see two strings and two beads where there is only one?"

"Yes, the string and beads really appear to double. You know you have lost focus when the bead you are looking at starts to double."

"This string exercise may be fun! I want to try," Sophie giggled.

"The exercise was challenging for me when I first started. However, if you really want to give it a go, I think I may have some string around here and that bookshelf across the room would be a good place to hold one end of the string. If you help me find some string, a clamp and some beads, we can get started." Sean and Sophie began opening drawers to look for some string.

"Found some." Sophie held up a long piece of string she found in one of Sean's desk drawers.

"There's my bag," Sean said as he reached down to pick up his black bag off the floor. "I normally keep a clamp and beads in here." Sean reached into the bag.

"What is this bread doing in here? I do not remember…"

Sean threw the bread in his trash bin and continued to search through the bag for the clamp and the beads. "There they are," he said with a smile as he reached into a zipped pocket in the inside of his bag.

Sean clamped the string to the bookshelf. He then pushed one bead to the end of the string and the other two to different points on the string. He backed away from the bookshelf and pulled the string to his nose to demonstrate the proper position and posture for the exercise. "To start off, hold the string to your nose and look at the bead at the end of the string. You should see two strings all the way to the bead at the end of the string and the other beads should have doubled. Once you see two strings and the other beads have doubled, you are ready to focus on the next bead. Look at the bead in the center of the string. The bead closest to you and farthest from you should appear double. The string on either side of the bead you are looking at should also appear double. Once the bead in the center appears single and the other two beads appear double, focus your eyes on the bead closest to you. If you are looking at the bead it should appear single and the rest of the beads should appear double.

You can also do the exercise by pushing all the beads to the end of the string. You focus your eyes to look at the beads at the end of the string and the string should appear double all the way to the beads. Then start to look at points on the string moving towards you. The point on the string where your eyes are looking should appear single; however, you should see two strings along the rest of the string."

Sophie tapped Sean's shoulder. "Let me try, please." She eagerly looked at him.

"Here you go," Sean stated as he handed the string to Sophie. "Remember the string will be single at the point where your eyes are looking on the string and the beads you are not looking at should appear double. Start off looking at the bead at the end of the string," Sean advised Sophie.

Sophie followed Sean's directions exactly, but could only see one string and three beads all the way down the string. "I must be doing something wrong," she thought. "Or maybe…"

"You're not just teasing me? Are you really supposed to see two strings?" she asked slightly perplexed.

"I am not teasing you Sophie," Sean declared. "Do I look like a joker?" he asked with a smile.

Sean placed a finger on the bead at the end of the string. "Look at my finger. How many strings can you see now?"

Sophie looked at his finger. "One…No, I see two…I see two strings… it is like magic," Sophie yelled as she jumped up and down in the air.

"Good Job! And how any beads do you see?"

"Five! I see two beads close to me, two beads in the center of the string and one bead at the end of the string."

"That's great Sophie! When you look at the bead in the center of the string how many beads do you see?"

"I'm not sure, just give me a second."

"Sean, Sean, are you there?" Sean and Sophie heard his bedroom door open.

An older looking lady with vibrant green eyes and white hair stood in the doorway. She had a shocked expression on her face, which had turned slightly pale.

"Grandmother, are you okay? You look as if you have seen a ghost."

Sean's grandmother stared at Sophie, "I feel as if I have seen a ghost. You look so much like your mother except your hair has more red in it and you have your father's chin. You are Sophie, I presume? I am Mrs. MacTavish, Sean's grandmother."

"Nice to meet you, I have heard a lot about you. I was wondering when we would finally meet."

"The pleasure is mine," Mrs. MacTavish said in a slightly hesitant voice that seemed to be a mixture of gladness, sadness, and possibly a little bit of fear.

As Sophie reached out her hand to shake Mrs. MacTavish's hand, her bracelet moved forward on her wrist. Mrs. MacTavish looked closely at the medallion on Sophie's bracelet. "Where did you get that medallion?" Mrs. MacTavish asked in a calm, but serious voice.

"From my mother," Sophie replied.

"I have a medallion similar to yours. I keep it on a chain around my neck." Mrs. MacTavish grabbed her medallion and pulled gently on the chain. She held the medallion up so Sophie could get a good look at it.

"That's interesting, Helen and you have a medallion similar to the one my mother gave me."

"Yes, interesting," Mrs. MacTavish repeated.

She then turned her attention to Sean. "And you are late for dinner. I came to check on you to make sure everything was alright. I did not expect to find both of you here."

Mrs. MacTavish then looked back at Sophie. "And, Helen was looking for you. She has been searching for you on and off for most of the day. Where have you been and why are you in Sean's room?"

When Sophie hesitated to speak, Sean spoke up. "I was just telling Sophie about my visual training and showing her some exercises. She never heard of visual training and was curious why I was not at this morning's lessons."

"Well, at least you were not getting into trouble! I hope she learned something. I hear from Mr. Fitzpatrice she is behind in her lessons," Mrs. MacTavish said sternly.

Mrs. MacTavish then cleared her throat and said, "We are holding dinner for you both. You have five minutes to get to the dining room, if you want to eat tonight. The staff will not be bringing any trays to your rooms tonight. They are too busy preparing for the party."

Sophie looked at Sean with big eyes. She had not eaten since breakfast and she was starving. She dashed to the door. Suddenly, she remembered she did not know where the dining room was located. She looked back at Sean. "Are you coming?"

"Sure am," Sean replied. "I am a little hungry myself." He said as his stomach started to growl.

"Good thing, because I am not sure where I am going," Sophie laughed. "We better hurry," she said as her stomach also growled. She grabbed Sean's arm and laughing they both ran to the dining room.

They entered the dining room red faced in a fit of giggles. Mrs. MacTavish appeared not too happy with their behavior. She ordered Sean to take his seat and directed Sophie to sit in the seat across from him. As she took her seat at the head of the table, Mrs. MacTavish was secretly smiling. She noticed Sean having fun for the first time in ages and was happy to see Sophie having fun, as well.

Sophie reminded Mrs. MacTavish so much of Emma, Sophie's mother. As Mrs. MacTavish thought of Emma her eyes got a little misty. She still could not believe that their precious Emma was gone. Now they had to ensure that Sophie remained safe and protected. They owed it to Emma.

YMIR LEGACY

It has been years since I've seen anyone. To be honest, I didn't expect regular visits from anyone; but it would be nice to hear someone's voice—even if it is only once in awhile. I have kept an eye on my daughter. Well, she isn't really my daughter, but she seems like my daughter. From the moment I heard about her, I have been following her life and watching her grow.

-The Mirror Image

vij : a mother's Love

Sophie returned to her room after dinner. Zoey was sitting on her bed waiting. "Where have you been all day?" Zoey scolded.

Sophie wondered if she should tell Zoey where she had been and hesitated. Would Zoey believe her? Then she thought, "I am talking to a dog, why wouldn't she believe what I have to say. Besides, what harm would it do to tell Zoey? And, I really want to share my adventure with someone."

"If you promise to be nice and stop giving me that dirty look, I will tell you all about the amazing place I was today." Sophie smiled at Zoey.

Zoey opened her mouth to say something and closed it quickly. She really was curious. She looked for Sophie all day and didn't want to do anything to keep Sophie from telling her where she had been.

"I promise," Zoey said in a pretend sweet voice with a fake smile, which looked hilarious on a dog.

Sophie just shook her head at Zoey and laughed to herself. She told Zoey about all the wonderful things she saw in the ForEverNever, the Land Beyond the Mist and Fog. She mentioned the Egg of Triumph, the journey to find it and the fight she witnessed. She told Zoey about the talking horse that acted like a gentleman and the man-boy-Faerie who could find things simply by thinking about them and who could fight like a seasoned warrior.

"I wonder if he can find humans and animals as well," Sophie thought.

"Was the man-boy-Faerie cute?" Zoey asked interrupting Sophie's thoughts.

"Hmm?" Sophie thought out loud. "He did have beautiful eyes. They were green with specs of blue. He also had wonderful black wavy hair. But he was very annoying, always telling me what to do. And he had this annoying habit of laughing at me and thinking he knew best."

Zoey started to laugh. Sophie gave her a stern look. Changing the subject, Zoey asked about the horse. "Was he fast? What did he look like?"

"He was as fast as the wind," Sophie recalled. "He had a beautiful white coat and mane. He was rather large with serious brown eyes. He was charming and treated me like an old friend."

Sophie spent hours sharing her adventures with Zoey. She talked until she couldn't stay awake any longer. As she drifted off to sleep she remembered she had to endure another round of Mr. Fitzpatrice in the morning. Sean had more visual training the next morning, so she would be alone with Mr. Fitzpatrice, again.

Before Sophie knew it, Helen woke her when she brought in her breakfast tray. The sun was shinning through her bedroom window, and the aroma of her breakfast filled her room. Yet again, it was French toast and hot chocolate. Sophie took a sip of the hot chocolate and then wiped some chocolate and cream off her top lip with the back of her hand.

"Thanks Helen…my favorite breakfast! You are too good to me," Sophie said with a huge grin. She really liked Helen and didn't want to cause her any worry or extra work.

"Sorry, if I caused you any inconvenience yesterday. In the future, I will try to do better," Sophie told Helen with an apologetic look on her face.

Helen winked at Sophie. "I am all for you enjoying yourself, but do try to keep the trouble to a minimum TODAY. You had Mr. Fitzpatrice in a fitful state for most of yesterday. It was not fun for anyone," Helen said as she walked out the door.

Sophie ate quickly and drank all the hot chocolate in less than seven gulps. Thankfully, it was not too hot. It was just the way she liked it.

After she got dressed for the day, Sophie snuck back into Sean's room to grab his bag. If she had the opportunity, she planned to return to the ForEverNever, today.

As she hoped, the bag was back in the same place it was yesterday. It still had all the items she put inside, except for the bread. She grabbed a flashlight off Sean's shelf and dropped it in the bag. She took the bag to her room. She poured the leftover water in the container on the flowers on her dresser and filled the container with fresh water from the pitcher on her breakfast tray. She grabbed a roll from the tray and placed the roll and water container in the bag. She went to her dresser and took out several pairs of socks and threw them in the bag. Then she grabbed the blue shoes, gently placed them in the bag and ran out the door. Mr. Fitzpatrice was already irritated with her, so she did not want to be late for the morning lesson.

When Sophie reached the library Mr. Fitzpatrice had already written the morning's lesson on the blackboard. Sophie read the blackboard: Zeus, Poseidon, Hades, Aires, and Apollo.

"Looks like today is going to be an introduction to the Greek Gods," she thought as she cringed remembering what Zoey said about how boring this lesson would be.

Mr. Fitzpatrice began to talk about Zeus. His voice still had not gotten any easier on her ears. Thankfully, his next sentence was interrupted by a knock on the library door. When Mr. Fitzpatrice answered the door, Helen stood in the doorway.

She motioned for him to step out in the hallway. "We need an extra pair of hands for a few minutes to hang up some of the decorations for the party. You are tall enough to reach some of the higher places in the hall. Will you help?"

Helen promised it would not take more than 15 minutes.

Mr. Fitzpatrice pointed his finger at Sophie, "No disappearing acts today young lady. I will be standing right outside the door."

He handed her a book. "Read from this while I am out in the hall. I will ask you some questions when I return."

He walked out the door, murmuring about falling further behind schedule. He did not slam the door, but he closed it firmly behind him. As soon as Sophie heard the door close, she got up and put her ear to the door. It sounded like Mr. Fitzpatrice locked the library door.

"Like that is going to keep me in this room," Sophie grinned. After a minute or so had passed, Sophie decided it was safe for her to make her escape. She ran over to the far side of the room and pulled back the tapestry. This time she was prepared. She pulled the flashlight out of the bag, turned it on and stepped into the hidden room behind the tapestry. With the light, she easily saw the door at the other end of the room. She headed to the door and stopped when the light sparkled off something on the walls. She took a closer look at the walls and saw there were designs etched in gold.

The designs were similar to the ones in her room and over her door frame. There were also brightly colored depictions of elaborate scenes on each wall. As far as Sophie could tell, each of the scenes represented one of the four seasons in a forest setting, with strange creatures. Sophie didn't recognize many of the animals. Sitting next to a pond, was an enormous white tiger with crystal blue eyes, whose paws were covered with long black hairs. There was a large purple lizard with a red and black-striped tail, and a creature with the head of a lion and the body of a horse. There were also snow white and yellow bunnies with long curly white tails on one of the walls. On the back wall was a beautiful black panther with piercing green eyes. Sophie stared a little longer at the panther than any of the other images. For some reason the panther almost seemed familiar.

The scenes were in the center of each wall, with elaborate gold-etched scrollwork surrounding them. The door that led to the hidden garden was in the middle of the scene on the back wall, which seemed to represent summer.

There was a large circle on the door, which appeared to have English writing inside of it. Sophie shined the light on the door and read:

Once opened, anyone is able to pass through these doors; but only the most courageous and the pure of heart individuals are able to see what truly lies behind them and reach into the unknown world.

After she finished reading the words on the door, Sophie looked around to see if there was anything else in the room to explore. She didn't see anything on the floor or in the corners. Since there was nothing else in the hidden room, she opened the door and stepped into the garden. She thought about looking around the garden, but she was too anxious to see if the shoes worked again. She went over to the bench by the pond and sat down. She put the flashlight back in the bag and took all the socks she packed out of the bag. She then put on the socks and took the blue shoes out of the bag.

Sophie made sure the bag was secure on her shoulders and then carefully put on the shoes. Holding her breath, she prayed the shoes would work again. All of a sudden her surroundings began to spin around her. She saw the bright colors and felt the electricity. She heard the buzzing sound.

"This is it! It is working!" Sophie thought. But when the world stopped spinning and the bright colors disappeared, she was still sitting on the bench.

Sophie looked around and what she saw looked just like the hidden garden. "It did not work," Sophie sighed in desperation. I won't be able to get back to the ForEverNever. She felt a great sadness overcome her. She so wanted to see Simeon and Polleux again.

"I bet they are off on another big adventure and I'm missing it," Sophie said aloud in a sad voice.

Sophie's thoughts were interrupted by a beautiful voice, singing a lovely song. "I know that song," Sophie thought. "My mother used to sing it to me. It's one of the songs with words I didn't understand, but always calmed me."

Sophie looked around to see who was singing. She could not help but to start humming the melody. If she tried hard enough she might be able to remember some of the strange words. However, since the words were not in English, they were more difficult to remember.

On the far side of the pond Sophie spotted a woman with long blonde hair. The woman looked vaguely familiar, but she was some distance away and the light was so bright.

"Who is she?" Sophie wondered. Her voice…makes me think of my mother. What should I do? Should I go over and say hello?

Curiosity made the decision for her. Slowly, Sophie started to walk around the pond towards the woman. The closer she got, the faster her heart beat.

"Could it really be? Is this woman my mother? She looks and sounds so much like her. Am I dreaming?"

Sophie could not contain her excitement. She ran up to the woman. The more she looked at her, the more she was convinced the woman was her mother. But the woman looked younger than Sophie remembered her mother looking. Sophie rubbed her eyes to clear them. The woman was still there.

Sophie closed her eyes again—only more tightly this time—and threw her arms around the woman. All she felt was air. She opened her eyes and looked up to make sure the woman was still there. The woman looked lovingly at Sophie and reached out her hand. Sophie tried to grab the woman's hand, but the woman's hand went right through her hand like there was nothing there.

"Mama?" Sophie asked in a weak and confused voice.

"Not exactly," the woman reached out to Sophie again and smiled down at her.

"Please follow me. I have a story to share with you. Some parts of the story will be difficult to believe, so you may want to sit down. I heard the bench over there is pretty comfortable. However, I have never been able to try it out. Every time I try to sit on it, I just fall through."

Sophie reached out and tried to touch the woman again, but her hand just went through the woman. She did not know why she thought anything would be different this time, but she so wanted to touch the woman, to hold her. She wanted to believe it was her mother and touch her at least one more time.

The woman looked down at Sophie with sad eyes. "Come on child. Please sit. We need to talk," the woman expressed in a sad voice, to match her eyes.

Sophie followed the woman and sat on the bench. "This was going to be some story," she thought. She just hoped that once she heard the story, she would be able to understand what was going on.

"Sophie, I am your mother, in a way," the woman started to explain.

"There is much about your mother you don't know. I think it is now time for you to know the truth. Your mother, was a Faerie from the ForEverNever, the Land Beyond the Mist and Fog," the woman explained.

"I know the place," Sophie said. "Aren't we there now?"

"Yes and no. But before I continue with the story, may I ask a question of you?"

"Yes," Sophie replied in an enthusiastic voice.

"How did you get here?"

Sophie raised her legs and pointed to her shoes. "I put on these shoes," Sophie replied.

"My shoes!" the woman gasped. "That explains a lot."

"I just knew they were your shoes. Where did you get them?" Sophie asked.

"I will tell you, but first I want to let you know that I am not exactly your mother, but rather a mirror image of her. I know that really does not make any sense right now, but let me start at the beginning.

"Your mother was a Faerie in the ForEverNever. But unlike other Faeries she was never able to travel from the ForEverNever to Earth. The knowledge of her power was kept from her for a very long time. Her power was so valuable to the Faerie World that it had to stay there. Her power was needed to help ensure there was a balance in the Faerie world and that Faeries were given the opportunity to choose to either be kind or selfish."

"Kind Faeries are known as Enlightened Faeries and selfish Faeries are known as Shadow Faeries." The woman smiled at Sophie.

Sophie smiled at the woman, eager to hear more about her mother.

"How much do you know about Faeries and the ForEverNever?" the woman asked.

"Yesterday, I went on an adventure with Simeon and Polleux to find the Egg of Triumph. Simeon told me a little about the Enlightened and Shadow Faeries during our adventure. When they heard I may be your daughter, they were very anxious for me to leave the ForEverNever."

"Of course, Simeon and Polleux, my faithful friends, would be looking out for you. Know that you can always trust them and turn to them for help, if you ever return to the ForEverNever. But you should not return to the ForEverNever... unless you have the ring."

"The ring? What ring?" Sophie asked.

"Your mother's sapphire ring. But wait, I am getting ahead of my story," the woman said.

"Your mother was not able to leave the ForEverNever, but she was fascinated by the human world and what was happening on Earth. She would often come to Crystal Pond, this pond. From this pond, she could see into the human world. She couldn't use the pond to leave the Faerie World, but she could watch and hear the daily happenings on Earth whenever she looked into the water."

"Have a look for yourself," the woman said to Sophie. Sophie jumped off the bench, leaned over the pond and hesitantly looked into the water. At first she didn't see anything, but after a few seconds the water seemed to disappear. She found herself looking at a scene in downtown Dublin.

"Can you see other towns, on Earth, in the pond?" Sophie asked.

"That's a little tricky," the woman replied. "The ancient Faeries who created the pond, connected it to the land on Earth that is now known as Dublin, Ireland. However, the powers of the pond are strong. If you focus on a place really hard and you see it in your mind, you are able to see that place in the pond. The trick is you have to know what the place looks like, in order to form the picture in your mind. Your mother was the only Faerie who could see anywhere on Earth or in the ForEverNever without first knowing what the location looked like."

The woman smiled at Sophie. "Now back to the story. One day the pond showed your mother your father. He was the most fascinating creature she had ever seen. She was drawn to him instantly. So much so that everyday for months, she asked the pond to show her what was happening in his life. She watched him walking around the city, at work and coming and going from work. She saw how valiant he was, and how kind he was to all those around him. She even saw him put his life in danger for others he barely knew. In all the years your mother watched humans, she had never seen a man more generous or noble than your father. Since your mother was attracted to goodness and kindness, she knew she had to meet him.

"However, your mother was not aware of any means to travel to the human world. She also knew she was not permitted to leave the ForEverNever; but she did not understand why she was the only Faerie who was not permitted to leave the ForEverNever. Your mother went to her father and explained how she had seen this wonderful, amazing human and it was her greatest desire to meet him. Her father was very angry to discover she had been peering into the human world. He then told her that it was foretold she would have to make a choice between worlds and the plain on which she lived. He was afraid that what she saw in the pond would somehow influence her choice and she would choose to leave the ForEverNever.

"At first, your mother did not understand. She asked her father more about the choice she would have to make. Would she have to choose between the human world and Faerie World?

"'No,' her father told her. 'Your choice is more crucial than choosing between living on Earth or in the ForEverNever. You will have to choose between the human, the Faerie or the heavenly plain.'

"You see Faeries do not die of old age or diseases like humans. There are only two ways for a Faerie to die. They die if all their powers are taken from them, so they begin to age like humans and they become susceptible to diseases, or they are killed. Once a Faerie is killed, the materials from the Faeries' bodies turn to particles and return to Earth to nurture it. And since Faeries have no souls, the Faeries cease to exist if they are killed. However, if you look closely you can see their essence in the trees, flowers, ground and waters on Earth.

"Faeries are not necessarily purely good or purely bad. Enlightened Faeries are generally fairer and less self-serving than Shadow Faeries. Enlightened Faeries also choose to honor their responsibilities and do what they can to protect Earth. Shadow Faeries always put themselves before others. However, all Faeries are known to cause mischief. You see, being an Enlightened Faerie or a Shadow Faerie is a choice a Faerie makes.

"Like all Faeries, when your mother was created she was given the freedom of choice, but she learned her choices were different from other Faeries. As a young Faerie, although she had no recollection of the event, she chose to accept the power of pure love and true goodness. She also accepted the responsibility that came with the power. From that point on, she did not have to choose between acting kind or selfish; she was just always kind, good and pure of heart. She loved all those around her. She was the only Faerie gifted with the power of pure love and goodness. And because of her goodness and pure heart, she developed a soul.

"However, because of your mother's unique gifts and the enormity of her choice, it was written that there would come a time when your mother would have to make another choice. She would have to choose if she wanted to remain a Faerie or live with the humans or the angels.

"Your mother never realized she had this power until she expressed her wishes to meet your father. Her father told her that if she wanted to meet your father, she would have to go to Earth. And if she wanted to stay with your father on Earth, the human world, she would have to become human and voluntarily choose to give up her power.

"When her father told your mother about her choices, she was not sure, what it meant to give up her power. She did not even know she had any powers. And she still could not understand why she could not travel to the human world like other Faeries. She was aware that those around her had incredible powers and could do amazing things. She also knew that some Faeries had powers or knew of portals or gateways that allowed them to freely travel between the Earth and the ForEverNever.

"Your mother even heard stories of Faeries permanently living in the human world. Her father explained she was different and her power was uniquely special. He stressed to your mother that she was the only Faerie in the ForEverNever who had the power of pure love and true goodness. As long as she was in the ForEverNever, selfishness could not corrupt the whole Faerie World.

"Even after her father's explanation, your mother still did not fully understand her power. She was just herself and never did anything special to enact her power. She did not see the results of her power. Her father further explained that she did not have to do anything to demonstrate her power, she just had to live and goodness flowed from her into the Faerie World. That was why she was so special and why many of the Shadow Faeries wanted to destroy her. That was also why everyone around her worked so hard to protect her all of her life.

"When your mother was young, she chose to give up her original powers for a power that the creator of the Faerie World, the "Power of All," decided was needed in the ForEverNever. "The Power of All" was concerned all the Faeries may become corrupt and totally selfish because there was no such power as goodness and pure love in the ForEverNever. Like the angels and humans, the Faeries, were given the freedom of choice between kindness and selfishness. Over time, "the Power of All" could see that without souls most of the Faeries were choosing selfishness. Without a soul, the Faeries were unable to understand the consequences of their actions. They could not see the value of helping others, serving others and doing something for the betterment of all. They had no concept of love. But, for some unknown reason, your mother was different from other Faeries. She truly cared for others.

"However, just like it is for all Faeries, angels and humans, there would come a time when your mother would have to choose if she wanted to remain good. It was foretold, that the Faerie of pure love, your mother, would be faced with a choice that could forever change her and the ForEverNever.

"Your father played a role in your mother's choice. There was something about him that drew your mother to him. Some voice deep inside of your mother told her that she had to choose him. I know all this to be true because your mother's memories are my memories.

"Your mother's father asked her to carefully think about her choice. He wanted her to make sure she truly understood what she would be giving up. Your grandfather told your mother that if she could figure out a way to travel to Earth for no more than a day to meet your father he would not stop her.

"Your mother went to the Faerie of the Woods, a gatekeeper between worlds, for help. The Faerie of the Woods gave your mother a magic red cloak, which made it possible for her to temporarily travel to Earth to meet your father. As long as your mother wore the magic red cloak, she could walk in the human world. However, once she removed the cloak, she would immediately return to the ForEverNever. The magic cloak was only good for one trip to Earth.

"Your mother spent a wonderful day with your father and after she returned to the ForEverNever she knew she had to be with him. Three days passed and the feelings inside your mother only grew stronger. After speaking with the Faerie of the Woods, your mother went to her father and told him she decided she wanted to live on Earth to be close to your father.

"Your grandfather was saddened by your mother's choice, but he accepted it. He knew that the only way she could remain on Earth for any significant amount of time was for her to become human. Your grandfather knew your mother loved your father, and he believed she would not be able to find the love she was looking for in the ForEverNever. He decided to help her discover a way to become human.

"There was only one spirit in the ForEverNever who could permanently transform Faeries to humans, Isadorella, the keeper of the four winds. Isadorella advised your mother and your grandfather that your mother must choose a location for her transformation. The place she chose could affect her transformation and would likely be her last reminder of the Faerie World. She recommended this place, Crystal Pond. Isadorella told your mother she needed to be prepared to leave the ForEverNever at the time the transformation ceremony occurred.

"Your mother was ready for the ceremony to occur right away. She was eager to see your father again. She had already said goodbye to her family and closest friends. But, her father wanted her to wait. He had a few things he needed to address before he felt it was safe for her to leave the ForEverNever.

"After three weeks, your mother and your grandfather returned to Crystal Pond with Isadorella. Isadorella walked around purifying the area and placing protection wards. When she was done, she indicated that it was time to perform the transformation ceremony. They all stood by the pond. She asked your mother to state what she desired.

"Your grandfather looked at your mother with sad eyes and silently mouthed 'Goodbye.' With a big smile, she waved goodbye and in return mouthed, 'I love you.'

"In a loud, clear voice your mother stated, 'I want to be human.' There was a large, bright streak of light and a strange hissing sound. Her body started to glow and vibrate. She felt incredible pain all over, a feeling she never experienced before. The pain was more distracting than all the light and the noise. The pressure and pain in her body grew stronger. It felt like she was ripping in two. She looked at her body and saw an image of her hands and arms floating above her hands and arms. An image of her chest was pulling away from her body. The bright light began to intensify and she had to close her eyes. The next thing she knew there was a loud snapping sound, similar to when you break a branch in half, only louder. Even with her eyes closed, she could tell that the bright light had intensified, then faded away. When she opened her eyes, standing in front of her was a mirror image of herself, me.

"'It is done,' Isadorella said as she fell to the ground completely drained of all her energy. 'There is no turning back now. You are human. Since your power is too important for us to lose, an image or mirror copy of you has been created, which now holds your power, your goodness. It looks like you physically, but since it is only made up of your power, which is an energy force, there is nothing physical about the image. The image can be seen and can see, but it cannot touch or be touched. It is similar to a hologram; but since your power of goodness was so strong, it has your memories and knowledge. The image or mirror copy of you can learn new things and interact with others. Similar to your former self, this newly created image can only think, say and do good things… it is not capable of selfishness. The image is bound to the area around this pond where wards and protective spells have been cast.'

"So you see Sophie, as I explained before, I am not really your mother. I have no physical presence. I am the copy, a mirror image, of your mother that was created when she willingly became human. I know all about your mother's past because I have her memories and feelings. I know all about your father and you because your mother told me about you and showed me photographs of you and your father. And I watched you grow while looking in Crystal Pond. You were such a cute, adventurous child. So many times you got out of trouble by just smiling.

"But I still have a little more to tell, before I finish with your mother's story." The mirror image of Sophie's mother continued with a smile and pointed at Sophie's shoes.

"Isadorella then held up a pair of beautiful blue shoes, a large lovely ring and a cape. She gave your mother the shoes and told her that once she left Crystal Pond and the ForEverNever she might be able to return by wearing the shoes, but only to visit for a short time. She also told your mother she was not exactly sure the extent of the shoes' powers, but they may also help her return to other areas in the ForEverNever.

"Isadorella then gave the ring and the cape to your grandfather and told him he could not return to the pond unless he was wearing either the cape or the ring. She cautioned him to be careful with the ring and the cape because anyone wearing either could enter the area surrounding the pond. If the ring or the cape fell into the wrong hands, your mother could be harmed.

"Isadorella then threw her hands in the air and said, 'My work here is done. As long as you do your part, the power of pure love and goodness will forever be protected and preserved in the ForEverNever.' She then disappeared with a gust of wind.

"Your mother remained at the pond after Isadorella disappeared. Her father rushed to her side. He could not figure out why she had not already transitioned to Earth. She had given up her power and was now human. He had prepared himself for your mother to be gone. He thought Isadorella's transformation ceremony would transport your mother to Earth instantly.

"Now that your mother was human, she had to return to Earth immediately. Although she was safe around the Crystal Pond, because no other creatures could enter the area unless they broke Isadorella's protection spells, if other faeries learned she was human they would do anything in their power to get to her.

"Since she was human, Earth was the safest place for your mother. Your grandfather had spent the last three weeks doing everything in his power to make sure she would be safe and cared for once she permanently entered the human world. He refused to let her go to Earth alone without any protection. Without your mother's knowledge, your grandfather questioned his staff and family. He found three loyal individuals who agreed to accompany your mother to Earth as her companions, guardians and friends. However, they were warned that they may lose some of their powers.

"Since it was not certain your mother's companions would be able to retain all their powers, your grandfather, with the assistance of Isadorella, gifted each of them with a magic box from the Faerie World. Each magic box contained several items that were enchanted with special powers. The items would enable them to better protect your mother and themselves in the human world. The items were also meant to help make life a little easier for all of them.

"Your grandfather also ensured a house, with enchantments and protections, was created for your mother and her companions on Earth. Evanswood was the product of his efforts. Evanswood is a very special house and holds many hidden secrets. Those who call Evanswood home will always be safe in its walls.

"At the time of her transformation ceremony, your mother's companions were already at Evanswood. Your grandfather had sent them there a week earlier so they could prepare things for your mother's arrival. In the Faerie World there are several portals that faeries can use to move between the ForEverNever, the Land Beyond the Mist and Fog and Earth. Your mother's grandmother, your great grandmother, is the Keeper of the Willow Trees and the Guardian of the Willow Portal. She agreed to allow your mother's companions to transit through the Willow Portal.

"However, it is important to remember, that nothing in the Faerie World comes without a price. Your great grandmother demanded that your mother's companions give her one of their powers in payment for entry into the portal to Earth. Your mother's companions agreed, and each forfeited one of their powers. Like your grandfather expected, they were allowed to keep their boxes when they entered the portal.

"Now that your mother was human, your grandfather did not think she could use the Willow Portal. Travelling through the portal could kill her. Plus, getting her to the portal would be too dangerous. Once the other Faeries learned there was a human in the ForEverNever, they would be after her with the intent to trap her in a rock or turn her into a tree. And your great grandmother would be one of the Faeries leading the charge. As the Keeper of the Willow Trees and the Willow Portal, she was responsible for protecting the ForEverNever from all outsiders, including humans.

"I watched as your grandfather wracked his brain to figure out a way to get your mother out of the ForEverNever.

"Then your mother hugged your grandfather and said, 'Why don't I just try these on?' as she lifted the blue shoes in the air. Your grandfather handed her a light blue box Isadorella had given him. He told your mother to sit on the bench and hold the box tightly in her lap when she put on the shoes.

"The next thing I knew the air was filled with bright lights and colors. Your mother was gone and it felt like a piece of me was missing. Your grandfather stood and stared for several minutes at the spot where your mother had been only moments before. Then he turned and left. Your grandfather has been back many times since, to speak to me and make sure I was still safe. He also uses the pond to watch your mother and you. Your mother also used to visit me regularly when she was in Ireland and every year after she moved to the United States, but I have not seen her for a while. It has also been some time since I was able to see you in the pond."

With tears in her eyes, Sophie told the woman her mother had died a year ago in a horrific car accident. She had been living with her grandmother for the last year. After her grandmother passed away, she moved to Evanswood to be with her father.

"I am sorry," the woman said. "I thought I would have felt her loss, once she was gone; or that I might not be here anymore once she died." Then the woman was quiet for a very long time.

THE SACRIFICE

I can't believe I lost my best friend and she never knew how much I truly cared about her. Life is funny that way. Those that we think will be around forever, sometimes just suddenly disappear... Or they make choices that take them away from us. I have learned that it is essential to let those important to us know how much they mean to us. When you think you are going to live forever, it is easy to take those around you for granted; however, I have never found anyone or anything that has meant as much to me as she does.

- Simeon DeLuc

viij : the Ring of Incognito

"**Y**ou must have found your mother's box. You are wearing her shoes," her mother's mirror image said to Sophie with a smile. "Do you know what the shoes say?"

"Oh! Those silver loops and lines are writing. I thought they might be, but I wasn't sure. What do they say?" Sophie asked with interest.

"Mrs. MacTavish did not tell you?" her mother's mirror image curiously asked.

"No!" Sophie, replied. "She does not even know I found the shoes or that I am here in the garden at Crystal Pond. In fact, I only just met her last evening."

"Well, that may be a problem," the woman playfully laughed.

"Mrs. MacTavish is going to very angry you used the shoes without telling her. And she certainly will not be happy you traveled to the ForEverNever. There are things about these shoes you need to know. You must understand that wearing the shoes is not a game," the mirror image of her mother expressed in a firm voice.

"The writing on the shoes is Fea-oldist, it is the ancient Faerie language. All Faeries can understand the language, but few can read it anymore. The inscription on the shoes says, 'Protection on the journey and a safe return home for the traveler of pure intent.' The shoes don't work for everyone; they are only meant to work for those who are pure of heart. They must work for you because you are Emma's daughter."

"As to how the shoes work... no one really knows. Similar to how the human world is divided into continents and countries, the Faerie World is divided into realms and kingdoms. Each Faerie realm shares an invisible bond with a land area on Earth. Where the shoes allow you to travel in the ForEverNever is linked to where you put them on in the human world. More specifically, the Faerie realm you travel to is determined by the country you are in when you put on the shoes. Although you may know which Faerie kingdom you will travel to once you put on the shoes, there is no way to determine where in the Faerie kingdom the shoes will take you. There is also no way to know into what type of situation you will appear. Wearing the shoes can lead to unknown dangers. There is always risk involved with putting on the shoes."

"I can reassure you, however, that putting the shoes on in Evanswood is a lot safer than putting them on in other locations. With Isadorella's help, your grandfather established connections in Evanswood that linked locations in Evanswood to areas in the ForEverNever he knew would be safe for your mother, if she ever returned for a visit."

"I should probably tell you about the other items in your mother's magic box," the mirror image of her mother expressed to Sophie. "Each item has a unique ability."

"Uhm...I need to remember what items were in the box and what your mother told me about each one." The mirror image of her mother pondered as she moved her hand to her forehead, which looked a little funny because her hand passed right through her forehead.

"There was the tapestry that now hangs in the library. The tapestry helped your mother create and protect the hidden room and hidden garden. The hidden garden is the only place your mother could go in Evanswood to connect with me and look in on others in the ForEverNever. Only your mother and those sent to Earth to protect her, have the ability to move the tapestry. They were all given medallions in their magic boxes. When they are in possession of their medallions they are able to pull back the tapestry. I see your mother's medallion is on the bracelet you are wearing."

"There was also a mirror, with gold writing inscribed around it: 'Trust not only what the eye sees, but look deeper still for the truth.' The back of the mirror was also inscribed with a saying, 'Have faith in the invisible, the world unseen, to the pure of heart all will be revealed.'"

"Your mother was able to use the mirror in the box to peer in on the Faerie World. The mirror allowed your mother to check on those she left behind. The pond in the hidden garden works similar to the pond here. The trick is that in order to see into the ForEverNever, you need to sit with your back towards the pond, hold the mirror up in front of you and find the reflection of the pond."

"And hold your nose," Sophie interrupted with a giggle.

"No nose holding or strange breathing is needed, silly," the mirror image of her mother said with a smile.

"Once you see the reflection of the pond in the mirror, you will be able to see the happenings in the ForEverNever, but it takes a few seconds. All you have to do is visualize the place or Faerie in the ForEverNever you want to see and the place or the Faerie will materialize before your eyes."

"One thing to remember," the mirror image of her mother stressed. "The hidden garden is the only place on Earth that is connected to this garden. The only way you can get back here is if you put on the blue shoes in the hidden garden on Earth."

"There seemed to be a spot in the box for a ring. Was there a ring?" Sophie asked.

"Yes, there was a ring…it was a beautiful blue sapphire mounted in yellow gold. The ring was a special gift to your mother from her father," the mirror image of her mother responded. "The ring is called the Ring of Incognito."

"There was an inscription inside the ring, but I cannot remember it right now. I do, however, remember the story of the Ring of Incognito and can tell it to you now, if you would like."

"Yes, I would very much like to hear the story," Sophie exclaimed. "Please tell it to me."

"Very well," the mirror image smiled, pleased with the opportunity to share the story.

"When your grandfather learned your mother wanted to become human, he knew she would not be able to return to the ForEverNever without the aid of a little magic. The magic in her blue shoes originally transported your mother to Earth, but she was able to stay there after she took off the shoes because she was human and she now belonged in the human world. The magic in the shoes also allowed your mother to return to the Faerie World when she put them on.

"But, humans aren't allowed in the ForEverNever and the few that have made their way to the ForEverNever were hunted and disappeared. They were likely turned into a tree or a rock. Your grandfather could not risk your mother's life. He would never ask her to return to the ForEverNever if her life was in danger. Your grandfather remembered the story of the Ring of Incognito.

"Each of the seven royal Faerie Houses in the ForEverNever possesses a ring that has the power to make it possible for a Faerie to pass as human. If a member of one of the royal families wears the ring they are able to travel around the human world without being detected by other Faeries or the rare human who can see Faeries. It is believed that the ring would have the opposite effect in the ForEverNever. The theory is, if a human wore the ring in the ForEverNever, the Faeries would not be able to tell that the human is human. However, no Faerie knows for sure if this is true. No Faerie from any of the royal houses has allowed a human to wear their ring.

"Believing the Ring of Incognito could provide your mother with enough magic to return to the ForEverNever without being in danger, your grandfather made a space in her magic box to hold the ring.

"You see your mother could only bring the items with her that had a place in her box. There was one problem, however, your grandfather did not have his family's Ring of Incognito. The ring had disappeared years before. It was rumored the ring had been stolen.

"In order to find the ring, your grandfather went in search of your mother's personal guard and protector, Simeon DeLuc. Your grandfather knew time was of the essence. He was sure Simeon could find anything."

"I know a little bit about Simeon's abilities," Sophie declared.

The mirror image looked over at Sophie. "How did Simeon describe the way his ability to find things works?"

Sophie thought a minute. "He told me that if he visualizes an object, he is able to establish a connection with the object. Based on the connection he is able to determine an approximate location for that object. I also think there is some luck involved, but I don't think he will admit it."

The mirror image of her mother raised her eyebrows. "Insightful." She then continued with her story.

"Well, based on Simeon's abilities your grandfather asked him for help to locate the ring. He told Simeon he was willing to pay any price to get the ring. At that time, many of Simeon's abilities were still new to him. He was not sure exactly how to use them. He had only tried them out a few times, but he really wanted to help your mother. Your mother meant, and I wager still does, a lot to Simeon. He put aside the risk of any danger to himself and agreed to search for the ring using his abilities.

"However, there was another problem. Your grandfather had never seen the ring, so he could not describe it to Simeon. If Simeon can't form a picture of the object in his mind, he can't connect with the object. If he can't connect with the object, he is not able to find the object using his abilities."

The mirror image of her mother paused a moment to see if Sophie was following the story. Once she was certain Sophie had understood her words, she continued with the story.

"There was only one place your grandfather knew they could find a picture of the Ring of Incognito. The next day he took Simeon to the royal library to search for the Keeper of Royal Artifacts, the book that held photos, descriptions, and the history of all royal objects since the creation of the ForEverNever.

"The first books your grandfather and Simeon encountered when they entered the library were the newer books. The books said they wanted to help. The newer books asked your grandfather and Simeon what they were looking for, but once they got their answer none of the books seemed to recall a book, Keeper of Royal Artifacts. They guessed the Keeper of Royal Artifacts was a very old book, but they couldn't agree where to begin searching for it. They started to argue loudly amongst themselves. They caused so much commotion the librarian asked your grandfather and Simeon to leave."

"Wait a minute, books talk?" Sophie interrupted.

"They do in the ForEverNever," her mother's mirror image replied. She then continued with the story.

"Your grandfather was very charming and convinced the librarian to let him and Simeon stay in the library. The librarian even offered to help your grandfather find the book for which he was looking. However, like the new books, the librarian had never heard of the Keeper of Royal Artifacts.

"After hours of searching, your grandfather was starting to think that the Keeper of Royal Artifacts did not exist, but rather the story of its existence was something told to mischievous young Faeries to get them to behave. The book contained the history and description of several items that were capable of causing a lot of problems for Faeries.

"Simeon, however, was convinced the book existed. But try as he might, he could not locate the book. As he scanned the library he felt a void where some books should be. The feeling led him to a dusty shelf at the back of the library. A spell had been placed on the book, so no one in the library knew of its existence, and it was also well hidden and very small.

"Book in hand, with a big grin, Simeon headed for a group of tables at the back of the library. As he walked the book began to get larger and larger and heavier and heavier. Simeon and your grandfather struggled to lift the now huge book onto the library table. It took both of them to heave open the heavy leather-bound cover. He and your grandfather flipped through thousands of pages. Finally, on page 777777, there was an ornate drawing and complete description of the Ring of Incognito.

"Simeon focused on the picture of the ring. Suddenly an image flashed in his mind. Simeon saw a cave in the hills of Escondria, which was far… far away. Your grandfather did not care that the ring was in another realm. He wanted Simeon to find it and return with it quickly. There was not much time left before Emma would travel to Earth, the human world.

"Simeon enlisted the help of your mother's horse Polleux. But even with Polleux running full speed the entire way, it would likely take over ten days to get there and ten days to get back.

"Your grandfather knew it was unlikely Simeon and Polleux would make it back before your mother's transformation ceremony. Isadorella told your grandfather there had to be a place in your mother's magic box for her to keep all the items from the Faerie World or over time they would lose their power and likely disappear into thin air. So your grandfather ensured there was a slot for the ring in your mother's magic box. He hoped Simeon and Polleux would make it back in time to place the ring in the box before your mother left for Earth, the human world.

"However, Faeries are tricky, and your grandfather had a plan in mind if Simeon and Polleux did not make it back in time. For now, he decided to keep his alternate plan to himself.

"Although, it was his desire, your grandfather could not ask your mother to wait until Simeon and Polleux returned with the ring. Your grandfather had promised your mother she only had to wait three weeks before Isadorella performed the transformation ceremony. One thing about Faeries you must always remember, Faeries can never go back on their word. While it is hard to get a Faerie to promise anything or even give you a straight answer, once a Faerie agrees to something and says the words aloud, it can never take it back, no matter how much it wants to or what damage its promise may cause.

The mirror image of her mother looked into Sophie's eyes, "So always be careful of what you ask a Faerie, because they can never go back on their word."

————————————————————————————————

"In spite of the possible danger and the small window of time before your mother left for Earth, the human world, Simeon and Polleux set off on their journey in search of the Ring of Incognito. They traveled night and day, stopping only long enough for Polleux to rest. Neither Simeon nor Polleux had ever been to Escondria. They had no idea what landmarks or natural wonders to look for to let them know they had arrived at their destination. Simeon depended on his innate gifts to lead him straight to the ring.

"Simeon and Polleux were not sure if they were in the right place when they came across a small village with four houses and a pub. Simeon saw a cave on a hill above the village, which looked similar to the cave he saw in his vision. Simeon thought it likely they were in the right place. He convinced Polleux they should search the cave.

"When they reached the cave Simeon and Polleux encountered a big, ugly troll with orange fur, yellow teeth and bulging blue eyes. The troll, with a menacing face, blocked the entrance to the cave. Simeon and Polleux whispered and even used gestures to work out a plan to knock out the troll.

"The troll gruffly asked 'What are you doing at my home?' Simeon looked at the troll with a tentative grin 'We are here because...' The troll smiled back, 'You are lost aren't you? My wife made dinner before she left for work. It's heating on the stove. Please join me.' The troll opened his arms wide in invitation.

"As the troll turned his back to walk into the cave, Simeon and Polleux looked at each other surprised and mouthed, 'his wife?' Simeon shook his head in disbelief while they followed the troll into the cave.

"The troll pulled out a chair from the table, 'This one's for you,' he motioned towards Simeon. 'Please sit'. He walked around to the other side of the table and removed the chair from the table so Polleux was able to get close to the table. 'The stew is almost hot,' the troll pointed to the pot heating above the fire. After a few minutes, the troll grabbed the steaming pot and carried it to the table. The troll's hands were so padded the heat from the pot couldn't burn them. However, since he had so much fur on his hands he wasn't able to get a firm grip on the pot. As he moved to the table his large hands fumbled on the side of the pot and it slipped out of his hands. Thankfully, the pot didn't break and he was able to flip it over before too much of the stew spilled out on the floor.

"The troll laughed at himself, 'I guess what they say about trolls is true. We are large and clumsy-handed.' He looked at Simeon. 'There is a towel on the cabinet. Would you get it and use it carry the pot to the table?'

"Simeon placed the pot in the center of the table and used the ladle in the pot to stir the remaining stew. 'Please take as much as you like,' the troll told Simeon, 'And pour some for your friend.'

"'What about you?' Simeon asked.

"'I will take what ever is left,' the troll continued to smile. Simeon only half filled his and Polleux's bowls to ensure the troll had enough to eat. The troll grabbed the ladle. It kept slipping out of his hand. Simeon reached for the ladle, 'Looks like you could use some help there.'

"The troll held out his hands, 'Because of these, I'm used to my wife serving the food,' the troll laughed. Simeon filled the troll's bowl. The troll's hands were too big to hold a spoon, so he had to hold the bowl up to his mouth to eat. The troll's action didn't bother Simeon or Polleux, since Polleux didn't have any hands to eat with and he was eating directly out of the bowl.

"They all enjoyed a wonderful dinner and friendly conversation. The troll was funny and shared interesting stories about his childhood horse. When he was younger all the other children were afraid to play with him, so his uncle got him a beautiful, large, black horse. The first time the horse saw him the horse fainted in fright. When he recovered, the horse saw the troll sitting on the ground, with his back turned to him, about fifteen feet away. The troll sat there with his back to the horse all night. The horse curiously watched him all night. In the morning, the horse's curiosity won over his fear and he moved closer to the troll. The troll slowly turned and held out an apple for the horse. Once the horse got accustomed to the troll, and was given hundreds of apples, he and the troll became good friends. The troll told Simeon and Polleux he felt very honored when the horse trusted him and he was able to name him. He named the horse Mountain because he was so large in size.

"After they finished their stew, Simeon offered the troll some chocolate cake he had brought. The troll enjoyed the cake so much he did not realize Simeon and Polleux had not eaten any. Before he was able to finish a second piece, the troll's head hit the table with a loud thud. He was fast asleep and snoring loudly.

"The cake was laced with a sleeping potion. Simeon brought it along as an after-thought, thinking he and Polleux might find themselves in a situation where it would come in handy.

"'Who doesn't like chocolate cake?'

"Simeon and Polleux did not want to hurt the troll; he was friendly and kind to them. They only wanted to find the ring. As the troll snored, Simeon and Polleux began to search the cave. They searched every inch of the cave, but could not find the ring anywhere.

"'It's not here,' Polleux neighed.

"'I don't understand,' Simeon rubbed his chin. 'I know this is the cave where the ring is located. This cave is the right size and all the items are in the exact spot as in my vision. The ring should be here.'

"Simeon grew frustrated as he threw a pillow back on the bed. He went over and checked the troll one more time, to make sure he didn't have any hidden pockets.

"'To bad your powers can only give you an approximate location instead of exactly where the ring is located,' Polleux said dejectedly. Polleux used his height to look above the cabinets and on the beams supporting the ceiling, but still no ring.

"At a loss for what to do next Polleux and Simeon decided to leave the cave, but before they left Simeon laid the troll in his bed, took off his shoes and covered him with a blanket. 'I feel bad about giving him that sleeping potion. He is going to have a terrible headache.' Simeon shrugged and turned to Polleux, wondering what to do next.

"'Maybe there is another cave close by.' Polleux suggested. 'It's possible we just got the wrong cave. I saw a pub as we passed through the village, let's go check it out and see if we can get anymore leads on the ring.'

"Halfheartedly Simeon agreed to check out the pub. Even though, he still believed the ring was somewhere in the troll's cave, the pub might be a good place to find additional information about the ring. Simeon touched the bag of gold hanging from his belt, which Emma's Father had given him before he set out on his journey. He had plenty of gold to pay for information."

I have all these powers, but when will I learn how to fully control them? I try not to doubt myself, but it is hard when I can't find a single ring. I need to find the ring. It is the only thing that will ensure I can see Emma again once she is human. I can't let her down. After my father was killed, when I was young, she was the only friend I had. When I moved into her family's home, she always watched out for me and made sure I was treated fairly.

- Simeon DeLuc

ix : the Fᴂrie Pub

Sophie listened intently as the image of her mother continued the story of Simeon and Polleux's search for the Ring of Incognito.

———————————————————————————

Simeon looked around the village. "This really is a small village," he thought. "It is very likely I won't find anyone at the pub. It may not even be open."

"When have you not known a pub to be open?" Polleux chided. "You head on in and see what you can find out. I will wait out here. I don't think they allow horses inside and besides I do not think I can fit through there." Polleux motioned towards the door.

Simeon slowly walked into the pub to search for a table. The pub wasn't packed, but it was very dark, which made it a little challenging to find a seat. It took a few seconds for his eyes to adjust to the darkness. There was only one candle burning on the bar. Once he spotted an open table, Simeon carefully walked over to the table and sat down. He quickly realized the only other person in the pub was a female Faerie standing behind the bar. "She must own the place or work here or probably both," Simeon thought.

The Faerie had a slim build and long blonde hair. She smiled at Simeon and headed over in his direction. When the blonde Faerie reached his table, Simeon realized she was a pixie Faerie and was beautiful. Pixie Faeries can glow when they move, make themselves smaller and fly.

"No wonder there is not a lot of light in here," Simeon thought as the pixie faerie moved closer. "She can make her own light."

In the dim light, Simeon could make out the pixie Faerie's delicate bone structure and shinning blue eyes. When she opened her mouth to ask what he wanted to drink, Simeon was greeted by the sweetest voice he had ever heard. He was speechless and could not help but stare.

After he found his voice, Simeon jokingly stated, "I see the pub is packed tonight. What's the occasion?"

The pixie Faerie laughed and replied, "To be honest, you are the first costumer who has been in this lovely establishment in a week. It does pick up a little over the weekend, though."

"Since I am your first costumer in a while, I better order something. What's the most expensive drink you have on the menu?"

"The Heather Mead." The Faerie glowed as she spoke. "The drink is made of blue Heather, which is difficult to find in these parts. The drink is also not easy to make. I have been told it has the ability to take away concerns without making the drinker addle brained."

Simeon took two gold coins out of his bag and laid them on the table. With a charming smile he said, "Make it the Heather Mead then."

"You, charmer! If that is what you want. That is what you shall have." The Faerie winked at Simeon. "Just give me a moment. I need to go to the back to get the good stuff."

The Faerie collected the bottle from the back room and returned to the table. As she poured Simeon a glass, she asked, "Do you mind if I sit with you a while?"

"Pull up a chair and have a glass," Simeon said as he motioned to one of the chairs.

The pixie Faerie was glad and somewhat surprised Simeon was so accommodating to her request. "Thanks! Sometimes it gets a little lonesome being here night after night without anyone stopping in. I am Gwyneth from the Faerie House of Attewater. What's your name?"

"I am Simeon DeLuc from the Faerie House of Ymir. Pleased to meet you." Simeon placed his hand over his heart then grinned at Gwyneth.

"You were right; this Heather Mead is very good. I have almost forgotten all my troubles."

"What concerns could a strong, young Faerie like you have?" Gwyneth asked.

Simeon was hesitant to provide the reason for his troubles, but the Heather Mead made it a little easier for him to speak. "I have this friend," Simeon sighed, "Who is counting on me to find something for her and I don't want to let her down."

"This Faerie must be very important to you, for you to travel such a far distance." Gwyneth looked directly in Simeon's eyes and smiled.

Simeon proceeded to tell Gwyneth all about Emma and how she wanted to become human and live in the human world. Simeon also explained how he and Polleux came to search for the Ring of Incognito. Gwyneth listened in silence until Simeon mentioned the cave and the troll.

"You did not hurt the troll?" Gwyneth asked in a concerned voice.

"No, we didn't hurt him. We only gave him a sleeping potion before searching the cave. We put him in his bed so he would be more comfortable. He is going to have one killer of a headache when he wakes up, though. He may be hiding the ring, but he was very kind and his wife is a great cook!"

Simeon took another sip of his drink then put down his glass. "Are there any other caves in the area?" he asked.

Gwyneth placed both hands on her hips. "No, that is the only cave in the kingdom; and you can thank me for the stew."

Simeon looked at Gwyneth in shock. He couldn't figure out if she was bragging or upset. And how did she know they ate stew?

"How do you know what we had for dinner?"

"I know the cave well. It is my home. That was my husband you tricked. I cooked the stew before leaving for work this evening. It was warming over the fire when I left home."

Simeon leaned back in his chair, embarrassed and not quite sure if Gwyneth was going to be mad at him or not. He thought, "Thank goodness I said she was a good cook."

Then Gwyneth stared directly at Simeon, forcing him to maintain eye contact with her. She placed her elbow on the table as if to arm wrestle and spread her fingers apart. "And I think this is the ring you are looking for." Resting on her ring finger was a blue sapphire stone in a gold setting. It was identical to the ring Simeon had seen in The Royal Artifacts.

Now it made sense to him. If Gwyneth was married to the troll, she lived in the cave and the ring was in the cave whenever she was in the cave. His powers had not led him astray.

"The Ring of Incognito," Simeon gasped. "Where did you get it?"

Gwyneth eyed the ring on her finger. "My husband gave it to me when we were married."

Simeon anxiously exclaimed, "The ring's rightful owner is the King of Ymir, the High King of the Enlightened Faeries. His daughter needs it to avoid potential danger. How much will you take for it? I can pay you in gold."

"There is not enough gold in the ForEverNever, to buy this ring." Gwyneth declared.

Simeon could not let Emma down. If Gwyneth refused to sell him the ring for a bag of gold, what else could he do? Then he remembered his gold chain. The one he never took off, the one around his neck at that very moment. The chain was very special. He had worn it for so long that it had become a part of him.

Simeon reached behind his neck and opened the clasp on his chain. He took the chain off and laid it and the bag of gold on the table. "I will give you this bag of gold and chain in exchange for the ring."

Gwyneth laughed. "Why should I help you, when you tricked my husband? I should have put something in YOUR drink."

"Please!" Simeon pleaded. "This chain is the only item of value I own. It belonged to my father. When he was killed, this chain was handed down to me. I have not taken it off since. The chain is charmed and protects the wearer from danger. Please, take the chain and bag of gold in exchange for the Ring of Incognito."

Gwyneth held the ring close to Simeon's face. "Put your chain back on. I will not take the chain in exchange for the ring."

"I have nothing else to give. Please take the chain and gold."

Gwyneth studied Simeon. "Answer these questions for me."

Simeon didn't know where this was going. "Of course! I will answer any questions."

"Did you wreck my home?"

"No! Polleux, my friend waiting outside, and I left everything in your house the way we found it."

"Would you have hurt my husband to get the ring? And I am warning you to think hard before you answer. I will know if you are telling the truth."

"I would have done everything in my power to get the ring without hurting your husband. As a matter of fact, we put him in bed to sleep off the sleeping potion we gave him. However, I must tell you if he attacked, we would have defended ourselves."

"I appreciate your honesty. That is worth far more than gold. I am very thankful for the kindness you showed him. Many would only see a monster when they looked at him. They would not think twice about hurting him. Others rarely treat him kindly. That is one of the reasons we live in such a small village. Only some family and a few close friends live around here. Even those close to us feel more comfortable with us living outside the village, so we live in the cave on the hill."

"You are a rare Faerie, Simeon. You are very kind and devoted to others. I have never met a Faerie quite like you before. I will not take your chain in exchange for the ring. I will give you the ring in exchange for the bag of gold and your friendship."

Simeon pushed the bag of gold across the table to Gwyneth as she carefully and reverently slid the ring off her finger. Simeon was stunned. He couldn't believe his good fortune.

"I have not taken this ring off since my husband placed it on my finger years ago when we were married. I am going to miss it. I hope your friend is worth the sacrifice you were willing to make for her."

"Emma is worth so much more than a bag of gold and a gold chain. She is gentle, kind and truly good. Her goodness washes over all those around her. She inspires others to want to do good and be kind."

"Good luck to Emma and to you," Gwyneth said as she took a few gold coins out of the bag. "The Heather Mead is on the house. Glad I recommended it. Without it I may not have gotten the story out of you and made a trustworthy friend. Here, take these in case you need any money on your journey home," Gwyneth handed Simeon the coins.

Simeon put his right hand over his heart and smiled. "Friends!"

Gwyneth returned his farewell gesture with her hand over her heart and wished him well.

Simeon left the Pub and met Polleux outside.

"What took you so long? You know we don't have a lot of time to find the ring," Polleux said as he walked towards Simeon.

"We can head home now." Simeon held up the ring for Polleux to see.

"Where did you get that?" Polleux looked at the ring in amazement.

"It seems I was not wrong about the location of the ring. We were just looking in the cave at the wrong time. The pub owner, a pixie Faerie, is the troll's wife…if you can believe? She had the ring and gave it to me. The trade was the bag of gold and my friendship."

Polleux laughed with delight. "It appears you also have the power to charm! We still must hurry. If we leave now we may make it back in time to give Emma the ring before she heads to Earth, the human world."

————————————————————————————————

"That's an incredible story." Sophie gave the mirror image of her mother an enormous grin. "Although I don't want to, I think I need to return to Evanswood."

The mirror image of her mother smiled at Sophie, "I think that is a good idea."

Tears of happiness welled up in Sophie's eyes as she waved goodbye to her mother's image. To have her mother's image to talk to was more than she had ever hoped for. Sophie reluctantly reached down to take off her shoes. Once both shoes were removed, her world started spinning, she heard a loud noise and saw flashes of brightly colored lights.

When Sophie's head stopped spinning, she looked around and realized she was still in a garden, but knew the shoes worked. She was confident she returned to the garden at Evanswood, the human world. Sophie stood up and walked to the other side of the pond, back through the door and into the hidden room behind the tapestry. She entered the dark library. Hours had passed since she had snuck out of the library.

She looked around and saw no one. She exited through the open door of the library and quietly made her way to her room.

Memories From the Past
Years Before Sophie

I know I can go faster than this, but how? Are there some magic words I have to say or think? Some white horses like me can even fly. Simeon worked so hard to find the ring. We are so close to making it back in time to get Emma what she needs to be safe. I am going to miss Emma so much when she is gone. We have to make sure she gets the ring, so she can return to the ForEverNever. I just need to push myself a little harder and everything will be okay.

- Polleux

x : Journey Into the Unknown

Simeon and Polleux headed for home as quickly as they could. Exhaustion forced them to stop for a few hours to rest. In spite of their efforts, Simeon and Polleux did not make it back in time. When they got home Emma had already left for Earth, the human world. Disheartened Simeon gave the ring to Emma's father, the King of the House of Ymir.

"Sorry, we failed you and Emma," Simeon said to the King. "We will likely never see Emma again."

The King of Ymir was not worried. He reassured Simeon. "I have a plan. Have you ever been to Earth, the human world, Simeon?"

"No, I didn't even know Faeries were allowed in the human world," Simeon replied.

"There are many Faeries in the human world. Some Faeries have even lived there all their lives, never knowing of the ForEverNever," the King of Ymir replied.

Simeon must have looked like Polleux just stepped on his foot. "Faeries that have never seen or heard of the ForEverNever! How can that be?"

It was unthinkable that there were Faeries that did not know where they came from. He would feel like a piece of him was missing, if he could not live in or even visit the ForEverNever.

"There is much about the Faerie World and the human world for you to learn. All the Faeries in the ForEverNever know they are Faeries. There are a few Faeries in the human world who don't know they are Faeries; and some Faeries in the human world know they are Faeries, but they don't know about our world here in the ForEverNever. I wager you will soon find out about the human world and the Faeries in it," the King of Ymir told Simeon.

"I want you to travel to the human world and give my daughter the ring," the King continued. "I already sent several Faeries to the human world to protect her. You may be able to travel there the same way. Would you agree to bring the ring to Emma? I would go myself, but as king I cannot leave the ForEverNever."

"I would gladly do anything to help Emma. I'm not scared of the possible danger. I will bring Emma the Ring of Incognito," Simeon replied.

"Before you get ahead of yourself young one, there is one thing you must know. There may be a price for traveling to Earth and it can be fairly high. You may have to freely and willingly give up one of your powers," the King of Ymir stressed in his booming voice.

Simeon pondered this new information. But he wasn't deterred, he already knew he was willing to take the risk to help keep Emma safe. She had looked out for him for years. She was his most trusted and dearest friend.

"My mother, the Keeper of the Willow Trees, is the Guardian of the Willow Portal. She is the only guardian of a portal to Earth that I know of and she has already allowed others to pass through to the human world to protect Emma, but she required payment She may allow you to travel through the portal, but she will likely require payment for use of the portal," the King of Ymir explained.

"Let's go speak with your mother then." Simeon looked directly at the King of Ymir with a determined look in his eyes and a giant grin on his face. He was all about adventure and he felt this might be one of the greatest adventures of his life.

Simeon, Polleux and the King of Ymir hurried to the Willow Portal knowing that Emma may need Simeon's help in the very near future. They knew they didn't have time to find another portal to Earth. Emma's father, had left a note in her magic box. He warned her not to contact or travel back to the Faerie World unless she wore the Ring of Incognito.

It didn't take Simeon, Polleux and the King of Ymir long to reach the Willow Portal. Simeon noticed Emma's grandmother, the Keeper of the Willow Trees, and Guardian of the Willow Portal was an ancient Faerie. She was covered in rolling tree bark-like wrinkles and was tall as a 200 year-old tree. Her long flowing white hair draped over the branches of her body and her deep and raspy voice sounded like the howling of a strong wind.

When the Guardian of the Willow Portal saw Simeon, Polleux, and her son, her ancient dark green eyes sparkled with greed. "What is it you have come to ask of me? I can tell it is something very important to you," she said gleefully as she rubbed her long leaf-like hands together.

"O, most gracious Guardian of the Willow Portal, I have come to ask you to allow me to enter the portal and travel to Earth, the human world," Simeon responded in his charming way.

The Guardian of the Willow Portal continued to rub her long leaf-like hands together with a gleeful twinkle in her eyes. "There is a price to enter my portal, young Faerie, are you sure you are willing to pay it?"

"I will pay your price," Simeon responded in a firm and deliberate voice.

The Guardian of the Willow Portal triumphantly laughed. "I can sense other Faeries' powers and I have never met a young Faerie with as many powers and abilities as you, other than my son, the King of Ymir. At this point, because of your age, I suspect you are not even aware of the extent of all your powers and abilities. Let's see, I sense you can find objects that are lost, you have incredible strength and speed, you know what your opponents are going to do before they do it, you can talk to animals, move things with your mind, and you are a Mesmer—you have the ability to hypnotize others and you can control them with your mind. I am also sensing another power not fully developed. All of which are extraordinary powers. Hmm, what new power do I want? Which power is the greatest?" The Guardian of the Willow Portal thought for a while.

"I have decided the price for your entrance to the portal, young Faerie. You will freely give me your power of controlling others with your mind. I have always wanted to be a Mesmer."

"You are correct. I did not even know I had that power. I guess I will not miss something I didn't know I had. I will freely give you my power to make people do things using only my mind. What do you need me to do?" Simeon asked.

"You need to say the words aloud. You need to say: I Simeon DeLuc freely grant the Guardian of the Willow Portal my power to make people do things using only my mind." The Guardian of the Willow Portal pointed her long leaf-like, willowy fingers towards Simeon as she spoke.

Simeon said the words and there was a large flash of blue light. The Guardian of the Willow Portal laughed greedily. "Your power is now mine. You are free to travel through the Willow Portal when you are ready."

Simeon took the Ring of Incognito from the King of Ymir and placed it on the chain around his neck. The King of Ymir showed his appreciation to Simeon by putting his hand over his heart and said with reverence, "Awaetuawe." He then spoke softly, "I am not sure where you will end up when you walk through that portal. It may take you some time to find Emma. She is living in Dublin, Ireland, in a house called Evanswood. The house is very large and made of red brick. It has vines growing on the front and is surrounded by a large iron fence, painted dark green. The house is located near a park not far from a large building humans call a church. It is near St.. Stephen's Green and not far from Leinster House. I wish I could give you more details, but that is all the information I have."

The King of Ymir continued, "I already sent Helen, Mrs. MacTavish and Mr. McGuire, to protect and take care of Emma. But I have not been able to communicate with them since they left the ForEverNever. Before they left they were each given a magic box containing charmed items. One of the items placed in each of their boxes was specifically charmed with the power to help them stay connected with the ForEverNever. But there just was not enough time for them to learn about the powers of each object before they left for Earth, the human world."

"Be on the lookout for Helen, Mrs. MacTavish and Mr. McGuire once you reach Dublin."

"You do remember what they look like?" the King of Ymir asked.

Simeon pictured each one in his mind, "Yes, I remember. Mrs. MacTavish practically raised Emma and me; and Helen was always there to make sure we had everything we needed. I only saw Mr. McGuire a few times, but I would recognize him if I ran into him on the street."

"Good, I am glad you remember them. You will also need some money. Here is another bag of gold, but be careful with it. Humans nowadays don't typically pay for things with gold. They use paper money and coins made out of other cheaper metals. If you are paying for things with a lot of gold people may get suspicious. A little gold goes a long way. I advise that you sell some of the gold for paper money when you get a chance."

Simeon stroked Polleux's neck, "Until we meet again." Simeon placed his hand on his heart. "I think I am ready to go through the portal now."

"One last thing," the King of Ymir called out just before Simeon entered the Willow Portal.

Simeon turned around to look at the King.

"Be cautious when using your powers," the King warned. "Most humans will not realize you are using special powers, but some may. Using your powers will announce to the Faeries in the human world you are a Faerie. If the wrong Faeries get word you are in Ireland, it could be dangerous for you and may expose Emma. I have enemies everywhere and if the Shadow Faeries get a hold of Emma, they would not think twice about hurting her or using her against me."

As long as the Ring of Incognito is in your possession, other Faeries will not be able to sense you are a Faerie unless you use too much power or they get really close to you." The King of Ymir winked at Simeon. "If you wear the ring other faeries will not be able to detect you at all. However, don't forget, only members of the royal houses can wear the ring without serious consequences."

Simeon thought, "How could Gwyneth, the pixie Faerie, wear the ring for all those years? She must be a Faerie princess. Imagine a Faerie princess married to a troll...or maybe, the troll is really a prince. Who knows? Wait, I shouldn't be thinking about this." Simeon scolded himself as he focused his attention back on the King of Ymir.

"Is that all you have to tell me?" Simeon asked thoughtfully.

The King of Ymir pondered for a moment. "That is all." As Simeon turned to walk through the portal the King of Ymir yelled, "Be safe and return home successful."

Just like that, Simeon disappeared through the portal.

"Good luck, my friend," Polleux said to the space where Simeon had stood only moments before.

———————————————————————————————

"What a rush!" Simeon rubbed his head. He felt a little confused and disoriented as he looked around at his surroundings. The floor and ceiling below and above him were blue. The walls were light blue on the bottom and yellow on top. There were odd pictures on the walls and white molding framed the ceiling. The floor was a little darker than the ceiling and was covered by a strange material that Simeon had never felt before. He reached down to feel the floor. It was soft and felt a little fury.

"You, young man. What are you doing here?" The voice came from behind him. He stood and turned around slowly to find a large man, in some type of uniform, pointing a small strange looking metal object at him.

"This cannot be good," Simeon thought.

"Don't make me ask you again. How did you get in here?"

"At least I can understand, what he is saying," Simeon thought.

"Sorry Sir, I feel a little disoriented. I am not sure how I got here." At least that was the truth Simeon thought. "I must have wondered in here accidently."

"Were you on the tour?" the man asked somewhat skeptical.

"Is this my way out?" Simeon wondered. "Yes, I was on the tour and somehow got separated from the group."

Thankfully, Emma had told him a few things about the human world. For example, humans like to travel together in something they call "groups" when they visit places.

"I guess that explains why you are here." The man lowered the strange looking metal object, but still held it in his hand. "But that does not explain how you got in this room. The doors were locked."

Simeon quickly looked around the room. He spotted a door on the other side of the room. It was opposite from the door the man must have used to enter the room. He focused on the door with his mind. It was locked. He decided to risk using one of his powers, one time, in a room with only one person. With his hand pointed to the ground he quickly made a small circle with his finger, which went unnoticed by the man. And with his mind and the movement of his finger, he unlocked the door.

"I came in that door." Simeon pointed at the door he just unlocked.

"I could have sworn that door was locked." The man went over to the door to check his suspicions. He was surprised to found the door unlocked and strangely enough there were no odd marks anywhere on the door to indicate it had been tampered with.

The man scratched his head and looked at Simeon. "You really should not be in here. I will help you find your group." The man directed Simeon out of the room and locked the door.

Simeon and the man walked around for a few minutes until they came across a group of people. "This must be your group. Have a good day and try to stay out of trouble."

"Thanks," Simeon replied as he joined the group. A small lady standing in front of the group with bright red hair and large black glasses held up her hand and started to speak:

Richard Cassels designed Leinster House. It was built in 1745-47 by the Earl of Kildare and was the former residence of the Duke of Leinster. Since 1922 Leinster House has served as the parliament building of the Irish state. The building is the meeting place of the Lower House and the Upper House, the two houses of the National Parliament of Ireland.

"Well, I guess this is a tour! I wonder what is a Parliament," Simeon thought to himself.

The small lady continued:

Following the Truce between Britain and Ireland in July 1921, ending the War of Independence, peace negotiations between the two countries were initiated. The "Articles of Agreement for a Treaty between Great Britain and Ireland" were signed on 6 December 1921. The Treaty provided for the establishment of the Irish Free State with jurisdiction over twenty-six of the thirty-two counties. In accordance with the terms of the Treaty a meeting of "the members elected to sit in the House of Commons of Southern Ireland" was held on 14 January 1922.

As the lady continued to speak, Simeon stepped away from the group desperately searching for a way out of the building. He had learned enough for one day. As he turned his head to the right, Simeon saw another large group of people exiting the building. He headed towards the exit door and walked outside.

Simeon lifted his head towards the sun and began to look around. Everything was strange to him. He was startled by the city's sudden loud noises and the hustle of people all around. Simeon lowered his head and pondered what he was going to do to find Emma. At a loss for where or even how he should begin his search, Simeon stopped a man walking briskly by him and asked him how to get to Merrion Square or St.. Stephen's Green.

"You are not from around here, are you?" The man pointed in front of him, "St. Stephen's Green is in that direction."

He then pointed behind him, "Merrion Square is in that direction." He then scurried down the sidewalk.

"Well, that didn't help matters. I still don't know which way to go," Simeon thought. He stared at the tall buildings and all the people. "Where could Emma be?"

He decided to use his powers once more to find Emma, ignoring the King of Ymir's warning. He pictured Emma in his mind and focused on her intently. A strong feeling inside of him told him to head down Kildare Street towards St.. Stephen's Green.

Simeon reached a large park area that had to be Stephen's Green and walked along side the park until he saw a sign that said Grafton Street. Just as his inner voice was telling him to turn down Grafton Street, a stray dog ran passed him.

"Please wait a moment," he yelled to the dog. The dog stopped suddenly and turned towards Simeon.

Taken aback by someone talking to him, the dog stood still and just stared at Simeon for a moment, thinking, "What a wonder, I can understand you! This is great!"

"Thank you for stopping," Simeon said. "If I am trying to find someone on Grafton Street, where would you suggest I look?"

"If I were you, I would start at Brown Thomas Department Store, it is very popular and is always packed with people."

Simeon scratched the dog on its head, "I am Simeon DeLuc and I am not from around here. Your help is much appreciated. What is your name?"

"I don't really have a name," the dog replied.

"Since I was fortunate to run into you, how about I call you Fortune?" Simeon asked.

The dog thought on the name for a moment. "Umm...that seems too upscale for me, how about Lucky?

"That sounds like a great name." Simeon patted Lucky on the head.

"And since you have been so kind to me, how about I take you to Brown Thomas Department Store," Lucky volunteered.

"That will be great! Thanks Lucky," Simeon smiled. "By the way, what is a department store?"

"What is a department store? You must be from somewhere far away. You really are going to need my help. Who knows what kind of trouble you can get into on your own?" Lucky shook his head then answered Simeon's question. "A department store is a place where humans go to buy things like food, clothes, and toys."

As they walked, Lucky continued to tell Simeon about all the things you could find in a department store. Before Simeon knew it, Lucky was motioning towards a large building with a big sign in front. "That's Brown Thomas Department Store. I will wait for you out here. Dogs are not allowed in the store." With that, Lucky lay down on the sidewalk in front of the store.

"Thanks again for your help. I will try not to take too long," Simeon declared as he walked into the store.

The store was packed with people. Simeon found himself surrounded by strange objects, most of which he had never seen before. There were glass bottles with colored liquids and odd tops on the counter. He picked up one of the bottles, pushed down on the top and liquid shot out into the air. He jumped back with his arms extended holding the bottle as far in front of him as was possible without dropping it. He looked around. No one seemed to notice. He slowly replaced the bottle back on the counter.

"Thank goodness that didn't squirt in my face. What is that smell?" He moved his left hand back and forth in front of him in an attempt to clear the air.

"Can I help you Sir?" Simeon turned and saw a young lady standing behind a different counter. "Excuse me…Can I help you Sir?" the young lady asked again.

"Oh, I am sorry. I did not realize you were speaking to me." Simeon walked towards the young lady and smiled. "What do you have at your counter?"

"Only the finest watches in all of Ireland. Come have a look." The young lady held up a watch.

Simeon took the watch from the young lady so he could study it more closely. He had never seen a watch before. Faeries didn't worry about time. However, he had heard of them. Emma had told him about watches a long time ago. He had always wanted to see one and was fascinated that a small piece of machinery that fits on your arm could tell you what hour it is during the day. Simeon was intrigued by how humans were always so focused on time. Most wore watches to keep them from being late. He and Emma had several long discussions on the topic of time.

"How much for the watch?" Simeon asked as he pulled out his bag of gold. He laid one piece of gold on the counter.

"That should cover it," the young lady said with a big smile on her face. She examined the gold piece. "What if I pay for your watch with my own Irish money and keep the gold piece in return?" The woman said as she waved the colored paper at Simeon.

She then put 70 Irish pounds in the cash drawer and handed Simeon the watch. "It's yours now," she said with a smile.

Simeon thanked the young lady and put on the watch. As he turned from the counter, Simeon bumped into a lovely woman with blond hair and green eyes. He reached out to stop her from falling. Looking at the woman more closely Simeon sensed something very familiar and somewhat inhuman about her.

"Can it be? Simeon, is that you?" the woman asked with disbelief echoing in her voice.

Simeon was taken aback. The woman looked very familiar. Simeon studied her for a moment. Could he really have found Helen, one of Emma's companions?

"Helen is it really you?" Simeon gave her a big hug. "Am I ever glad to see you!"

"What are you doing here Simeon?" Helen asked perplexed.

"It is a long story," Simeon said as his stomach started to growl.

"Let us get something to eat and you can tell me all about it," Helen replied. "I know a great place called Bewley's. It is right down the street."

When Helen and Simeon left the store, Lucky was still waiting out front. "Well, it looks like you are in good hands. I guess you don't need my help anymore." Lucky turned to leave.

"Lucky stop. Please! We are going to get some food in a place called Bewley's. I would be more than happy if you joined us," implored Simeon.

"Are you crazy? Bewley's is one of the nicest cafes on the street. Dogs are definitely not allowed in there."

"Well, please come with us and I will make sure you get a nice meal," Simeon said.

Helen just stared at Simeon and Lucky when she heard Simeon speaking. Because she knew about Simeon's abilities, she could tell Simeon and Lucky were communicating. She just wasn't sure what Lucky was saying.

After Simeon told Helen he invited Lucky to lunch, they all headed towards Bewley's. When they got to the café, Simeon realized Helen and Lucky were right. There was a big sign out front that said *No Dogs Allowed*.

"I guess you are going to have to wait out here. However, I promised you a lunch and you can be sure you will get a nice meal."

Helen and Simeon headed into the café and found a place to sit. "What would you like to eat?" Helen asked.

"I am not sure. I've never had human food. What would you recommend?" Simeon asked.

"I think you would like the salmon. It is very good here," Helen advised. When the server arrived at their table, Helen asked for two ginger ales, and two platters of salmon and chips.

"Now that we have ordered, tell me what you are doing here in Dublin."

Hidden in his shirt, Simeon pulled out the chain around his neck. "Emma's father sent me here to give this to her," he said as he dangled the Ring of Incognito before her eyes.

Helen reached over the table and gently held the ring in her fingers. "Where did you get this? It has been missing for thousands of years."

"It is a long story, but the short of it is, I used my powers for finding things to track down the ring. It was owned by a pixie Faerie who lives in a cave and is married to a troll. Since the pixie Faerie wore the ring on her hand for many years, it is possible she is a Faerie princess."

"I tried to get the ring to Emma before her transformation ceremony, but I was not able to get back before she left for Earth."

"How is Emma?" Simeon anxiously asked.

"She is doing well and is adjusting to the human world with little difficulty. It's almost like she has been human all her life."

"Really?" Simeon questioned. "Both her father and I have wondered how she is doing, since she left the ForEverNever."

"Once we finish here, I will take you back to our house and you will get to see her for yourself."

A big grin formed on Simeon's face as he thought about seeing Emma again. He was glad she was doing well; he had been worried about her. "Why have none of you made contact with the Faerie World and let us know how you are doing?" Simeon asked.

"We do not have the ability to contact anyone in the Faerie World," Helen responded slightly confused.

"What about the objects that were in the magic boxes you brought with you? The King of Ymir told me that each of you has an object in your box you can use to connect with the Faerie World. You just need to figure out which one it is and how to use it."

"So far, I have not had any luck figuring out how to use the objects in my box." Helen appeared a little frustrated. "Since you are here, maybe you can help me? You have always been good at figuring things out."

"Sure, I would be glad to help you. Are you ready to head out now?"

"Yes, just let me pay the bill." Helen motioned for the server.

"You were right about the salmon; it was great. Can we order one for Lucky before we leave?"

"Lucky? Is that the dog who accompanied us?"

"Yes, and he is waiting outside. I promised him a nice lunch for his help."

"You have always had a soft spot for animals," Helen laughed. "I guess that is likely to happen when you can actually communicate with them. Of course, we can get Lucky an order of salmon."

THE SACRIFICE

This world is so different than my world. When I look around I see so many things that I have never seen before, and yet they look oddly familiar. I am told it takes great courage to venture from what is known, to the unknown. But I am not here because I am courageous, I am here because an old friend, who I would do anything for, needs me. And, being here is an adventure. I have never been one to shy away from an adventure. I am sure I will learn a lot being here and I am confident that I will find a way to get home. Although this place is growing on me, I don't want to be stuck here forever. And even if I wanted to stay here, I could not. My king and homeland need me. They rely on me to protect them. I could never turn my back on my purpose and those who need me.

- Simeon DeLuc

xi : Reunion of Old Friends

Salmon in hand, Helen and Simeon left the café.

"Here you go Lucky. I told you I would get you a nice meal. Hope you like it," Simeon said as he leaned down and placed the Salmon in front of Lucky.

"Simeon, it is not a long walk back to the house, but I know a way to get there even quicker," Helen exclaimed as she raised her hand and walked towards the street.

A large, shiny, metal machine that looked a little like a carriage stopped in front of them. The machine made a strange noise. Helen opened the door to expose places to sit inside the machine. In the front of the machine was a man wearing a hat. He sat behind a circular shaped object that was connected to the machine.

"Care for a ride?" the man sitting behind the circular shaped object asked.

"I am not getting in that!" Simeon stated with conviction.

"It's fine Simeon. This machine is called a taxicab and the man up front is the taxicab driver. It's safe and will get us to the house much faster than walking. I really do not feel like carrying these bags for blocks." Helen held up her shopping bags.

Simeon hesitantly followed Helen into the taxicab. "What about Lucky?"

"Sorry, dogs are not allowed in the taxicab," the driver said emphatically.

"Lucky seems to be able to take care of himself. He should be fine," Helen reassured.

"See you around Lucky," Simeon said as he squeezed into the taxicab.

"Where to Ms.?" The driver asked.

"29 Merrion Street Upper, please," Helen responded.

Simeon's body jerked backward when the taxicab took off. Then he settled comfortably in his seat. Simeon was not used to traveling at such a speed. He looked out the window and watched as they quickly passed buildings and people. Helen was speaking to him, but he was so distracted by what he saw that he had no idea what she was saying. Before Simeon knew it, the driver shouted as the taxicab stopped. "This is it, 29 Merrion Street Upper."

Helen gave the taxicab driver some of the strange looking paper the girl at the department store had shown Simeon when he bought his watch. Then Helen and Simeon got out of the taxicab, went up the stairs and walked to the front door of 29 Merrion Street Upper. Helen smiled at Simeon, "Welcome to Evanswood! Everyone is going to be so glad to see you."

Simeon and Helen entered the house and ran into Mrs. MacTavish in the entrance way.

Smiling, Mrs. MacTavish gave Simeon a big hug. "Is that really you, Simeon? I never thought I would see you again. What brings you to the human world?"

Simeon reached into his shirt and held up the ring for Mrs. MacTavish to see.

"The Ring of Incognito," Mrs. MacTavish gasped. "You brought it for Emma? What a great friend you are!"

"I vowed years ago that I would give up my life to protect Emma. You know, as a Faerie, I can never go back on my word. Emma's father is also very worried about her. He has not heard from any of you."

"Not heard from us?" Mrs. MacTavish was obviously a little irritated. "And just how are we supposed to get in contact with him?"

"Before I left, the King told me that you, Emma, Helen and Mr. Maguire are able to contact the ForEverNever using the objects in the magic boxes you brought with you. Since you came to Earth in a rush, there was no time for the King to explain how to use the objects in your magic boxes. The King hoped each of you would figure out how the objects from your boxes provided you with the power to connect with the ForEverNever.

"There are several objects in our magic boxes, but as far as I know, none of us have been able to determine how to make them work," stated Mrs. MacTavish.

Simeon sensed her frustration, so he attempted to change the subject. How is Emma? Is she home?"

"Emma is doing well. She is out with William St. Clair. They have spent a lot of time together lately. He really seems to like her. He is very kind and friendly, and he goes out of his way to help others. Besides being extremely loyal, he is also intelligent, trustworthy and has a great sense of humor. He spends time at the local orphanage every Sunday. He has even taken Emma a few times. Just the other day when he came to pick her up, he brought Helen and me flowers. And when he heard the faucet in the kitchen was broken, he fixed it. Now I understand why Emma was so willing to give up her powers. William St. Clair is a wonderful man."

Simeon was curious as he listened to Mrs. MacTavish's description of William. He was eager to ask Emma questions about him.

"When do you expect Emma to return?"

"She should be back in about an hour," Mrs. MacTavish responded.

Simeon looked at the new watch on his wrist. If he remembered correctly, the long hand had to make a complete circle before an hour passed.

"Are you tired or hungry?" Mrs. MacTavish asked.

"I just ate, but I do feel a little tired," Simeon stifled a yawn.

"I will give you a quick tour of the house then take you to your room. You will have some time to rest before Emma gets home."

———————————————————————————————

Simeon had just fallen asleep when he heard a knock on the door. In a groggy voice he yelled at the door, "You may enter." He rubbed his eyes as he sat up in bed, put his feet on the floor and stood up to walk towards the door.

Before Simeon had taken a step, the door opened and standing in front of him was Emma.

"Simeon, it really is you! You're here in the human world! I could scarcely believe it when Helen told me you were here. I am so happy to see you." Emma ran over and gave Simeon a big hug.

"What brings you to the human world?"

"You," Simeon said as he grinned and poked Emma in the arm.

Emma gently hit him on the arm. "Stop teasing Simeon! What really brings you here?"

"Seriously Emma, I came here for you. Your father asked me to bring you this." Simeon reached into his shirt and pulled out a ring.

Emma stared questionably at the Ring of Incognito as it sat securely in Simeon's hand sparkling as it caught the light coming in from the window.

For a brief moment Simeon just stared back at Emma. He still could not believe she was standing right in front of him.

"When you wear this ring, you should be able to move through the Faerie World without being detected as human. You can now safely return to the ForEverNever!" Simeon took the ring and the chain off his neck and handed both to Emma.

"I can't take that," Emma pointed to the chain.

"The chain is to remember me by," Simeon winked.

"But, the chain belonged to your father! I can't take it Simeon," Emma stressed again.

"I want you to have it," Simeon reassuringly smiled at Emma.

"Thank you Simeon, I will treasure it always." Emma held the ring and chain to her heart as she returned Simeon's smile.

"Did you get here the same way Helen, Mrs. MacTavish, and Mr. McGuire got here?" Emma asked. She was grateful Simeon had brought the ring, but she wanted to make sure he did not have to sacrifice too much to get it to her.

"Yes, I saw your grandmother and came through the Willow Portal." Simeon winked again.

Emma sighed. "Oh Simeon, did you have to give up all your powers?"

"No need to worry. I only had to give up one power and it was a power I didn't know how to use anyway. A small sacrifice, well worth making, to know you will be safe."

"My hero," Emma said as she pinched Simeon's arm and gave him another hug.

"And how is my father?"

"He is doing well, but he misses you. He's concerned about you and wonders how you are doing."

"Life is fantastic! I am gloriously happy! You could not have arrived at a better time."

Emma held up her hand. "William asked me to marry him today."

"Congratulations! I am glad it has worked out for you. Your father will be happy to hear this news and glad to know you are safe. When is the wedding?"

"There really is no reason for us to wait. It's in a few weeks. When do you have to return to the ForEverNever?"

"Since you are here now, I really want you at the wedding. William and I can get married sooner, if you have to return earlier than a few weeks."

"Well, I don't quite know how to get back to the ForEverNever, so I think I can be here for the wedding." Simeon grinned at Emma.

"I will let you rest now, but later I want to hear all about what is going on in your life and especially how my father is doing."

Emma turned to leave the room then looked back over her shoulder at Simeon. "Dinner is at 6:00. Just a warning, Mrs. MacTavish will not hold dinner for you, but Helen may sneak you something, if you miss it. Even after all these years, she still makes sure I'm comfortable and have all I need," Emma smiled.

"Just like when we were younger!" Simeon lightly chuckled.

"Emma," Simeon called out before she closed the door behind her, "When you are not wearing the ring, make sure you keep it in your magic box. I am not sure how being on Earth, without the touch of Faerie power, will affect it."

Emma turned back around to look at Simeon. "I will. Thankfully, my father had the foresight to make sure there was a spot in my box for the ring."

"And if there is ever a time when you need the ring close by, but you don't want to wear it on your finger, keep it on the chain. In fact, you should always wear the chain, it will protect you."

"And don't forget, we still have to figure out how the other objects in your magic box work," Simeon teased.

Emma fingered the chain around her neck. "I will always wear the chain. Thank you Simeon. And, I was able to use one of the objects from my magic box."

"Which object is that?

"The tapestry," Emma grinned in satisfaction.

"There were two strings hanging out of a slit in my magic box. I pulled on the strings and a beautiful cloth came out of the box. As I continued to hold the strings, the cloth started to grow. Next thing I knew, I was holding an elaborate tapestry. There seemed to be a perfect spot in the library for the tapestry. As I hung the tapestry, I heard a loud cracking and clicking sound. When I moved the tapestry aside to see what made all the noise, I discovered a strange room behind it with several doors. I am not sure what the room should be used for or where the other doors lead. The only one I was able to open was on the far side of the mysterious and hidden room leading to a beautiful garden."

"My box has a place for the tapestry, the ring, my shoes and a medallion, which I placed into this custom-made bracelet." Emma lifted her wrist for Simeon to get a better look at her bracelet.

"The only other object in my magic box is a mirror, but I am not sure what it is for or how to use it."

"Did you try saying mirror, mirror?" Simeon laughed.

Emma looked directly at Simeon and raised her eyebrow. "That only works in make believe stories, and this is very real!"

However, she thought, "Maybe I will try that once I get back to my room. What could it hurt?"

I'm afraid neither Helen nor Mrs. MacTavish has figured out the powers associated with the objects in their boxes either. I am not even sure if they have tried."

"Well, at least now you can safely return to the ForEverNever."

"What about Mr. McGuire, does he know how to use any of the objects in his box?"

"I don't know. His responsibilities keep him away from Evanswood for long periods of time. We don't see him very often. However, he will be returning for the wedding," Emma said with a big smile.

Simeon wondered what could keep Mr. McGuire away and where he might go, but he held his tongue as Emma spoke.

"Simeon, we also need to figure out how to get you home," Emma said in a concerned voice.

"However, let's not worry about that now." Emma patted Simeon's shoulder. "I'm just thankful to be able to spend time with my oldest and dearest friend." Emma hugged Simeon and pulled on his ears. She then turned and walked out of the room.

—————————————————————————————————

After dinner, Emma, Helen, Mrs. MacTavish and Simeon all sat by the small fireplace in the library closest to the wall with the tapestry. There were three boxes neatly lined up on the table in front of them. Each box was a different color. Emma's box was a beautiful blue with a touch of silver and was covered in gold writing, which said, anithey. Helen's box was a vibrant green with silver writing that said, sywueth, and Mrs. MacTavish's box was a muted pink with silver writing, which said, fethewey. The writing on the magic boxes was in Fae-oldish an ancient Faerie language, which many Faeries understood when spoken, but very few Faeries could read. Mrs. MacTavish was the only one in the group who could read it, so she translated for the group. Anithey is love, sywueth is heal and fethewey is guide.

Emma, Helen, and Mrs. MacTavish knew it was past time they figured out how to use the objects in their magic boxes. Their safety could depend on the powers the objects held. Emma's box was open. Emma put her shoes and ring in her box, and showed everyone the objects. The only object that was still a complete mystery to Emma was the mirror.

Emma chuckled as she pointed at the tapestry hanging on the wall beside them. "That was also in my box, but I can't remove it from the wall. After I hung it, I thought about moving it to the other side of the room just to see how it looked. But, I was unable to get it off the wall. It seemed liked the tapestry was gripping onto the wall and wouldn't let go. The harder I pulled, the more firmly the tapestry clung to the wall, as if it were alive. I was, however, able to push the tapestry aside like a curtain. That was when I discovered a beautiful hidden room and garden behind it.

Helen and Mrs. MacTavish looked at each other in surprise.

"Follow me, I want all of you to see something," Emma said excitedly. She pulled back the tapestry and exposed the hidden room behind it.

As they entered the room, Emma continued to hold back the tapestry and light filled the room. Emma pointed out the door at the back of the room. "That door leads to a beautiful garden. But, I couldn't open the other two doors."

Simeon closely examined the two doors on the sides of the room and tried to open them. Neither door would budge. He made his way to the back of the room. "Surely, this door will open," he thought. He tried to open the door and it too would not budge.

"How odd," Emma said aloud. She stepped up to the door and turned the handle. The door opened with very little effort.

Simeon gasped, "Well, I'll be!" He had Emma close the door then he tried to open it. Again, it would not budge. Both Helen and Mrs. MacTavish also tried to open the door, but neither of them had any luck. Emma tried the door again, and for a second time the door opened with ease.

"Incredible!" Mrs. MacTavish expressed in awe. "The garden is hidden behind this room. I wonder its purpose, other than looking and smelling beautiful."

"I haven't a clue, but isn't it wonderful?" Emma laughed as she turned her palms upward, extended her arms from her side, raised them to just above her waist and spun around in the brightly lit garden. She took a deep breath and could smell a hint of jasmine and lemon in the air. A gentle breeze brushed by her face filling her nostrils with an even stronger scent of jasmine and lemon. Two small fountains framed the door leading back into the hidden room. The sound of flowing water created a soothing effect. The vibrant blue, purple, pink and yellow flowers scattered throughout the garden seemed to be humming. Emma reached down to put her hand in the narrow brook that ran through the garden.

"Emma, I think you are going to have to ask your father about this garden and the mirror. Let's get back to the library, so we can check out the other boxes. Maybe if we all put our minds to the task we can figure out what some of the objects in the other boxes can do," Simeon suggested.

They all walked back through the hidden room and returned to the library. Emma noticed Mrs. MacTavish appeared uncomfortable with sharing.

"I think Helen should open her box next," Emma stated as she moved towards the small fireplace next to the tapestry. They all sat back down in front of the fireplace.

Helen smiled at Emma and took out a key in the shape of a four-leaf clover, which she had hidden in her apron. "Let's see if this works." She pushed a button at the bottom of the box to expose a keyhole. She gently placed the key in the lock. The box made a quiet popping sound as the key turned in the lock and the lid to the box opened. Helen cautiously lifted the lid and raised her magic box so everyone could see the contents. Inside were bandages, a small empty glass bottle, a needle and thread, an hourglass and a small gold medallion. Helen took the hourglass out of the box and discovered an inscription on top. She did not know what the words meant so she handed it to Mrs. MacTavish to read.

"Time is but an illusion, which can be reshaped or reordered at any moment. There is no past or future, there is only the now," Mrs. MacTavish read aloud and handed the hourglass back to Helen.

Helen decided to flip the hourglass over. At that moment everything in the room froze in place. Helen was the only person or thing in the room moving. Emma's mouth was wide open in the process of speaking.

Simeon's hand was reaching towards Emma. Mrs. MacTavish was sitting back on the couch with her legs crossed looking somewhat less entertained than the rest of the group.

The hands on the clock on the mantle above the large fireplace in the center of the room also stopped moving. Helen stood up and walked over to the clock to get a better look. The clock was not making any noise. Intrigued, she tried to move one of the dials, but she couldn't get it to move. She wondered how long this would last. Then she saw the hourglass sitting on the table. The sand in the hourglass was moving. She walked back over to the table and picked up the hourglass. She flipped it back over and everything started to move again as if nothing had been interrupted at all. Emma finished her sentence and Simeon's hand moved back in front of him.

"How strange." Helen flipped the hourglass back over and everything froze in place again.

"I can stop time! I guess the saying time waits for no one is no longer true for me," Helen laughed.

Helen flipped the hourglass over several times. When she finally stopped playing, having fun watching everyone stop and go and the funny expressions on their faces when they were frozen in time, she told everyone what happened.

Emma thought it was incredible, Mrs. MacTavish was skeptical and Simeon wanted to try it out. Simeon lifted the hourglass and flipped it over. Nothing happened. The sand in the hourglass was moving and so was everything else in the room. Everyone glanced in Helen's direction with a questioning look.

"Let me see that." Helen grabbed the hourglass and flipped it. Again everything froze in place. "This must only work for me like the door to the garden only works for Emma." Helen flipped the hourglass back over and explained to her friends what she discovered.

Interesting," Simeon said as he rubbed his chin. "Let's see what else is in here!"

"Except for the obvious, I'm not sure what else you can do with these." Simeon held bandages and a needle and thread in his hands and placed them on the table.

"What else do you have in there? A glass bottle...hmm?" Simeon rubbed his chin again. "I think I have an idea. Everyone follow me! And Helen bring your glass bottle."

Simeon tried to pull back the tapestry, but it would not move. "Emma, can you move this thing?"

Emma easily pulled back the edge of the tapestry to reveal the hidden room.

Simeon looked around. "Ok, things are starting to make a little more sense to me. Helen, I think you are the only one who can open the door to the left inside the hidden room. See that groove or indention above the door? What does it look like to you?"

"My glass bottle!" Helen expressed excitedly.

"But I can't reach that high. Simeon would you put the bottle in the groove for me?"

Simeon paused a moment to think. "I have a feeling this is something you have to do. Here, I will give you a lift." Simeon held out his arms to Helen.

But Simeon could not lift Helen high enough for her to reach the groove above the door. Simeon lowered Helen to the ground and got down on his knees. Helen sat on Simeon's shoulders. She held on tightly to the glass bottle as Simeon quickly stood up. Continuing to hold tightly to the glass bottle, Helen grabbed Simeon's head so she would not fall off. Within seconds Simeon was standing at his full height.

"You tease." Helen patted Simeon on the head, not too gently.

Helen was now eye level with the groove above the door. She carefully reached her hand out and placed the glass bottle in the groove. There was a sudden flash of light and a loud ringing noise like wind chimes, but magnified.

Helen covered her ears. "I suspect that worked. Let's see."

Simeon held onto Helen's legs with one arm and used his other arm to help him kneel to the ground.

Once Helen slid down from his shoulders, Simeon stood and tried to open the door. The door would not open for him. Emma enthusiastically tried to open the door, but she couldn't open it either.

"My turn," Helen said. She reached out and gently turned the handle on the door. There was a clicking sound and the handle continued to turn. Helen turned the handle as far as she could and slowly opened the door.

A sudden rush of steam and warm air hit Helen in the face. She began to cough. "What's inside that room? What could create so much steam?" Helen wondered.

Simeon, would you check out what is behind the door?" Helen pleaded.

Simeon intently stared at Helen, but there was a sparkle in his eyes as he walked into the space behind the door.

"It is a room full of steam," Simeon yelled.

"Tell us something we could not guess," Emma yelled back.

As Simeon moved closer to the center of the room he saw water. "It looks like there is a bath or a pond of some kind in the middle of the room."

Simeon stuck his hand in the water. "Ouch! That's hot!" Simeon shook his hand.

Helen and Emma cautiously ventured into the room. "What an interesting room. There sure is a lot of steam." Helen waved her hand in front of her face to push back a thick blanket of mist.

Emma put her hands in the water. "Boy, that is hot. Helen, you should test the water."

Helen placed both of her hands in the water. "The water is not too hot to sit in. It reminds me of a hot spring I used to visit when I was younger. The waters had healing properties."

Helen cupped some of the water in her left hand and let the water trickle through her fingers onto a small scratch on her right arm. Helen curiously watched as the scratch completely disappeared instantly.

"Just as I thought, the water does have healing properties." Helen rubbed the spot on her arm where the scratch had been.

"It's getting a little stuffy in here," Emma coughed. "I am going to head back out into the other room."

Simeon and Helen also left the steam filled room. "I wonder if I can still open the door if the glass bottle is no longer in the groove?" Helen said aloud as she rubbed her hands together.

"Let's see what happens," Simeon kneeled down again so Helen could get back up on his shoulders.

"Wait!" Helen took a small container from her apron pocket and went back into the room. She returned holding up the container, which was now filled with water. "Just in case."

"Let me see that. I have a theory." Simeon took the container and poured the water on another scratch on Helen's arm. Nothing happened.

"Just as I thought. The water will likely only retain its healing powers if it is held in your glass bottle." Helen grabbed the container from Simeon and dumped the rest of the water from the container on the ground. She then returned the container to her apron.

Helen then climbed up on Simeon's shoulders. He raised her up again, slower this time. Once she was eye level with the glass bottle, Helen was able to remove it from the groove. She slid off Simeon's shoulders and immediately tried to open the door. The door easily opened as steam and hot air came rushing out again. Helen went back into the room and filled her glass bottle with water. She then returned to the hidden room holding up the glass bottle for everyone to see. "Just in case I need this healing water in the future."

After Helen closed the door, Simeon tried to open it. Again, he was unable to make it budge. Helen reached in front of him, and opened and closed the door one more time.

"I guess you don't have the magic touch." Helen smiled at Simeon.

Helen, Simeon, Emma and Mrs. MacTavish all returned to the library. "It's your turn." Emma looked at Mrs. MacTavish and smiled. Mrs. MacTavish reluctantly removed the star-shaped key from her dress pocket. She pushed the button to reveal the keyhole then stuck the star-shaped key in the lock at the bottom of her box. After hearing the quiet popping sound Mrs. MacTavish gently opened the lid of her box. Everyone leaned over to see what was inside.

This was the first time Mrs. MacTavish had opened her box. She thought about opening the box and seeing the objects inside earlier, however, she didn't want to think about all she had given up. She had been a powerful Faerie and member of the Royal House of the Faerie House of Ymir. Of all the Faeries who had given up their powers to help Emma, Mrs. MacTavish had sacrificed her one most significant power. Mrs. MacTavish could control other Faeries' and humans' emotions. She could make them feel sad, mad, angry or happy at will.

Mrs. MacTavish knew it was time to face the pain of all she lost and embrace her future. She opened the box and was surprised. As she looked inside she only felt curiosity. She was eager to discover the powers the objects held.

"What's inside your magic box?" Emma asked.

Mrs. MacTavish held up her magic box. "There is a book with writing and blank pages, a few pieces of paper, a pen, a miniature mirror and a pair of binoculars."

Emma pointed to the gold medallion in the corner of Mrs. MacTavish's box. "Look you have a medallion too! It looks very similar to Helen's and mine, but I think it has a different symbol."

Mrs. MacTavish opened the book and was delighted to see it contained pictures and descriptions of different Faeries. An odd saying written in Fae-oldish that slightly resembled poetry was inscribed in the book. Mrs. MacTavish translated:

Think not about the future
Dwell not on the past
To the present hold fast

Dare to ask your questions
And all will be revealed

At the back of the book were a number of blank pages. Picking up the pen Mrs. MacTavish decided to write something on one of the blank pages. The words began to vanish after she finished the sentence. "How odd," she thought. Then she tried writing a question. As soon as she placed the question mark on the page, the question disappeared.

"What is this book for?" Mrs. MacTavish rubbed her chin.

In a few seconds words began to appear on the page. Mrs. MacTavish looked at the writing carefully. She could not believe it.

"All the answers to my questions just appeared in the book. This book can help me protect Emma. The answers this book provides will enable us to better understand the potential dangers surrounding us."

Mrs. MacTavish was enthralled with the book. A little piece of her Faerie world was with her and with it came a power. This was a different kind of power, but a power just the same.

"I know what to do with that." Simeon pointed to the mirror inside Mrs. MacTavish's magic box and had that mischievous look on his face that always made Emma laugh. "Is everyone ready for another trip back into the hidden room?"

"Yes!" Emma said with a big smile as she clutched her fists and bent her elbows raising her hands towards her face.

"This should be fun!" Helen laughed as she rubbed her hands together.

"I guess so," Mrs. MacTavish sighed as she grabbed the mirror. As she pulled it out of the box, it lengthened in size right before her eyes.

Emma, Helen and Mrs. MacTavish gasped in surprise.

"Your mirror grows in size just like my tapestry," Emma smiled.

"I thought something like that would happen," Simeon laughed.

They all hurried to the hidden room.

"It goes right there." Simeon pointed above the door on the right side of the hidden room. "And now that it has gotten a little larger in size, the mirror should fit perfectly in the groove."

"Well, I guess we know how to do this now. Do you want a lift?" Simeon asked Mrs. MacTavish.

Mrs. MacTavish confidently shook her head yes. "And I am warning you, no funny business." Mrs. MacTavish shook her finger at Simeon as he got down on his knees.

Emma and Helen helped Mrs. MacTavish onto Simeon's shoulders. Holding Mrs. MacTavish's legs Simeon stood very slowly. Once Simeon had fully stood and she was no longer swaying, Mrs. MacTavish reached out her arms to put the mirror in the groove above the door. When the mirror was firmly placed in the groove, there was a bright flash of light and a loud noise that sounded like paper being ripped in two, only amplified.

After checking to make sure Mrs. MacTavish was securely positioned on his shoulders, Simeon lowered himself back down on his knees. Mrs. MacTavish slowly climbed down off his shoulders with the help of Emma and Helen.

"You're up," Simeon said as he looked at Mrs. MacTavish and pointed at the door handle. Mrs. MacTavish purposefully turned the handle. The door opened and a cold air rushed out of the room.

"Do you want me to go in first?" Simeon asked smiling.

"No, I can do it," Mrs. MacTavish replied as she rolled her eyes at Simeon and added, "Thanks for the offer though."

Mrs. MacTavish stepped through the door. It was cold and very bright. She looked around. The same ray of light was reflecting off each wall in the room. She felt the surface of the walls. They were cool and smooth, like glass. I think the walls of this room are made of mirrors. "What could the purpose of this room be?" Mrs. MacTavish thought.

"Maybe we should say mirror, mirror in this room," Emma said as she entered the room after Simeon.

Helen was the last to enter. "This is incredible! In all my years, I have never seen anything like this."

Mrs. MacTavish said aloud, "Mirrors show me the cliffs of Moher." The room lit up and an ocean appeared on one of the walls. A massive cliff and bright green grass appeared on the other three walls. The ceiling seemed to vanish and the sky on a sunny summer day was revealed.

"Amazing," Emma whispered. I wonder if we can see the ForEverNever in this room.

Emma looked a Mrs. MacTavish. "I would like to see my father. Please see if it will work," Emma pleaded.

Mrs. MacTavish nodded. "Mirrors show me the King of Ymir in the ForEverNever."

Again, a bright light flashed in the room and then an image of the ForEverNever appeared on all four walls of the room.

Emma sighed and her eyes became a little misty. She knew the images on the walls well. They were of her home in the ForEverNever. Her eyes were drawn to the image of a lone figure standing on top of a hill with its shoulders slightly hunched and its head down.

Emma reached her hand out towards the image. "Father, what's wrong?" She whispered.

Simeon put his hand on Emma's shoulder. "No need to worry. He will be alright as soon as I get back and reassure him you are safe and happy. Let us return to the library and see if we can figure out how to use any of the other objects in your magic boxes."

Simeon whispered in Emma's ear, "You know, if you want to visit your father you can return to the ForEverNever whenever you want now that you have the Ring of Incognito and your magic shoes. Unlike me, who doesn't know how to get back, you may be my only hope for figuring out how I can return home." Simeon winked at Emma.

"Mrs. MacTavish, do you want to see if the door still opens, if you take the mirror down from above the door?"

"I think it would be a good idea to know if it does, especially since I have you here to help me."

Mrs. MacTavish got back on Simeon's shoulders and carefully took down the mirror from above the door.

Simeon lowered Mrs. MacTavish to the ground. Once on her feet, Mrs. MacTavish slowly walked to the door, reached out her hand and turned the handle on the door. The door opened and exposed the bright, cold room behind it.

The light from the Mirror Room lit up the walls around the hidden room. Beautiful pictures were revealed on each of the walls.

"These pictures were not here before!" Helen exclaimed.

Simeon looked around. "I remember seeing the scene on the wall that contains the entrance back into the library and the picture on the far wall when we went into the hidden garden, but I did not see the other pictures before. I think they appeared once Helen and Mrs. MacTavish unlocked the doors with the objects from their magic boxes."

"The pictures are lovely and seem so lifelike and real," Emma exclaimed.

An elaborate winter scene was on the wall with the door to the Mirror Room. A summer scene was on the wall with the door to the healing waters. The wall with the door leading to the hidden garden was covered in a spring scene. The wall with the opening that led back out to the library was decorated with a fall scene.

Simeon studied the wall that led back towards the tapestry. "Maybe that wall and what's behind it, the library, is somehow connected to Mr. McGuire's magic box. Do you see that groove above the opening to the library? I can't exactly make it out, but it is circular."

"Speaking of the library," Mrs. MacTavish stated, "I think it is past time we return. Emma, do you not have plans with William this afternoon?"

"Yes, I do. I need to get ready!"

"Let me help!" Helen offered.

"And I should be trying to figure out a way to get home," Simeon expressed.

Emma, Helen, Simeon and Mrs. MacTavish, with mirror in hand, all left the hidden room behind the tapestry. Emma and Helen headed upstairs so Emma could get ready for her outing with William. Simeon headed towards the kitchen to get a snack before he tackled the problem of how to return to the ForEverNever.

Mrs. MacTavish remained in the library. She still had one object in her box that she had yet to explore. The binoculars looked like any normal pair of binoculars. She held them up to her eyes and they seemed to work like normal binoculars. The books across the room appeared a little larger and so did the furniture in the room. Mrs. MacTavish decided to go over to the window to try them out. When she looked out the window with the binoculars she saw William walking down the street. Then right before her eyes, the street surroundings began to change. She removed the binoculars from her eyes and the street and its surroundings returned to normal.

When Mrs. MacTavish put the binoculars back up to her eyes the strange surroundings around the street reappeared. William was no longer walking alone. He was walking with Emma and a little girl. Mrs. MacTavish removed the binoculars again and she only saw William approaching the house. She could not believe what she was seeing. Again, she held the binoculars to her eyes and William was walking down the odd street with Emma and a young girl by his side.

Mrs. MacTavish smiled. She knew she was seeing the future. Now, Mrs. MacTavish knew for sure that everything was going to be all right. Emma and William were going to have a beautiful little girl someday. Mrs. MacTavish felt overjoyed for both of them.

Mrs. MacTavish walked out of the library just in time to see Emma hurrying to the front door to meet William. Emma had a big smile on her face. She looked lovely. Helen was amazing. With her help it only took Emma a few minutes to get ready.

Emma normally took a few hours to get ready. Not because she was overly concerned with her appearance, but Emma was still getting use to the clothing worn in the human world. She was still learning how to put together pants and dress outfits and what was worn on which occasions. At home, in the ForEverNever, Emma always wore brightly colored, loose fitting, long flowing gowns.

———————————————————————————————

Emma left with William, and Mrs. MacTavish returned to the library to pick up her magic box and mirror. Mrs. MacTavish was glad she finally opened her box. She returned to her room with a contented smile. She felt happier and more relaxed now that she could see her Faerie world through the Mirror Room. She could also see the future with her binoculars, and she could have any of her questions answered simply by writing them in her book. However, she still had to figure out what the extra paper and medallion were for.

Mrs. MacTavish hung the mirror on the wall in her bedroom. There was a loud hissing sound and bright colors sparked out of the wall next to where the mirror hung. The next thing Mrs. MacTavish knew a door appeared next to the mirror. "What is it with all these appearing doors," Mrs. MacTavish thought. She hesitantly opened the door and apprehensively peeked her head in the room to see what was inside. Cold air hit her face. Mrs. MacTavish was excited to discover that the door led to her Mirror Room.

Mrs. MacTavish was curious to see if she could still get in the mirror room from the hidden room off the library. She tried to pull back the tapestry in the library, but the tapestry would not move. She returned to her room and wrote the question in her new book, "How do I pull back the tapestry?" After the question vanished, the following response appeared on the page: Make sure you have your medallion. Only those in possession of a medallion can pull back the tapestry.

Mrs. MacTavish grabbed her medallion and hurried back down to the library. She pulled back the tapestry and entered the hidden room. She then went to the door that led to the mirror room and quickly opened it. When she looked inside, there was nothing in the room. It was completely empty and the air was no longer cold. It was much warmer and only felt a little damp.

"This is more than odd," Mrs. MacTavish thought. "Now what am I supposed to do with this room?" Mrs. MacTavish didn't ponder her question for long. She felt she had experienced enough excitement for one day and she was tired. She returned to her room to rest.

I can't believe he came all this way because he was concerned for my safety and wanted to bring me a means to visit my father. He even sacrificed one of his powers. And now, he is not sure he can get home. Don't get me wrong, I am very glad to see him. In fact, this is one of the best surprises I have ever had—and I have been around for more than a few years. I am also glad he will be here for my wedding. I can't wait to marry William. Simeon's presence at my wedding will make the day that much more special. I only wish my father could be here. Although, I know with all of his responsibilities it is impossible for him to leave the ForEverNever. But Simeon will be here to celebrate with me. I just hope he can find a way home soon after the wedding.

- Emma

xij : the Search for a Way Home

Simeon waited for Emma and William to leave before he headed out the front door. He didn't want to take the chance of having William see him do or say something that might somehow jeopardize Emma's future happiness. However, he was curious about William and was tempted to use his powers and abilities to follow the young couple. "I want to make sure he is good enough for Emma."

"William and Emma would never know they were being followed," Simeon thought. But Simeon stopped himself from walking out the door after them. He reminded himself that Emma had made her choice and he needed to respect that.

Simeon waited for ten minutes after Emma and William left, before he walked out of the house. And Simeon was sure it had been ten minutes because he watched the time slowly pass on his new watch.

Simeon had no idea where to go in the city to look for other Faeries. He decided to head back towards Leister House, thinking he might be able to find another portal around there.

"I wonder if there is a cost to get home. Nothing in the Faerie World comes without a price," Simeon thought as he walked towards Leister House.

Simeon hoped he was walking in the right direction. If he remembered correctly, all he had to do was walk along the street he was on and he would run into Leister House. "Not too complicated," he thought, "and it should not take too long to walk there."

About 30 minutes after he started walking, Simeon heard a bark. He looked over and a dog with the same build and fur color as Lucky was barking at him, but the dog was too far way for him to be sure it was Lucky. The dog trotted closer to Simeon.

"Lucky, is that you?"

"Of course it's me. How many other dogs do you know in Ireland that would be greeting you?"

"You are the only dog I know," Simeon laughed. "I was wondering about you. I hope you have been well."

"Things have been acceptable, not exceptional. My mouth is still watering from that wonderful meal you gave me. What was it called…, salmon? Are you a Faerie?" Lucky asked.

Simeon took a step back. "Wow, that's a jump! Way to discreetly slip that question in. What makes you think I am a Faerie?"

"Well, you can talk with me. I have never met a human who could talk with an animal."

Simeon was intrigued. "How do you know what Faeries are? Have you met one before?"

"Sure, I have seen tons of Faeries. I've even spoken to a few over the years. But, you are the only one kind enough to ask me how I'm doing."

"Well, you were there to help me when I was in need." Simeon petted Lucky on the head. "Do you know where I can find other Faeries?"

"I have seen many Faeries in Iveagh Gardens, a hidden paradise right in the center of Dublin where the gardens' high walls block out the world. The gardens are known to be very quiet and peaceful. A magnificent waterfall, rose gardens, open fields, intricate gravel walkways, wooded nooks and a charming set of classical statues are all found in the gardens. Iveagh Gardens is a magical place—the perfect place for Faeries to play," Lucky said as he wagged his tail.

"Sounds like a wonderful place. Do you know how the Faeries get there?"

Lucky cocked his head to one side making his ear droop a little. With a twinkle in his eyes he replied, "I am not sure where the Faeries come from. During the day I like to take naps in Iveagh Gardens and these Faeries just appear. I think they may come out of one of the trees or the waterfall in the garden, but I am not sure. For all I know they just walk in the front gate. I can take you to Iveagh Gardens if you like, but how about a nice meal first?"

"Thankfully, Helen gave me some paper money earlier today. She's in charge of the household accounts and had a few extra bills lying around. Where do you want to go for lunch?"

"I really like salmon." Lucky eagerly wagged his tail.

"The Bewley's on Grafton Street it is then. But, if I remember correctly no dogs are allowed in the restaurant." Simeon leaned over and scratched Lucky's head. "I'll go into the restaurant and get the food. We can eat in a nearby park."

"To Grafton Street," Simeon said as he started walking down the street whistling.

———————————————————————————————

After Simeon and Lucky finished an amazing lunch, Lucky led Simeon to Iveagh Gardens.

"How do you get in this place?" Simeon looked up at the high walls surrounding the Iveagh Gardens.

Lucky nudged Simeon's leg. "Don't worry! The entrance is right around the corner. It's sort of hidden. That is why not many people know about it, which is probably one of the reasons you can find Faeries here and so few humans."

Lucky led Simeon around the corner. Briefly visible, behind two tall trees was the entrance. Simeon walked into Iveagh Gardens with long confident strides. He knew he was close to finding a way home. He could just feel it.

Lucky followed close behind. Simeon looked down at Lucky. "You know most Faeries appear just like humans, how do you know you actually see Faeries?

"Faeries may look like humans, but they do not smell like them. Faeries have a fainter, sweeter smell than humans. When you are around a Faerie you can smell a light scent of lavender. I knew you were probably a Faerie before I even saw you," Lucky explained. "Either that or you wash with lavender soap."

Simeon found Lucky's observations interesting. He stowed away this new bit of information. It might prove useful in the future. He then asked, "What is lavender?"

"Lavender is a beautiful plant with various shades of purple and blue. Humans use extracts from lavender plants to make fragrances and bath products. They sometimes put it in food. Lavender is also known to have a calming effect. It is also used to…"

"Ok, ok…Enough about the lavender," Simon interrupted. "Where are those trees or waterfall you were speaking of?"

"They are up here a ways," Lucky replied. "Just, look around for a moment. Aren't these lovely gardens? I always feel at peace when I'm here."

Lucky lifted his head and raised his nose in the air sniffing. "There are Faeries on the other side of those bushes. If you take the next turn on the gravel path, you should run into a pair of Faeries."

"That's a pretty good smeller you have there, Lucky." As Simeon rounded the corner, he wondered how Lucky knew there were two Faeries.

Sure enough there was a male and female Faerie siting on a bench close to the waterfall. They had their heads bent over looking at a strange book with shiny pages and pictures. When they heard Simeon approach, they looked up. Simeon could tell they were Faeries by looking at them. A bright gold and silver light glowed around their bodies. From his brief encounters with humans, Simeon knew various colored lights surrounded humans, but none of them were surrounded by a bright gold and silver light. As far as he could tell, only Faeries were surrounded by a bright gold and silver light along with the color of light associated with the Faerie House they belonged. The female Faerie was surrounded by a bright gold and silver light, as well as a red light. The male Faerie was surrounded by a bright gold and silver light, and multi-colored lights. Because of the color of light surrounding them, Simeon knew that the female Faerie and the male Faerie were from the Faerie Houses of Ashbel and Erion respectively.

"What do you want?" The male Faerie was clearly annoyed with the interruption. "Can't you see we are busy?" He glared at Simeon. The female Faerie just ignored Simeon and returned to the brightly colored, shiny pages sitting in her lap. She laughed at something she read and the male Faerie looked down to see what made her laugh.

"Excuse me," Simeon said, "I was just wondering how you got into the gardens?"

"We walked in through the entrance like everyone else," the male Faerie responded coldly with a little sarcasm.

"Well, how did you get here in the human world?" Simeon asked.

"What do you mean, how did we get here in the human world? What kind of question is that?"

Simeon scratched his head. "I guess they have always lived here or they have lived here so long they have forgotten how they got here. It's likely they can't asker the question, but I have to ask it." he thought.

"Do you know how I can get back to the ForEverNever?"

"The ForEverNever? What a silly name. I've never heard of a place called that. I would wager you made up the name," the male Faerie huffed annoyed.

Simeon was taken aback by the male Faeries response and attitude. "You have never heard of the ForEverNever, the home of the Faeries?" Simeon asked in awe.

The male Faerie just stared at Simeon like he was crazy.

Simeon mumbled as he turned to walk back to Lucky. "Well, I'll be, they do exist. I guess I just met some of the Faeries, the King of Ymir told me about. They don't even know where they came from. I suspect they have lost their powers and think they are humans."

"Well, Lucky these two aren't going to be helpful. And even if they were friendly enough to offer help, they don't even know what they are."

Lucky sat close to Simeon's leg. "Where do we go now?"

Simeon wrinkled his brow. "Let's wait around here for a little longer. Where is that tree you were talking about earlier?"

"It's just a few paths over. Do you want to head over there for a while and see what we see? Maybe you will find what you are looking for." Lucky tried to sound encouraging.

Simeon and Lucky sat by the tree for hours waiting.

"We are not going to see any other Faeries here today," Simeon said as the sun set in the West.

"I think it is time I return to Emma's. I didn't tell anyone I was leaving. They may be a little concerned. Would you like to come with me?" Simeon asked Lucky.

"With pleasure!" Lucky wagged his tail with delight.

"Good," Simeon said with a grin, "Because I don't think I can get back to Emma's without your help."

————————————————————————————

Simeon and Lucky made it back just in time for dinner. As Simeon suspected, Emma and Helen were a little concerned about him.

"Where have you been all day?" Helen asked.

"And who is this you have with you? Is this the dog you told me about when you first arrived?" Emma asked.

"Yes, this is Lucky. I was hoping he could stay with us for a while." Simeon looked at Emma with pleading eyes.

"Sure Lucky can stay," Emma said with a smile. "But you still have not told us where you were all day." Emma playfully raised her eyebrows.

"I was trying to find a way back to the ForEverNever. Lucky knows about Faeries and has seen many over the years at Iveagh Gardens. He took me there today."

"And were you successful? Did you figure out a way to get home?" Emma asked enthusiastically.

"I saw two Faeries, but they were not able to help me. In fact, they were a little rude. And, they have never even heard of the ForEverNever."

"Faeries that have never heard of the ForEverNever? How can that be?" Emma and Helen asked in unison. Helen shook her head and Emma had a very odd expression on her face.

"How can they not know of the ForEverNever?" Emma asked again confused.

"Yes, these Faeries exist! Before I left home your father told me all about Faeries who had never heard of the ForEverNever. Apparently, some Faeries were created here on Earth and have never been to the ForEverNever. However, these Faeries generally live in the hills, forests, deserts, mountains and oceans, away of humans. There are also other Faeries who have been away from the ForEverNever for so long they have no memories of it. They forgot how to use their powers or just stopped using them and over time their powers weakened and eventually disappeared. Without their powers these Faeries think they are humans, and like humans they are susceptible to illness and aging. And the answer to your question is, no! I was not able to find a way home," Simeon said discouraged.

"We will find you a way home Simeon," Emma promised.

"Tomorrow, I will see if I can find my father. I am not exactly sure how the shoes work, but they can't be too difficult to figure out. I think I'll start by putting them on my feet." Emma winked.

Simeon laughed as he pictured Emma putting the shoes on her hands.

"I have to admit, I'm very glad you are here. I missed our talks and your teasing. And now you can give me away when I marry William in a few weeks."

"Give you away?" Simeon repeated confused. "I never want to give you away! You will always be important to me and I always hope to carry your friendship with me."

"Silly," Emma teased Simeon as she gently pinched him arm. "You will always be important to me too. Giving the bride away is something humans do at weddings. The father or a close male relative or friend walks the bride down the aisle to her soon-to-be husband. William insists he doesn't want me to walk down the aisle alone. He says it's bad luck to break with tradition. Mr. McGuire was going to walk me down the aisle, but since you are here, I would prefer my oldest, dearest friend have the honors."

Simeon gave Emma a big grin and winked at her. "It will be my greatest pleasure to walk you down the aisle."

Emma smiled back at Simeon and gave him a big hug. For a moment she let herself think about all she was getting ready to give up and how much she had missed Simeon. His quick wit always made her laugh. She wished he could stay forever, but she knew he had to return to the ForEverNever soon after the wedding. He had a job to do and he had Faeries to protect.

I am so glad I have been able to spend time with Simeon again. However, as the days pass I realize how crucial it is that we find a way to get him home. I know he is always up to facing a challenge and he never gives up. Simeon is a force all his own, with more powers than even he has figured out how to use. He likely has other powers that he is still unaware of. It is possible that when he is older, he will be the most powerful Faerie in the ForEverNever. I am still a little shocked father allowed him to leave the ForEverNever to bring me the Ring of Incognito. Father needs Simeon and all his powers. It must have been very important that I receive the ring. He must know of dangers I'm unaware of. But I don't have time to think about that now, I must find a way for Simeon to get back to the ForEverNever so he can return home after my wedding.

- Emma

xiij : the meaning of friendship

Emma woke early the next morning. She had wrestled most of the night with what to do to help Simeon. And it didn't escape her that if he found a way home she could use the way to return to the ForEverNever, if her shoes didn't work. She wasn't going to let either her father or Simeon down. She took the Ring of Incognito out of her box and placed it on her finger. It was a little big, but it didn't slip off her finger when she shook it.

Emma grabbed her shoes out of the box and headed down to the hidden garden. She figured that trying on the shoes in the garden would get her to where she wanted to go in the ForEverNever. Emma sat on the bench near the pond in the garden and slowly and carefully put on the shoes one at a time. After both shoes were securely placed on her feet, there was a bright flash of light. Color orbs of blue, red, green, yellow and purple floated around the garden like tiny bath bubbles. There was a loud humming sound and Emma began to fade in and out. Then she completely disappeared. The next thing Emma knew; she was in the garden in the ForEverNever standing face to face with the mirror image of herself.

After she had a chance to adjust to her surroundings and remember who and what she was looking at, Emma asked, "Have you seen my father? I mean our father? Is he anywhere around here?"

"I have not seen him since you left the ForEverNever. Why are you looking for him? Is there something I can help you with?" Emma's mirror image asked.

"Yes, I could use your help. I am trying to find my father because I was hoping he would know of a way for Simeon to get home. Right now, we can't figure out how to get him out of the human world and back to the ForEverNever. I was hoping my father knew of a portal or an alternate way for Simeon to return home."

"I can try to send word to him that you are here, but there are no guarantees. Remember, a protective spell was placed around the land surrounding this pond. You can't leave here. The best and easiest way to reach your father may be for you to return to Earth and put on the shoes in another location," Emma's mirror image advised her.

"Thank you. I think I will try that." Emma sat down on the bench close to the pond and slowly removed both of her shoes, careful not to drop one. She saw the bright lights again and her surroundings began to spin. Before she knew it, Emma was back in the hidden garden at Evanswood.

The next best place Emma could think of to put on the shoes was her room. Emma hurried up the steps, closed the door and sat on her bed to put on the shoes. Having a better idea of what she would experience after she put on the shoes, Emma tightly closed her eyes right after she slipped the second shoe on her foot. All the bright lights and spinning made her a little sick to her stomach.

As soon as she felt her body stop spinning, Emma opened her eyes. She was in the ForEverNever, at a place she knew well. Emma looked up the hill and she could see Polleux running swiftly in the meadow. She hurried up the hill and whistled. Polleux stopped running and jerked his head to the side. There was only one Faerie he knew who whistled like that.

"Emma, girl, what are you doing in the ForEverNever? You should not be here lassie…unless you have seen Simeon."

Polleux was now standing in front of Emma. She held up her hand to pet his magnificent head. The ring on her finger sparkled in the sunlight. "It is because of Simeon that I am here. I am trying to help him find a way to get home. Have you seen my father?"

"I believe your father is currently at home. Would you like a ride?"

"I would be most grateful for a ride, my dear friend. It will be just like old times. I have missed you so." Emma hugged Polleux's neck.

"How have you been?"

"Things have not been the same around here without you, Emma, but we are managing."

Polleux lowered his front legs and bowed his head. Emma hugged his neck again and jumped on his back. Once Emma was securely on his back, Polleux took off at a fast pace. In no time, Polleux was standing in front of Emma's old home.

Just as Emma was about to knock on the gate, the gate opened and her father appeared before her.

"Welcome daughter! I have been waiting for you. I knew you were in the ForEverNever as soon as you arrived in Polleux's meadow. What brings you here? Wait; let me guess. You are here for Simeon, right?"

Emma just smiled at her father as he sighed.

"I never thought about a way to get Simeon home before he left for Earth, the human world. I was so concerned about getting you the ring that we forgot that little detail. Your well-being is very important and we had to ensure you were able to get back to the ForEverNever, safely, in case you had to return for any reason."

With an intense look on her face, Emma asked, "Father, why is everyone always so concerned for my safety?"

"Emma, I do not think you understand how special you are. Because of your sacrifice many years ago, you and the members of our house were granted privileges and abilities over the years. We all promised the "Power of All" that we would keep you safe. Even though you have become human, Shadow Faeries, fallen angels and dark forces in the human world may want to harm you. Also, since you are my daughter, my enemies may try to hurt you to get at me. And if you are killed, your mirror image and the power of pure love and goodness may disappear from the ForEverNever. Members of our house and I will always do everything in our power to keep you safe from any Faerie, human or other worldly threat.

Emma's father looked down at her hand. "I see Simeon was successful in getting you the Ring of Incognito. But you still need to be careful while you are here. You are safe with me and no other Faeries should be able to detect you are human. However, there are some who may recognize you as my daughter. I do not want others to know you are here and try to follow you back to Evanswood. The only way I can protect you in the human world is with the objects in your magic box." Emma's father sighed.

Emma reached over and gave her father a big hug. Of all her friends and family from the ForEverNever, it was her father she missed most.

Emma's thoughts were interrupted by her father's next words. "I have been expecting a visit from you. Shortly after Simeon left for Earth, the human world, I went in search of Isadorella to see if she knew of a way to get Simeon home. Thankfully, she was in a good mood and decided to share her knowledge about additional portals. She also told me about gateways as another means of traveling between the ForEverNever and Earth. She told me that close to your house there is a small public garden hidden behind high walls. Inside the gardens is a waterfall.

In a hidden chamber, at the back of the waterfall is a secret gateway. The gateway is behind an oddly egg-shaped white rock. For Simeon to get home, he must find this gateway and walk through it. Once Simeon pushes the rock out of the way, the gateway is revealed. The twist to the gateway is that it can only be used during…"

"…the nights of a full moon," Emma continued.

Her father smiled down at her. "Yes, that is correct. How did you know?"

Emma mischievously smiled, but said nothing.

"Emma what I have to say is very important. Please listen carefully. Isadorella also told me the purpose of the mirror in your magic box. Do you remember the pond you loved to spend hours at here in the ForEverNever? Looking into the pond you could see any location in the world, as long as you had an idea what the location looked like. All you had to do was visualize a place and it appeared. Well the same is true with the pond in your hidden garden at Evanswood. The catch is that you can only see the places in the reflection of the mirror. You still can see any place you think of, but in order for you to see it, you need to sit with your back to the pond and hold up the mirror so you can see the pond behind you. Once you can see the pond reflected in the mirror, think of the place you want to see and you will see it in the mirror."

Emma stared at her father, "Seriously, that's incredible! I will try it out soon after I get home."

Emma's father smiled at her enthusiasm and gave her another hug. "Emma dear, you should be leaving now. But please come back to visit soon. Only check in the mirror first to make sure I am home."

"Does it matter where I take off these shoes?" Emma asked.

"Yes, you should take the shoes off anywhere in this house or in Polleux's meadow. These locations are tied to locations in Evanswood. If you take off your shoes in any of these places you will return to Evanswood. If you remove the shoes in any other location in this kingdom, I am not sure where you will end up."

Emma turned to find a place to sit to take off her shoes.

"Oh Emma, I forgot to tell you one more thing about the gateway," her father said in a forceful, booming voice. "Tell Simeon that the gateway will bring him back to the ForEverNever, but I have no idea where in the ForEverNever it leads. When he chooses to travel through the gateway he needs to be prepared for anything. His journey home could be dangerous. Remind him to bring his bag of gold when he returns. He may need it."

"I almost don't want to leave," Emma said as she hugged her father one last time.

She sat on the steps outside her old home and carefully removed her shoes one at a time. Her surroundings began to spin around her. She saw the streak of light and the colored lights floating in the air while hearing the loud humming sound.

Emma's father watched as she faded in and out before his eyes. A sudden wave of sadness washed over him as he watched Emma clutch her shoes to her chest. Within moments Emma was standing in the dining room at Evanswood.

"I am home," Emma said with a smile to the empty room.

Emma rubbed her head and let her eyes adjust to the bright light in the room. The trip home left her with a slight head and stomachache. As she sat down in a chair at the table, Emma realized she already missed her father. She was so thankful she had the shoes. But she could not think about that now, it was time to find Simeon.

Emma was excited to tell Simeon what she learned. "The walled garden near Evanswood couldn't be too hard to find," Emma thought. "We are going to have another adventure like the ones we had when we were young. And I can't wait."

Emma was so eager to find Simeon, she ran down the hallway and up the flight of stairs to his room. She knocked loudly on the door. There was no answer, so she knocked again, harder this time. The door opened just as she raised her hand to knock for a third time.

"Where's the fire?" Simeon asked. "I was trying to sleep." He rubbed his eyes with a mischievous grin.

"I saw my father!" Emma was hopping up and down with excitement. "He told me about a gateway you can use to get home. He also told me how to use the mirror from my magic box. If it works the way he described, it will be one incredible trick.

"Tell me more about this gateway."

"The gateway is close to here. My father said it is behind an oddly egg-shaped white rock hidden behind a waterfall in a walled garden close to Evanswood."

"Am I going to have to give up anything to gain access to go through?"

"No, since it is a gateway not a portal, I don't think you'll have to give up anything or pay a price to go through. However, there is no way to know where you will end up in the Faerie World once you go through the gateway."

Enthusiastically Simeon told Emma, "I know the place. It has to be Iveagh Gardens. Lucky took me there yesterday. It is the walled garden I told you about. There is a beautiful waterfall. That is where I ran into those two Faeries who didn't know they were Faeries. I can take you there later today."

"Oh, I almost forgot," Emma said as she stepped away from the door, "You can only go through the portal during the night of a…"

"…full moon," Emma and Simeon said at the same time.

"So when is the next full moon?" Simeon asked.

"Fortunately for you and me it happens to be the day after my wedding. Let's go see if we can find that portal now. I have a few hours before I am supposed to meet William."

"Ok, but may I get dressed and have a little breakfast first? I also need to track down Lucky. I think I can get back to the walled garden without any problems, but with Lucky guiding us it will be a lot easier and probably more fun. Have you seen Lucky around?

"I think you will likely find Lucky in the kitchen when you stop by for breakfast. He is probably there trying to get Cook to feed him. Boy, that dog really likes human food and Cook has a hard time saying no to him. Whenever Lucky begs, with his big brown eyes and floppy ears, Cook always slips him a little food. I will meet you in the main hall in about 45 minutes."

Simeon looked down at his watch. Again, he was thankful he bought it. He knew Emma would not be upset if he was a little late, but he would have had no idea what 45 minutes was if he didn't have the watch.

Simeon got dressed and headed towards the kitchen. Sure enough Emma was right. Simeon found Lucky in the kitchen enjoying a few pieces of crispy beacon. As Simeon began to gobble up a plate of eggs and bacon, Lucky turned to leave the room. "Don't leave yet," Simeon said with a mouth full of food.

"What? Sir, I was not planning to leave," Cook said in a confused voice. "I was just getting ready to start preparing the afternoon meal."

Simeon stopped eating and turned to Cook with an apologetic look, "I am sorry, I did not mean you, I was talking to him," Simeon said as he pointed at Lucky.

"Does the dog really understand you?"

"He seems too," Simeon replied with a laugh. Lucky came over and plopped down next to Simeon's feet. "We are in for a little adventure today." Simeon patted Lucky's head.

After he finished eating, Simeon walked to the kitchen door and motioned for Lucky to follow him. He didn't want to confuse Cook again.

"So, what's up?" Lucky asked once they reached the hallway.

"Emma found a way to get me home," Simeon said with a big grin. "Guess where we are going."

Before Lucky could respond, Simeon yelled, "Iveagh Gardens!" Simeon then pointed at Lucky. "And we need your help getting there, if you don't mind?"

Lucky bowed his head, lowered his front legs and with lighthearted sarcasm said, "My pleasure."

"Thanks, Lucky. Let's grab Emma and we can be on our way. She should be waiting for us at the front door."

Simeon met up with Emma in the main hall and they both followed Lucky out the front door. "Iveagh Gardens is not too far from here. We should be there in less than thirty minutes," Lucky told Emma and Simeon.

———————————————————————————————————

Before they knew it Lucky, Simeon and Emma were at the entrance of Iveagh Gardens.

"Here you go," Lucky barked. "We all made it here safe and sound without getting lost once. Boy, I'm good!" Lucky wiggled around in a circle.

Simeon was glad to see the gate to the gardens was open. As he got closer to the entrance, he saw a familiar symbol at the top of the gate. He tapped Emma on the shoulder then pointed, "Do you remember that symbol, we saw it many times on our adventures when we were younger?"

Emma rubbed her eyes and looked at the entrance again. Reluctantly she asked, "Simeon, are you feeling ok? There are no designs or symbols on the gate."

Simeon took a deep breath. "You can't see the two trees that twist around each other with enough space between their trunks that there is a pathway between them?"

"There's nothing there Simeon," Emma repeated.

"How about you Lucky, can you see anything?" Simeon asked.

"I'm with Emma, there's nothing there," Lucky looked at Simeon, then at Emma.

"Umm! Maybe only Simeon can see the symbol because he is the only one among us who is a Faerie," Emma expressed out load.

"I think Emma has a point," Simeon said as he made a mental note to remember the symbol. He then led the way into the gardens. As Simeon, Emma and Lucky got close to the waterfall they ran into the same Faerie couple Simeon spoke to the other day. He tried to get their attention by waving at them, but the Faeries just ignored him.

"I guess they are too busy reading their magazine to be bothered by anyone or anything else," Emma stated.

"Is THAT what that is called, a magazine?" Simeon pointed at the item in the male Faerie's hands. "That's what they were looking at the last time I was here.

Simeon, Emma and Lucky walked right past the Faeries and headed towards the waterfall. Simeon hopped over the fence surrounding the waterfall and started to climb up the hill.

"Hey man, what are you doing? You really are crazy! You can't be up there," the male Faerie yelled.

"Of course now he is paying attention," Simeon thought. "Go back to reading your magazine," Simeon yelled back.

Emma decided to say something to get the couple to leave them alone. "He is afraid of water. A friend bet him he would not get close to the waterfall. I am here to witness whether he completes the bet or not."

The couple abruptly got up off the bench and quickly left the gardens in a huff. They were annoyed their quiet spot had been disturbed.

Simeon was relieved he no longer had an audience. He didn't want any distractions. If he made a misstep, he could slip and maybe fall down the waterfall. The waterfall was not that high, but he didn't know how deep the water was below. Plus, he really didn't want to get wet.

Simeon followed the path along the side of the hill towards the waterfall. As he got closer, water began to splash on his legs. "So, much for not getting wet. I guess, no matter how careful I am, I'm not going to find this hidden pathway without getting some water on me."

Water splashed on his arms, back and legs as he moved forward. The space around him began to get dark and he realized if he reached out with his other hand he could stick it through the falling water. Simeon took a few more steps and found the hidden pathway. "Now, to find the white rock in the small chamber."

Simeon continued to feel his way along the dimly lit path. Before he knew it, he was inside the small chamber. As he breathed deeply, cool, damp air filled his lungs. The water wasn't crashing down on him anymore, but all the rocks were slippery and appeared to be a grayish color. Then his hand brushed across an oddly egg-shaped rock that didn't feel damp and was slightly warm to the touch. The rock was glistening and appeared white. A hint of lavender filled the air. "This must be the rock!"

He tried to move the rock side to side, but it would not budge. He pushed harder, but the rock still would not budge. He then tried moving the rock by pushing it up from the bottom with no success.

Simeon wiped his head with the back of his hand. Despite the cool, damp air inside the chamber he was sweating from his effort to move the rock. "This is tough work trying to get this rock to move," he mumbled.

Simeon reached his hand out and rested it near the top of the rock. As he slid his hand down the rock, there was a slight ringing sound as it began to slip down. Simeon couldn't believe it. Before he knew it, the rock completely slid down the wall to reveal an opening. The opening did not look like anything special. It was dark and did not seem to go back very far into the rock wall. Simeon stuck his arm into the opening, but could only fit half his arm into it before he encountered another wall.

"How am I supposed to get my whole body in there when I can't even get my whole arm to fit in the opening? I guess I'm going to have to wait until the night of a full moon to figure that out."

Simeon removed his arm and took a step away from the wall. The rock moved back up the wall to cover the hole. "Well, that was easy."

Once he made his way out of the chamber and back along the pathway, he waved at Emma signaling he had found the gateway. He quickly ran down the hill and joined Emma and Lucky at the bottom of the waterfall.

As Emma and Simeon turned to go back to Evanswood, they talked about how relieved they were to have found a way back to the ForEverNever. Lucky followed close behind. His tail stopped wagging.

I'm still not sure why I was entrusted with the important job of keeping Emma safe. But I was, and I will do everything in my power to keep her safe. Even if that means constantly traveling back and forth between the ForEverNever and Earth, the human world, to ensure that no Faerie knows where she is located or that she has become human. And what I learned from my last trip to the ForEverNever is that Emma is no longer safe in Ireland. I am so glad she and William are getting married. He can take her back to the United States, where she will be safe—at least for now.

- Mr. McGuire

xiv : the Wedding

Emma married William in the outside gardens at Evanswood. As the guests cheered the bride and groom, nature joined the festive occasion. The sun shone brightly in the sky, which was a rare sight in Dublin. The flowers were in full bloom. Bright pinks, blues, reds yellows, purples and oranges could be seen throughout the garden. A slight breeze carried a faint scent of lavender through the air and birds sang a lovely melody in the distance.

The day and the ceremony were beautiful. Simeon walked Emma down the aisle. Mr. McGuire even made it on time for the wedding. However, no one was sure how he got there or when he arrived. All of a sudden, he just walked out of the library.

After the ceremony, Mr. McGuire pulled Simeon into the library to speak with him about how important it was to get Emma out of Ireland.

"Many of the Shadow Faeries have heard Emma is now human. There are rumors several Shadow Faeries are getting close to finding her. This could mean serious trouble for Emma."

"How do you know this? Did you just return from the ForEverNever?"

"I will tell you Simeon, but you mustn't tell anyone else. I have been in the ForEverNever to make sure none of the other Faeries have learned where Emma is currently living. Right now she is safe, but as I stressed earlier, some of the Shadow Faeries are getting close to figuring out her location."

"How did you get back to the ForEverNever?" Simeon asked.

"This is something else you must keep to yourself," Mr. McGuire whispered. "There is a gateway in this room which leads back to the ForEverNever."

"Where is it? Can I use the gateway to get home?" Simeon was thinking a gateway in the house was a lot easier than making his way along a slippery path under a waterfall and having to wait for a full moon.

"No, I think only I can use the gateway," Mr. McGuire gave Simeon a sympathetic look.

"I am sure you are aware of the magic boxes Helen, Mrs. MacTavish and I received before we left the ForEverNever. Well, my box had this," Mr. McGuire held up a gold pocket watch.

"I know where that goes," Simeon declared. "On the top of the door frame right on the other side of the tapestry."

Mr. McGuire raised his eyebrows in surprise.

Simeon explained. "Emma, Helen, Mrs. MacTavish and I explored the other magic boxes when I arrived. We figured out how to use most of the objects in the boxes. Each of the boxes contained an object that fit into a groove above one of the doors in the hidden room. I remember seeing a circular shape above the doorway leading to the library. A pocket watch would fit perfectly into the space above the door."

"How did you find the hidden room?"

"One day, shortly after Emma arrived at Evanswood, I walked into the library and discovered a tapestry hanging on the wall opposite the windows. The tapestry looked so lovely and soft, I wanted to feel it. When I touched it, I realized the wall behind the tapestry was gone. The space was hollow. I pulled back the tapestry and saw the hidden room. I was a little confused since I had thoroughly searched the house looking for anything suspicious before Emma arrived. I didn't remember a door on the wall before the tapestry was hung. I spent the next few days exploring the hidden room. I realized the pocket watch from my magic box would fit neatly above the doorway behind the tapestry."

"What other objects were in your magic box?"

"There was a black top hat, a black cape, a walking stick and this medallion," Mr. McGuire said as he pulled the medallion out from under his shirt.

Simeon took a close look at the medallion, "Emma, Helen and Mrs. MacTavish all have medallions similar to yours."

"I thought the medallion was very important. As soon as I discovered the medallion in my magic box, I put it on this chain. It's been around my neck ever since."

"What about the other objects in your magic box? Did any of them have any interesting powers?"

"I thought I would become invisible if I put on the cape, so I stood in front of a mirror and put on the cape. And behold! When I looked in the mirror, I saw a man wearing a cape. I wasn't invisible." Mr. McGuire chuckled.

"So I decided to see what I looked like with the hat and cape. I put on the hat, and that is when I disappeared. I took off the hat and I reappeared. It was incredible!"

"Wow, it sounds amazing. So, what power did the cape have?"

"I had an idea of the cape's power. I had seen a few capes in the ForEverNever that protected the wearer from harm; however, I was a little hesitant to try out my theory. You see, it involved poking myself with a knife."

Simeon stared at Mr. McGuire incredulously, "You didn't stab yourself with a knife, did you?"

"Not exactly. While wearing the cape I slowly and carefully tried to stick a knife into my upper arm, which was covered by the cape. The knife didn't pierce the skin even when I pushed down hard."

"So, the cape can protect you from injury? That will likely come in handy if you are attacked by any Shadow Faeries."

"And what about the walking stick?"

"That one was easy to figure out. I unscrewed the top of the walking stick and found a sword. The sword can cut through anything."

Simeon smiled. "I wish I had one of those walking sticks. I could have fun with one of those. How did you figure out how to use the pocket watch?"

"I took the pocket watch out of my magic box and carried it everywhere with me. When I saw the grooves above the doorways, I thought the grooves might have something to do with all of our magic boxes. The circular groove looked like it might be the right size for the pocket watch, so I gave it a try. The next thing I knew there were sparks of bright light and a loud crash of thunder. Then a bright light shined across the floor creating a lit path from the hidden room to the grandfather clock.

"This clock?" Simeon asked as he walked over to the grandfather clock sitting in the corner of the library.

"Yes! When I first stood in front of this clock there were small dull green orbs floating behind the glass door." Mr. McGuire put his finger on the glass door.

"I opened the glass door and the orbs turned into a bright green light that completely filled the inside of the clock."

"I remembered the back of the pocket watch said 'thou shall not pass and return, if thou are not holding me as the key'."

Simeon interrupted in awe, "You can read Fae-Oldish?"

"Yes, I learned how to read Fae-Oldish when I was younger. Now, do you want to hear how I used the gateway in the grandfather clock to return to the ForEverNever?"

Simeon simply shook his head yes in response.

"I went back to the hidden room and removed the pocket watch from the groove and returned to the grandfather clock. The inside of the grandfather clock was still filled with the green light. Holding the pocket watch tightly in my hand and closing my eyes, I walked into the green light. When I opened my eyes, I was standing in the ForEverNever, close to Emma's old home.

"Since I was in the ForEverNever, I figured I would visit the King of Ymir, but no one was at home. Then I remembered his warning. 'I should never meet with him in a familiar or public place if I ever made it back to the ForEverNever.' I have been traveling regularly between the ForEverNever and the human world, but haven't been able to contact the King."

"During my trips, I learned the Shadow Faeries are getting closer to discovering Emma is in Dublin. All through the ForEverNever, I tried to mislead them as to her whereabouts. It has worked up until this point, but I think our luck may be running out. The best way to ensure Emma stays safe is to make sure she leaves Ireland. The Shadow Faeries shouldn't be able to track her if she is no longer here. You need to help me convince William and Emma to leave Ireland soon. I believe William plans to ask for an extension at his job, so he can stay in Ireland longer. He thinks that's what Emma wants. We have to get him to change his mind." Mr. McGuire's voice sounded urgent.

Later that day Simeon and Mr. McGuire pulled William into the library to speak with him man to man. Mr. McGuire told William he had something important to tell him, although he could not provide a lot of details or answer any questions. He told William to get Emma out of Ireland soon. He had learned through his travels that Emma could be in serious danger if she stayed in Ireland. Individuals from her past were searching for her and they were close to finding her.

Simeon looked directly at William and stressed, "The danger is real, and you need to get Emma out of Ireland immediately."

William thought, "Who is hunting Emma and how close are they to finding her? Surely, if Simeon or Mr. McGuire could provide additional details concerning the danger to Emma, they would. However, based on what they said, I know I have to act quickly."

William needed no further explanation. Emma's safety was the only thing that mattered. "I will immediately begin making plans to move back to the United States. We can live with my parents for a few months in New York while we find a new place to live," he told Simeon and Mr. McGuire.

Back to the Present

It is wonderful to be so powerful, but even those as powerful as I fall victim to loss. I lost my wife and my daughter, and war has taken my brother and best friend. I wonder if Simeon knows how much he means to me. He is like my own son. I still remember the day his father, my best friend, died. I held him in my arms as he took his last breaths. I promised to take care of his son. As Simeon and my daughter grew up they were inseparable. I thought they might end up together, but things don't always happen the way we expect. The unexpected is often right around the corner and even the most powerful of beings—like me—can be surprised.

- The King of the Faerie House of Ymir

xv : the Dance

Dublin, Ireland 1958

Sophie was surprised to see her father come into her room to speak with her before the party started. She didn't think he would have enough time to see her before he had to go downstairs to begin the celebration. However, since her father was in her room, Sophie took the opportunity to ask him if he knew where the ring and gold chain were that her mother always wore.

Sophie's father reached down his shirt collar and pulled out a ring connected to a gold chain. "You mean this ring?" he smiled. Sophie stared at the ring in awe as it glimmered in the afternoon light coming in from the window.

"Your mother would have wanted you to have this." He took his chain off and placed it around Sophie's neck.

Sophie just stared at her father, unable to say a word.

"Your mother wore the chain all the time; however, she gave it to me to wear shortly before she died. Remember when I had to leave the country? Your mother thought I may be in danger, so she gave me the chain to wear to keep me safe."

Sophie's father smiled at her and turned to leave the room. As he headed out of the room to get ready for the party, Sophie's father looked over his shoulder and gave her another smile. "I promise to teach you how to dance a few steps at the party."

———————————————————————————————————

The evening passed, but Sophie's father was too busy talking to people to find any time to dance with her. In fact, he hadn't spoken with her once since the party started. However, he had spent a lot of time with "that" woman. Sophie had no idea who the woman was and she didn't want to meet her.

Sophie began to think, "The ForEverNever would be a much better place than this boring old party. Thankfully, my father gave me the Ring of Incognito."

Sophie hurried up to her room and put on several pairs of socks and the blue shoes. She saw the colored lights and heard the loud buzzing. The scenery around her started to change. Before she knew it, Sophie was back in the ForEverNever.

"I'm so glad my father gave me this ring." Sophie turned the ring on her finger. She was wearing the gold chain around her neck. Sophie then smiled, as she looked around, she knew exactly where she was. Up the hill, in the distance, she could see Polleux running in his meadow.

"Being here is going to be much more fun than the party at Evanswood," Sophie thought to herself as she hurried up the hill.

"Polleux," Sophie yelled, as she got closer to the meadow.

Polleux lifted his head, saw Sophie, and ran in her direction. "So you made it back here, young lady. I am glad to see you. You know, however, it isn't safe to be here unless..."

Sophie held up her finger and winked, "Unless I have the Ring of Incognito."

"I see you were able to find the ring. What brings you to the ForEverNever and to my meadow?"

As Polleux and Sophie were talking, Simeon walked up the path and joined them. "Good to see you again, Sophie. You weren't foolish enough to return to the ForEverNever without the Ring of Incognito, were you?" Simeon playfully asked as he noticed the ring on Sophie's finger.

"What brings you back here so soon?"

"I wanted to see Polleux again," Sophie grinned at Simeon. "And since I have the Ring of Incognito and my father was busy with his party at Evanswood, I thought this would be a good time to return."

"Sophie, your mother kept the Ring of Incognito on a gold chain. Have you seen it?" Simeon asked.

Sophie pulled the gold chain out from under her shirt. "Not only have I seen the chain, I'm wearing it," Sophie smiled.

Simeon stared at the chain with reverence. He still remembered when he received the chain after his father's death. He remembered giving it to Emma to help keep her safe. "If only Emma had been wearing the chain the night of her accident, maybe she would still be alive," Simeon thought. He wondered why Emma had taken off the chain.

"Sophie you must wear that chain always. It will protect you. And when you aren't wearing the Ring of Incognito on your finger, you should wear it around your neck on the chain or keep it in your mother's box where you found your blue shoes."

"If your father has returned to Evanswood, why aren't you spending time with him?" Polleux asked concerned for Sophie. "Something has to be wrong," he thought.

"He is very busy with his party. He doesn't have time for me tonight. He promised he would teach me how to dance, but he was too occupied with his guests to even talk to me."

"So, you want to learn how to dance. I think Polleux and I can help with that," Simeon smiled. He pulled two spoons out of his pocket and began to tap them together.

"Polleux, a little help with the music please." Polleux began to tap his foot and beat his tail against the fence.

Once he felt confident Polleux had the beat down, Simeon put the spoons back in his pocket. Sophie stared at his pocket in awe. She couldn't figure out how he kept one spoon in his pocket, let alone two.

"What are you looking at?" Simeon asked with a mischievous grin. He pulled his pocket inside out and nothing fell out. Sophie gasped.

"Neat trick, huh? Sometimes I just have to think about an object and it appears in my pocket. When I am done with the object, I put it back in my pocket and it simply disappears.

Sophie raised her eyebrows. "Another one of your powers?"

Simeon laughed as Polleux continued to play music. "If you want to learn how to dance you need to come here." Simeon held out his arms opened wide.

"Here, put your right hand in my left hand and put your other hand on my shoulder. Now, we just move to the beat provided by Polleux. One, two, three, one, two, three, one, two, three. See, dancing is very easy," Simeon said teasingly as Sophie stepped on his foot again.

Sophie smiled. "Yes, very easy! I hope I don't step on your foot again." Sophie laughed as she and Simeon continued to move to the music Polleux enthusiastically provided.

Suddenly, they heard a loud booming voice. "What is this?" Sophie looked at Simeon and Simeon looked in the direction of the loud voice. They both stopped dancing.

Simeon immediately took a step back from Sophie and looked at the ground. "Hello Sire. I am trying to teach Sophie, how to dance."

"With that noise?" The loud voiced visitor looked at Polleux. He was an older looking Faerie with deep, ageless, green eyes. He was tall with a strong build, a full beard and long, white flowing hair. His body shimmered, almost radiating as he moved closer to Sophie.

"I know Polleux is trying, but that really doesn't sound like music. Just give me a moment and I will get you some real music," the bearded Faerie boomed. He raised his hands and announced, "Music, please." An assortment of instruments appeared right before their eyes. There were flutes, drums, trumpets, a harp, bagpipes, guitars, fiddles and several instruments Sophie couldn't name.

"For the final touch!" The bearded Faerie's eyes sparkled as he rubbed his hands together, "A piano."

Simeon laughed, "Now you are just showing off, Sire. The next thing you will ask for is the Faerie choir to appear in all its grandeur."

"What a splendid idea! The Faerie choir, please, minus the grandeur," the bearded Faerie commanded with a big grin on his face.

Simeon rolled his eyes. "All we really needed was a one-man band."

Then in his rich booming voice the bearded Faerie instructed, "Music... begin." As the music played, he held out his arms to Sophie. "Young lady, may I have the pleasure of teaching you how to truly dance?"

Simeon nudged Sophie forward. "It's okay. He means you no harm and I know he would be honored to dance with someone as lovely as you."

Hesitating a moment, Sophie stepped forward and wrapped her small hands inside the bearded Faerie's larger ones.

"Don't worry about the one, two, three, one, two, three. Trust me and just follow my lead," the bearded Faerie smiled.

"Oh, and I do not mind if you step on my feet a few times." He winked at her.

Sophie was overjoyed. Before she knew it, she was actually dancing. And she had not stepped on the bearded Faerie's feet. She laughed out loud. "I'm dancing. I'm dancing. I'm truly dancing!"

The first song ended and Sophie and the bearded Faerie continued to dance, as the second song began to play.

"You know, I once taught my daughter to dance. You remind me of her." His voice became wistful. A far off expression came over his face.

"Simeon, come here," the bearded Faerie yelled.

"Yes, Sire."

The bearded Faerie stepped away from Sophie. "You should dance with her now. I think she has the steps down." The bearded Faerie walked away to speak with Polleux. Sophie and Simeon danced for several more songs. They continued to dance until they were both out of breath. After they caught their breath and the music stopped, Sophie and Simeon walked over to the fence and joined Polleux and the bearded Faerie.

"That was so much fun," Sophie laughed. "Thank you for the music and the dance lesson. The whole thing was incredible." She hugged the bearded Faerie.

"Only the best for you, young lady. Speaking of the best, have you ridden Polleux yet?"

"Yes, I rode him briefly with Simeon, during my first visit to the ForEverNever. I can't recall seeing another horse run faster. But, it was also the first time I ever rode a horse. Before I met Polleux, I was a little afraid of horses. However, Polleux is so kind and gentle. Being around him has taught me I have nothing to fear from horses."

"Be advised little one, most animals are more than they appear and Polleux is no different. He is more than just a horse; he is a Faerie horse. And he is not just any Faerie horse; he is a white Faerie horse. He can run faster than the wind and can jump over anything."

The bearded Faerie leaned down and whispered in Sophie's ear. "On occasion, he can even fly."

In a loud voice so everyone could hear, "Would you like to ride him?" the bearded Faerie asked. "I am sure he would be happy to give you a ride."

"I am still not really sure about riding a horse, even if it is Polleux. I have to confess, I was terrified when Simeon and I rode Polleux to retrieve the Egg of Triumph."

Sophie quickly put her hand over her mouth with a guilty expression on her face. She looked at Simeon and mouthed, "I am sorry. I didn't mean to say that."

"What are you sorry for?" the bearded Faerie asked.

Sophie looked down and kicked the ground with her foot. "I am not supposed to talk about our adventure to retrieve the Egg of Triumph."

"It's okay Sophie, he already knows all about our adventure." Simeon's voice was surprisingly quiet and then there was a long silence.

The bearded Faerie broke the silence. "If you want to learn how to ride, Simeon and I can teach you. There is no need to be afraid of riding a horse."

Sophie looked up at the bearded Faerie, not knowing what to say. She wanted to please him, but at the same time she still felt a little intimidated about riding.

The bearded Faerie saw her concern. "But, right now you should return home. I am sure there are people there who are worried about you and probably looking for you."

"I don't think anyone there has noticed that I am gone," Sophie sounded dejected. "But you are right. I probably should be heading home. It's most likely really late by now. I haven't completely figured how the passing of time here equates to the passing of time at Evanswood."

Sophie followed the bearded Faerie's suggestion and started to sit on the ground to take off her shoes. But before she did, she walked over and gave the bearded Faerie, Simeon and Polleux a big hug.

Sophie heard the bearded Faerie yell as she began to take off her shoes. "I am so glad you found the Ring of Incognito." Within moments, Simeon, Polleux and the bearded Faerie were staring at only green grass where Sophie had been sitting only moments before.

THE SACRIFICE

I am so glad I'm back at Evanswood and my daughter is here. I know Sophie isn't very happy with me right now and may not act too excited to see me. And I feel bad I haven't been able to spend too much time with her over the last few days, because of my work and the party. I really didn't want to have the party, but the Ambassador insisted. As soon as I returned to Evanswood shortly after Sophie arrived, I had to make sure everything was prepared for the party. And I had to spend quite a bit of time with the Ambassador and my guests while at the party. If things didn't go well at the party, my job would have been much more difficult.

- William St. Clair

xvi : the færie Princess

William St. Clair burst in the dining room where Mrs. MacTavish and Sean were having breakfast. He was out of breath and wore a panicked look on his face. He had been running through the house for at least thirty minutes.

"Have you seen Sophie?" William asked in a breathless voice.

"No, I haven't seen her since yesterday," Mrs. MacTavish replied.

Sean subtly shook his head no and looked down at the table to avoid any further eye contact with Sophie's father. Sean was not afraid of Sophie's father, but he was a little apprehensive of him. Looking into Sophie's father's intense blue eyes made Sean squirm in his seat.

"Well, she is not in her room," William stressed. "And it doesn't look like she slept in her room at all last night." William almost yelled as he ran his fingers through his hair.

Mrs. MacTavish stood up from the table and gently led William by the arm to the library. "We need to talk," she said in a calm, but firm voice.

Once William and Mrs. MacTavish reached the library, Mrs. MacTavish closed the library door. She motioned for William to sit on the couch, "I know you needed to get out of New York after Emma's death, but I still cannot believe you brought Sophie here to Ireland. With your current job and knowing who her mother was and her grandfather is, Dublin is not safe for her."

"What are you talking about?" William blankly stared at Mrs. MacTavish.

Mrs. MacTavish began to open her month as if she wanted to say something. She stopped herself from speaking and just shook her head in disbelief.

"Even after all your years together, Emma never told you, did she?" Mrs. MacTavish questioned in a quiet voice.

"Told me what?" William was obviously agitated.

"Emma never told you who she really was or what she gave up so the two of you could be together. She never told you about her father or where he lives?"

"I have no idea what you are talking about. I thought her parents died years ago," William responded.

Mrs. MacTavish sat down on the couch next to William and took a deep breath. The expression on her face softened and she gently gazed into is eyes.

"Emma was not born in this world. She was the daughter of one of the most powerful kings in the Faerie World. To state it simply, Emma was a Faerie Princess. As a young Faerie, she was fascinated by humans and the human world. Every day, she used to go to a magical pond in the Mystical Forest called Crystal Pond to see what was happening on Earth, the human world. The pond's water shines like a crystal with rainbow colors bouncing off its surface. When Emma looked in the pond, she could see what was happening anywhere on Earth or in ForEverNever, the Land Beyond the Mist and Fog."

"The Land Beyond the Mist and Fog? There is no such place," William shook his head in disbelief.

"Yes, there is. The ForEverNever, the Land Beyond the Mist and Fog is where we Faeries live. It coexists in another dimension parallel to Earth, the human world."

William's jaw dropped as he stared at Mrs. MacTavish in disbelief. She continued with her story.

"One day when Emma was looking in the pond, she saw you walking out of your office building. She saw a man push a woman down on the sidewalk and steal her purse. You helped the woman up, chased the man down the sidewalk, caught him and returned the woman's purse. You then made sure she was okay and helped her home. After she saw how brave you were, Emma watched your building every day to see how you were doing. She always told me what she saw, even when I begged her to stop. She would just laugh, and continue telling me all the new things she saw each day. The day she first saw you, she ran into my room and told me she just saw the most handsome, kindest man she had ever seen. She was convinced, and tried to convince me that she had to meet you. I told Emma it was not a very good idea for her to leave the ForEverNever to meet you."

William sat listening, trying to wrap his head around what he was hearing. He thought to himself, "Should I believe this? Has she lost her mind?"

Instead, he asked out loud, "Why would you tell Emma she should not meet me?"

"I wasn't warning Emma against meeting you, William," Mrs. MacTavish smiled at William. "I was warning Emma against leaving the ForEverNever. Even though she desired to travel to other worlds, she was never allowed. Her place was in the ForEverNever at her father's side."

"As I said, once she saw you, Emma knew she had to meet you. After Emma spoke with her father, she sought out the Faerie of the Woods, a guardian between worlds. The Faerie of the Woods gave Emma a magic red cloak. The magic cloak made it possible for Emma to temporarily travel between worlds. As long as Emma was wearing the red cloak, she could walk on Earth. However, once she removed the cloak, she would instantaneously return to the ForEverNever. The cloak was good for only one trip to Earth."

"I remember the red cloak. It was lovely. Emma wore it the whole time we were together. At the time, I thought it a little odd she would not take off the cloak when we were inside." William smiled at the memory.

Mrs. MacTavish could tell William was beginning to believe her.

"Emma felt a little silly wearing the cloak inside. She laughed when she returned home and told me the story." Mrs. MacTavish chuckled.

William looked at Mrs. MacTavish and almost burst out laughing when he heard Mrs. MacTavish chuckle. Her chuckle sounded a lot like a cat squealing. William realized he had never heard her chuckle before and he rarely heard her laugh.

"Do you remember Emma looked a little different when you saw her the next time?"

"Yes, her hair was longer. The first time we met was the only time I ever saw Emma with short hair," William recalled.

"That's right, Emma's hair was short. Her hair was the payment for use of the cloak. You know, nothing in the Faerie World is given without a price. The Faerie of the Woods wanted Emma's hair to make a potion. I think it was a love potion."

"How could Emma's hair make a love potion?" William asked.

"That's a long story for another day, but back to how Emma was able to return to Earth and ended up with you. After Emma had spent time with you, she knew she was in love. She was the only one in the ForEverNever that could feel true love. She knew humans can feel love and she wanted to feel it forever. She returned to the Faerie of the Woods and told her she wanted to be with you always. She asked if there was a way she could permanently live on Earth. The Faerie of the Woods told Emma she was too important to leave the Faerie World forever. The Faerie of the Woods also told Emma that even if there were no issues with Emma leaving the Faerie World, it was beyond her power to grant Emma the means to permanently live on Earth. The Faerie of the Woods advised Emma that she should turn to her father for help.

"Emma spoke with her father and told him how much she cared for you. She told her father she wanted to live with you on Earth. He was not happy with her choice. He tried to talk her out of it. Her goodness resonated throughout his kingdom and she brought light and love to everything and everyone she touched. As such, he deeply cared for her. And 'caring' is not everywhere in the ForEverNever. But because of his devotion to her, Emma's father decided to help. He knew allowing Emma to permanently remain on Earth would not be an easy task.

"Emma had a very special power, which helped to maintain the balance between kindness and selfishness in the Faerie World. Shadow Faeries, with their selfish deeds, were always trying to upset the balance. Emma's father knew that the balance between kindness and selfishness could be in jeopardy if Emma was no longer in the ForEverNever. He also knew that once Emma left the Faerie World, his ability to protect her would be very limited. He suspected she would be in great danger if any of his enemies, the Shadow Faeries or unkind forces in the human world, discovered she was permanently living on Earth. Therefore, he sent Helen, Mr. McGuire and me to Evanswood to help keep her safe."

"Shortly before your wedding, Mr. McGuire learned the Shadow Faeries where getting close to discovering Emma was in Ireland. For that reason, he convinced you to leave Dublin right after you and

Emma were married. And now you have brought Sophie right back into potential danger."

William was stunned by all Mrs. MacTavish told him. His mind was frantically trying to process what he had just learned about Emma. He had so many questions. What are Shadow Faeries? How are they different than humans? And if her father was a powerful Faerie, why could he no longer protect her in the human world?

But the question that pushed to the forefront of William's mind was why hadn't Emma told him any of this?

William knew all his questions would have to wait. Right now they had to focus on finding Sophie. If all of what Mrs. MacTavish said was true, Sophie could be in serious danger.

William looked anxious. "Where should we start looking for Sophie?"

"I think we should start by asking Sean some questions," Mrs. MacTavish replied. "He seemed awfully quiet when you asked about Sophie earlier. If you remember, he would not even make eye contact with you. Stay here, I will get him."

Mrs. MacTavish left the library in search of Sean. William stayed on the couch with his head in his hands. He couldn't remember ever being so worried. He had already lost his wife and mother. He couldn't handle losing his daughter too. They had to find Sophie. She couldn't have just disappeared. People didn't just vanish. As he looked up, William saw Mrs. MacTavish walking back into the library with Sean a few steps behind her.

"Sean, we can tell you know more than what you told us earlier. It is very important that we know all you know. Sophie could be in serious danger and may need our help. Go sit on the couch next to Sophie's father and tell us all you know," Mrs. MacTavish commanded.

Sean hesitantly moved towards the couch. Sophie had trusted him with her secret and he didn't want to rat on her, but he knew he was going to have to tell her father and his grandmother all about his and Sophie's adventures. If anything happened to Sophie, Sean would never forgive himself.

"It's okay Sean," William said. "You can come closer. I won't bite. I am only concerned about Sophie's safety. We want to find her before she is injured or worse."

Sean cautiously sat on the couch next to William and stared at the floor. He slowly began to speak in a quiet voice. "The last time Sophie was missing she told me she had fallen asleep in the hidden garden behind the tapestry."

Mrs. MacTavish gasped. "She knew Sophie wore Emma's medallion. Could it really be, had the children found the hidden room? If they had found the room, what else had they discovered?"

William stood up and walked over to the tapestry. He tried to pull back the tapestry, but it would not move. He gave Sean a questioning look and pulled a little harder.

Sean shrugged. "I also tried to pull back the tapestry. I've only seen Sophie be able to move it. But I really don't think Sophie was in the hidden garden the whole time. I think she put on those blue shoes."

"What shoes?" William asked.

"The shoes we think used to belong to her mother."

Mrs. MacTavish gasped even louder this time. "What are you talking about Sean?"

"Could Sophie have found Emma's shoes?" Mrs. MacTavish asked herself.

Mrs. MacTavish recalled, "After Emma left for the United States she requested that the shoes be hidden. She didn't want to take the chance other Faeries might track the magic signature left by the shoes. She knew there was no danger of leaving the shoes at Evanswood, because her father had fortified it and no other Faeries couldn't sense the magic in the house."

Sean looked down at the floor, "We found the shoes in the hidden room behind the tapestry. I am sorry I can't show you the room. I really can't move the tapestry."

"William, I can show you the room," Mrs. MacTavish said as she walked over to the tapestry and easily pulled back the corner. "But I cannot open the door to the hidden garden. Only Sophie can do that, since she wears her mother's medallion in the bracelet on her arm."

William was distraught. "So we cannot check to see if Sophie is in the garden?"

Mrs. MacTavish raised her hand to calm William and replied in a soft voice. "I did not say that. I simply said that I could not open the door to the hidden garden."

"Well, if you can't open the door, how are we going to look inside the garden to see if Sophie is there?" William asked almost at the point of hysterics. Mrs. MacTavish wasn't making any sense and he did not have time for word games. William was getting frustrated.

"I can look into the hidden garden without opening the door. It should not take too long. While I am looking, you and Sean should search the house again. Sean, can you search some other places in the house where you may have not looked? I will meet you back here in about an hour."

Mrs. MacTavish quickly left the library and headed to her bedroom. She didn't think Sophie was in the hidden garden. If her gut was right, Sophie was in the ForEverNever, and could be in more danger than William had imagined.

Mrs. MacTavish entered her room and swiftly closed the door. She walked straight over to her mirror hanging on the wall and asked, "Show me the hidden garden in Evanswood." The mirror turned gray and in moments went completely black. Then a faint image began to form in the mirror. As Mrs. MacTavish continued to stare in the mirror, the image became clearer and clearer. Before she knew it, she could see the entire hidden garden. Just as she suspected, Sophie was nowhere in sight. Mrs. MacTavish sighed.

Mrs. MacTavish thought back on all the places Emma visited when she put on her shoes. Polleux's meadow was the first place she remembered. She asked the mirror, "Show me Polleux's meadow in the ForEverNever." The image of the hidden garden in the mirror faded away. The mirror went gray than black again. Within moments, the image of the hidden garden was replaced by an image of a lovely meadow on top of a hill. As the image became clearer, she saw Simeon and Polleux. Then see saw Sophie laughing. Sophie walked over and hugged Polleux and Simeon. It looked like she was saying goodbye. Mrs. MacTavish let out a sigh of relief. She knew Sophie was safe. She also knew Sophie could not be in the meadow without her grandfather knowing. He must be somewhere close by.

YMIR LEGACY

174

She is so much like her mother, with her daring spirit and constant search for adventure. She has only been here for a short time and Sophie has already sent this house into a panic more than once. I remember the hours I spent searching for her mother in the ForEverNever, only to find her staring into Crystal Pond or returning from an escapade with Simeon. I still cannot believe that Emma is gone. I owe it to her to make sure Sophie stays safe. Sophie is all that we have left of Emma. I will do everything in my power to make sure she remains safe.

- Mrs. MacTavish

xvij : Defending Yourself

Mrs. MacTavish hurried back down to the library to meet up with William. She found him pacing back and forth in front of the fireplace in the center of the room. "Is Sophie in the hidden garden?" William asked louder than he intended.

William continued, "Sean and I searched all over the house and found no trace of her."

William lowered his head as he rubbed his hands through his hair and took a deep breath. He then looked at Mrs. MacTavish for reassurance, as his heart beat franticly and his mind raced with thoughts of the possible dangers to Sophie.

"Sophie has to be in the hidden garden, she just has to be."

"Let us have a seat." Mrs. MacTavish motioned to the couch.

"I don't want to sit. I want to know where Sophie is!" William yelled as he continued to pace.

Mrs. MacTavish motioned to the couch again. "William, please sit down." She said in a firm yet gentle tone.

William hesitantly sat down. He knew he wasn't going to get any answers until he sat.

"No, Sophie is not in the hidden garden," Mrs. MacTavish finally said in a calm voice.

"Then why aren't we still looking for her?" William questioned as he jumped off the couch. "I will call the police. And I have a few friends, with connections, who I can call."

Mrs. MacTavish grabbed William's arm. "Please, sit back down and I will continue."

William sat half on and half off the couch, ready to spring at the first opportunity.

"We are not searching for her any longer because I know where she is," Mrs. MacTavish assured.

William stared at Mrs. MacTavish, very perplexed.

"Sophie is no longer in this house or even in Dublin, she is in the ForEverNever. And I know she is safe."

William continued to stare at Mrs. MacTavish. He opened his mouth to say something, then shut it, not knowing what to say.

Mrs. MacTavish dismissed William's stare with a wave of her hand. "I have a feeling Sophie will return shortly. When she does, we must have a serious conversation with her. The ForEverNever is not a safe place for her. If any of the Shadow Faeries realize she is there, she could be in serious danger."

"How do you know she is in the ForEverNever?" William asked incredulously. "I am still not convinced the ForEverNever really exists. And I certainly find it very unlikely my daughter is there."

"I saw her there." Mrs. MacTavish interrupted William. "She is with Emma's horse Polleux and Emma's best friend Simeon, who you met many years ago. I promise you, a more loyal two you could never find. They will protect Sophie with their lives."

"Saw her, what do you mean you saw her? That doesn't make any sense." William shook his head and replayed in his mind what Mrs. MacTavish had said.

William scratched his head. "Wait a minute, how do you know they will protect Sophie? They don't even know who she is."

"They know Sophie is Emma's daughter. She looks just like Emma. I guarantee as long as Sophie is with Polleux and Simeon, she is safe. They are not going to let her out of their sight as long as she is in the ForEverNever."

Mrs. MacTavish stopped mid-sentence. Spheres of colored light began to float around her and William. Sophie appeared and disappeared right before their eyes like a blinking light. William reached out to grab her, but she just disappeared again. Sophie reappeared and Zoey started to bark. This time William jumped off the couch to run to his daughter.

Mrs. MacTavish looked puzzled. "I did not realize the dog was in the room."

William engulfed Sophie in his big, strong arms and held her tight. He then held her out in front of him. "Are you hurt?"

Sophie shook her head no.

"Don't you ever disappear like that again!"

"I am sorry. I didn't think you would miss me. You were so busy with your friends at the party. And I didn't think I was gone that long."

"You were gone all night and half the day," William scolded. "You don't think that is long? And what makes you think I would not miss you?"

William gently shook Sophie and pulled her tightly into his arms again. "Of course I missed you, you are my little girl and I love you more than anything in the world. I had no idea where you were." Tears began to well up in his eyes. "If it wasn't for Mrs. MacTavish, I would have gone crazy with worry."

Sophie heard Mrs. MacTavish's loud clear voice, "I am glad you returned home safely Sophie. You must never return to the ForEverNever. It is dangerous. There is so much you do not know about your family and its history."

"But, I have the Ring of Incognito." Sophie held up her finger for Mrs. MacTavish to see. "And Simeon and a kind, older bearded Faerie who shinned like gold when he moved, agreed to teach me to ride Polleux. The bearded Faerie told me Polleux can even fly."

Mrs. MacTavish interrupted Sophie. "An older bearded Faerie who radiated a golden light? Mrs. MacTavish was curious. She didn't remember seeing a bearded Faerie when she saw Sophie in her mirror.

"What was his name?"

"I never learned his name. Simeon only called him, Sire."

Mrs. MacTavish smiled at Sophie. "Well it might not be so bad after all for you to return to the ForEverNever and learn to ride Polleux. It sounds like fun."

William was stunned. "What are you talking about? You just got through telling her how dangerous the ForEverNever is. She is never going back. I will not allow it."

Sophie was relieved Mrs. MacTavish had come to her rescue. She knew her father would eventually calm down. Right now he was upset and difficult to reason with.

Mrs. MacTavish cut the tension with a question. "Sophie, are you hungry? Let me call Helen so she can take you to the kitchen to get something to eat. I know it is well past breakfast, but I think Cook made cinnamon rolls for breakfast this morning and there are still some left."

Mrs. MacTavish went over to the desk and pushed the button on the intercom. "Helen, Sophie has been found. Can you please meet us in the library? I think Sophie may be hungry."

William gave Sophie another big hug just as Helen entered the library. Sophie smiled at him. She had decided to wait to convince him to let her return to the ForEverNever until after he calmed down.

"Where have you been child?" Helen walked over and hugged Sophie.

Sophie enjoyed the attention. She had no idea they all cared so much about her.

"She can answer your questions on the way to the kitchen," Mrs. MacTavish interrupted. Mrs. MacTavish then motioned for William to stay behind in the library.

"I guess we are headed to the kitchen." Helen laughed and grabbed Sophie's arm pulling her towards the kitchen.

Sophie looked up at Helen. "I'm glad, because I really am hungry."

William was annoyed with Mrs. MacTavish. He could tell she still wanted to speak with him, but he was not ready to let Sophie out of his sight.

"Why did you want Sophie to leave the room?"

"I needed to speak with you about Sophie's trips to the ForEverNever without her present. I have a few things to say that maybe she does not need to know at this time."

Mrs. MacTavish paused. "I think she should continue her trips to the ForEverNever."

"Why?" William asked in disbelief.

"There is only one Faerie Simeon would ever call Sire. Sophie met Emma's father, her grandfather. As long as she is with her grandfather, no harm will come to her in the ForEverNever. Sophie can learn a lot from her grandfather. And he did give up his daughter so she could be with you. Do you not think it is time he got to know his only granddaughter?"

"I'm not taking any chances with Sophie's safety. She means too much to me. I will not permit her to return to the ForEverNever or whatever it is called. I don't care if her grandfather is there and has a whole army to protect her. Sophie isn't going back," William commanded. "I forbid it."

"I believe you meant to say the ForEverNever," Mrs. MacTavish sounded slightly annoyed.

"The ForEverNever is the home of the Faeries. It is just as much a part of Sophie's heritage as the human world. She needs to learn about the Faerie World so she can protect herself. You endangered Sophie by bringing her to Ireland. There are things her grandfather can teach her that can keep her safe. Things you could not possibly teach her. Things you could not possibly imagine."

Mrs. MacTavish's voice softened. "And I don't think you can keep Sophie from returning to the ForEverNever even if you wanted to."

William lowered his head into his hands. He knew Mrs. MacTavish was right. And he knew the only descent thing to do was to allow Sophie to get to know her grandfather. He was however, determined to set boundaries when she could and could not go.

"Very well, Sophie can return to the ForEverNever; however, she is not permitted to return there until she has learned Martial Arts."

"Martial Arts?" Mrs. MacTavish questioned.

"Yes, Martial Arts!" William repeated. "I insist on Sophie learning how to protect herself before I permit her to return to the ForEverNever. She and Sean will take lessons from my good friend Sadao Kimoto. Once Sadao says she is ready, Sophie can return to the ForEverNever."

"What does Sean have to do with any of this? And isn't Sadao Kimoto Japanese?" Mrs. MacTavish questioned William. She didn't understand how he could be friends with someone who was Japanese when the United States had been at war with Japan.

"Don't look at me like that. The war was over years ago. Sadao may be Japanese, but he has been my friend for as long as I can remember. I want Sophie to learn Martial Arts from a grand master and Sadao Kimoto is a grand master. He can teach her a lot. And as you pointed out, Sadao is Japanese. The war may be over, but there are some in government circles who would think it suspicious if Sadao regularly came to my house. No matter how much I would like for him to be able to drop in and just visit, Sadao Kimoto shouldn't come to Evanswood unless on official business and we all know he isn't a diplomat."

"As for what Sean has to do with this..."

William explained, "Sophie will have to have lessons somewhere other than here. However, I will not allow her to leave Evanswood alone. I want Sean to accompany her to her lessons. And he may be able to use what he learns to protect himself and Sophie in the future."

"Knowing Martial Arts may or may not be helpful to Sophie in the Faerie World, but it would not hurt her to learn some sort of self-defense. This would also be good for Sean. Maybe it will make him a little tougher," Mrs. MacTavish thought to herself.

"Sophie can return to the ForEverNever, once Sadao Kimoto gives the go ahead. Do you think we should tell her that the bearded Faerie she met is her grandfather?" William asked.

Mrs. MacTavish thought a moment. "No, I do not think it is our place. He should be the one to tell Sophie.

"I will contact Sadao Kimoto right away. Thankfully, he is currently working in Dublin."

William already began to feel a little better about the situation. "A Faerie World? And all this time…!"

———————————————————————————————

William stared into the fire in the small fireplace across the room from his desk thinking of his oldest and dearest friend, Sadao Kimoto. They were young boys when they met many years ago. William and his family had just moved to Japan. His father's company sent his father to Japan to work for several years. William and his mother left New York to join him. They had a nice house by the water. William attended an international school where all the lessons were taught in English. He liked Japan and his school, but he missed all his friends he had to leave behind in the United States.

William first met Sadao Kimoto about three weeks after he moved to Japan. He was walking home from school. There was a gentle, misty rain in the air, but the sun was shining. The cherry blossoms with their light, pinkish white petals, were in full bloom. William stopped to admire one of the cherry blossom trees and saw a group of boys beating up another smaller boy across the street. The smaller boy was wearing the same uniform as William, and William recognized him as someone he had seen earlier at school. William could hear the boys yelling at the smaller boy. Although he couldn't understand a word, he knew they were not kind words. Plus, four against one was not a fair fight. Without another thought, William ran across the street and joined the fight.

Thanks to his father William knew how to box. He was excited he was finally going to get to put the boxing skills to good use. The tall thick-headed boy aimed a punch at his head, but William ducked. William returned the punch and hit the boy square on the chin. The boy fell to the ground making a grunting sound. William looked around prepared to fight the other three boys. In disbelief, he saw the other boys sprawled out on the ground. None of them were able to move. William looked at the smaller boy who just smiled.

"Thanks for the help."

"You are more than welcome; although, it really doesn't look like you needed my help. Your fighting skills are impressed. Your probably could have fought all four boys without any assistance. That was incredible!"

"Yes, I needed your help. I can handle three by myself, but four may have been one too many. I was just trying to figure out what to do when you came along."

"I am Sadao Kimoto. Pleased to meet you." The small boy bowed.

William was amazed how well Sadao Kimoto could speak English. All the diplomats' and foreign businessmen's' children went to an international school in the center of Tokyo. Some of the wealthy Japanese paid a large amount of money so their children could attend the school to master the English language. The fact that Sadao Kimoto spoke English wasn't what surprised William. He was surprised that Sadao Kimoto spoke with hardly any accent.

"I am William St. Clair and the pleasure is mine. How did you learn to fight like that?" William reached out his hand to shake Sadao Kimoto's hand.

Sadao Kimoto stepped back, "In Japan, we bow." He smiled and bowed at William again.

"My grandfather and father are teaching me our family's Martial Arts secrets. My great-grandfather was a Samurai warrior and my grandfather has been training since he was my age."

William and Sadao Kimoto quickly became the best of friends. For the six years William lived in Japan, William and Sadao Kimoto were inseparable. Sadao Kimoto even convinced his grandfather and father to teach William some Martial Arts. Normally, Martial Arts masters didn't teach anyone outside their families and it was unheard of to teach a foreigner any Martial Arts, but Sadao Kimoto was very persuasive.

"I need to call Sadao Kimoto right now," William said to himself as he continued to stare into the fire. As the fire died down, he walked over to the desk in the library and picked up the telephone.

Sophie was sitting up at the counter eating a peanut butter and jelly sandwich when Zoey walked into the kitchen. "Causing trouble again, I see. You had everyone looking for you all day. You went back to that Faerie-Land didn't you?"

Sophie laughed, looked down at Zoey and petted her head. She reached into the bowl of popcorn on the table and gave Zoey a handful. "Sure did, and I had so much fun. I met an older, bearded Faerie. He was very kind to me. He and Simeon are going to teach me to ride Polleux. They tell me Polleux can even fly. Can you image, a flying horse?"

"Horses can't fly," Zoey said. "However, I also never met a human who could talk with animals. So, maybe in this Faerie-Land horses can fly. But, I won't believe it until I see it."

"And dogs can't talk." Sophie grinned at Zoey while she licked some jelly off her finger.

"Ok, point taken." Horses can fly and so can pigs!" Zoey laughed.

"And what is more impressive than a flying horse?" Sophie asked Zoey.
"I don't know, what?"
"A spelling bee!" Sophie cracked up with laughter.
"Is that your attempt at a joke?" Zoey rolled her eyes.
"Come on Zoey, that was a funny one. Or do you only laugh at your own jokes?"

Zoey couldn't help herself. She looked up at Sophie and laughed.
Sophie reached down and gave Zoey another handful of popcorn.
"I want to hear more about this Simeon character," Zoey said changing the subject.

"Simeon and the bearded Faerie taught me how to dance. The bearded Faerie made these instruments appear out of nowhere. There were about twenty instruments and they played the most beautiful music."

Zoey began to move to imaginary music teasing Sophie.
"I am sorry. I didn't mean to make anyone worry. I didn't realize how much time had passed. In the future, I need to remember that time passes a lot quicker when I am in the ForEverNever."

"Who are you talking too?" Sean asked, as he walked into the kitchen. "And what is the ForEverNever."

"I was just talking to myself." Sophie smiled at Sean. She wasn't sure she wanted Sean to know she could speak to animals.

"What have you been up to all day?"
"What have I been up to all day?" Sean incredulously looked at Sophie and threw his hands in the air. "I have been looking for you all day.

Just like everyone else in this house. Please don't just disappear like that again. We were all worried."

"I am sorry!" Sophie felt like a recording. "I didn't realize how long I was gone. I was in the ForEverNever. The next time, I will let someone know where I am going." Sophie looked at Zoey and mouthed, "I promise."

"The ForEverNever! What is the ForEverNever?"

Sophie opened her mouth to answer Sean's question, but stopped suddenly.

"I am glad you are both here." Sophie's father entered the kitchen. "I have something to tell you."

"Starting tomorrow you will begin learning Martial Arts with my old friend Sadao Kimoto."

Sophie and Sean stared at Sophie's father. "Why can't you teach us?" Sophie asked. "I remember when you would practice in the garden at our old house in New York. You looked pretty good."

"Martial Arts? I am not really much of a fighter." Sean started to fidget. "Do I have to learn Martial Arts?"

"Sadao Kimoto will teach both of you Martial Arts starting tomorrow and I don't want to hear any complaints from either of you. Sadao Kimoto is doing this as a favor to me, so I want you both on your best behavior. Besides, learning Martial Arts should be a lot of fun and gives you the opportunity to get out of the house."

Sean just looked at Sophie's father but didn't say a word. Sophie on the other hand looked at her father with suspicion. She wasn't happy about the situation and had many questions she wanted answered.

Sophie asked again, "If you want us to learn Martial Arts, why can't you teach us?"

"I would love to teach you Martial Arts, but I don't have time. Besides, Sadao Kimoto is a master. He is the best one to teach you."

Sophie's father gave her another big hug and pinched her nose. He tousled Sean's hair and walked towards the kitchen door. "You two should get to bed soon. Tomorrow is going to be a big day for both of you."

After her father had left the kitchen Sophie turned to Sean. "Before my father walked in, I was going to ask you how your visual training is going. Have you made any improvements?"

"The training is going well." Sean smiled at Sophie. "It has really helped me improve my juggling."

"Juggling?" Sophie questioned. "Now, you are teasing me."

Sean continued to smile at Sophie. "Yes, juggling. You know when you continuously toss objects into the air and catch them without dropping any of them."

Sean took three apples out of the bowl on the kitchen table. He held two apples in his right hand and one in his left. He threw the first apple in the air and then the second. Sophie watched in awe as he threw the third apple in the air and caught the first. She tried to figure out how Sean was able to keep the apples in the air without dropping any.

After Sean had juggled for a few minutes, he put two apples back in the bowl. He then threw the third apple up in the air, caught it and took a big bite. As he chewed the apple he smiled at Sophie. "How do you like them apples?"

Sophie just rolled her eyes at Sean and grabbed the apple out of his hand.

Sean reached for the apple and grabbed it back. "You know your father is right. We should get to bed soon." He took another bite of the apple.

"I know, but there is one thing I want to do before I turn in for the night. And since I promised to tell someone the next time I return to the ForEverNever, I am telling you. I plan to return to the ForEverNever tonight."

"Oh, no you're not! We spent all day looking for you. You are going to get up to your room and go to bed, like your father said."

"I will not be gone long. Just about an hour. I promise you, I will be safe."

"I am with Sean and your father on this one," Zoey said. "You should head right up to bed and keep out of trouble for the rest of the night."

"Thank you for your concern." Sophie looked at Sean then Zoey, "But I am returning to the ForEverNever tonight. I just need to get my shoes and go to the hidden garden."

"Why do you need to put on your shoes in the hidden garden?" Sean just shook his head. "Never mind, don't answer that. I am going with you to the hidden garden," he insisted. "And nothing you say is going to change my mind."

"Ok, you convinced me. You can go with me to the hidden garden. Just wait for me here and I will return with my shoes in just a moment."

Sophie grinned. "This really will not take long."

THE SACRIFICE

You learn, as you get older, things aren't as simple as when you were a child, especially when there is a war. Those who were once your friends, somehow, without your choosing, become your enemy. Although my country was at war with my friend's country, we could never see each other as enemies. Now, my friend has called on me for help. He was by my side all those years ago. Now is my time to stand by him. I have no children. It will be an honor to pass along my family's secrets to those I know and trust. In many ways I think of William as my brother and his daughter as family.

- Sadao Kimoto

xviij : Learning from the Master

Zoey walked with Sophie up to her room. "I don't think this is such a good idea. We were all very worried about you today. You really should just head up to your room for the night and go to bed."

Sophie just smiled at Zoey and shook her head. "I have to return to the ForEverNever. There is something I need to do."

"Do you really have to return to the ForEverNever tonight?" Zoey asked.

"With my Martial Arts lessons, it may be months before I have time to return to the ForEverNever. I really need to see the mirror image of my mother. I want to tell her all about my day. I know she isn't my real mother, but when I am with her, it makes me feel like I'm with my mother."

"I wish I could go with you. I want to make sure you stay out of trouble," Zoey said.

"There is no need to worry. I will be safe when I am there. Magical wards protect the place where the mirror image of my mother is located. Only those wearing a special ring or cape, or my magic blue shoes, can enter the garden."

Sophie grabbed her shoes and the flashlight from her room and headed back to the kitchen to get Sean. "Are you ready? Let's go to the hidden garden before it gets any later."

Sophie walked over to the tapestry and pulled it back revealing the hidden room. "I forgot the room doesn't have any light," Sean groaned.

"I didn't." Sophie turned on the flashlight.

Sophie, Sean and Zoey made their way to the door at the end of the hidden room. Sean tried to open the door, but again, it wouldn't budge. Sophie handed the flashlight to Sean and put her shoes on the floor. She pulled back her sleeves and reached up to turn the doorknob. The door opened with ease. Sophie turned and smiled at Sean and Zoey. She picked up her shoes and entered the garden as Zoey and Sean followed close behind.

Sophie made her way over to the pond and sat down on the bench. She looked down at the shoes in her hand. "I guess it's time to put you back on."

Sophie wiggled her toes into two pairs of socks. She carefully put on the first shoe then the second. The world around her began to spin. She saw the flash of light and spheres of colored lights. A buzzing noise filled the air.

"Here we go again," Zoey said as Sophie began to fade in and out then disappear completely.

Sophie's head stopped spinning, the buzzing stopped, and the colored lights were gone. She rubbed her eyes and looked around. The mirror image of her mother was walking towards her.

"You are back! I am glad to see you, but take care for the ForEverNever is not a safe place for you," the mirror image of her mother warned.

"Look, I have the Ring of Incognito." Sophie grinned as she held up the ring, which was on the chain around her neck.

"Isn't it lovely?" Sophie took the ring off the chain and put it on her finger. "And look, it almost fits my finger!"

The mirror image of her mother smiled in approval. "I really am glad you are back to visit. I was watching you at Evanswood. It did not look like you were having a lot of fun at that party the other night."

"You are right! I didn't have any fun at the party. But I really don't want to speak about that. I came to talk about the wonderful time I had after I left the party. I returned to the ForEverNever. It was great being there. I met an older, bearded Faerie when I was there. He and Simeon taught me how to dance and they are going to teach me to ride Polleux."

"That sounds exciting," the mirror image enthusiastically smiled at Sophie.

Acting like her mother the mirror image asked Sophie, "What does your father think of all of this?"

"My father has reservations, but he agreed I can return to the ForEverNever, if I learn some Martial Arts."

"Martial Arts? What is your father thinking?" The mirror image of her mother shook her head and laughed.

"Tell me a little more about this older, bearded Faerie you met."

"He was very kind to me and had a nice smile. He was taller than you with a strong build. He had lovely long flowing white hair, a beard, shimmered a gold light when he moved and he dances elegantly. That's all I remember. Oh, I remembered one more thing. He had bright green eyes."

"Was he wearing a ring?" the mirror image of her mother inquired.

Sophie thought a moment. "I am not sure. I didn't really look closely at his hands."

"Well, if you see him again, look for a ring. If he is wearing a ring, take a close look and see if it is similar to the ring your mother wore when you were young."

Sophie appeared disappointed in herself for not being more observant or remembering her mother's ring.

"No need to worry," the mirror image of her mother soothed. She reached out her hands to Sophie, but was not able to touch her. "Have you seen the portrait of your mother when she was young?"

Sophie shook her head up and down. "I have the portrait. It is hanging in my bedroom."

"Next time you are in your room look closely at the portrait. Your mother is wearing the ring with her family crest. Your grandfather wears a ring that looks exactly like your mother's except his ring is larger and sparkles like the stars. Your grandfather had both rings enchanted. He never takes his off. Because of the rings' enchantment, your mother could always find her father and her father could always find her as long as they both were wearing their rings. Having the rings enchanted was just one of the many things your grandfather did to ensure your mother's safety. He stills wears his ring. I think he wears it in memory of your mother."

"Thank you! I'm going to check out the portrait as soon as I get back." Sophie's mind was a blur. She couldn't wait to get back to her room. Could the bearded Faerie really be her grandfather?"

"Speaking of my room, I should be heading home. I told Zoey and Sean that I wouldn't be gone very long. Tomorrow Sean and I start our Martial Arts lessons with a master, Sadao Kimoto. My father says he is one of his oldest friends, but I never met him."

The mirror image of her mother attempted to reassure Sophie. "Your father loves you very much. He wants what is best for you."

Reluctantly, Sophie said goodbye to the mirror image of her mother and returned to the bench to carefully take off her shoes. Once she was clutching both her shoes close to her chest, she saw the bright flashes of light and colored spheres of light. She then heard the buzzing sound. The next thing Sophie knew she was sitting on the bench in the hidden garden at Evanswood. Sean was sound asleep, curled up next her.

Zoey started to bark when she saw Sophie. Zoey's barking woke up Sean. Startled, he looked over to see Sophie sitting next to him. "Oh, you are back," Sean yawned and stretched his arms. "I hope you were able to do that important thing you just couldn't wait another day to take care of."

Sophie ignored Sean's sarcasm. "Mission accomplished! Thanks for your concern. Now it's time for bed. But, it looks like you've already been asleep for hours." Sophie poked Sean in the chest. "Let me help you to your room, sleepy head."

Sean pushed Sophie's hand away and gave her an annoyed look. "I can make it back to my room without your help, thank you very much!"

Sean stood and stumbled to the door leading to the hidden room. He was having a little trouble getting his legs to wake up, so he stopped to shake them out a few times.

"A bit wobbly there, are you? Sure you don't want any help making it back to your room? On those legs you may not be able to make it there," Sophie teased.

Sean looked over his shoulder and glared at Sophie. His legs were working better. Sophie followed behind Sean as they made their way through the hidden room and back into the library.

"Good night Sophie. I hope you still have that grin on your face when I beat you at Martial Arts tomorrow."

"I thought you weren't a fighter." Sean heard Sophie laughing as he walked to his room. At least she was laughing again. He really liked to hear her laugh. He then smiled to himself. There was no chance she was going to beat him at Martial Arts.

Sophie continued laughing as she and Zoey headed back to her bedroom.

"Time for bed, right?" Zoey said.

"Sorry, not yet. I still have one more thing I need to do before I go to sleep," Sophie insisted.

"Oh, no!" Zoey barked. "That's what you said the last time and that was over two hours ago."

"This will be quick." Sophie promised. "I just need to see if my mother is wearing a ring in the portrait hanging in my bedroom. I won't have to leave my room to accomplish the task. Once we go through that door, I am only steps away from going to bed."

Excited, Sophie walked in her room and turned on the light. She headed straight to the portrait of her mother. Just as the mirror image of her mother had told Sophie, her mother was wearing a beautiful ring on the ring finger of her left hand. Etched into the ring was her family crest. A gold lion stood in front of a large blue moon. The background was black. There was a silver lily in the right top corner and a gold crown in the left top corner. Sophie took one last look at the ring. Alright Zoey, "Now it's time to go to bed."

"It's about time," Zoey barked as she jumped on the bed, circling around before finally laying down for the evening.

"Don't forget your morning lesson with Mr. Fitzpatrice starts an hour early tomorrow, since your first Marital Arts lesson is in the early afternoon."

"I haven't forgotten!" Sophie crawled into bed and rubbed Zoey on her head.

Helen knocked on Sophie's door, but there was no response. When she knocked again and there was still no response, she walked into Sophie's room singing, "Good morning, good morning, it's time to wake your sleepy head. Good morning, good morning, it's time to start the day."

Smiling, Helen put the breakfast tray on the table as Sophie began to sit up. "I brought you breakfast."

"Yum, breakfast. I hope there is some bacon on that tray." Zoey wagged her tail.

Sophie rubbed her eyes then stretched her arms. "G-o-o-d m-o-r-n-i-n-g."

"French toast and hot chocolate?"

"What else would it be?" Helen cheerfully answered as she walked towards the door.

"I know it is early in the morning, but you need to hurry. Mr. Fitzpatrice is already waiting for you in the library."

Sophie groaned, "I don't think I can take his voice this morning. Do I have to go?"

Helen just smiled.

Sophie dressed and ate her breakfast. She saved her bacon and last piece of French toast for Zoey. After eating, she headed to the library for her morning lesson with Mr. Fitzpatrice. Sean was already sitting in his seat at the table, glasses on his head, when Sophie entered the library.

"You are late young lady," Mr. Fitzpatrice admonished. "Although we are starting earlier than usual, we still have less time than normal for our lesson, since your father wants you to have a Martial Arts lesson today. I guess we should all feel privileged you even made it to our lesson today." Mr. Fitzpatrice held the teacher's philosophy that only his class was important.

As Mr. Fitzpatrice scolded her, Sophie looked at the clock on the mantle of the fireplace in the center of the room. She was surprised to discover the image at the base of the clock appeared to have changed. She recalled seeing a rooster the last time she looked at the clock, but now she thought she saw a bear resting in a cave. Although she was unable to more closely examine the clock at that moment, she made a mental note to check out the clock at a later date.

When Mr. Fitzpatrice was done scolding her, Sophie walked over and took her seat next to Sean. Surprisingly, Sophie didn't feel like she had to cover her ears when Mr. Fitzpatrice spoke. "I guess Sean was right," Sophie thought. "Mr. Fitzpatrice's voice really does grow on you."

The lesson was on the Greek Goddess. This time Sophie found she was truly interested. Mr. Fitzpatrice began his lecture on Nike, the Greek goddess of victory, both in battle and in sport.

Mr. Fitzpatrice stated in his somewhat less annoying voice, "Nike was one of four children of the Titan god of war Pallas, and the Naiad Styx. Nike's siblings Kratos, Bia, and Zelus, represented Strength, Force, and Rivalry."

Mr. Fitzpatrice looked up and saw Sophie was actually listening to him. He continued on with his lesson. "Most stories associated with Nike are intermixed with tales of the Greek goddess Athena. I will tell you more about her in a moment."

"Nike and Athena were said to be among the few gods to stand by Zeus' side in the famous war against Typhon for control of Olympus. Since you already know who Zeus is, I will not spend any time talking about him today."

192

Mr. Fitzpatrice looked directly at Sophie. "Now back to Nike. It is said Nike, along with her siblings, were the first to join Zeus in the battle against the Typhon. They are often depicted standing by his throne as his sentinels. Nike herself was given a golden chariot to lead Zeus' troops into battle.

"However, little else is known about Nike. As I said before most accounts of her are intermixed with stories about Athena, the Greek goddess of wisdom, courage, inspiration and justice. Athena was the favorite child of Zeus and sprung fully grown out of his head. The Classical Greek Myths tell the stories of her coming to the aid of several famous Greek heroes. Legend tells that she guided Perseus in his quest to behead Medusa and instructed Heracles, her half-brother, on how to skin the Nemean Lion by using its own claws to cut through its thick hide. Athena also helped Heracles defeat the Stymphalian Birds, and navigate the underworld to capture Cerberus."

Mr. Fitzpatrice stopped to take a breath and looked up to find Sophie staring at him intently. "She truly is listening to me. This is a change for the better. I can work with this."

Mr. Fitzpatrice enthusiastically continued telling the stories of other Greek goddesses. However, none of the others intrigued Sophie like Athena. Sophie admired Athena's wisdom, cunning, and bravery.

After he stopped talking about Hera and reached Aphrodite, Mr. Fitzpatrice could tell he had completely lost Sophie's interest. "Well, I am glad I was able to keep her attention as long as I did. Hopefully, she learned something."

"So, are you both ready to begin your Martial Arts lessons?" Mr. Fitzpatrice asked Sophie and Sean. "I know your father is glad his old friend Sadao Kimoto will be able to teach you both. He was talking about it this morning at breakfast, before he headed out to work."

"It should be fun." Sean looked at Sophie then back at Mr. Fitzpatrice. "I can't wait to beat Sophie." Sean grinned. He was only teasing Sophie, but deep down he thought he could be really good at Martial Arts.

Sophie couldn't believe it. She wasn't bothered by Mr. Fitzpatrice's voice and she didn't mind his questions. "There is hope! Mr. Fitzpatrice is growing on me," she thought. However, Sean was another story. She was a little annoyed with him at the moment. Beat her was he? She was going to show him.

Sophie smiled. She had to admit that she was glad Sean was starting to show a little spunk. She knew it was there, somewhere under his manners.

"Yes, we should be heading to our Martial Arts lesson soon. However, my father neglected to tell us where we are supposed to go." Sophie looked at Mr. Fitzpatrice to see if he knew the answer.

"No need to worry. Your father's driver is taking you. I think you may have met him the night you first arrived. He was probably the one who picked you up at the airport."

"Oh, him!" Sophie sighed.

"This is going to be a pleasant experience. I can't wait to see him again. He was so kind and welcoming." Sophie thought as she rolled her eyes.

"While I wish my lesson was not cut short today, I am sure you both will learn a lot at your Martial Arts lesson. I have heard Sadao Kimoto is a very wise and interesting man."

Thirty minutes later Sophie and Sean were waiting outside the house for their ride to their first Martial Arts lesson. They still didn't know where they were going, but they didn't let that or the stern, bulky driver dampen their excitement. Sophie smiled at the man and said hello. He simply grunted in response and motioned for her and Sean to get in the car.

"Well, at least I tried," Sophie thought.

The driver drove about twenty minutes and stopped the car. "You can get out here," he grumbled, "I will park the car across the street and wait for you."

Sophie and Sean stepped out of the car onto a sidewalk next to a high wall. Leaning up against the wall was a skinny, short Japanese man with graying hair and a strange looking mustache that curved and hung below his upper lip. He was dressed in an all-white, loosely fitting outfit.

Sean whispered to Sophie. "If he is our instructor, he looks a little older than I expected."

He is supposed to be the same age as my father, and my father doesn't have any gray hair," Sophie silently observed.

The man stepped away from the wall. "You must be Sophie and Sean. I am Sadao Kimoto. Pleased to meet you."

"Sophie, I have known your father for many years. And yes, we are the same age."

"You may call me Sensei," the man said to Sean and Sophie.

Sophie stepped back a little embarrassed. Had Sadao Kimoto heard her thoughts? If so, how was that possible? Sophie took a deep breath thinking, "Since I can speak to animals, I guess it isn't impossible Sadao Kimoto can hear my thoughts." She made a mental note to try not to think anything bad around him.

Sean stepped forward to shake Sadao Kimoto's hand. Sadao Kimoto stopped him. "Lesson number one, you don't shake your Sensei's hand, you bow."

Both Sophie and Sean bowed at the same time.

Sophie stepped forward. "Where are we?"

"Behind this high wall is Iveagh Gardens, a hidden paradise. Sadao Kimoto pointed at the high wall behind them. "The gardens' high walls block out the world. It is very quiet, peaceful and not often used. It is the perfect location to learn Martial Arts. There is also a magnificent waterfall in the gardens. Let's head in and begin your training."

Sophie and Sean followed Sadao Kimoto through the gate into the gardens. They saw the rose gardens, open fields, intricate gravel walkways, and a charming set of classical statues. They also saw the waterfall.

"So that is a waterfall! I have never seen one before. It's wonderful!" Sean proclaimed.

Sitting on a bench close to the waterfall was a couple reading a magazine. The oddly dressed couple were the only other individuals Sophie and Sean saw in the gardens.

Sadao Kimoto directed Sophie and Sean to an open space close to the waterfall. "Now what was lesson one?"

Both Sophie and Sean bowed.

"Since you have mastered lesson one, let's move onto lesson two. Clear everything from your mind. Block out all distractions and focus on your breathing. Once your mind is clear, close your eyes and pay attention to all your senses. Feel the heat of the sun on your skin, the cool breeze on your face. Hear the noises around you, the rustling leaves and the sounds of the animals moving in the distance. Now, simply focus on the feel of the air and warmth on your skin. Try to determine from which direction the wind is blowing and the sun's ray are coming. Next, focus solely on the noises made by the animals without opening your eyes. Point in the direction the animals are located."

"Lesson two is knowing your surroundings, recognizing any changes in your surroundings and always being present in them."

Sophie and Sean looked to Sadao Kimoto for further direction. "For the rest of the lesson, the remaining thirty minutes, I want you to stand in this spot with your eyes closed, taking in your surroundings."

I cannot believe my daughter is gone. I did everything in my power to keep her safe. I should not have let her go to Earth, the human world; but it was beyond my power to say no to her. And if I did not help her, she would have figured out another way to get to Earth. She was very strong willed and determined. I have really missed her over these last few years. And now that she is truly gone, any hope of seeing her again is gone. I am so glad her daughter, my granddaughter, has found her way to the ForEverNever. She is so much like her mother. Sometimes it hurts me to look at her. She is beginning to mean a great deal to me. It is only fair to her that I tell her who I am, and soon.

- The King of the Faerie House of Ymir

xix : Truth Revealed

When Sophie returned from her Martial Arts lesson she headed to her bedroom to get her blue shoes. Zoey met her in the hallway.

"How was your lesson? Did Sean beat you? Did you learn anything new you can show me?"

"All we did today was close our eyes, breath and focus on our surroundings. I really feel like I can protect myself after today's lesson!" Sophie laughed.

Zoey wiggled her ears as she followed Sophie to her room. "What are you up to now?"

Sophie held her blue shoes in her arms. "I am going to return to the ForEverNever and see if I can start my riding lessons."

"You know your father doesn't want you to return to the ForEverNever until you can protect yourself. You need to complete more Martial Arts lessons with Sadao Kimoto," Zoey stressed as she moved in front of Sophie.

"If the rest of my lessons are like today's lesson, I don't think I will ever learn how to protect myself. I can't wait any longer to see the bearded

Faerie. I need to check if he is wearing a ring. I have to know if he is my grandfather." Sophie was hopeful and a little excited.

Zoey sat at the edge of the bed looking at Sophie with worried eyes. "I can understand your desire to know if the bearded Faerie is your grandfather. However, you did promise to tell someone, human, before you returned to the ForEverNever."

"Oh, yes!" Sophie had momentarily forgotten her promise. "I will inform Sean I'm returning to the ForEverNever. He should be in his room."

Zoey stood by Sophie as she knocked on Sean's bedroom door. There was no answer. She knocked again and still no answer. She reached down to turn the doorknob.

"Are you sure you want to do that?" Zoey questioned.

"Yes, I am sure. I know he is there. He must be asleep," Sophie replied as she turned the doorknob. She opened the door carefully and quietly walked in the room. Sean was standing on the other side of the room doing eye exercises. Sophie walked closer and yelled, "SEAN."

Startled, Sean dropped the string out of his hand. "Sophie, what are you doing in my room? And why are you yelling at me?"

"I knocked two times. You didn't answer, but I knew you were here. Why didn't you answer?"

"Oh, I am sorry! I was so focused on my eye exercises I just didn't hear you. So where is the fire?"

"It's not urgent. It's just that I promised to tell someone before I returned to the ForEverNever. So I am telling you. I plan to return to the ForEverNever right after I get back to my room."

"Do you think that's such a good idea? We haven't gotten very far in our Martial Arts lessons. You know your father doesn't want you to return to the ForEverNever until Sadao Kimoto has confidence in your ability to take care of yourself."

"You're right. We haven't gotten very far in our lessons," Sophie agreed. "But, I will be careful. There is no need to worry. I will be back before you even realize I am gone."

"I don't believe that for a second. However, I really can't do anything to stop you, unless I tell your father and I really don't think that will stop you anyway. That will just make him and you mad, then you will not tell me when you are leaving in the future," Sean thought to himself.

"Just be careful," Sean pleaded.

"I will." Sophie ran over and gave Sean a quick peck on the cheek before she ran out of his room.

Sean intently stared at the door Sophie just ran through and shook his head. "That girl really is trouble, but she is growing on me."

———————————————————————————————

Back in her bedroom, Sophie grabbed her blue shoes, put on two pairs of socks and sat on her bed to put her shoes on one at a time. The room started to spin, there was a flash of light and multi-colored spheres appeared. There was the familiar buzzing sound. Sophie heard Zoey barking as she faded in and out, and then finally disappeared. Zoey jumped up on the bed to wait until Sophie reappeared.

Sophie rubbed her head and looked around. "I can't believe that trip still makes me so light-headed and disoriented. You would think my body would get used to making the trip to the ForEverNever by now." Sophie cleared her eyes and Polleux's meadow came into view. She could see Polleux in the distance and ran up the hill towards him.

"Hello, young lady. It is a pleasure to see you." Polleux slightly bowed. "What brings you to my meadow?"

Sophie smiled at Polleux. "I thought I might start my riding lessons today."

"I think that is a wonderful idea. Let's go get Simeon. I think he is home." Polleux and Sophie started to walk down the hill to Simeon's house. Before they were halfway down the hill, they saw Simeon walking towards them. Sophie and Polleux stopped. Within moments Simeon reached them on the hill.

"I had a feeling you would be in the meadow with Polleux. It is good to see you again. I bet you want to start learning to ride. Let's get started," Simeon grinned.

"I can't wait. It is all I have thought about. What about the nice bearded, Faerie, who taught me how to dance? Should we get him too?" Learning how to ride wasn't all Sophie had in mind.

"No!" Simeon replied. "He probably already knows you are here and is on his way to see you."

"Look there he is now." Simeon pointed to a glowing figure in the distance walking towards them.

Sophie took a closer look. That sure looks like him. Should we wait here or head up towards the meadow?" Sophie asked.

"Let's meet him in the meadow. By the time he makes it up to the meadow, we should have you already on my back."

Sophie looked at the sleek horse without a saddle. "How am I supposed to get on your back, Polleux? You are so big and tall. I don't think I could make it up there even if I jumped."

"No need to worry. I will give you a lift." Simeon grabbed Sophie around the waist and lifted her up on Polleux's back. Polleux stood very still until he was sure Sophie was balanced.

"I see you are ready to ride." The bearded Faerie was now beside them. "No need to worry. You are perfectly safe on Polleux."

Polleux could feel Sophie gripping his sides. "Relax, I will not let anything happen to you."

"Nice to see you Sire," Simeon bowed. "Polleux would also bow, but as you can see that would be a little difficult for him right now."

"What do I do next?" Sophie asked with a smile.

"Squeeze tight with your legs and grab a hold of my mane. It won't hurt if you pull tight on my mane." Polleux started walking.

"Look, I'm riding a horse!" Sophie smiled. She was so excited she almost forgot about the ring.

"Keep your head up instead of looking down at the ground." Simeon instructed. "You can tell Polleux which direction to go with your knees. If you want Polleux to go to the right add a little more pressure with your left knee and if you want him to go to the left add a little more pressure with your right knee. If you want him to go faster, lean forward and add a little more pressure with both knees. And if you want him to stop, pull back on his ears."

Polleux slightly turned his head and stared at Simeon. "Just kidding Sophie, don't pull back his ears to make him stop. He normally knows when to stop. But if you need to stop, add more pressure with both your legs and lean back slightly. You can hold onto Polleux's mane to help you keep your balance."

Polleux spoke up. "Or you can just tell me which direction you want to go."

Simeon laughed. "Yes, but learning to ride with her legs will help ensure Sophie is able to ride other horses."

Circling Simeon and the bearded Faerie, Polleux picked up speed. Sophie yelled with delight. "This is so much fun!"

Sophie held on tighter with her knees as Polleux ran a little faster.

"Looking good young lady!" The bearded Faerie's voice boomed. Sophie smiled and cautiously waved at them. Polleux circled one more time around the meadow and returned to where Simeon and the bearded Faerie were standing.

"I think that is enough for today, young lady." The bearded Faerie lifted Sophie off Polleux's back. As he lowered her to the ground, Sophie noticed a ring sparkling on the ring finger of his right hand.

"May I see your ring?" Sophie asked when her feet were firmly planted on the ground.

"Of course you can." The bearded Faerie took the ring off his finger and handed it to Sophie. The ring had the lion, the blue moon, the flower and a crown in the top corners."

Sophie looked at the bearded Faerie with an enormous smile on her face. "This has the same crest as my mother's ring."

"Yes, I gave your mother her ring when she was about your age." The bearded Faerie's eyes sparkled.

Sophie had to make sure. "If you gave my mother her ring, then you must be her father, and if you are my mother's father, that would make you my grandfather."

Sophie looked directly at the bearded Faerie. "Are you my grandfather?"

"Yes, Sophie, I am your grandfather. I am so glad you found your way to the ForEverNever. I thought I might never get to meet you."

Sophie gave her grandfather a big hug. His coat was velvety soft. He smelled of smoked hickory wood and pine. His long white beard was full and very soft and his body shined with a gold light.

"I have the best grandfather in the whole world," Sophie thought as she hugged her grandfather again. "Why didn't you tell me who you are when we first met?"

"I was not sure it was my place to tell you, or how much you knew about your mother's family. I figured it was better to wait for you to ask the questions. You need to keep in mind that it is best no one in the ForEverNever, other than Polleux and Simeon, knows who you are and that I am your grandfather."

Sophie was confused. She just found her grandfather and now she had to keep it a secret. "Why can't other Faeries know I am here?"

The bearded Faerie looked down at Sophie with wise, gentle eyes. "To start with, did you forget humans are not allowed in the ForEverNever? But more importantly, you still do not know who I am, do you child?"

"Yes, I do. You are my grandfather." Sophie smiled and gave him another hug.

"Yes, I am your grandfather, but I am also the King of the Faerie House of Ymir and High King of the Enlightened Faeries. Your mother was a well honored and loved princess."

Did she hear right? Her grandfather was a king? Her mother was a princess? Sophie felt like she was in a fairy tale. This was all so wonderful. "Does this make me a princess too?"

"Yes, you are my little princess. However, I have to warn you if other Faeries know who you are, you could be in serious danger. You must promise to never tell anyone you are my granddaughter."

Sophie didn't understand the seriousness of what her grandfather was telling her. What possible danger could there be? She looked up at her grandfather not wanting to disappoint him. "I promise."

The realization she was a princess was beginning to sink in. "So, you can tell Simeon he has to be nice to me and do what I tell him?"

Sophie's grandfather laughed. "Even I have a difficult time getting Simeon to do what I want. The only one he really listened to was your mother. They were the best of friends until your mother left the ForEverNever. Simeon may give you a little attitude, but I have a feeling he will do whatever you ask of him."

Sophie looked at Simeon, who was pretending as if he was not paying attention. "Smash in Squash! Is that true, Simeon?"

"Princess or not, I would do anything for you. All you need is ask." Simeon wanted to make sure Sophie knew his loyalty wasn't in response to her title, it was given because he cared for her mother and he was beginning to care for her.

"I want to talk to you about something," Sophie's grandfather motioned for her to follow him.

"Okay!" Sophie skipped after her grandfather and grabbed his hand as they started to walk down the hill. "What did you want to talk about?"

"How much do you know about your mother's past, before she met your father?"

"Not too much, but I met her mirror image. She told me about the Ring of Incognito and the ring with the family crest. I also know my mother's power was the power of pure love and goodness."

"You met your mother's mirror image?" her grandfather questioned before Sophie could voice her next thought.

"Yes, she seemed very kind and I enjoyed listening to her stories about my mother." Sophie's grandfather could tell she was very proud of her mother; but he was not sure how she could see her mother's mirror image. He was positive that if his daughter was dead, her mirror image should have disappeared. However, he decided now was not the time to dwell on the discovery that Sophie had seen her mother's mirror image. He had several important things he needed to tell Sophie. Although, he was already making plans to visit Crystal Pond as soon as Sophie left the ForEverNever.

"You are right. Your mother was gifted the power of pure love and goodness after she willingly gave up the power she was given at the time of her creation. Your mother could do no evil and she was unable to do anything that would cause harm to another Faerie, human, animal or spirit. Your mother gave up her power of pure love and goodness to become human. However, your mother had other unique abilities. I think you may have inherited some of these abilities."

"What abilities?" Sophie asked as she and her grandfather continued to walk away from Polleux's meadow. "I can't do anything special."

"You can talk to animals, can you not? That was one of your mother's first abilities. The first animal she spoke to was Polleux. A short time later, we realized she could sometimes hear other Faeries' thoughts. After that she started to have dreams about the future. Have you had any interesting dreams lately?" her grandfather asked with a grin.

"No, I haven't grandfather," Sophie replied a little disappointed. "But if my mother gave up her powers to become human, how could she pass them to me?"

"Your mother gave up her power, but not her abilities. Her powers were in her Faerie Energy, but her abilities were in her blood. The same blood, she passed along to you, Sophie. Since you have your mother's ability to talk to animals, it is very likely you inherited her other abilities. I guess we will have to wait and see. If you discover you are able to hear others' thoughts, you must let me know immediately. This is a very powerful ability. You will need to learn how to control it and use it wisely, to avoid getting hurt."

"If I am able to hear others' thoughts or if I have any strange dreams you will be the first to know, other than me, of course." Sophie looked up at her grandfather and giggled.

"Good to know." Sophie's grandfather directed her to turn around and head back towards the hill leading up to Polleux's meadow. "I have thoroughly enjoyed this visit young lady, but I think it is time for you to head home."

"You are probably right, but I don't really want to go." Sophie gave her grandfather a big hug. "I did tell Sean I wouldn't be away too long. But, before I go I want to say good-bye to Simeon and Polleux."

"I am sure they would appreciate that."

Sophie and her grandfather walked back up the hill to Polleux's meadow in silence.

Sophie said her good-byes. She sat on the ground and slowly took off her shoes, careful not to drop either of them. Her surroundings started to spin around her as she closed her eyes. She waited for the buzzing to stop and counted to thirty. When Sophie was done counting, she opened her eyes and found herself sitting in her bedroom.

"Well the trip is a little easier if I keep my eyes shut. Now, I need to find Sean and let him know I am home."

Sophie quickly made her way to Sean's room and knocked softly. This time he answered right away.

"Sophie, I am so glad it is you. You made it back just in time for dinner." Sean wiped his hand across his forehead. "I wasn't sure what I was going to tell everyone if you weren't at the table for dinner. I could have stalled for a few minutes by not heading down to the dining room right away, but you know how my grandmother is about dinner. After dinner, she would be in my room asking why I wasn't at dinner. I can't lie to my grandmother, Sophie."

"Well I am here now." Sophie smiled as if she had won a race. "Let's head down to the dining room before anyone starts asking questions." Sophie grabbed Sean's arm and pulled him out the door. "I'm starving."

———————————————————————

Sophie woke up in the middle of the night in a cold sweat. "What's wrong?" Concerned was etched on Zoey's face.

"It's nothing," Sophie replied in a sleepy voice. "I just had a bad dream. Go back to sleep. Everything is okay."

Zoey thought it might help if Sophie talked about her bad dream. "Well, what was your dream about?"

"I don't remember all of it. But I do remember there was a darkness that I could feel surrounding me. The darkness had a presence and a will all its own. It pulled me into this cold damp place, with no light. I couldn't see anything around me. I remember sensing large, dark, blurry figures moving in the shadows."

"Can you remember anything else?" Zoey appeared calm, but was somewhat bothered by Sophie's dream.

"No, not really. Wait, I saw some water falling before the darkness surrounded me. That's all I can remember."

"That doesn't sound like too bad of a dream. Do you think you will be able to get back to sleep?" Zoey stretched out next to Sophie to comfort her while she slept.

"I'm already back asleep," Sophie mumbled to Zoey as she rolled over, closed her eyes and pulled the blanket up to her chin.

Zoey on the other hand wasn't ready to fall back to sleep. She recalled Sophie saying she possibly had the ability to dream about the future. "Sophie may have had a dream about a potential danger to herself. But, what did the dream mean?" Something about Sophie's dream really concerned Zoey. After several hours of trying to figure out what bothered her about Sophie's dream, Zoey succumbed to sleep.

Helen woke Sophie the next morning with breakfast and her morning song. "You need to hurry today. Mr. Fitzpatrice is in one of his moods and is anxious to get started with your lesson."

Sophie ate a few bites of her French toast and took a drink from the cup on her tray. She looked at Helen with a confused expression on her face.

Helen smiled at Sophie. "Sorry, we are out of hot chocolate. Today you are going to have to make due with milk."

"I have to stop at the bank before I head to the store this afternoon. And I can't forget to buy bread, milk, cheese and chocolate."

"What did you say Helen?" Sophie asked.

"I didn't say anything, why?"

Sophie wrinkled her brow. "Oh, I thought you said something about going to the bank and the store to buy bread, milk, cheese and chocolate. I must be hearing things."

"Yes, you are young lady. I didn't say anything about going to the store or the bank, at least not out loud," Helen thought to herself.

"Did you hear me say anything else?" Helen asked.

"No, I just thought I heard you say something about going to the store and the bank, but I guess I was wrong," Sophie replied.

"Has this happened often, that you think you hear things, but no one is saying anything?"

"I don't remember this happening in the past. No, this has never happened to me before. I had a bad dream last night. This morning I'm probably just feeling the after effects of a restless night sleep. You must think I'm losing my mind. Even I think I'm losing my mind."

Helen moved closer to Sophie and patted her on the shoulder. "It's all right Sophie, I'm sure you will feel better after you finish your breakfast."

"I think something deeper is going on here," Helen said to herself as she used her skills to block Sophie from reading her mind. "I need to speak to Mrs. MacTavish about this. We are going to have to start watching Sophie more closely. It is starting to look like she has inherited some of her mother's abilities."

Sophie got dressed and looked at the clock. Helen had woken her up a little earlier than normal. "Why did Helen tell her to hurry when she still had a little over thirty minutes before her lesson started?"

Sophie crawled back in bed to read for a little while before she headed downstairs for her lesson.

Sophie walked into the library and was just about to take her seat when the clock on the mantle struck seven. She couldn't believe Mr. Fitzpatrice insisted on starting his lessons so early in the morning.

"You are late again!" Mr. Fitzpatice scolded in his high-pitched voice. He really sounded annoyed today.

"Sorry I am not in my seat, but I am on time. The clock just struck seven." Sophie walked over to the table to sit next to Sean.

Sean whispered in Sophie's ear. "You really are late today. We were supposed to start our lesson thirty minutes earlier."

Sophie looked at Sean bewildered. "I didn't know. No one told me."

"Can she ever make it to a lesson on time? This is getting a little tiresome," Mr. Fitzpatrice thought as he turned to write on the blackboard.

"No need to be rude Mr. Fitzpatrice," Sophie said defensively. "I said I'm sorry and I didn't know we were starting our lessons early today."

Mr. Fitzpatrice continued to stare at Sophie. "Pardon me young lady. I did not say anything to you."

Sophie looked confused, "I…I… thought I just heard you say something to me."

"Well, you are mistaken young lady! I said nothing and you should learn to be polite. Especially, when you are the one in the wrong," Mr. Fitzpatrice scolded.

Sean looked at Sophie with a strange expression on his face. "What's wrong Sophie? I am concerned about you. Mr. Fitzpatrice hasn't said anything since you sat down."

Sophie rubbed her forehead. "I don't know Sean, but my head is starting to hurt. I think I need to return to the ForEverNever, now. My grandfather said this might happen. Please help me figure out a way to get out of here."

"I have a feeling Mr. Fitzpatrice isn't going to let you out of here until the morning lesson is over."

"Sean, I really have to get out of here, now. My head is killing me and I think my grandfather is the only one who can help me."

"Ok…ok, let me think." Sean grabbed his stomach. "I have an idea." Sean started to moan. "My stomach, my stomach, it hurts. I think I'm going to be sick. I know I am going to be sick." He ran to the trash can.

Mr. Fitzpatrice rushed over to check on Sean. Sophie jumped at the opportunity. "I'll go get help." She leaned down and whispered in Sean's ear, so Mr. Fitzpatrice couldn't hear her. "Thank you!"

Sophie ran out of the library yelling. "Helen, Helen, I think Sean is going to be sick." Instead of heading towards the kitchen where she suspected Helen was, Sophie hurried up the stairs to her bedroom. She felt a little dizzy and her head hurt terribly by the time she got to her room. Thankfully, there was still a glass of water on her breakfast tray. Sophie hoped that if she drank some water the ache in her head would go away.

Zoey jumped off the bed. "What are you doing back here? Aren't you supposed to be in your morning lesson with Mr. Fitzpatrice? He is going to be really irritated, if you miss another lesson."

"I have to make a quick trip to the ForEverNever." Sophie grabbed her shoes and an extra pair of socks, and sat on her bed. With her head already hurting, she really wasn't going to enjoy this trip to the ForEverNever.

She carefully put on the socks and both shoes. Immediately after the second shoe was placed on her foot, she closed her eyes and held her breath. She could hear the buzzing and feel her body shifting as it transitioned through space.

Sophie knew she couldn't deal with the bright lights, so just to be safe she counted to one hundred before she opened her eyes. After her eyes cleared, Sophie looked up and realized she was right where she wanted to be, on the path leading up to Polleux's meadow. She was glad the walk up to Polleux's meadow wasn't very far because her head continued to pound.

Polleux saw Sophie stumbling up the hill and ran over to the fence to meet her. Looking at Sophie, Polleux was concerned. Sophie was really pale. "Hi young lady. Is everything ok?"

"I'm not quite sure. My head really hurts and I have been having strange, for lack of a better word, interactions with people. I think I hear them say things they aren't really saying. When I ask them about what they said, they give me strange looks. I suspect I am really hearing things they are thinking, not what they are saying. The odd thing is I can't tell the difference. My grandfather told me that if this happened, I needed to let him know right away."

Polleux was about to ask a question, when he was interrupted by a loud whistling sound. Polleux and Sophie looked down the hill and saw Simeon walking briskly up. He continued to whistle until he reached them.

"Glad to see you! What brings you here so early?" Polleux asked Simeon.

Simeon looked at his watch and then at Sophie. He was still glad he decided to pick up the fashionable item when he was on Earth all those years ago.

"I saw Sophie appear in the meadow, so I decided to head over early. What brings you back so soon?" Simeon asked Sophie.

Sophie was hesitant to talk about what she had experienced, but she trusted Simeon and Polleux. "I believe I have been hearing other's thoughts. I keep getting odd looks. I also have a terrible headache. We need to go find my grandfather."

"The headache is to be expected, but everything will be okay. Let's go to my house and I will fix a tonic for you that will help your head. Your grandfather knows you are in the ForEverNever. Once we reach my house, I will send him a message asking him to meet us there."

Sophie let out a little moan and grabbed her head again. Her headache was getting worse and she wanted the pain to stop. Sophie shut her eyes hoping if she blocked out the light, the pain would lessen, or at least wouldn't get any worse.

"We should go now," Polleux said.

"You aren't going to hear any objections from me." Simeon picked up Sophie and put her on Polleux's back.

"Sophie, grab a hold of Polleux's mane," Simeon yelled as he jumped on behind Sophie and grabbed onto her. "We are ready, Polleux, let's go."

Polleux took off running while Simeon held on tightly to Sophie. "We are good back here. You can go a little faster."

Polleux picked up speed and within moments they were out in front of Simeon's house. Simeon jumped off Polleux's back then helped Sophie down. Simeon and Sophie left Polleux at the fence and headed into the house.

"No need to worry. My grandmother is not home. You can sit at the table in the kitchen, while I mix the tonic. I just need to get seven Zumberries, a little honey, some water and a pinch of salt." Simeon poured the ingredients in a big pot on the stove.

"Don't worry, Sophie, it won't take long and your grandfather should be here before the tonic is ready." Simeon lit the stove and started to mix the ingredients.

"What is that horrible smell?" Sophie asked in a faint voice as she pinched her nose.

"It's the Zumberries. Don't worry it tastes much better than it smells, and with the honey and a pinch of salt, some even like the taste of the tonic."

Sophie crinkled her face. "I'll have to take your word on that one! What is a Zumberry, anyway? I have never heard of them." She pinched her nose again. "And thankfully I never had to smell them before."

Simeon raised his hand so Sophie could see the oddly oval shaped green berry with small yellow and red spots. "This is a Zumberry. They are very rare and can only be found in the Helo Mountains here in the ForEverNever. The Helo Mountains are some distance from here. After you spoke with your grandfather during your last visit, he let me know that you may have the ability to hear others' thoughts. Your mother realized she could hear others' thoughts within days after she learned she could speak to animals. As soon as your grandfather told me of his suspicions, Polleux and I took a trip out to Helo Mountain. I collected a whole basket of Zumberries, just in case your grandfather's suspicions were right."

"The rumor is someone has a bad headache." Sophie heard her grandfather's loud booming voice from behind her.

"Ohhhh! I'm dizzy." Sophie's hands instinctively flew to her head as it began to spin even worse. She lifted her head to greet her grandfather. "Grandfather, I think you were right. I can hear other individuals' thoughts. And I do have a horrible headache. Simeon is making me a tonic. He says it will make my head feel better, but it smells awful."

"Here, give it a try." Simeon held out a cup of the greenish, brown tonic for Sophie to drink. "If you want your headache to go away, you need to drink the whole cup."

Sophie grabbed the cup from Simeon and crinkled her face again. She really didn't want to drink the foul smelling liquid. A thick steam rose from the greenish, brown, gooey liquid. Sophie lightly shook the cup back and forth, causing several odd looking brown and black clumps to make their way to the surface.

"I guess I better drink this…quickly, in as few gulps as possible." Sophie pinched her nose and gulped down the tonic. Surprisingly, Simeon was right. Thankfully the tonic tasted much better than it smelled.

Sophie's grandfather reassured her. "Give it about thirty minutes and your head should start to feel better. Now, tell me about your experiences of hearing others' thoughts."

"Just this morning, I heard Helen and my tutor, Mr. Fitzpatrice's thoughts. I made some comments to them in response to the things I thought they said. Helen told me she had not said anything and Sean told me Mr. Fitzpatrice hadn't said a word."

"Yes, it sounds like you have inherited your mother's ability of hearing others' thoughts." Sophie's grandfather seemed pleased. "You need to learn how to control your ability or you may end up with a permanent headache. Simeon and I will teach you, but right now, you really need to head home."

"Yes, I should be getting home. Sean is probably really worried about me."

"When you get home, you need to spend the remainder of the day resting. You also need to return to Polleux's meadow early tomorrow, so we can begin your lessons."

They all headed back outside and Simeon jumped on Polleux's back. He reached down, grabbed Sophie's hand and pulled her up in front of him.

"Your trip home is going to bother your head a little more than normal. Remember to keep your eyes closed," Sophie's grandfather boomed as Polleux took off down the road.

Polleux moved a little slower heading back to his meadow than he did getting to Simeon's house. Simeon held on tightly to Sophie, who was enjoying the ride back even though she was growing very tired.

Once they reached the meadow Simeon jumped off Polleux's back and reached up to help Sophie down. "Remember what your grandfather told you. You need to rest this afternoon. See you tomorrow morning, first thing, your time." Simeon winked at Sophie.

Sophie looked at Simeon and tried not to smile, but the expression on his face looked so silly she couldn't help herself. She walked over to Polleux, gave him a hug and thanked him for his help. She then sat down on the grass to take off her shoes.

"What about my thanks?" Simeon yelled as he walked over to Sophie.

"Oh! Thanks to you too," Sophie grinned. She proceeded to carefully take off one of her shoes. Tightly holding the shoe against her chest she reached out to take off her other shoe. As soon as she had a tight hold on her other shoe, Sophie closed her eyes. She didn't see the flashing light or the colored orbs, but she did hear the buzzing. She started to hum to herself and continued to keep her eyes closed until she finished the song. When Sophie finally opened her eyes, she was sitting on the floor in the middle of her bedroom.

Zoey barked and ran circles around her. Once she was confident Sophie was not going to disappear again, Zoey sat down on the floor next to her. "How are you feeling? Were you able to see your grandfather? Could he help you?"

"I am doing much better. Simeon gave me a tonic to help with my headache. I saw my grandfather. He and Simeon are going to help me learn how to use my ability to hear others' thoughts." Sophie rubbed Zoey's back.

"Are you able to hear everyone's thoughts or just some individuals? Can you hear my thoughts?" Zoey asked as she curled up her lip in an attempt to smile.

Sophie laughed and thought to herself. "It seems talking isn't enough for Zoey, now she thinks she can smile."

"I am not sure how this all works, or if in time, I will be able to hear everyone's thoughts. I just know occasionally others' thoughts pop into my head. And I think I have heard your thoughts once or twice," Sophie teased as she continued to rub Zoey's back.

"I need to find Sean. Have you seen him today? Do you have any idea where he might be?"

"I think he mentioned something about going to his room to do some eye exercises."

Sophie slowly stood up. "I think I better go find him and let him know that I am fine. Then I am going to climb into bed and go to sleep for the rest of the day."

With my new friends and being able to spend time with my father again, the days are getting a little easier. Although, I still miss my mother terribly. I am so glad I have learned about who she was and where she came from. To get to spend time with Simeon and Polleux is a wonderful gift that I'm grateful for every day. And there are no words to express how thankful I am to have gotten to meet my grandfather and the mirror image of my mother. Although I was hurt and angered by my father's decision to move us here to Dublin, I'm beginning to realize it was one of the best things for us. If we had not moved here, I would have never learned who I am, the granddaughter of a Faerie King. And I certainly would have had no one to teach me about my abilities.

- Sophie St. Clair

xx : Gifts Come to Light

Sophie knocked loudly on Sean's door. Sean pulled the door open quickly after the first knock. "Sophie, it's you. I was hoping it was you."

Sean looked down at Zoey. "And I see you are being followed by your constant companion."

Sophie followed Sean's gaze and saw Zoey sitting at her feet. Sophie affectionately patted her on the head.

"Are you talking about Zoey? She is not around all the time," Sophie teased.

"May we come in?"

"Sure thing!" Sean opened his door further and stepped aside so they could enter the room. Sophie could see he had a piece of string attached to the bookcase on the other side of the room.

"You were doing your eye exercises weren't you?" Sophie said enthusiastically. "Would you like me to come back?"

"No, I am glad you are here. I was worried about you. Are you feeling better?"

"I am feeling a lot better, thanks for asking."

Zoey found a comfortable spot on the rug in the middle of Sean's floor to lie down. Sometimes she really liked being a dog; she could rest anywhere.

Sophie asked if she could try the string, eye exercise, again. While Sean handed her the string, Sophie couldn't help but remember how he really helped her out earlier in the day. Although he sometimes annoyed her, Sophie was learning she could count on him. Sophie was glad she could call Sean her friend.

"Do you remember what you are supposed to do?"

"Sure do," Sophie replied as she pulled the string to her nose.

"Easy, peasy!" Sophie smiled at Sean. She really enjoyed the challenge of the string exercise.

"Looks good! Pretty soon, I'll show you how to add different head positions. But, right now, you really look tired. You should head to bed."

"You're right, I am very tired. I just wanted to thank you again for your help today. I couldn't have gotten past Mr. Fitzpatrice without your quick thinking." Sophie turned to walk out of Sean's room.

Before she made it through the door, Sean expressed his relief. "I am really glad you are feeling better."

"Thanks," Sophie replied as she stopped at the door and turned around. "Oh, and I just want to let you know that if I don't make our morning lesson tomorrow, I am okay. I just returned to the ForEverNever."

"Now I've told someone," Sophie winked at Sean and quickly turned and walked out of the room before he could say another word.

———————————————————————————————————

Sophie left Sean's room and walked slowly to hers. She noticed Zoey was close to her heals the whole way. She thought, "Maybe Zoey is my constant companion. I'm so glad my father gave her to me."

Sophie was exhausted. As soon as she reached her room, she crawled into bed and turned off the light. Zoey jumped up on the bed to lie down next to her. "Goodnight, Sophie. Sleep well."

"You too," Sophie said as she pulled the blanket up to her chin.

Later that night Sophie started to roll in her sleep, kicking her legs and punching her arms. "No!" She yelled, waking Zoey from a sound sleep. Zoey looked over at Sophie and realized she was still asleep. Sophie yelled out again "No! Please let me go."

Zoey inched closer to Sophie rubbing her nose against Sophie's face. Sophie began to toss her head from side to side. Zoey rubbed her nose against Sophie's face again. Sophie slowly opened her eyes and gently pushed Zoey away. "What is it Zoey?"

"You were yelling in your sleep. Is everything ok?

Sophie sat up and rubbed her eyes. "I think so. I must have had another bad dream."

"Do you remember anything about the dream?"

Still half asleep, Sophie wrinkled her eyebrows trying to remember. "I think someone was trying to grab me. I saw darkness and water, but I cannot remember any more."

Zoey yawned. "Well, dream about something fun and let's go back to sleep. It's still dark out. There are still a few hours before morning."

Sophie instantly fell back to sleep. Zoey nestled at her side, but had trouble falling back to sleep. She spent hours racking her brain for any possible dangers she had seen or heard about that could affect Sophie. Exhausted she finally fell back to sleep.

Several hours later, as the morning sun shone through the bedroom window, Helen entered Sophie's room, breakfast tray in hand. Helen called Sophie's name but she didn't wake up. Helen placed Sophie's breakfast on the table then gently shook her arm. "Sophie, it's time to wake up. You need to get ready for your morning lesson."

Sophie slowly opened her eyes and stretched her arms above her head. "I am not feeling very well this morning. I think I am just going to stay in bed for a little while longer." Sophie rolled over, pulled up the blanket, and closed her eyes.

"Please let Mr. Fitzpatrice know I will miss his lesson," Sophie mumbled at Helen from under her blanket.

Zoey opened her eyes and briefly lifted her head off the blanket. Helen's attempts to wake Sophie were of no interest to her. She turned over on her side and went back to sleep.

"Sophie sick? That child is as healthy as an ox," Helen thought to herself as she walked towards the door.

Sophie heard Helen's thoughts and said out loud, "I may not be sick, but I had a horrible headache last night and my stomach is still a little upset."

Helen smiled as she turned around and looked directly at Sophie. She just had her confirmation. Sophie had inherited her mother's ability to hear others' thoughts.

"In case you were wondering, your shoes are in the corner near your door," Helen said with a wink. "And I left your breakfast on the table. It's the usual. There's even hot chocolate today."

Although many years had past, Helen still remembered how bad the headaches were when she began involuntarily hearing other's thoughts. Her headaches lasted for weeks until she learned how to control her ability. She rarely listened to others' thoughts now. To her it was an invasion of privacy. Maybe it was time to start up again.

———————————————————————————

To Zoey's surprise and delight, Sophie went back to sleep for a few hours. Zoey was more than a little concerned by Sophie's dreams. She wished Sophie could remember more of the details. "I'm going to have to keep a closer eye on Sophie," Zoey thought as she closed her eyes to get a little more rest.

Sophie woke up, for the second time that morning and stretched her arms above her head. She knew she was going to have to get up this time. Her grandfather and Simeon may already be waiting for her in Polleux's meadow. She got dressed, making sure to put on several pairs of socks and walked over to the table where her breakfast sat completely untouched. She was starving and her stomach was growling. "I guess that's what you get when you miss breakfast."

Sophie sat at the table to eat. She poured a little syrup on her French toast and took a sip of the hot chocolate. She discovered the French toast and hot chocolate were no longer hot.

Sophie's stomach growled again as she took a large bite of French toast. She was hungry and tried to ignore the fact that all her food was now cold. The cold "hot" chocolate wasn't too bad.

"It's not popcorn, your favorite, but I know you also really like bacon. Enjoy!" Sophie smiled as she left two pieces of bacon on the floor for Zoey.

Sophie finished the glass of water that was sitting on the table and looked at Zoey with an expression that said, "all done."

She grabbed her shoes from the corner by the door. "I'm glad Helen told me where these were, it would have taken me awhile to find them."

She held the shoes close to her chest. She was ready and eager to return to the ForEverNever. She didn't want to keep her grandfather and Simeon waiting any longer and her head was already starting to hurt a little.

Zoey was still in bed, trying to get a few more minutes of rest.

"I am getting ready to put on my shoes Zoey. I will see you later today." Sophie looked at Zoey and waved goodbye.

Zoey sat up and watched as Sophie put on her right then her left shoe.

"Here it goes again!" Zoey watched as a bright light flashed across the room. She heard the slight buzzing noise get a little louder. The red, blue, purple, green, orange and yellow orbs appeared in the room. As Zoey admired the colored orbs, Sophie began to fade in and out. She appeared one more time then completely disappeared.

Sophie closed her eyes, which had become her habit when traveling to the ForEverNever. However, she still didn't know how to block out the buzzing sounds. Holding her hands over her ears had no effect. When the buzzing stopped Sophie opened her eyes. She was at the bottom of the hill leading to Polleux's meadow. She looked up and saw Simeon, her grandfather and Polleux waiting for her. Sophie walked towards them.

"What took you so long?" Simeon yelled down to Sophie. "We have been waiting for you for some time now."

"Sorry, I was still recovering from my headache this morning and I found it a little difficult to get out of bed. My headache is also starting to return.

"I thought that might happen." Simeon grinned as he held up a steaming cup. "That's why I brought you some of this."

"More Zumberries? Yuck!" Sophie made a sour expression and stuck out her tongue.

"If I have to, I guess I will drink more of this stuff. But, that doesn't mean I have to like it." Sophie stuck her nose in the air and looked at Simeon. She pinched her nose and downed the smelly mixture in three gulps.

Sophie made a few gagging sounds and looked directly at Simeon with blazing eyes.

Simeon shrugged, "Don't look at me like that. I am here to help get rid of your headaches."

Sophie looked away ignoring him.

Sophie's grandfather boomed, "Your head should start feeling better in about 15 minutes. Then Simeon will start with your training."

"Sorry, I am going to miss your first lesson. I need to return to the castle; there is something I must take care of. I guess I must assume some responsibility along with the title," he winked at Sophie.

"Come here Sophie girl, and give me a hug. I will see you soon, promise."

Sophie walked over and gave her grandfather a big hug. "You better. I enjoy spending time with you."

She gave her grandfather another hug and walked towards Simeon. She wobbled a little as she approached him. "Are you ready to begin?"

"I am, but I don't think you are." Simeon reached out to stabilize Sophie after she stumbled. "I think you should sit down and give the tonic a few minutes to take effect. Stay here with Polleux. I need to go get you something to eat. Once that tonic starts to work you will be very hungry and you will not be able to focus on your lesson. I will be back shortly, just in time for your head to start feeling better."

Simeon winked at Sophie and set off down the dirt path whistling.

"But, I just ate," Sophie yelled after Simeon. However, he seemed not to hear her over his whistling.

"Young lady just close your eyes and rest," Polleux said in a soft voice. "I will be standing close by and will not allow anything to happen to you. With me here, you have nothing to worry about." Polleux nudged Sophie with his nose.

"I think that is a great idea." Sophie closed her eyes and breathed deeply.

"Would you like me to sing to you? I don't have the greatest voice, but I have received a few compliments over the years."

"That's okay Polleux, no songs are necessary. I really just want to rest my eyes."

With her eyes closed Sophie shook her head. "Not only am I talking to a horse, but now he wants to sing to me as well. My friends back in New York would never believe this. Sometimes I even find it hard to believe all this is happening to me."

"Well, if you don't want me to sing, how about letting me entertain you with some jokes."

"You don't give up easily. Just one joke, then I really would like to just sit here in peace and quiet with my eyes closed for a while."

"If one joke is all I get, then I better make it a good one. Let's see... got it! Why couldn't the pony sing?"

"I don't know, why?"

"Because he was a little horse," Polleux laughed.

Sophie stared at Polleux not knowing what to say. It wasn't exactly a horrible joke, but she had heard better. However, when she looked at the expression on Polleux's face, Sophie couldn't help but laugh.

"At least Polleux was trying to poke fun at something he knew a little about, horses," she thought and as she reached up to rub Polleux's leg. "Thanks for trying to make me feel better."

"You are welcome. But my joke really wasn't that funny was it. I am trying to work on my sense of humor, but I don't have anyone to practice on."

Now, Sophie truly laughed, thinking of this noble horse, the epitome of formality, trying to mix a little comedy in his life. Simple jokes didn't exactly fit him. If he wanted to add more humor to his life a few sophisticated jokes were more apt to suit him. Sophie would keep Polleux's goal in mind in case she ever heard a joke she thought would suit him.

Moments later, Sophie felt someone shake her arm. She slowly opened her eyes and saw Simeon staring down at her. "I must have fallen asleep. Simeon, how long have you been back?"

"I just got back and I brought you some soup and bread to eat. I thought something light would be best for you, since you just ate breakfast." Simeon winked.

Sophie rolled her eyes. "He really thinks he's funny."

"Here, have something to drink before you have a bite of soup." Simeon held up a canteen for Sophie to take a drink. "And I'm chivalrous as well as funny," Simeon proclaimed in response to Sophie's thought about his lack of humor.

Simeon lifted the canteen to Sophie's lips for her to take a sip. Sophie took a few sips of water and motioned with her hand she had enough.

Sophie then held the soup up to her lips to see how hot it was. "Prefect." She dipped the bread into the soup and took a small bite. "This tastes great! What's in it?"

"You really don't want to know." Simeon grinned at Sophie.

"More teasing," Sophie thought. "I better not push for an answer."

"Feeling any better?" Simeon asked.

"Yes, much better. Thanks for the soup!" Sophie finished her last bite of soup and smiled at Simeon.

"Now, we are both ready to begin your first lesson."

Simeon helped Sophie up and led her to the middle of Polleux's meadow. "Stand still and take a few deep breathes."

Sophie closed her eyes and breathed in deeply about ten times. "Now you need to clear your mind," Simeon spoke softly.

"What is it about clearing my mind? My Martial Arts instructor told me to do the same thing."

"I guess you can do a lot with a clear mind." Simeon laughed.

Sophie glared at Simeon. "You know, you really aren't that funny."

"Ok, but in all seriousness it is very important that you clear your mind and focus on your breathing. This will help you learn how to block out others' thoughts."

Sophie was surprised. "I assumed these lessons were about me learning how to hear others' thoughts, not block them out."

"The most important thing you need to learn about hearing others' thoughts is how to block them out."

Simeon gave Sophie a very serious look. "If you cannot learn how to block others' thoughts, you will never get rid of your headaches. After you have mastered blocking out others' thoughts, I will teach you how to purposefully hear others' thoughts at will. Having a clear mind also helps to mentally connect with those you wish to connect. It will be a while before you are ready to mentally connect with others with abilities similar to yours and have a conversation without even saying a word."

Simeon continued. "Have you cleared your mind and blocked out all other sounds?"

Sophie kept her eyes closed and nodded her head, yes, in response.

"Good! Now open your eyes and look at me. Focus only on me. Block all other images from your mind. Continue to focus on me until I am the only thing you see and my image starts to go a little blurry. You should see me, but it should feel like you are looking through me. Do you understand what I am saying?"

Sophie was so intently focused on his image that she could only respond by shaking her head.

"You are getting it." Simeon was impressed how fast she was learning.

"Continue to focus on my voice and note how it sounds. It is loud and clear, right?" Simeon looked at Sophie for confirmation. Again she responded by simply shaking her head.

"Now, try to focus on my voice a little more intently. Listen to the sounds I am making and note the sound you hear when I pause...like now." Simeon repeated. "It is very important you focus...on the...pauses."

"You can stop focusing now," Simeon thought. He walked towards Sophie hoping his movement would break her intense focus. She was almost in a trance like state.

Somewhat startled and slightly off balance Sophie asked "What did you say?"

"I did not say anything," Simeon replied. "Do you hear the difference between the sound of what I am saying now and the statement you just thought you heard me say?"

"Yes, I do hear a difference," Sophie responded in a surprised voice. "What you are saying now sounds much clearer and there was no faint humming or static sound when you paused in the middle of your sentence."

"Bingo! That is exactly correct and you just heard my thought. When you hear others' thoughts the sound is not as clear and pronounced as when you hear them speak. Also when you are listening to others' thoughts, you will hear a slight static sound when there is a pause in their thoughts, because their mind is still working to develop their next thought. To successfully hear the change in tone and the faint humming or static sound you must block everything else out and be solely focused on the individual's thoughts you want to hear."

Sophie started rubbing her head and sat down on the grass. Polleux walked over and stood next to her. He nudged Sophie's hand with his nose. Sophie continued to rub her head and closed her eyes. "My head is really starting to hurt again."

"That is to be expected young lady, this is all new to you." Polleux rubbed Sophie with his nose again. "Once you practice and you are used to hearing others' thoughts, the effort and the intrusion in your brain of another's thoughts will no longer cause your head to hurt."

Simeon proclaimed, "You are doing great! Now that you learned what it sounds like when you are hearing another's thoughts, I will teach you how to the block the noise and thoughts when you hear them involuntarily. It's very simple."

"Right, very simple," Sophie said sarcastically.

"Yes, it is. You focus on everything else around you except for the individual's thoughts you are hearing. If you are indoors, focus on the noise; don't focus on the individual speaking. Listen to the ticking of the clock or the sound of someone walking. If you are outside, intently listen to the animals and the sounds of nature. Purposefully, block out unwanted thoughts in your head and intently focus on other noises. This will help you break the connection to the individual whose thoughts somehow made their way into your head."

Sophie looked at Simeon with a blank stare and rubbed her head. She felt her head start to hurt again, but this time it wasn't from someone else's thoughts, it was because of all Simeon was telling her.

"No need to worry Sophie," Simeon said in a calming voice. "It isn't as difficult as it seems. With a little practice the only thoughts you are going to hear are the ones you want to hear. But I think that is enough for today. You should be going home."

"I think you are right. It is probably almost evening at Evanswood. Someone is bound to check on me soon, if they haven't already."

"After today's lesson you will need a little break. I want you to rest this evening and return in three days. Tomorrow you can continue your lessons with Mr. Fitzpatrice and your Martial Arts lessons."

"I will return here in three days. However, since time passes differently in my world than your world, how will you know when it is the third day?"

Simeon held up his wrist and pointed at his watch. "Thankfully, I have this. Remember, it keeps time with the time in your world. With the help of this nifty little gadget and a few marks on a piece of paper, I will know when it is the third day."

Sophie rubbed Polleux's head as he nudged her to say goodbye. She then took off the shoe on her right foot.

"Wait!" Simeon yelled. "You can't leave without this." He reached into his pocket and pulled out a small blue thermos.

"More Zumberry tonic?"

"Yes! You need to drink a cup before you go to bed tonight and another cup tomorrow morning."

Sophie looked at Simeon's pocket and a puzzled look came over her face. Simeon's pocket didn't look large enough to hold the thermos.

"Don't look so surprised," Simeon laughed. "Don't you remember, sometimes things that I need just show up in my pocket. It's another one of my many powers."

Sophie started to roll her eyes at Simeon. Then she thought about all he had done for her throughout the morning. "Thank you for all your help today." Sophie smiled up at Simeon.

She then tucked the thermos under her arm, held on tightly to her right shoe, closed her eyes and took off her left shoe. She waited for a few moments then heard the buzzing sound. Although her eyes were closed, Sophie could still sense she was moving. She could feel herself physically transfer from the ForEverNever back to Earth. Sophie opened her eyes and found herself sitting on the floor in her bedroom. The first thing she saw when she was able to focus her eyes was Zoey sitting on the floor next to her.

"Welcome back! Did you learn anything?"

Sophie heard Zoey speaking to her and found it a little odd that she could hear animals speak without it affecting her head, but listening to other human or Faerie thoughts gave her a horrible headache. She was going to have to remember to ask Simeon why hearing animals didn't bother her, but hearing human and Faerie thoughts did.

"Simeon taught me a few things and gave me this to help with my headache." Sophie held up the blue thermos. She opened the lid to show Zoey the liquid inside.

"What is that horrible smell?" Zoey scrunched up her nose.

"It's the Zumberries." Sophie laughed. They are very rare and are good for headaches."

"But it smells really, really bad. How can you drink that stuff?"

"It tastes much better than it smells. I am supposed to drink a cup tonight and another cup tomorrow. Although, I have to admit I am thinking about dumping the whole thermos down the sink, but I really don't want my headache to come back."

"Well then, I guess you have to drink that awful smelling stuff. I think there is still a cup on the table near the window."

Sophie sat down in a chair and set the thermos on the table. She placed the cup in front of her, lifted the thermos and attempted to pour the Zumberry tonic into the cup without spilling a drop. A brown, greenish vapor like substance filled the air around the cup as Sophie poured some of the contents from the thermos into the cup.

Sophie finished the tonic in her cup and changed for bed. "Are you going to bed now?" Zoey asked. "It's still a little early."

"I know, but Simeon said I needed to rest when I got home. Tomorrow I have another Martial Arts lesson." Sophie crawled into bed. Zoey jumped up on the bed with her.

"I hope she has a restful night sleep," Zoey thought, "with no bad dreams."

Although, I don't know much about her, I can tell she is very special. Sophie caught on very quickly on how to quiet her mind. She must take after her mother in that regard. I remember how difficult it was for her father to learn how to clear his mind and anticipate what others would do. But, boy could he fight. I suspect she got her fighting spirit from her father. From the first day I met him, I knew William St.. Clair pulled for the underdog and was willing to sacrifice a lot, especially a few bruises, for those in need. I am honored to call him "friend," and glad to have this opportunity to help him. I am also glad to have this opportunity to get to know his daughter, Sophie. I know there is something great in her future.

- Sadao Kimoto

xxi : Martial Arts Lesson Two

Rays from the sun shone brightly into Sophie's room. She rolled over in her bed and stretched her arms. As Sophie moved to sit up, Zoey woke up. "Any bad dreams?"

"No bad dreams. I had a wonderful, restful night of sleep."

Sophie stretched again. "It must be really early; Helen hasn't been here yet."

Sophie got out of bed and dressed for the day. She made her way to the dining room for breakfast. The food was set out on a side table under the window. Sophie was surprised no one else was in the dining room. She finished her breakfast and headed into the library for her morning lesson.

"No one is here either. I guess I am a little early." Sophie looked up at the clock. "Looks like I have about 20 minutes before the lesson begins."

Sophie then noticed that the image at the bottom of the clock was of a bear resting in a cave, which was the same as the day her morning less started a little earlier. This image was different than the image of the rooster, which was at the bottom of the clock when she saw it the morning of her first lesson. She walked over to get a better look at the clock. She touched the image at the bottom of the clock and it moved slightly. "It looks that the inner piece of the bottom of the clock with the image on it may turn."

Confident that she had discovered how the image at the bottom of the clock kept changing, Sophie grabbed a book off one of the shelves and sat down at the table in front of the blackboard to read. "Mr. Fitzpatrice is going to be surprised I am reading, Yeats. And he will be shocked to discover I made it to a lesson early."

Some time later, Sean walked in the library and saw Sophie sitting at the table. "What are you doing here?"

Sophie was so engrossed in her book she didn't hear Sean enter. Startled by his voice, she slightly jumped in her seat and quickly turned around to see him smiling at her.

"Helen said you were not in your room when she went to check on you this morning. I thought you might be down here. I guess you didn't hear that we aren't having our morning lessons for a few days."

Sophie looked at Sean confused. "What do you mean? Mr. Fitzpatrice was so concerned we were behind schedule."

"After you missed our lesson yesterday, Mr. Fitzpatrice told your father he couldn't take it anymore. He was tired of you being late and missing lessons. He had enough and was leaving the city for a few days. I think he just needs a little time; then he will be back to normal, and you will have the opportunity to listen to him squeak, I mean speak all you want." Sean winked at Sophie.

"What about our Martial Arts lesson, do we still have that today?"

"Sure do!" Sean replied. "Are you ready to spend an hour or so clearing your mind?"

Sophie laughed. Sean had no idea how much time she had spent over the last few days learning how to clear her mind. "What time do we need to be outside to catch our ride?"

"The driver will be here to pick us up at the same time as before. You have a few hours before we need to leave. I am going to head back up to my room and work on my eye exercises."

"Can I join you? Now that you've interrupted me, I don't think I can get back into this." Sophie held up the book for Sean to see, and huffed teasingly.

"You seem to be feeling much better today. I am glad."

"I am feeling much better. Thank you for noticing. Which reminds me, I must get something from my bedroom. I'll meet you in your room when I am done, if that is ok?"

Sean just shook his head, yes. "See you in a few."

Sophie returned to her room and noticed Zoey was still in bed. "Are you having a lie-in today?"

Zoey barely looked at Sophie, rolled over to the other side of the bed and tried to go back to sleep. "I guess that answers my question."

Sophie ignored Zoey's efforts to go back to sleep and continued to talk. "Just so you know my morning lesson with Mr. Fitzpatrice was cancelled. I still have my Martial Arts lesson and I am going to practice eye exercises with Sean until it is time to leave for our Martial Arts lesson. I just come back here to drink another cup of my Zumberry tonic."

Sophie poured the remainder of the tonic into her cup from yesterday.

"Not that horrible smell again?" Zoey stretched her back. "All I wanted to do was get a few more hours of sleep before I headed off with you to your Martial Arts lesson. What does a dog have to do around here to get left in peace, and not woken by horrible smells?"

"I am sorry Zoey, but you know I have to drink this stuff for my head. Thankfully, this is my last cup. Fingers crossed I don't get any headaches over the next few days."

Sophie finished the tonic and put her cup back on the table. Zoey just looked at Sophie. "Now that the awful smell is gone, I am going back to bed. I will meet you downstairs when it is time to leave for your Martial Arts lesson. Enjoy the eye exercises."

Zoey rolled back over and closed her eyes.

Sophie left her room quietly. She didn't close her door, so Zoey could leave the room whenever she woke up.

When Sophie got to Sean's room he was standing in the middle of it with a string pulled tightly to his noise. "There you are. I'm almost done. I was starting to think you weren't going to show up."

"I wouldn't miss the string exercise for anything," Sophie said with a wink. "It's my fa-vor-ite."

Sean handed Sophie the string. "Go for it. It is all yours."

Sophie spent about fifteen minutes looking up and down at different spots on the string.

After Sean and Sophie had several turns with the string exercise Sean advised, "We should probably head downstairs to meet the driver soon. He may be a little testy if he has to wait for us. You want to stop by the kitchen to get a snack before we leave for our Martial Arts lesson?"

Sean moved his hands back and forth in a chopping motion to emphasis the Martial Arts lesson part of the question. He thought about kicking out his leg, but decided against it.

Sophie laughed at Sean's antics. "That's a great idea!" Sophie rubbed her stomach. "Plus, I think Cook made cookies this morning. I'll beat you down stairs." Sophie dropped the string and ran towards the door.

Thirty minutes later, with a full stomach of cookies, Sophie and Sean were waiting out in front of the house to be picked up for their lesson. Within minutes a big black car pulled up to the curb in front of the house. This time the driver didn't get out of the car to open the door, so Sean opened it.

"Good morning," Sophie smiled at the driver. "Thanks for picking us up."

"Like I had a choice," the driver mumbled under his breath.

Traffic was light. They made it to the gardens in less than twenty minutes. For some reason the drive stopped across the street from the gardens, instead of dropping Sophie and Sean off right in front of it, like he had done for their first Martial Arts lesson. But again the driver didn't open the door for them; however, he did get out of the car.

Sean opened the back car door on his side and he and Sophie got out of the car. Sophie wasn't exactly sure why, but something inside her told her that she should try to hear the driver's thoughts. She blocked out all the other noise around her and focused on the driver.

"I'm heading across the street. Are you coming?" Sean asked.

"I'll be right behind you. I just need to tie my shoes."

As she pretended to tie her shoe, she focused on the driver. At first she couldn't hear anything, so she tried to strengthen the connection by focusing harder on the driver's face. She then started to hear a static sound and within moments she heard a faint noise she suspected was the driver's thoughts. She shuffled a little closer to the driver pretending she was having trouble tying her shoes. She was somewhat surprised the driver didn't notice it was taking her an awfully long time to tie her shoes.

"How did I get stuck with this job? I am one of the senior guys in the organization. I shouldn't be driving kids around. The girl is a little annoying. She thinks I don't understand what she is doing with those smiles and friendly hellos. If she only knew what was planned for her, she wouldn't be smiling anymore."

The hair stood up on the back of Sophie's neck as she continued to try to listen to the driver's thoughts. She hesitantly moved closer to the driver, but all she could hear was static. To top it off, her head was starting to hurt again.

Since Sophie could no longer hear the driver's thoughts, she finished tying her shoes and then crossed the street to meet Sean in front of the gardens.

"You were really having some trouble with your shoes back there. I was about to head back across the street to check on you."

"No need to worry," Sophie said with a half-smile trying to hide how upset she truly was by the driver's thoughts.

"It is past time to start our lesson. Have you seen Mr. Kimoto?" Sophie asked trying to distract Sean and herself.

"Not yet. He is probably waiting for us inside the gardens. Let's head in." Sean entered the gardens as Sophie followed close behind.

Sophie and Sean found Sadao Kimoto, their Sensei, waiting in the open grassy area by the waterfall. Strangely the same couple were sitting on the bench by the waterfall looking at magazines.

Sophie and Sean walked past the couple to meet their Sensei in the open grassy area. After greeting their teacher, Sophie and Sean closed their eyes and began to block out the sounds of the world around them.

"Very good," Sadao Kimoto said. "Now let's see if you can do that for the rest of the hour. I am going to be over there under the tree if you need me."

"What kind of lesson is this?" Sophie thought, but she continued to keep her eyes closed trying to block out all the noises except for the ones she wanted to hear.

Sophie could hear the birds in the tree Sadao was sitting under. She focused on the birds for a few minutes. Then she expanded her focus to include Sadao Kimoto. She realized she could hear his thoughts:

These children may think my methods are a little crazy, but they are getting it. Learning to quiet oneself teaches an individual discipline and helps make them truly present in the moment, so they are better able to recognize and react to the dangers around them. Learning how to quiet their minds will not only protect them from their enemies and the dangers in the world around them; but more importantly, it has the power to help protect them from themselves. Youth are often impassioned to make rash decisions when chasing after adventure. They are known for not weighing the consequences of their actions.

Because of who she is, Sophie must learn there are consequences to all her choices.

Next week, Sean and Sophie will be ready to learn some simple moves.

————————————————————————————————

Zoey greeted Sophie and Sean in the main hall when they returned home. "You were supposed to come back to your room and get me before you left for your Martial Arts lesson," Zoey scolded Sophie.

"I was worried about you."

"No need to worry. And I specifically recall you saying you would meet us downstairs before we headed outside to catch our ride. When you didn't show, I thought you had changed your mind." Sophie tried to whisper under her breath so Sean couldn't hear.

"Pardon, what was it you said?" Sean asked Sophie.

"Oh, sorry, I must have mumbled." Sophie looked down at the ground. "What I said was, I should be heading to my room. I'm feeling a little tired."

Sophie tapped her leg and looked directly at Zoey, "Coming?"

She then smiled at Sean. I think I'm going to relax in my room this afternoon. Enjoy the rest of the day. See you tomorrow."

"Sure, you are just going to relax in your room." Sean eyed her suspiciously.

"What about dinner?" Sean asked.

"I'll just ask Helen to bring me up a tray."

Sophie returned to her room with Zoey following close behind. Within moments Sophie was resting comfortably in her bed. In no time at all, she fell asleep.

Zoey watched as Sophie tossed and turned. Zoey stayed close enough to Sophie to provide her some comfort, but not so close that Sophie rolled over her. Zoey could tell Sophie was having another bad dream. She wanted to wake her before Sophie became too distressed. Zoey suspected she was having dreams about a possible danger in the near future.

When she finally stopped tossing and turning, Zoey nudged Sophie with her nose. "Are you awake?'

"Of course I'm awake. You just woke me," Sophie yawned.

"What were you dreaming about?" Zoey asked.

"I really can't remember much of this dream. I just remember seeing darkness and a police station next to a large cathedral. Can I go back to sleep now?"

Zoey was concerned by what Sophie had told her. What could Sophie's dream mean and what was the significance of the police station near the cathedral? Zoey knew exactly where the police station was located.

"Yes, you should go back to sleep. You need your rest. I will be right here beside you if you remember anything or need to talk."

I am really worried about her. These dreams mean something, but what? I haven't figured them out yet, but I will. If only she could remember a little more from her dreams when she wakes. But then again maybe it's good she can't remember any more. If they distress her too much she may not be able to fall asleep in the future. Sophie is my friend and I just want to be able to help her. From what I've heard Mrs. MacTavish say, I know Sophie is in some danger being here in Dublin. And she is so stubborn and spirited she may not realize when the danger is staring her directly in the face. Well, at least she has Sean and me to look out for her. Hopefully, we'll be enough.

- Zoey

xxij : the Disappearance

Sophie, Sean, and Zoey waited outside Evanswood for their driver to come and pick them up for their Martial Arts lesson. The driver was about 20 minutes late when the car pulled up to the curb in front of the house. The driver got out of the car to open the back door on the right side of the car.

"Who is that?" Sean asked Sophie.

Sophie shrugged her shoulders and smiled. "It looks like we have a new driver. I am glad, the other one creeped me out."

Sophie and Sean crawled in the back of the car. Zoey jumped in right before the tall, lean, blond haired driver closed the door.

As Zoey jumped in the car, the driver mumbled, "I don't remember anyone saying anything about a dog."

Sophie heard the driver, but paid not attention to his comment. As soon as the driver took his seat behind the steering wheel, Sophie started to ask him questions.

"Where is the other driver today?"

"He left town to visit his family in the south and asked me to fill in for him for a week or so," the driver answered Sophie's question as he continued to look down the road in front of him.

"Oh, I don't recall my father mentioning that we would have a new driver," Sophie said curiously.

The driver hesitated. "I'm sure Carl told your father I would fill in for him. If your father had not notified the garage I was picking up the car, they never would have let me into the garage. And I wouldn't have been able to give you a ride to your Martial Arts lesson today."

Sophie smiled at the driver and rubbed Zoey on the head. "I am glad you made it downstairs in time to go with us to Iveagh Gardens today."

"Don't forget to scratch behind my ear." Zoey slanted her head sideways so Sophie had easier access to her ears.

Sophie and Sean sat quietly in the back seat for the rest of the drive. Within 20 minutes the driver pulled into a space across the street from Iveagh Gardens. The driver got out of the car and it looked like he leaned down to do something. Sean tried to open the door, but it was locked.

"What's he doing?" Sophie was anxious. They were already late for their Martial Arts lesson and the driver was acting strangely.

Sean moved closer to the window and looked out. "He is bending down, but I can't exactly see what he is doing. Stuff on the sidewalk is blocking my view."

Finally, the driver opened the back door so Sophie, Zoey and Sean could get out of the car. The driver then looked down and kicked the front tire. "Shucks, how did that happen?"

He went to the trunk of the car to get the car jack.

There were no cars coming in either direction. Sophie looked down at Zoey. "Ready to cross?"

"Sure, lets go," Zoey barked as they ran across the street.

Sean started to follow Sophie, but the driver reached out and put his hand on Sean's shoulder. "Can you help me with something before you go to your lesson? It shouldn't take more than a few minutes."

"If it's only going to take a few minutes, I guess I can help you. I just need to let Sophie know." Sean started to cross the street again.

The driver stopped Sean again. "It really won't take that long. We will probably be done before you have time to run across the street and back. There is no need to tell Sophie. She can see us and she is only on the other side of the street."

"Okay, what's the problem?" Sean asked as he lifted both of his hands out to his sides palms up.

The driver pointed to the front tire. "We appear to have gotten a flat tire. There is no way we will be able to get home if it isn't changed. I don't think I can work the car-jack by myself."

"I can help you change the tire, but I still need to let Sophie know what I'm doing."

Sean yelled across the street to Sophie. "Come back. I have to help the driver change the tire before our lesson. It is only going to take a few minutes, but I'd feel more comfortable with you on this side of the street with me."

"I'm not running back across the street. We are late and I need to find Mr. Kimoto to let him know we are here. I'll meet you in the gardens by the waterfall," Sophie yelled.

As Sean helped the driver change the tire, Sophie and Zoey entered Iveagh Gardens to find Sadao Kimoto. They walked around the waterfall, but Sadao Kimoto was nowhere in sight. However, the same couple was sitting on the bench in front of the waterfall looking at a magazine. "I wonder if they have been looking at the same magazine this whole time?"

Sophie laughed to herself as she continued to look around for Sadao Kimoto. When she didn't see him she looked down at Zoey. "We normally, meet him right here. I don't know where else he would be."

Sophie made one more trip around the gardens, calling for Sadao Kimoto the whole time. When she returned to the waterfall, she saw a policeman. She went up to the policeman to ask if he had seen Sadao Kimoto. The policeman put his arm around Sophie while talking to her and stuck a large needle in her neck.

As far as Zoey could tell, the policeman was injecting a clear liquid into Sophie's neck. Zoey barked at the policeman and bit his leg to try to stop him from injecting anymore of the liquid into Sophie. The policeman kicked Zoey and she flew into the bushes. Zoey yelped in pain as she tried to get up. Sophie grabbed at her neck to remove the needle. As she pulled out the needle, she fell to the ground unconscious.

Another man in a police uniform turned the corner and walked towards Sophie.

"Good, Sophie will be all right," Zoey thought as she struggled to get up again. "This policeman will help her."

Zoey watched helpless as the policeman who just turned the corner greeted the other policeman. The policeman who had just turned the corner then placed a large black bag on the ground.

"Something isn't right. Why isn't the policeman who just arrived helping Sophie? And why does he have a large black bag?" Zoey continued to watch helplessly.

Zoey tried to move again. This time she was able to roll onto her stomach and crawl under the bush. "These guys are going to put Sophie in that bag. I have to get Sean."

Once she was on the other side of the bushes and out of site, Zoey ran out of Iveagh Gardens. She barked loudly at Sean across the street to get his attention.

Sean looked up when he heard Zoey barking. Sophie was not anywhere around. "Sophie must be in trouble," Sean thought as he ran across the street towards Zoey.

"Wait, we aren't done changing the tire."

Sean ignored the driver and continued to run towards Zoey. He reached the other side of the street just in time to see two policemen loading a big black bag into a white van.

Sean ran into Iveagh Gardens yelling for Sophie, but there was no response. When he reached the waterfall, there was no sign of Sophie anywhere. Zoey stood barking at the entrance of the gardens. "What is it girl? What are you trying to tell me?"

Zoey was beside herself, "How am I going to get Sean out of the gardens and back to the white van? He needs to go get help. We have to save Sophie."

Zoey ran back and forth from Sean to the entrance of Iveagh Gardens barking madly. "Alright girl, where do you want me to go?"

Zoey ran to the back of the white van and started to bark even louder. "Thankfully, the van is still here," Zoey thought.

She then ran to the side of the van to look in the window. "Good, only one of the policemen is in the van and he isn't the one who kicked me."

Sean remembered the big black bag the policemen were loading into the white van before he entered Iveagh Gardens. "What Zoey? Are you telling me Sophie is in that big black bag?"

Zoey barked louder and jumped at the back of the van. "Why am I asking a dog? She can't tell me." Sean scratched his head. "However, she sure is making a lot of noise. I have to be on the right track."

Sean motioned for Zoey to be quiet before the policeman discovered them. He looked across the street and noticed the car and driver who brought him and Sophie to Iveagh Gardens was gone. He then quickly and quietly snuck into the white van and gently closed the door behind him leaving Zoey outside to keep watch. Zoey stepped away from the van and hid in the bushes where she could see everything that was going on. She prayed Sean and Sophie would exit the van shortly.

The black bag was lying on the middle of the floor in the van. Sean examined the bag and saw tiny holes on the sides. He felt around and found a zipper at the top of the bag. He slowly moved the zipper down the bag.

After the bag was completely unzipped, Sean pulled back both sides. He was a little afraid of what he would find and hesitantly looked inside. It was dark inside the van and even darker inside the black bag. At first Sean couldn't see anything, so he pulled the sides of the bag further apart to let in as much light as possible. There was a body inside the bag. Although he couldn't make out the face, he knew it was Sophie. Gently and as quickly as possible he pulled the body out of the bag. Sophie's face stared back at him. A strange sense of fear settled in Sean's stomach. "She can't be dead. She really can't be dead. I was supposed to protect her."

Sophie wasn't moving. Sean felt her wrist for a pulse, but couldn't feel one. Almost in a panic, he nervously used his fingers to find a pulse in her neck. "Thank goodness she has a pulse. It is very faint, but I still can't tell if she is breathing." He held his cheek to her nose and felt a slight breath. Relieved, he shook her. "Come on, Sophie you need to wake up. We have to get out of here, now."

Sophie did not move. Sean then shook her with more force, but still she did not move.

Sean couldn't get Sophie to wake. He wiped his forehead with his arm. "Somehow, I have to get you out of here."

With much effort, Sean lifted Sophie over his shoulder; he held on tightly to her legs as Sophie's body dangled down his back. Remaining on the floor of the van, Sean scooted over to the door tightening his grip on Sophie's legs to ensure she didn't fall. Sean tried to open the door, but it wouldn't budge. He pushed a little harder and still the door wouldn't move. Sean gently rolled Sophie back onto the van floor, careful not to bang her head. He looked for a hidden latch on the door, but couldn't find one. He leaned with all his strength, but still couldn't open the door.

Desperate, Sean got a tighter grip on the door and started to shake it with all his might. When the door refused to open, he hit it a few times for good measure. "This can't be happening," Sean yelled. "I can't get the door to open from the inside. We are now both stuck in this van."

Just then the van started to move. Sean fell backwards and landed on Sophie. "Good thing you are still unconscious," Sean said as Sophie remained motionless on the van floor.

"I have to come up with a plan." Sean rubbed his head. "Think! Who knows how much time we have before this van stops."

Sean closed his eyes to collect his thoughts. "Holding Sophie, I can't take on two grown men by myself. And, there could be more to fight once we arrive at wherever they are taking us. However, if I remain hidden in the van, I will likely get stuck in here after the men remove Sophie from the van. I would lose track of her and not be able to figure out where they took her. Although I don't want to and it creeps me out a little, the only plan I can think of is for me to crawl inside the black bag with her."

Sean gently put Sophie back in the bag. With care he ensured her head was resting comfortably at the bottom of the bag. However, he wasn't ready to crawl into the bag quite yet. Sean studied the bag. "The bag is more than big enough for two people, but I still need a few minutes before I cram myself in that thing."

Sean took a few deep breaths and counted to one hundred. "I guess I have to do this. I'm not sure how much time I have left. I better crawl in the bag now."

Sean opened the bag wide and crawled inside, cautious not to kick Sophie in the head. "I really don't like this. And how am I supposed to close the bag when I am inside?"

Sean sat up and reached for the zipper, but couldn't find it. He then crawled back out of the bag and kneeled down in front of it. He found the zipper at the end of the bag and zipped the bag up a little less than half way. He then crawled back in the bag, extra careful not to kick Sophie.

Sean sat up in the bag again, but this time he was able to reach the zipper. He scooted as far up in the bag as he could and pulled the zipper up. He then scooted his body further down in the bag. The zipper was about even with his forehead when he reached his arm outside the top of the bag and grabbed the zipper. With his arm outside of the bag he pulled the zipper up as high as he was able.

The bag was almost completely zipped except for a little gap at the top. "Looks like that's going to have to do. There is no way I can completely zip the bag while I'm lying inside of it."

Sean moved his head and shoulders to get as comfortable as he possibly could lying in a big, black bag—with little light and air and another person inside. "What did they keep in this bag? Boy, it smells dreadful in here."

Sean was grateful he wasn't able to zip the bag all the way. He pinched his nose and was just getting to the point where he could tolerate the smell when the van suddenly stopped. Both he and Sophie were tossed around in the bag. "Jeepers, creepers, I have run out of time. I hope the bag is zipped up far enough, so they don't think anything is out of place."

Sean heard the van door open and someone entered the van. He remained as still as possible as the footsteps got closer. The man looked down at the bag, took off his police uniform cap and scratched the side of his head. He was a little confused. He thought he completely zipped the bag, but wasn't entirely sure. Sometimes he easily forgot things. He suspected it was caused by too many knocks on the head when he was younger.

The other man kneeled down beside the first man and looked at the bag. "Clifton, I'm glad you didn't completely zip the bag. The girl needed a little air to breath. We want her alive not dead. I thought you might have zipped the bag all the way up."

Glen snickered. "Well, if she died from lack of air, at least the boss couldn't blame me."

"Should we open the bag to check on the girl?" Clifton asked slightly concerned.

Sean's body stiffened a little in the bag. "No, the boss is waiting, let's carry her inside now."

"Whatever you think is best." Clifton positioned himself at one end of the bag. Glen grabbed the other end. "Lift on three...one, two, three."

"The girl sure seemed a lot lighter when we first carried her to the van," Clifton exclaimed.

"Don't be silly, Clifton, the bag weighs the same." Glen gritted his teeth.

Clifton and Glen carried Sophie and Sean into the building in front of them. They placed the big, black bag on a bench in one of the rooms at the front of the building. "Should we just leave the bag here?" Clifton asked Glen.

"The girl should be all right here for a few moments while we go get the boss. Plus, she should be knocked out for a few more hours, so there is no chance of her running away."

Again, Sean was glad he couldn't completely zip the black bag. He was able to hear Clifton and Glen's conversation and now knew Sophie's kidnappers wouldn't be back for a few minutes. He pushed his arm through the hole at the top of the bag and wrapped his fingers around the zipper. He pulled the zipper down slowly.

Sean fully unzipped the bag and carefully removed his legs and placed them on the ground in front of the bench. He stood up and stretched his body, which was a little stiff from being stuffed in the bag. He then walked back over to the bag and shook Sophie, but she continued to lie perfectly still.

Sean looked around the room. It appeared to be some sort of large bathroom with cubbies for holding cloths. There were numerous benches throughout the room. Sean poked his head outside the room and saw several men in police uniforms walking around.

"We must be in the police station. I wonder if these guys really are policemen," Sean thought as he quickly pulled his head back in the room and quietly closed the door. He looked around the room trying to figure out what to do next when he saw a few police uniforms in the corner.

"One of these uniforms has to be small enough to fit me." Sean held up the first uniform and laughed. "Well, this one is way too big. It will fall off my body." He tried on the jacket of another uniform. It fit loosely, but the pants were still too big for him. So, he picked up another pair of pants and tried them on. "Well, these fit better. They are a little big, but they aren't falling off. They will have to do."

Once he was fully dressed, Sean looked around for a cap to complete the uniform, but he didn't see one laying out anywhere. He looked through several of the cubbies and thankfully found a cap.

"Now that I am fully dressed, I may be able to carry Sophie out of here without drawing any attention or being stopped." Sean walked back over to the black bag to zip it back up again. He knew it would be easier to get out of the police station carrying a bag, as opposed to a lifeless body.

As soon as Sean finished zipping the bag, making sure to leave a small gap at the top to let air in, he heard a noise outside the door. "Had he run out of time? Were the two men who kidnapped Sophie already back?"

Sean moved behind a row of cubbies towards the back of the room where he wasn't easily seen. From his spot Sean could also see Sophie. He wasn't losing her again. He lowered his head and watched the two men who kidnapped Sophie enter the room.

"Have you even seen the room where the boss wants us to take the girl?" Clifton asked Glen.

"I have been to the downstairs room once. It's very dark down there and I wouldn't want to spend much time there," Glen responded.

Glen's revelation made Sean a little anxious for Sophie. He wanted to do something, but he wasn't sure what to do. If he was able to follow the two men downstairs, at least he would know where they put Sophie and he could figure out a way to rescue her.

Sean moved and the bench creaked.

Clifton pointed in the corner and whispered to Glen, "Look!"

"Hey, what are you doing in here? You look a little small to be a police officer?" Glen's voice was gruff.

Sean tried to speak, but it felt like there was a frog in his throat. He cleared his throat and stood up as tall as he could. He had to think fast. "I..I..I am just getting ready for my shift."

"Well, pay us no mind. We will be out of your way in a few moments." Glen motioned for Clifton to pick up the end of the black bag. Glen picked up the other end. "Let's go, Clifton. We have to get this bag down to the basement."

After the kidnappers left with Sophie, Sean sprung to his feet. If he wanted to rescue her, he couldn't let the black bag out of his sight. He stuck his head out the door and watched the kidnappers make their way to a door at the end of the hallway. Sean stepped out of what he suspected had to be the police officers changing room, and headed in the same direction as the kidnappers.

Sean passed several men dressed in police uniforms. "I wonder if those guys are real policemen? I don't know who I can trust."

Sean cracked the hallway door the kidnappers had opened and cautiously looked inside. The door led to stairs. Trying to make as little noise as possible Sean walked down the stairs. When he reached the bottom, he saw the kidnappers open and close a door at the end of the hall. He made his way to the door and cracked it open. He gingerly peeked through the door, hoping he could still see the kidnappers.

Cool, damp air immediately hit Sean in the face. He reached his hand up to pinch his nostrils closed. There was that horrible smell. The space beyond the door was also much darker than the hallway where Sean was standing. It took a few moments for his eyes to adjust to the dark. Once he could see in front of him, Sean realized he was standing at the top of another set of stairs. He cautiously made his way down the second set of stairs. There was a gate at the bottom of the steps.

Sean lightly shook the gate. "One of the kidnappers must have locked the gate."

A noise further down the hallway caught Sean's attention. However, it was so dark at the bottom of the steps that he couldn't see anything. He had no idea where the kidnappers went with Sophie.

"What do I do now? Do I go and get help or do I wait upstairs for the kidnappers to leave and follow them? Maybe they will set the key to this gate down somewhere where I can pick it up."

Sean reluctantly went back up the stairs. There was a bench across the hall from the door that led to the stairs. "I guess I'll sit here and wait for a while."

THE SACRIFICE

I am so glad my little one is starting to feel at home here in Dublin. And words cannot express how thankful I'm to have Sophie close to me again. Leaving her in New York with my mother was one of the hardest things I have ever had to do. However, it seemed like the right thing to do at the time, but I may have been wrong. Seeing how happy she is here at Evanswood and watching her learn more about herself and her mother's past has been a gift. If we hadn't returned to Dublin, she may not have ever had the opportunity to meet her grandfather. I can't believe it, my wife was a Faerie princess and her father is a powerful Faerie king. How wonderful and amazing, but at the same time, troubling. What I recently learned about the possible danger surrounding Sophie, because of who her grandfather is, makes me constantly concerned for her safety.

- William St.. Clair

xxiij : Lost in the Darkness

Sophie opened her eyes to a raging headache. The smell was horrible and she had no idea where she was. She rubbed her eyes and tried to see in front of her, but the room was too dark. She couldn't even see her hands when she held them up in front of her face. She tried to stand and stumbled because her feet were tied together. She scooted up against the wall and sat on the hard floor. Although she couldn't see the room, she knew she was in a cold, dark, damp place. "Just like in my dreams," she thought.

Sophie was really scared. She had no idea where she was. The last thing she remembered was going to her Martial Arts lesson with Sean.

"If I can get my head to stop hurting, I might remember how I got here." She rubbed her head and breathed deeply.

"Sean! Where is Sean? Is he okay?"

"SEAN!" Sophie yelled. Her voice echoed off the cold, stone walls. She listened for a minute, but there was no answer. Sophie leaned away from the wall and yelled loader. "Sean, where are you?"

There was still no answer. "Is anyone there?" Sophie screamed at the top of her lungs. Again there was no response.

She then heard a noise from somewhere on the far side of the room, like an animal scurrying across the floor. "I hope it's not a big rat. I can't stand rats."

Sophie leaned back against the wall for support. She closed her eyes in an attempt to calm the pounding in her head. She kept her eyes closed for awhile and thought about her father, her grandfather, Sean, Simeon, Helen, Mrs. MacTavish, and Zoey. Someone had to find her.

Moments after Sophie opened her eyes, they began to adjust to the dark. She rubbed them a few times hoping she could see things more clearly. Although the room was still dark, she noticed that on the far side of the room, tiny specks of light trickled through a few holes cut into the ceiling. Sophie heard drops of liquid hitting the ground somewhere close.

"I hope it's water making that noise," she thought as she scooted over to the specks of light on the floor. She stuck her legs into the sparse rays of light. She could vaguely make out the image of her legs and the rope wrapped around them. She stretched out her arms to pull on the rope, but she couldn't get it to budge. She tried pulling harder, but it was no use. The rope was strong, thick and heavy, and the knots were tied very tightly.

Frustrated, Sophie tried to pull her legs apart, but she couldn't move them. Sophie took a deep breath and turned to her side. She struggled even harder to pull her legs apart. It was like they were glued together. Try as she might, her legs would not budge.

Out of breath, Sophie finally gave up and scooted herself up against the nearest wall. She sat against the wall with her knees bent. She felt several knots in the rope on the back side of her legs. She pulled at the knots and tried to pick them apart.

"Where these knots are located... I can barely reach them. They are tied so tightly I will never be able to untie them without help or some kind of sharp object."

"Poor, girl." Sophie heard a voice from somewhere out in the darkness.

"Who is that? Whose here?" Sophie found herself feeling a little frightened.

Sophie heard the little voice again. "How could she hear me? She's a human and I didn't even make a noise?"

"Please! I can hear you and I really need your help." Sophie heard whatever animal it was scurry away from her.

"I bet you are a rat. I would be grateful to see even a rat at this point. Where did you go?" Sophie asked into the darkness.

The next thing Sophie heard was the door opening on the other side of the room. Someone stepped into the room. "I see you are awake girly. I bet your head hurts a little. I brought you some water and food."

The man pushed a tray of food with a cup of water towards Sophie. She wasn't sure what kind of food was on the tray. She picked up the cup of water and moved it to her nose to smell it. Then she moved the cup around in a single ray of light, swishing the liquid around to see what color it was. "No need to worry, girly. It's just water in the cup and there is nothing in the food that will hurt you. I promise, we will not hurt you and we will let you go once we get what we want."

Sophie took a sip of the water. It felt wonderful going down her dry, scratchy throat. Sophie looked down on the tray and could barely see what was on it. She began moving her hand over the tray. From what she felt, she guessed there was some kind of meat, bread and cheese on the tray.

She picked up the meat and took a bite. "Although, I can't exactly tell what kind of meat this is, it's not too bad. It might even be tasty, if I stick this meat between the bread."

Sophie added the cheese between the meat and bread and took a big bite. She immediately spat the food out of her mouth. "I guess even when I am starving, I still don't like cheese."

Sophie took the cheese out from between the pieces of bread and laid it back on the tray. She took a large sip of water and finished the meat and bread.

"I have a brilliant idea. I'm going to leave this cheese for that animal that keeps running around this room. Maybe then it will trust me enough to help me." Sophie scooted away from the wall and placed the cheese in the middle of the room. Then she returned to her spot against the wall and waited for the animal to return.

Sophie didn't have to wait long before she heard little feet scratching across the floor. There was quiet for a few moments; then Sophie heard a chomping sound.

"Tastes good?" Sophie asked in a gentle, calm voice.

The little animal sat up on its back feet and quit chewing. "How can I hear and understand her?"

"You can hear and understand me because I can talk to animals. Can you please step into the light so I can see you?

The animal didn't move. Cautiously, it said, "Don't worry, I am not a rat, I am a mouse.

Sophie breathed a sigh of relief.

Curious of Sophie, the mouse continued, "Thank you for leaving me some cheese, even if it is a little stale."

"So that's what's wrong with the cheese," Sophie stated as she looked in the direction of where she thought the mouse was located. She then took a deep breath. "Hey, can you help me get out of here?"

"I might be able to help you. I have some pretty sharp teeth." The mouse displayed its teeth with a big grin. "But, I don't think I will help you now."

"You won't help me now?" Sophie was confused.

The mouse moved into the light, stood on his hind legs and adamantly stated, "No, I won't help you out of the ropes now. I think the men who kidnapped you are still in the building. They are probably going to check on you again tonight and tomorrow. You don't want them to know you are untied. And even if I help you free your legs, you can't get out of here without the key."

Sophie sat in the dark for a few minutes contemplating what the mouse said. Within moments, her thoughts were interrupted by a noise that sounded like a key turning in a rusty lock. The mouse scurried into a dark corner, out of view. A shadowy figure of a man, faintly outlined in the dim light appeared in the doorway.

"I see you finished the food. Do you need any more water?" The shadowy figure held up a jug and shook it back and forth.

Sophie hesitated a moment. "Why yes, I…I…I would like some more water."

After the man entered, Sophie noticed there was a bag over his shoulder. The man laid the bag on the ground near Sophie. "Where's your cup?"

With shaky hands, Sophie held up the cup. In a friendly, reassuring voice the man said, "There is no need to be afraid. We won't hurt you."

The man filled Sophie's cup with water then pushed the bag towards Sophie. "Here's some stuff to help you sleep. You may be here a few nights. My boss says we won't let you go until we get what we want from your family."

The man then walked out of the room and locked the door behind him.

Sophie reached out and pulled the bag close to her. She opened it and found something that resembled a pillow and a blanket. Sophie hit the pillow with her hand. "How am I supposed to sleep in here?"

She arranged the pillow and blanket, to get as comfortable as possible on the hard, cold stone floor. She mumbled as she rested her head on the pillow, "I need to figure out a way to get that key from the man… if he ever comes back."

Sophie looked up to see the outline of the mouse standing in front of her. "It will be okay. I've told all my animal friends, especially the rats, to stay away from you tonight. You can rest in peace. I can stay close by if you like?"

"I can even sing you a song." The mouse opened its mouth to sing. A horrible, loud, high-pitch squeak echoed off the walls.

"Make it stop. Pretty please, make it stop. It's torture!" Sophie sat up and held the pillow to her ears.

The mouse laughed at Sophie's comical response. "Ok, no more singing. I have to save my voice anyway. Let's see…I'll hum instead."

Sophie didn't say a word. She found the humming soothing and was glad for the distraction. After a while, Sophie recognized the tone and started to sing along:

> *In Dublin's fair city,*
> *Where the girls are so pretty,*
> *I first set my eyes on sweet Molly Malone,*
> *As she wheeled her wheel-barrow,*
> *Through streets broad and narrow,*
> *Crying, "Cockles and mussels, alive, alive, oh!*
> *Alive, alive, oh,"*

The mouse joined in. "Crying, 'Cockles and mussels, alive, alive, oh'"

Sophie stopped singing and stared at the mouse. The mouse tapped Sophie's foot. "You have a beautiful voice."

"Thank you! I got it from my mother. She taught me Molly Malone when I was younger. We used to sing it when either of us had a bad day. Sorry, I really don't feel like singing any more. I'm very tired."

"How about we go to sleep and in the morning we can figure out a way to get you out of here. Oh, I forgot one thing. Stick out your legs," the mouse requested.

Sophie stuck out her legs and the mouse started chewing on the ropes. "Now that you have the blanket to hide your legs, you don't need to keep the ropes around them."

The mouse hid the chewed-up ropes in a dark corner of the room.

Once her legs were no longer tied together, Sophie was able to rub, scratch and stretch them. She positioned herself more comfortably on the floor. Although it took quite a while, Sophie was able to fall asleep. After Sophie had fallen asleep, the mouse crawled on the blanket and fell asleep at her feet.

———————————————————————————

"Sophie, Sophie where are you?" William St.. Clair yelled as he ran through Evanswood searching for her.

"Where could that girl be? I haven't seen her since breakfast. She has not disappeared since the last time she traveled to the ForEverNever without telling anyone. After that incident, she promised she would tell someone when she left the house and where she was going. So far she has been true to her word, always telling someone before she returned to the ForEverNever," William thought as his stomach tightened into knots.

As William passed the library door, his thoughts were interrupted when he heard, "Sean are you in here?"

William scratched his head. "Was Sean missing too?"

William stepped into the library as Mrs. MacTavish backed out. He caught her as she bumped into him.

"Thank you William." Mrs. MacTavish adjusted her jacket and skirt. She was noticeably concerned.

"Have you seen Sean? I have not seen him since this morning. He missed his visual training session this afternoon. This is not like him."

"Sophie is missing too." William was now alarmed.

Helen entered the library with a barking Zoey close on her heals.

"Helen, have you seen the children?" William and Mrs. MacTavish asked at the same time.

Helen raised her eyebrows and paused. "Hmm, I haven't seen either of the children since breakfast. Zoey just returned home and she's been barking like crazy since I let her in. I think she went with Sophie and Sean to their Martial Arts lesson today. Zoey never lets Sophie out of her sight these days."

Concerned Mrs. MacTavish exclaimed, "Something must be wrong for her to bark so much."

Helen suspected the children were somewhere in the house. She wasn't ready to get too concerned just yet. "I will head to the kitchen to check with Cook to see if she has seen the children this afternoon. You know they are always looking for food. I am sure she has seen them."

Mrs. MacTavish considered Helen's explanation for the children's absence. She was less convinced the children were in the house. "I will check to see if they are in the Hidden Garden or if Sophie has snuck off to the ForEverNever again. Sean may be hiding in his room covering for her. I will let you know what I find out."

William looked at both Mrs. MacTavish and Helen. "Sounds like we have a plan. I am going to call Sadao Kimoto. Let's meet back here in an hour."

———————————————————————————

A fire crackled in both the small fireplace in the library. William sat at his desk in the library and picked up the telephone to dial his good friend Sadao Kimoto. After three rings he heard someone pick up on the other end. "Sadao, I am so glad you answered your phone."

"What's the matter? You sound concerned."

William was too anxious to answer. "What time did the children leave your lesson this afternoon? Did you see them get into the car to return home?"

There was a long pause on the other end of the line. "We didn't have a lesson this afternoon. I called your home yesterday and left a message that I had business to attend to this afternoon, so I would not be able to meet with the children."

William's heart sank. After a long pause, he was finally able to speak. "What did you say?" He asked in a quiet, desperate voice that Sadao could barely hear.

"I did not meet with the children today," Sadao repeated.

William then took a deep breath, shook his head and frantically yelled into the telephone, "I didn't receive any message. Who did you talk with?"

Sadao understood William's panic. "I spoke to a man, but he didn't give his name. He told me he would pass the message along to you." Sadao now wished he had asked for the man's name.

"Something has happened to the children, hasn't it? Don't panic William. I am leaving for your house right now. I will be there in a few minutes. We will figure this out."

After William hung up the telephone, he wiped his head. He was sweating profusely.

"I lost Emma. I can't lose Sophie too," William thought as he briefly put is head on his desk. He felt at a loss as to what to do next.

William then took a few deep breaths and raised his head. He picked up the telephone and called his driver at home. There was no answer. He then called the garage where he kept his cars.

"Yes, Mr. St. Clair your car is here," the attendant told William.

"Has it been there all day?" William asked.

"Please give me a moment to check the log and I will let you know."

"According to the log your driver picked up the car this morning and returned it before two this afternoon."

"Did anything seem odd when the car was returned? Does the car look damaged in any way?"

"I don't see any damage on the car, Mr. St. Clair, but I wasn't here when it was dropped off. Please give me a few minutes and I will get Eddy. He is the one who logged the car in this afternoon."

William clutched the telephone as if his life depended on it. "If anything happens to Sophie, all the joy and light will be gone from my life."

As he rested his head on the desk again, William heard on the other end of the receiver, "Eddy, Eddy, come over here."

"Mr. St. Clair this is Eddy. I was told you wanted to speak with me. How can I help you Sir?"

"Eddy, can you tell me if you noticed anything odd when my car was returned this afternoon?"

"Nothing seemed out of the ordinary. There was no damage to it." Eddy paused for a moment, "But the man who dropped off your car wasn't your usual driver."

William's voice was shaking. "What did you say?"

"I have never seen the driver who returned your car. I asked him if everything was fine with your normal driver, because we weren't expecting a different driver and we hadn't received a call from you. The driver told me everything was okay, your normal driver was just sick and he was filling in for the day."

William couldn't speak for a few seconds and coughed to clear his throat. "Thank you Eddy. You have been a big help."

"Mr. St. Clair, I hope everything is okay."

"Thanks Eddy, so do I, so do I." William hung up the telephone and laid his head back on the desk. What was he going to do now? It looked like his daughter and Sean had been kidnapped.

———————————————————————————————

Four men sat in a dimly lit room discussing what they were going to do next. The tallest man sitting in front of the three other men had an enormous smile on his face. He was noticeably older than the others and was having difficulty containing his excitement. Their mission had been successful. After months of waiting and planning, they had the girl.

The smaller man, dressed in a police uniform asked, "Should we call the girl's father tonight and make our demands?"

The elegantly dressed, older man, in front of the group, grinned even larger and laughed. It was not a pleasant laugh, it sounded crackly and sinister. He rubbed his hands together and thought, "I have William right where I want him and I am going to make him sweat a little before I make any demands. I can't remember the last time I had so much fun. William is finally going to pay."

The older man then addressed the group. "No, we are going to wait a few days before we call the girl's father. That way he will be even more desperate and will give us anything we ask for."

The men chimed in. "Yeah, that's a good idea."

The older man stared at the other men thinking. "These fools. They think it is all about the money. Yes, William is very rich, but they have no idea what this is truly about. I am going to make William pay. He is going to be sorry for what he did to me all those years ago."

The smaller man in the police uniform asked, "Should we at least check on the girl to make sure she is okay?"

The older man contemplated. "You already gave her food and bedding for this evening. There is no reason to visit her again tonight. You can bring her more food in the morning."

He had to keep the other men convinced that this was all about the money and he was not going to hurt the girl. "I don't want one of these half-wits ruining my plans by become too fond of William's daughter."

After all the men left the room, Sean gave a sigh of relief. They had not noticed him quietly hiding. Sean couldn't remember ever being that still or quiet in his life. He hadn't moved since the two men in police uniforms walked into the room earlier that evening. Sean had entered the dimly lit room earlier in the day looking for a place where he could remain in the building without being noticed. He was waiting for the right opportunity to help Sophie. It was just his luck that Sophie's kidnappers chose to meet in the room where he was hiding. He was able to conceal himself behind a stack of boxes in the corner without being noticed.

Sean now knew Sophie was likely not in any danger this evening and one of the men was going to check on her in the morning. After some time passed and Sean felt confident the kidnappers were no longer in the hallway, he left the dimly lit room and made his way back to the police officers' changing room. He sat on a long bench in the back of the room, in front of some windows, and thought of a plan. He tried to stay awake, but he was just so tired. He stretched out on the bench and fell asleep.

After hours past, Sean woke to a bright light shining into the room. He left the changing room and waited on a bench in the hallway for the man in the police uniform to head downstairs. "I'm not going to miss the chance to find out where Sophie is being held."

Helen and Mrs. MacTavish joined William back in the library. Zoey was still barking incessantly. Mrs. MacTavish had enough of Zoey's barking. "Stop that barking, right now! We know something is wrong, but we cannot think with all that noise."

Zoey stopped barking and just stared up at Mrs. MacTavish. "I wish she could understand me."

"The children haven't been to the kitchen all afternoon." Now, Helen worried. "I searched the house and I didn't see any sign of them."

Mrs. MacTavish was also very concerned. "I did not see them in the hidden garden or in the ForEverNever. Although, I cannot see all of the ForEverNever, I do not think they are there. Anyway, only Sophie can travel there and Sean is missing too."

In a desperate voice William informed them, "I don't think they are in the ForEverNever. I believe they have been kidnapped."

"Kidnapped?" Helen gasped.

"Why do you think they were kidnapped?" Mrs. MacTavish asked in a pseudo calm voice.

"I talked to Sadao Kimoto. He told me he called the house yesterday to let us know he couldn't meet with the children. I also talked to the employees at the garage. They told me someone picked up my car this morning, and that someone, who isn't my normal driver, returned it this afternoon."

"Who would want to kidnap the children? And why?" Helen asked.

"We have to get a hold of Mr. McGuire. Someone has to let Sophie's grandfather know what is going on. I can write Sophie's grandfather a message, but it would be better if Mr. McGuire traveled to the

ForEverNever to tell him in person. We cannot rule out that Faeries could have taken the children."

Mrs. MacTavish walked over to the telephone. "I know he has been very busy and often away on business, but I must reach him now."

Mrs. MacTavish picked up the telephone to call the only number she had for Mr. McGuire. He advised her that she should only call the number if it was an emergency.

"Well, two missing children is certainly an emergency in my book," Mrs. MacTavish said as she dialed the number.

Mrs. MacTavish breathed a sigh of relief when she heard a voice on the other end of the telephone. It was not Mr. McGuire, but the person told her he could get a message to Mr. McGuire. She told the person to let Mr. McGuire know he was needed at Evanswood. She stressed he should arrive as soon as possible because Sophie had been kidnapped.

Mrs. MacTavish hung up the telephone. "Mr. McGuire should be here in the next few hours."

"Good!" William stated. "Sadao is also on his way."

"Should we inform the police?" Helen asked.

"No," William and Mrs. MacTavish responded at the same time.

Mrs. MacTavish became the voice of reason. "We should wait until we speak with Mr. McGuire before we involve the police. We have no idea who took the children or if they are still in the human world. There is also the possibility they were taken by a dead eye."

"A dead eye? What's a dead eye?" William asked.

"A dead eye is a human who is desperate, with no faith and has lost all hope. You can tell an individual is a dead eye by looking in their eyes, which appear cloudy, dull and lifeless. Unkind and manipulative forces of the Faerie World seek out these individuals. These forces easily influence dead eyes for their own selfish goals."

YMIR LEGACY

I can't believe her father risked bringing her to Dublin. What was he thinking? When the note arrived inviting me to the party at Evanswood to meet Sophie and consult with Mrs. MacTavish, I was out of town on business. By the time I received the note, the party had already happened. I have been the busiest I can ever remember over the last few weeks visiting the Faerie and human contacts I have established over the years. I have been working to ensure that no one has learned who Sophie is and I have been doing everything I can to make sure she remains safe in Dublin. One of these days, I will make it back to Evanswood to meet her. It has been years since I've been back at Evanswood. I feel I can help keep everyone who lives there safer if no one knows I'm connected to the individuals who live in the house. I watch them from afar and keep a close eye on others, human and Faerie, who appear to watch the residence of Evanswood too closely.

- Mr. McGuire

xxiv : Truth Comes to Light

Two hours later William, Helen, Mrs. MacTavish, Mr. McGuire and Sadao Kimoto sat in front of the fireplace, closest to the tapestry, discussing the situation. Within a short time, they had a list of possible individuals who could have taken the children.

"Who do we have on the list so far?" Helen asked.

William went through the list. "Well, there is Mr. Fitzpatrice, my driver, hmm…, a dead eye or someone from the Faerie World."

Mrs. MacTavish weighed in. "I think it is safe to mark Mr. Fitzpatrice off the list. I know he suddenly disappeared. But, I believe his story that he was truly frustrated and needed to get away for a few days. I know the children sometimes irritate him, but I think he genuinely cares for them and would not harm them in any way."

William didn't want to rule out Mr. Fitzpatrice just yet. "Are you sure, Mrs. MacTavish? I tried to reach him earlier today, but couldn't."

"I would bet my magic mirror that Mr. Fitzpatrice did not take the children. However, I will call his mother's house when we are done here. One way or the other, you will be able to confidently mark him off the list or pursue him as a viable suspect."

William was surprised to hear Mr. Fitzpatrice might be at his mother's, but didn't say anything out loud. "Sounds like a plan to me. Do any of you have any idea of who in the Faerie World might have taken the children?"

Mr. McGuire opened his arms wide. "The list of possible suspects could be very long. Being the King of the Faerie House of Ymir and High King of the Enlightened Faeries, Sophie's grandfather has many enemies. I plan to travel to the Faerie World and meet with the King. He may have some ideas and I am sure he will order his royal guards to search for the children."

Mr. McGuire looked directly at William. "I will leave as soon as we are done here."

Sadao Kimoto was thinking of what he could do to help. "And I will have my people look into your driver's history. William, you should also make a list of all your enemies who might know Sophie is here in Ireland with you."

They all agreed to return to the library once they completed their tasks. Before Mr. McGuire stepped through the clock in the library to return to the ForEverNever, he put on his cape, grabbed his top hat, and then pulled Mrs. MacTavish aside. "I see you decided to keep the boy."

"Keep what boy?" Mrs. MacTavish asked confused.

"Sean! You really have no idea who he is, do you? I thought you knew I left him at your door?"

Mr. McGuire searched Mrs. MacTavish's face for an answer as he rubbed his chin. "Didn't you find the note I left with Sean?"

Stunned, Mrs. MacTavish just stared. After a few seconds, she gained her composure. "Yes, I found a note, but I had no idea it was from you. I saved it all these years to give to Sean when he was older. I was hoping his true identity would come to light, before I told him he was left on my doorstep and I am not really his grandmother."

"I can tell you who he is and where he came from. Do you remember what the note said?"

"I remember reading: Keep him safe and one day he may save you or those you hold dear, once he knows his true propose."

Questioningly, Mrs. MacTavish raised her brow. "What does it mean?"

"I don't know yet. It is what his mother told me when she handed him over to me. I am sure the meaning will become evident when the time is right."

Mrs. MacTavish bunched up her shoulders and held her hands together in the middle of her chest, expecting the worse. "Should I even ask where Sean is from?"

"I came across his mother during my travels. She recognized me from the ForEverNever and asked for my help. She was the daughter of Urmiar, the King of the Faerie House of Attewater. Like Emma she left the ForEverNever for love. However, unlike Emma her father was not supportive of her decision and who she chose to love was not good. He left her shortly after Sean was created. Shadow Faeries quickly learned she was alone on Earth and came after her thinking they could use her to get money or power from her father. She and Sean were in terrible danger."

"When I walked into the restaurant, where Sean's mother was working, she saw me as the answer to her prayer of how to keep Sean safe. She handed him over to me and begged for my help. I took him, but I didn't know what to do with a baby. So I brought him to you and Helen. I figured keeping his identity a secret would ensure his safety. I thought you saw me place him on your doorstep and recognized my handwriting on the note."

Mrs. MacTavish opened her mouth to speak, but closed it suddenly and just shook her head.

"Now that you know who Sean is, you know he is almost as valuable to the Shadow Faeries as Sophie," Mr. McGuire continued.

Mrs. MacTavish stared at Mr. McGuire in disbelief. "How would I have known Sean has Faerie blood?"

"Haven't there been any indications over the last year that he is not a typical boy? He should have started to develop some of his powers and abilities by now."

"There have been little things, but nothing shouted at me that Sean has Faerie blood."

"We can talk more about this later. Right now, I need to return to the ForEverNever to talk with Sophie's and Sean's grandfather." Mr. McGuire bowed and walked into the clock.

Mr. McGuire focused his thoughts as he walked through the clock, which worked brilliantly because he ended up right where he wanted to be; the road leading up to Polleux's meadow. Mr. McGuire needed to find Simeon right away. He hoped Simeon was with Polleux. If not, he would seek out Sophie's grandfather.

Thankfully, Simeon and Polleux greeted Mr. McGuire when he reached the meadow. "Thank goodness you are here Simeon!" Mr. McGuire scratched Polleux on the head.

"I am glad to see you too, but something in your voice tells me there is a problem."

"Yes, we have a big problem. Sophie is missing."

"Sophie... missing?" Simeon gasped. "But how...when...who? I should have suspected something was wrong. She was supposed to arrive here hours ago."

"We don't know the answers to any of those questions. Sophie and Sean went to their Martial Arts lesson and never returned. We later found out from Sadao Kimoto, their Martial Arts instructor, that he had called the house and left a message advising the lesson was cancelled. The message was never passed to William or the children. William hasn't received any calls with demands. We really don't have much to go on. William and Sadao Kimoto are reaching out to their contacts in the human world and I am here in the ForEverNever to let you and Sophie's grandfather know she is missing. We need to start searching and asking questions here in the ForEverNever."

"I don't think Sophie is in the ForEverNever," Simeon responded. "I normally sense her presence when she arrives. However, it is possible that another powerful Faerie could mask her from me. Go with Polleux and let Sophie's grandfather know what has happened."

"And what are you going to do?" Mr. McGuire asked Simeon.

"Me?" Simone pointed at himself with a smile. "I'm returning to Earth."

"Shouldn't you ride Polleux, so you can get to the gateway much quicker?"

"No, you need him more than I do. Since we last met, I have mastered a new trick, which only took me a few hundred years to learn. I can now Easy Snap Travel. All I have to do is think of a place and in the time it takes me to snap my fingers, I am there. I call it Snap, Snapping or Snapped for short. It will only take moments for me to get to the gateway."

Mr. McGuire stared at Simeon in disbelief. Only the rulers of the Seven Faerie Houses and members of their immediate bloodlines were thought to have the ability to Easy Snap Travel. He knew Simeon was powerful, but not this powerful. He thought in time, Simeon could become the most powerful Faerie in the ForEverNever.

"Then why don't you just Snap to Dublin?" Mr. McGuire teased.

"I am still not able to Snap between worlds. I don't even know if I am able to Snap on Earth. However, I guess I am going to find out the answer to that question soon."

Simeon motioned towards Polleux. "Jump on and hold on tight. Time is critical. You must inform Sophie's grandfather immediately."

After Polleux and Mr. McGuire headed off down the road, Simeon Snapped to the closest gateway that led from the ForEverNever to Earth.

The young girl looks scared and alone. It is so dark and damp down here and she only has the floor and a thin blanket to sit on. I know she has to be cold. I feel like I should help her, but I don't help humans. Humans have never done anything for me, but chase me with brooms. However, the girl did give me cheese and actually spoke to me. I know she was only trying to get me to help her, but I have a feeling this one is different. She is kind and sings so beautifully. I think she could be a friend. I will help her if I can. I am sure I can think of something.

- The Mouse

xxv : Help from a new friend

Within a few seconds, Simeon was standing in front of the gateway leading to Iveagh Gardens. All he had to do was walk through and he would be on Earth again. Although he found the human world interesting, he really didn't like spending too much time there, but Sophie needed him.

Simeon stepped through the gateway and found himself in the chamber behind the waterfall in Iveagh Gardens. He left the chamber, followed the pathway from behind the waterfall and made his way down the hill.

He spotted the same Faerie couple who had been sitting by the waterfall years ago and shook his head in disbelief. "They are still sitting on the same bench, reading magazines. At least now, I know what those glossy paged things with pictures are called."

"Do you see that?" The male Faerie nudged the female Faerie's shoulder. "He is back. He is really back!"

"I almost can't believe my eyes, but it sure looks like him. Do you really think that's him?" the female Faerie asked.

"It's him alright, I would recognize him anywhere. Plus, the last time we saw him, he was going into the waterfall." The male Faerie smiled at the female Faerie. "And now he is coming out."

"I am so glad he is back. I don't know if I could take much more of looking at these magazines. Yeah, it was fun when we were first looking out for that guy years ago, but there is only so much reading magazines a person can take."

The male Faerie looked directly at the female Faerie. "You go let our boss know that the man has returned. I will follow him and report back once I have the location of where he is staying."

Simeon tried to Snap to Evanswood, but it wasn't working. He counted to ten then tried again. This time he focused all his mental energy and power on visualizing Evanswood, but still nothing happened. Simeon threw his hands up in the air in irritation. "I think I remember how to get to Evanswood from here, but it's a little bit of a walk."

Simeon left Iveagh Gardens in a hurry, setting a fast pace. He was so distraught for Sophie that he didn't notice someone following him.

The male Faerie continued to follow Simeon for miles. He practically had to run to keep up with him. "What is it with this guy? It's almost like he isn't human."

After taking a few wrong turns and about 30 minutes later, Simeon found himself at the front door of Evanswood. Before he could knock on the door, the door flew open and Helen was giving him a big hug. "You came, you really left the ForEverNever and you are standing in front of me. We are so happy you are here and you were able to find your way back to Evanswood."

Simeon looked uncharacteristically serious. "Emma's daughter needs me. Nothing was going to stop me from returning to Dublin."

"Still the same old Simeon. Always there to help a friend." Helen patted Simeon's arm as they heard Zoey barking behind them.

"Zoey is barking, again. I thought she was going to give us a break. She never barks, but she was barking up a storm after she returned home yesterday. Thankfully you are here Simeon. Maybe you can let us know what she is trying to tell us. She was the last one to see the children."

"Come!" Helen held the front door open for Simeon to enter Evanswood. "Let's join everyone in the library. We are trying to determine who took the children and where they might be."

Outside the house, the male Faerie stepped out from his hiding place, wickedly laughed and rubbed his hands together. He was finally going to be able to tell his boss exactly where the man he had been waiting for all these years was staying.

He was glad he ran into the strange man at the bar all those years ago and shared the story about the girl, the dog and boy at the waterfall. The man at the bar was so interested in the girl, the dog and boy at the waterfall, that he hired the male Faerie and his girlfriend to stand watch at the waterfall in case the boy or the girl ever returned. All his waiting was going to finally pay off. The male Faerie laughed again, only louder this time.

Sophie shivered and pulled the thin, worn blanket tighter to her body. She could hear footsteps in the distance. Then the door began to slowly open. "Smash in Squash! He's back earlier than I expected."

"We don't have time to come up with a plan." The mouse mumbled still half asleep.

Sophie made sure the blanket was completely covering her legs and then nudged the mouse before the man entered the room. "You seem to be an intelligent mouse. I think we can come up with something pretty quick."

Sophie was wide-awake and alert as the man moved towards her with a tray of food. It was the same guy who brought her food the night before. He closed the door behind him and then sat the tray down close to Sophie. She could hear the keys jingling in his front jacket pocket.

"Here we go," Sophie thought as she gestured for the mouse to move away from her.

"Mouse! Mouse!" Sophie yelled at the top of her lungs, as the mouse revealed itself on the blanket. "There's a mouse in here!" Sophie screamed as she dramatically pointed to the mouse standing on its hind legs on the corner of the blanket.

The man covered his ears, "Please... stop... screaming. I'll get the mouse. I see it... it's running across the room."

Sophie pointed. "Look, it just went behind the boxes in the corner."

"There it is!" Sophie pointed at the mouse again as it ran behind another box. The man took out a small flashlight from his jacket pocket and shined some light in the corner. "I don't see anything."

The man, holding the flashlight in one hand, started to move some of the boxes. The mouse ran to the side of the room farthest from the door. Again, the mouse disappeared behind other boxes. The man hung his coat on the doorknob, rolled up his sleeves and threatened, "I'm going to get you!"

The man returned to the far side of the room to find the mouse. Sophie looked over at his coat and realized his police baton was hanging out of one of the pockets. Intently focused, Sophie leaned back against the wall further into the shadows and slowly stood. While the man was completely distracted by the mouse, she crept over to the jacket. She reached for the baton, grabbed it firmly and carefully removed it from the jacket pocket without making any noise.

Holding the baton with both hands tight to her chest Sophie breathed a sigh of relief, "I'm so glad the keys weren't in the same pocket as the baton."

From the mouse's hiding place on a ledge on the far side of the room, it had a perfect view of the man and Sophie standing on the other side of the room holding the baton to her chest. It knew it had to continue to distract the man. The mouse quickly climbed down the wall, poked its head out, and ran in front of the boxes disappearing behind them again.

Sophie crept back in front of the blanket, sat back down and with one hand held the baton behind her back. The mouse ran across the room and disappeared behind another set of boxes in the corner. Sophie pointed. "It's over there! It's over there!"

The man hurried to the other side of room and began to move some of the boxes, so he could get to the mouse. As he leaned over to pick up one of the boxes, Sophie quickly stood up and snuck behind him with the baton tightly gripped behind her back.

Sophie really didn't want to do it. The man had been kind to her and she had never hurt anyone in her life. But she had to get away. As the man leaned over to remove another box, Sophie held her breath and soundly hit him on the back of the head. The man slumped to the ground. Fortunately for Sophie, the man was out cold with just the one hit. Sophie released the breath she didn't know she was holding and dropped the baton to the ground.

The mouse seemed to grin at her. "You did it; you really did it. I wasn't sure you had it in you."

Sophie smiled at the mouse. "I'm glad you picked up on what I was doing and were able to play along. I almost gave myself a headache screaming so loudly."

"Let's get the keys and get you out of this place." The mouse crawled into the man's jacket pocket and used its mouth to pull out the keys.

Sophie bent down to put her pillow under the man's head. "Sorry to hurt you, but I didn't have a choice. Hopefully, your head doesn't bother you too much when you wake up."

The mouse dragged the keys over to Sophie. "Hurry! You need to get out of here."

Surprised, Sophie looked at the Mouse. "Aren't you coming with me?"

"No, I think I have done enough to help you today. I am going to find a nice place in one of the corners and rest."

"Thank you for all your help." Sophie handed the mouse the cheese off her breakfast plate. "Always remember you have a human friend. If I can ever do anything to help you, just let me know."

Sophie waved goodbye to her new friend as she unlocked the door.

"Way to go Sophie. You got the right key on the first try." She was pretty proud of herself as she carefully slipped out into the dark hallway. In the distance she saw a dim light and hesitantly headed towards it.

I never thought I would be doing anything like this, but I have to save her. There is no way I'm going to let her down. She's my friend and she needs me. I've longed for a friend for years and I'm not going to lose her now. Even though she annoys me sometimes, she really makes me laugh. Admittedly, I haven't met many girls, but of the few I have met, none seem as adventurous as Sophie. She can also be kind of nice, when she wants to be. She has to be still unharmed. The two men in the police uniforms went downstairs. One of them just returned and headed into the room at the end of the hall. I can take on one guy. Time to act. I need to calm my nerves. Good thing I learned to focus in my Martial Arts classes.

- Sean MacTavish

xxvi : the Rescue

Sean walked to the bottom of the stairs. It was very dark and he could barely see in front of him. When he turned his head to the side, he saw a dim light coming off the wall. He moved closer to get a better look. "It's an oil lamp!" he mumbled. "I didn't know people still used these."

Sean took the oil lamp off the wall and used it to light the path in front of him. He noticed the gate at the bottom of stairs was closed. "This can't be, the gate locks from this side. If the guy in the police uniform just came down this way, he had to have unlocked the gate. Unless, the other guy in the police uniform re-locked it before he returned upstairs."

Sean shook the gate as hard as he could while still holding the oil lamp, but it was no use. The gate didn't budge. It made a squeaking sound, laughing at him, mocking him for his efforts. As Sean shook the gate again, he saw the faint figure of a person in the distance coming towards him. He wasn't sure if he should dim the light from the oil lamp and try to hide or run back up the stairs. He hesitated, as the figure got closer. "The figure is still too far away and it is too dark to be sure, but I think it could be Sophie!"

Sean followed his gut. "Sophie is that you? It's Sean!"

"Sean! It's me!" Sophie cried as she ran towards the gate.

"I'm so glad to see you, but the gate is locked. I can't get it to budge."

"That's okay Sean, I have these." Sophie dangled the keys in the light.

"Great! We just might get you out of here yet. Hand the keys to me Sophie. The gate can only be opened from my side."

Sean reached through the gate while Sophie held out the keys. She released her grip when she thought Sean had a hold of them. But, the light from the flickering oil lamp played a trick on her eyes. It was too late.

"Smash in Squish! Catch them! We don't want them to fall through the crack in the floor." Sophie squealed as the keys left her fingers, falling towards the floor.

Fast as lightning, Sean reached out and caught the keys. "Good thing I have been doing all my eye exercises." Sean winked at Sophie.

Sophie was amazed at Sean's quick reflexes. She had only ever seen Simeon move that quickly.

Sean tried the first key, but it wouldn't fit in the lock. The second key fit perfectly. He turned the key and the lock popped open.

"See, easy peasy." Sean opened the gate so Sophie could slip through.

Sophie gave Sean a big hug. "I am so glad to see you!"

"How did you get out of the room where you were held?"

"It's a long story. I will tell you once we are safely away from this place."

Sophie and Sean quickly made their way up the stairs. Sean slowly opened the door leading to the staircase and carefully stuck his head out the doorway to see if anyone was in the hallway.

"The hallway is empty. We need to try and make it to the main entrance of the building, now." He stepped out into the hallway holding the door for Sophie.

"The main entrance is right in front of us. Just walk slowly behind me. Everything is going to be okay." Sean gave a reassuring smile as they headed towards the main door.

"Stop!" Sean and Sophie quickly turned their heads in the direction of the person who made the command. They saw two men, one in a police uniform, running towards them. Sean grabbed Sophie's hand and ran towards the main entrance.

"We have to hurry!" Sean looked back and yelled at Sophie. He saw each man raise two knives to throw, but he wasn't quick enough to move Sophie out of the way before two of the four knives struck her body. One hit her in the back of the right knee, while the other hit her on her left shoulder.

Sean watched in horror as Sophie collapsed to the floor. He didn't know what to do. The two men were still running towards them. He couldn't lift Sophie on his back in fear of making her injuries worse, and he couldn't out run the two men. "How am I going to fight them?" Sean kneeled next to Sophie, defeated.

"Don't remove any of the knives from her body." Sean looked up to see a boyishly looking man standing over them. He then looked back towards the men who were just chasing them. They were no longer moving. One of the men's legs was lifted in the air. They were frozen in place. Sean looked around the hallway and no one else was moving, except the man who had just spoken to him.

"You must be Sean." The boyishly looking man spoke calmly and with confidence. "I'm a friend of Sophie's and I'm here to help."

"W...w...w...ho are you?" Sean stammered. "How did you do th... th...th...that?" He pointed at the two men frozen in place.

"I promise to tell you later, but right now I need to get Sophie home." The boyishly looking man carefully picked up an unmoving Sophie. As the man gently held Sophie to his chest she briefly opened her eyes and looked up at him. She mumbled, "Simeon how did you get here," before she went unconscious again.

At that moment, Simeon wished he had healing powers. He not only didn't have any healing powers; he couldn't tell how badly Sophie was hurt.

"Time is of the essence. I have to get Sophie back to Evanswood and to Helen as soon as possible," Simeon thought as he carefully pulled Sophie more tightly to his chest and looked down at her to make sure the knifes in her body had not moved.

Since he had Snapped to the police station, he knew he could Snap in the human world. He was just not able to Snap to Evanswood. There were too many protective spells around the house.

"I'm going to Snap to the café across the street from Evanswood," Simeon said out loud.

"Snap? What do you mean Snap?"

"Sean, don't freak out." Simeon took a deep breath and looked directly at Sean. "In just a moment you are going to see Sophie and me disappear. That's what I mean by Snapping. We are going to vanish right before your eyes and travel to Evanswood. Sophie's father, your grandmother, and a few other friends are waiting outside. I need you to tell them Sophie is hurt and that Simeon Snapped her back to Evanswood. Let her father know some of the men who kidnapped Sophie are frozen inside the police station. Then find your grandmother. She will make sure you get home."

Sean stared at Simeon in disbelief.

"Remember to stay calm and let Sophie's father know about the men frozen inside the police station right away. I don't know how much longer they will stay that way." Simeon yelled moments before he and Sophie vanished into thin air.

Sean continued to stare in disbelief at the empty spot where Simeon had just stood.

"If I hadn't spent so much time with Sophie the last few days, I might think I'm going insane," Sean thought as he ran out of the police station to find Sophie's father and his grandmother.

———————————————————————————————

Simeon arrived in front of the café across from Evanswood. He looked down at Sophie. She was still not moving. He gently pulled her tighter to his chest carefully of the two knives still in her body and dashed across the street. Helen was waiting for him with the door wide-open.

"You found her." Helen looked at Sophie with concern. "Bring her in the library, so I can see how badly she is hurt."

"How did you know we had arrived?" Simeon asked.

"I may no longer have all my powers, but I still have a few tricks left. Maybe one day I'll share my secrets." Helen winked.

"Now lay Sophie face down on the couch.

"The knife in her shoulder doesn't appear to have gone in too deeply and there isn't much blood, but the knife behind the knee looks a little more serious. Sophie may have some trouble walking for some time."

"If her injuries aren't that bad, why is she still unconscious?" Simeon asked with concern.

"It is very likely she is unconscious because the pain has caused her system to go into shock."

Helen pulled out a few cloths from her magic box. "As I remove the knives, I need you to quickly cover the wounds and press down hard on the cloths."

"Do the cloths have the power to make her wounds heal?" Simeon asked hopefully.

"No, they will just temporarily stop the bleeding. Once the bleeding is under control, carry her to the hidden springs in the room behind the tapestry. I will hold back the tapestry and open the door to the hidden springs, so you can carry her in. Sophie will be okay. I promise."

Things aren't always as they appear. People are sometimes afraid to look deeper and often try to hide the truth from those around them. And they especially like to hide the truth from themselves. Fear is always present, so there are always those easily manipulated and willing to cause harm to others. I knew if I was patient, I would find the information I sought. Now, I only have to be patient a little longer and I will find a way to get into Evanswood. With their chants, their powers and their money, they think they have protected it from all dangers. However, when they're not looking, I will find my way in and have my revenge.

- Patient Being

xxvij : Danger Surrounds

Sophie's wounds bled more than Helen expected after the knives were removed. However, after a few stressful minutes Sophie's wounds finally stopped bleeding. William, Mrs. MacTavish and Sean walked in the library right as Simeon was getting ready to carry Sophie into Helen's hidden springs.

William ran to Sophie. "Why isn't she moving?"

"Calm yourself William. Sophie's not dead, she is just unconscious. Simeon is carrying her to my healing springs. Don't worry, she is going to be okay."

William and Sean breathed a sigh of relief.

"Once Sophie sits in the healing waters for awhile, she will wake up." Helen reassured William.

Simeon looked at Sophie then reluctantly smiled at William, "You should take her." Simeon carefully handed Sophie to her father.

Helen pulled back the tapestry revealing the hidden room behind. Simeon walked into the room. William followed close behind holding

Sophie lovingly in his arms and kissed her on the forehead. "You are safe and everything is going to be okay. Your father's here."

Helen opened the door leading to the healing springs. Warm, damp air began to fill the room. Helen walked into the room motioning for William to follow. The warm, damp air immediately weighed heavily on William's lungs making it difficult to breath.

William coughed and cleared his lungs. "What do you want me to do, Helen? If I just set Sophie in the water, her body could slip down and she could drown."

"You can carry Sophie into the water and sit with her for a little bit. However, once she regains consciousness you need to get out of the water. Do you understand?" Helen warned.

William nodded his head, yes. As he walked into the water with Sophie wrapped tightly in his arms, he noticed the water was extremely warm. Thick fog filled the air around him. Sweat began to roll off his forehead as he sat on a bench in the water. William spoke softly as he held Sophie's head above the water, extended her arms and allowed the rest of her body to float in the water. "I love you so much! You are the most precious thing in the world to me. I was so scared when I couldn't find you. I swear I'll do everything in my power to always keep you safe."

Within a few minutes Sophie's eyes fluttered open. "Father, is that you?"

"Yes, it's me little one. I am here." Sophie's father smiled down at her.

With her head resting in her father's loving hands she moved her eyes to look around in the fog. "Where am I?"

"You are safe now. No one is going to hurt you. You are back at Evanswood." Sophie's father continued to smile at her.

———————————————————————————————

A dark shadowy figure gleefully watched the boyish looking male Faerie carry a wounded girl into the house, called Evanswood. He stepped out of his hiding place to get a better look. After all these years, he found them. Years ago he heard about a young male who disappeared behind the waterfall in Iveagh Gardens. He knew the young male was Emma's Faerie friend. He hated Emma. She had ruined his plans for the ForEverNever. She had to pay. He had lost track of her once she travelled to Earth, but he knew Emma's friend was the key to finding her. That's why he hired the male and female Faerie to keep watch in Iveagh Gardens for either Emma's or her friend's return.

Recently, the male Faerie was getting restless and tired of sitting in Iveagh Gardens every day. He already asked for another assignment. However, the dark shadowy figure would have ordered him back to Iveagh Gardens for a hundred years, if that's how long it took Emma or her Faerie friend to return."

Now all he had to do was sit back and keep an eye on the house. "It may take those inside the house awhile to let down their guard, but when they finally do…"

An hour after the dark shadowy figure turned to walk away from Evanswood, an elegantly dressed tall, older man stepped out of his hiding place from across the street. He had been intently watching the house for the last hour. The man scratched his head and sighed in disgust. "How could've my plan failed?"

The man had spent months laying the ground work for his plan. "I had the girl." Angrily he punched the air and stubbed his toes when he kicked the curb. "If only the men I hired weren't so incompetent. Really, how hard is it to keep a young girl captive?"

The man sat down on the curb to rub his sore foot. "Well, I have a few more plans up my sleeve. I will never forget what William did to me. I'm going to make him pay if it's the last thing I do."

While William was with Sophie, Simeon Snapped back to the police station. There he stuffed the two frozen men into a closet, so William could talk to them later. "Better they are questioned here than at Evanswood," he thought.

———————————————————————————

Sophie was resting in her bed with Zoey beside her. Simeon, Helen, Mr. McGuire and Mrs. MacTavish all sat on the couches in the library waiting to hear what William had learned. William stood in front of the fireplace closest to the tapestry hanging on the wall, as the fire crackled behind him. With Simeon's help, William had questioned the men who took Sophie.

"There are still a lot of pieces to the puzzle missing, but the guys who took Sophie told me their boss had someone working for him inside Evanswood, feeding him information. The two men never saw the person and didn't know who it was."

There were several loud gasps in the room. "Who do you think it is?" Helen quietly asked.

"It was probably your driver," Mrs. MacTavish affirmatively stated. "No one has heard from him in days and I always found him an odd sort."

"I think you are probably right, Mrs. MacTavish, but just to be safe we can't rule anyone out. The only people that I'm not suspicious of are those in this room, Sean, Sadao Kimoto and maybe Mr. Fitzpatrice. We all need to keep our eyes open."

Helen leaned forward on the couch to emphasize her point. "You can be sure I will keep a close watch on everyone in this house. Thank goodness Sophie is home and the healing springs nearly mended her injuries."

William nodded. "Yes, we are very lucky. I haven't asked Sophie anything about the kidnapping. I didn't want to upset her just yet. Hopefully, she has more information about the men who took her. However, I'm a little concerned that maybe she hit her head or was given something that affected her memory. She told me she had to tell her mother she was okay. When I asked what she was talking about, she mumbled something about seeing her mother in the ForEverNever and needing to talk to her."

Mrs. MacTavish looked directly at Simeon to gauge his reaction to what William had just told them. Simeon looked as confused as Mrs. MacTavish felt. She indicated to Simeon with her eyes that they needed to speak about this recent revelation.

William continued, "The individuals being held at the police station told me their boss was going to call me with demands, but they didn't know what the demands were. They said he often talked about how rich I am, so they thought their boss was going to ask for a lot of money. But I have a gut feeling this isn't about money. I am just not sure who would hate me so much they would try to hurt me through my daughter."

———————————————————————————————

Sophie was sitting up in her bed reading a book when Simeon went upstairs to check on her, one last time, before he returned to the ForEverNever.

"How are you feeling today squirt? Ready for another riding lesson?" Simeon smiled with a mischievous twinkle in his eyes.

Sophie returned his smile. "I am feeling much better. Thanks for asking."

With a more serious look on his face, Simeon moved closer to Sophie's bed. "I need to ask you something about what you told your father. Do you feel up for a conversation?"

"I'm fine Simeon. Just a little tired. What do you want to know?"

"Your father said you mentioned needing to speak to your mother about what happened to you. Do you remember this?"

"Yes, I remember. And as soon as my leg completely heals, I'm returning to the ForEverNever to talk to my mother," Sophie said matter-of-factly.

"Sophie, honey your mother is…your mother is…dead." Simeon said gently, as he sat down next to her. Simeon gazed at Sophie for a few moments trying to determine what to say next and then looked away.

Sophie put her hand on his shoulder and whispered. "Don't you think I know my mother is dead? Then louder she continued. "I don't really talk to my mother. I talk to my mother's mirror image."

Relief spread across Simeon's face. "Okay, now I understand. I know of your mother's mirror image. I am glad you found her."

Simeon stood-up and leaned over to give Sophie a hug, "I'm heading back to the ForEverNever shortly and wanted to say good-bye before I leave."

Sophie hugged Simeon. "Thank you so much for saving me. But please tell me, how did you know where to find Sean and me?"

"It was Zoey. She remembered that in one of your dreams you were being held at a police station. When you described it, she knew exactly which police station it was. She also followed the white van used to transport you to the police station. She watched your kidnappers carry the black bag into the back of the police station. Once I arrived at Evanswood, she told me exactly where you were being held."

Zoey sat up in bed and cocked her head to one side. "Lucky for us there are a lot of traffic lights between Iveagh Gardens and the police station. And, I knew where I was going because Sophie told me about her dreams."

Simeon rubbed Zoey's head. "Thank you for your help."

"Well, aren't you wonderful!" Sophie scratched Zoey behind her ears.

Sophie smiled at Zoey and then turned to Simeon. "Thank you again for saving me! I wish you could stay longer, but I know you can't. Have a safe journey home." Sophie gave Simeon another hug.

Simeon smiled and turned to leave.

Sophie called out, "See you soon!"

Simeon turned around, placed his hand on his heart and waved good-bye. He reluctantly turned back around and left the room.

Moments later, Sophie eased her way out of bed and headed down the stairs as quickly as she could with a bummed leg. She needed to catch Simeon before he left. She wanted to ask him to say, hello, to her grandfather and Polleux. When she reached the library, the door was slightly ajar. She could hear Simeon and Mrs. MacTavish talking inside the library.

"I understand what she told you, but she couldn't have seen the mirror image of her mother. You know the mirror image was connected to Emma's life force. Her father told me, that if Emma died, the mirror image would cease to exist." Mrs. MacTavish shrugged and raised her upturned palms in bewilderment.

Simeon stated a little louder than Mrs. MacTavish would have liked, "I'm not sure how the protected enchantment is supposed to work. No one has been back to the Crystal Pond since Emma died. None of us could handle it."

"Some Faerie must be playing a trick on Sophie. We need to get a handle on the situation. We need to figure out who is behind this. We have to protect her."

"You are right. We need to protect Sophie. However, we can't rule out that Emma may still be alive." Simeon sounded hopeful. "I will start investigating when I return to the ForEverNever."

Shocked by what she heard, Sophie backed up against the wall to catch her breath. "My mother could still be alive. But, if that is the case, then where is she?"

Not wanting to be seen, Sophie carefully slipped back up to her room.

THE SACRIFICE

Epilogue

After spending a few days in bed with her leg propped on a pillow, Sophie was finally feeling as good as new. She knocked on Sean's door. She hadn't seen him since Simeon brought her home. She needed to thank him for everything he had done for her. She also wanted to let Sean know she was going to the hidden garden to put on her shoes and return to the ForEverNever.

Sean was surprised to see Sophie when he opened his door. "Sophie, I'm glad to see you, but you should be in bed."

"Thank you for your concern, my protector."

Sophie placed her hand on Sean's shoulder. "But I'm feeling great and I'm tired of lying in bed. In fact, I was planning on returning to the ForEverNever today."

Sophie held up her shoes with a smile. "Do you want to go to the hidden garden with me?"

"I don't think your father would approve. I really don't think it is a good idea. But, now that you've told me your plans I can't let you head to the hidden garden alone."

Sean lifted his finger to his lips. "We are going to have to be quiet. If anyone sees you out of bed, they are going to send you back to your room."

Sean and Sophie snuck into the library and made their way to the hidden room behind the tapestry.

"Smash in Squash, I forgot the flashlight! We are going to have to find our way in the dark." Sophie was annoyed with herself.

Sean smiled. "I've got you covered this time." He held up the flashlight he had brought from his room.

"What would I do without you?" Sophie laughed as she grabbed Sean's hand and dragged him through the hidden room. They reached the door at the back of the room within seconds.

Sophie opened the door that led to the hidden garden. "I'm going to sit on the bench and put on my shoes."

Sean sat down on the bench next to her. He knew she would be gone for awhile.

Sophie put on the extra pair of socks. "This is going to be a lot easier when my feet finally grow!"

Sophie grinned at Sean as she put on the first shoe.

"Don't stay away too long," Sean begged. "Remember our lessons with Mr. Fitzpatrice start back up tomorrow."

"Mr. Fitzpatrice is back? When did he return to Evanswood?"

"He arrived late this afternoon," Sean replied.

"I won't be gone very long. I promise. I just have to ask someone a few questions, and then I'll be right back." Sophie put on the second shoe.

Sean heard a low buzzing sound, saw a flash of light and orbs of different colors floating in the air. Sophie disappeared right before his eyes.

When Sophie opened her eyes she was sitting on the bench in the garden in the ForEverNever looking straight into the eyes of the mirror image of her mother.

"Sophie, child it's good to see you. I was worried about you. Watching you in the pond, I saw you being kidnapped and there was nothing I could do to help you."

"I'm okay now." Sophie smiled at the mirror image of her mother. "I made a new friend who helped me escape from the room where I was locked up. Sean and Simeon were also there to help me out of the building. Simeon safely returned me home to Evanswood."

"I'm glad you escaped and Helen was able to help you with your injuries." The mirror image of her mother gave a look of wanting to hug Sophie. "Yes, I saw everything."

"So, what brings you to my garden?"

"I came to ask you…I know it sounds crazy, but do you know if my mother is still alive?"

"Why the question, Sophie?"

"Well, I heard Mrs. MacTavish say I shouldn't be able to see you if my mother was really dead."

"Sophie, I can't tell you if your mother is alive or dead." The mirror image of her mother said in a gentle, loving voice. "However, if she is dead, I'm not exactly sure how I'm still here right now. I never thought about it before you mentioned it. But if your mother is truly dead and her life force is gone, then there should be no energy in the human world or the Faerie World to keep me in a visible form."

"Perhaps I am still here because of the energy created by the intense love your mother felt for you, your father, and her father. For love doesn't remain within the heart. It doesn't just vanish when we are gone. It flows out of us and into the world around us imprinting an everlasting image on our loved ones' world. We are never truly separated from those we love. They remain in our hearts and in our memories. We hear their voices at unexpected moments; when we need them most and when we are on the verge of giving up. Even in death those we love remain close; watching us, protecting us, loving us."

Sophie stared at the mirror image of her mother. Even though the mirror image did not know if her mother was alive or dead, she had hope.

CPSIA information can be obtained
at www.ICGtesting.com
Printed in the USA
LVHW041931251218
601652LV00001B/51/P